A CASE OF ANXIETY

Dr. Alan Gregory has to find out why an enraged husband has turned his office into an abattoir . . . which of his colleagues is sexually exploiting and blackmailing a very troubled patient . . . what strange secrets are simmering in the most elegant restaurant in town . . . why his stunning wife is back in his life and wants to be back in his bed . . . what unspeakable horror young Randy Navens cannot remember . . . whether a mysterious killer is driven by greed, lust, guilt, madness, or all or none of the above . . . and how to keep himself from joining the mounting heap of victims.

"**Enough criminal behavior to fuel a minor crime wave . . . killer, conspiracies, child abuse, pornography . . . strong.**"
—*Mostly Murder*

"**The best thrillers now being written by a psychologist-turned-mystery-writer are Stephen White's novels featuring Dr. Alan Gregory.**"
—*Flint Journal*

"**Engrossing . . . Stephen White is a first-rate writer.**"
—Aaron Elkins

PRIVATE PRACTICES

Stephen White

A SIGNET BOOK

SIGNET
Published by the Penguin Group
Penguin Books USA Inc., 375 Hudson Street,
New York, New York 10014, U.S.A.
Penguin Books Ltd, 27 Wrights Lane,
London W8 5TZ, England
Penguin Books Australia Ltd, Ringwood,
Victoria, Australia
Penguin Books Canada Ltd, 10 Alcorn Avenue,
Toronto, Ontario, Canada M4V 3B2
Penguin Books (N.Z.) Ltd, 182–190 Wairau Road,
Auckland 10, New Zealand

Penguin Books Ltd, Registered Offices:
Harmondsworth, Middlesex, England

Published by Signet, an imprint of Dutton Signet, a division of Penguin
Books USA Inc. Previously published in a Viking edition.

First Signet Printing, February, 1994
10 9 8 7 6 5 4 3 2 1

PUBLISHER'S NOTE
This is a work of fiction. Names, characters, places, and incidents either are
the product of the author's imagination or are used fictitiously, and any
resemblance to actual persons, living or dead, events, or locales is entirely
coincidental.

to my brothers and sister

ACKNOWLEDGMENTS

Many gracious people assisted me during the preparation of this manuscript, including Tom Foure, Hal Nees, Stan Galansky, Mary Malatesta, Raetta Holdman Webster, Dana Shepard, and Judith Fisher. I thank them all.

My continued gratitude goes, as well, to the wonderful people at Viking, especially Al Silverman, Matthew Bradley, and Leigh Butler, and to my agent, Jean Naggar, and her hardworking staff. It is also a joy to thank my family for their encouragement and inspiration and to acknowledge those intrepid friends who read early versions. Their critiques and suggestions enhanced this book. A special note of appreciation to Patricia and Jeffrey Limerick, who approached this manuscript with particularly sharp eyes, and blue pencils to match.

And to Rose and Alexander—thanks always for believing. Your faith is my freedom.

1

Claire Draper's life was in danger. And she knew it. But the day the tall man showed up unannounced at my office, banging furiously on the back door, I didn't even know Claire Draper. And I didn't know the tall man had a gun.

Outside the French doors a woman stood next to the tall man, shivering. She stared at me with stuporous eyes, looking as perplexed as if she had found me sitting in my office naked. She wore a medium-weight, pin-striped black wool suit over a gray blouse adorned with an embroidered collar. Despite the aching cold and the falling snow, she had no coat and was swaying on two-inch heels. Evidently, loitering in the yard behind my office in a snowstorm hadn't been one of her considerations when she'd dressed that morning.

The tall man had edged his mouth to within an inch of the glass of the French doors, and his breath frosted the pane before I managed a good look at him. He raised a gloved hand to his brow to shadow the morning glare so he could try to peer inside. Getting up from my chair, I said, "Excuse me a moment, we appear to have visitors," to the young psychotherapist who was sitting opposite me and walked past him to talk to the uninvited pair outside. I twisted the gleaming brass knob on the deadbolt and cracked open one of the doors. The January air was bitter, and little snowflakes hurried to nest in my hair.

"May I help you?" I said, much more annoyed than my voice betrayed.

The man was thin and haggard. He leaned forward and looked over my shoulder. He didn't respond to my offer of assistance and looked so confused and distraught, I wondered momentarily if he spoke English. As he continued to ignore me and to focus all his considerable attention on the interior of the room, I began to feel a bit like a doorman at a members-only nightclub who was trying to find a polite way to coax the riffraff away from the door.

I decided to try acting more authoritative. "Sir, the waiting room is around front. You can't stay back here. The front door is unlocked. Please go in and have a seat."

"*Where is she?*" he screamed. The frozen woman next to him and I jumped in unison. She squeaked as well. I didn't. But close.

"I'm sorry, I don't know what you're talking about," I said, employing a practiced voice, one trained to stay calm in the face of incipient lunacy.

I heard faint sirens in the distance.

So did the man at the door.

His face contorted as he yelled, "*Where the fuck is Claire?*" The contortion fractured the unbroken ridge that bisected his face from the tip of his nose to his undulating hairline. His face was narrow, his convex cheeks ravaged by ancient acne. His sloping forehead and large nose conspired in a pitched descent to his shrieking mouth. His teeth were marvelous.

I yanked my attention back into the room momentarily and saw the top of my supervisee's head over the back of his chair, which sat at a forty-five-degree angle to the doors that led to the yard. I thought it odd that Eric Petrosian hadn't turned to observe the drama. I'd only recently begun a temporary stint doing prelicensing supervision of his clinical work after his previous supervisor died in a freak skiing accident over the holidays. This was just my second supervision appointment with Dr. Petrosian; I didn't know him well enough to understand his apparent paralysis. "Call the police, Eric," I ordered him. "Now!" I barked the last word and watched with some relief as he finally hurried over to my desk.

That's when I saw the gun. Actually that's when the tall man shoved it into my cheek.

"Now, asshole, where the fuck is fucking Dr. Beaner, the little spic who's fuckin' with my wife's head?"

"Dr. 'Beaner,' " I quickly surmised, was my longtime partner, Diane Estevez, Ph.D.

"Look for yourself, she's not here," I said loudly, hoping vainly Diane would somehow hear me through the ample soundproofing of the adjoining wall. I knew Diane was right next door. I thought, He's looking for you, my friend. I hope somehow you're managing to get the drift of this through the walls. And I hope you're getting the hell out of here.

I cracked the door open a little wider so that the tall man could survey the perimeter of the office and reassure himself that Claire wasn't there. I turned with him as he leaned in to search the space and watched with some relief as Eric Petrosian, his back to us, crouched behind the desk and began whispering into the phone.

As Eric made his call, the bitter bray of sirens wended through the neighborhood, louder, closer. And the red-faced man with the silver gun barged the rest of the way into the office. He shoved the woman in front of him harshly, momentarily oblivious of me and Eric. The woman's hair was capped with a veil of powdery snow, her face was blotched white and red from cold and terror. She whimpered and fought to maintain her precarious balance each time he jostled her farther into the room. When he had pushed her to the center of the office, he removed his arm from behind her and poked the barrel of the gun into the side of her neck. Slowly he rotated her 180 degrees and backed away toward the interior door that led from the office to the adjacent hallway.

"Stay here or I'll kill her. Got it?" he said to me, ignoring Eric.

I said, "Listen, I know you're very upset. Maybe it would help to—"

"*Got it?*" he screamed, veins popping to the surface of his red face.

Swallowing the words, I said, "I got it."

He backed out the door into the hall and reached in front of his hostage to pull the door shut. Eric Petrosian was still cowering behind the desk. It seemed like as good a place as any for him.

Dr. Diane Estevez's office was next to mine in the rear of the renovated 1890s Victorian house that housed the offices of our clinical psychology practices. My office was on the east side of the rear of the house and had French doors opening to the backyard. Diane's office was on the west side and had a single oak door leading to a small cedar deck at the corner of the house. Each office had an interior door that led to a narrow hallway that linked together all the rooms in the rear of the building. A locked door separated the office suite from the waiting room at the front of the house.

After turning the deadbolt on the door, effectively locking the man with the gun out of the office, I yelled at Eric to stay put, bolted out the French doors, my loafers instantly filling with icy snow, and jumped up onto the tiny deck outside Diane's office, desperately hoping to warn her before this crazy man busted in on her.

Too late. Through the beveled glass window I saw the man with the gun shove his hostage into Diane's office, watched as his prisoner stumbled to the rug, and registered the madness in the man's sharp face as he waved the pistol in an arc from woman to woman. He started the rotation with Diane and ended with Diane's psychotherapy patient.

I guessed that she was Claire.

Diane's patient was sitting in the corner of a deep burgundy sofa in the consultation area of Diane's psychotherapy office. Claire's right hand was covering her mouth, her left arm was curled around her abdomen in a pantomime of self-protection. Her long auburn hair swayed as she shook her head slowly from side to side. The look in her face was not pure terror. It was, instead, a mingling of fear and resignation. She looked doomed.

I knew the face. It was the face a battered woman turns to a raised fist.

Diane edged slowly between her patient and the man with the gun, saying, I imagined, some variation of the words I had vainly tried to use to calm him moments before. As I watched Diane's lips form the carefully chosen words, I willed her to step back out of the line of fire.

This had to be a domestic dispute gone mad. The man with the gun had to be Claire's husband. Claire was Diane's patient. I had no idea who the woman in the suit was. Through the glass I watched Diane's lips continue to move, her appraising eyes locked on the frantic face of the man with the gun. I knew the calm, reassuring tone Diane would be trying to coerce into her voice. I knew her voice would quiver anyway. Gently I tried the knob on the door. The cold, cold metal didn't budge.

Shrill sirens from emergency vehicles pulsed once more in a deafening peal, and then suddenly the sirens and the cars stopped close by, maybe on the street right in front of the building. In an instant a police cruiser blasted, siren off, down the long driveway on the west side of the house and skidded at an angle toward the backyard. The front passenger door flew open on the side of the patrol car away from the house. Two patrolmen jumped out, guns drawn, barrels pointed skyward.

"Get away from there," one hissed at me as I watched spellbound from the deck. I waved an arm to implore him to shut up and then raised a finger to my lips. "How many?" he whispered.

I wondered, How many what?

"How many hostages?" The sharp rasp in his voice told me that he wasn't pleased that it was I, not he, peeking through the window. I raised three fingers. "How many takers?"

Takers? I raised one finger and then made a pistol shape out of my hand and pointed at it with my other hand.

I returned my attention to Diane's office. The man with the gun wasn't talking to his hostages. That frightened me. He either wanted to take his wife somewhere, he wanted to talk to her, or he wanted to kill her. I couldn't imagine that he had any other intentions. It worried me that he wasn't leaving or talking. It suggested which option he had chosen.

The "taker" seemed oblivious of the tactics of the rapidly mobilizing authorities. His current reality apparently stopped with his hostages. I feared, mostly, that he was unconcerned about escaping.

I watched two more cops move into covered positions in the backyard, one each behind Diane's car and my old Subaru wagon. Then, without warning, an arm with the grabbing power of a Vise-Grip clamped over my bicep and yanked me off the deck. I scrambled to my feet, and then, while I was still crouched over, a cop tugged me toward the front of the house.

"Who the hell are you?" asked the cop with the pincer grip as she yanked me around the corner of the front of the building.

"This is my office. I'm Alan Gregory. That's my partner in there with that maniac." The cop finally turned to face me. She was a couple of inches shorter than I and carried a shotgun in the hand that wasn't pulling me around. The raised collar of her winter jacket hid bright blond hair.

"You can let go now. I'm not gonna run." The hydraulic pressure on my arm relented. At her urging I preceded her through the carved oak front door of the old house. Two more Boulder officers were in the waiting room, discussing the merits of knocking down the locked door separating the waiting room from the office suite in back.

I yelled, "Hey, hold it," dangling my keys. "You know there's a guy with a gun in there? And hostages? Maybe you wanna know the layout first?" Apparently even life-and-death situations failed to mute my sarcasm.

The cop with the shotgun acted as though she were in charge. "Wait," she said sharply to the other officers. "Stay right here until SWAT arrives. And call in again and make triple sure they know this is a hostage situation and we need a negotiator. Make sure he's been called. Everybody should be here in a few minutes." She shook her head just a little and said, "I hope." Her voice softened with the last sentence. I guessed she was trying to calm everybody down.

"Whatta we got so far, Charlie?" asked the smaller of the two sentries by the connecting door.

Charlie was listening to something on her radio. Static

caused the noise to sound like a chicken fight. After a final squawk she turned to her colleagues and told them what she knew. "The suspect grabbed the attorney in the hallway outside a courtroom at the Justice Center, threw her in his car, came over here, and broke into this office. The taker is armed—we think a small-caliber semi-automatic—and has three hostages. The attorney, a therapist, and an unidentified woman."

"Claire," I volunteered, "her name is Claire. She's Dr. Estevez's patient. I'd guess she's the guy with the gun's wife."

"Thanks for the guess," came the derisive response from the lady with the shotgun.

"Damn," I said, "my supervisee is still in my office. It's the one with the French doors on the east side of the backyard. His name is Eric Petrosian." She used her radio to relay the information to somebody else.

"*So,* you want to be helpful? You *seem* to want to be helpful," she asked me sarcastically.

I nodded.

"The floor plan? Draw it."

After searching around the waiting room for paper and finding nothing but magazines, I grabbed the pencil she was offering and drew a diagram of the back of the house on the waiting room wall. "The doors are solid core with gaskets, brushes, and deadbolts. The walls are all double-channeled," I added. She looked perplexed. And annoyed.

"Soundproofing," I explained.

She was quiet, but I read her face to say "So why are you wasting my time telling me this?"

I said, "Thought it might be important." It didn't seem to mollify her.

Another oversight crept into my awareness. "Wait, is Dana Beal upstairs? She's an architect, her office is up there." I nodded at the staircase.

"It's been secured. We didn't find anybody." I wasn't too surprised at that. It was only midmorning, a little early for Dana.

"Is there a phone in there?" Charlie directed the question at me.

"In Diane's office?" I asked.

"No. In the garage." She seemed to be considering the possibility that I had just wandered away from a sheltered workshop. "Of course I meant her office."

I said, "Yeah," and gave her Diane's private line number.

"Bring a cellular phone in here, too," she snapped into the transmitter. I had been assuming that the tone she had been using with me was reserved for civilians. I was apparently wrong.

I stood by my schematic and offered some tactics. "I think you could move into the interior hallway safely. Somebody out back can look through the window and tell you if the interior door to Diane's office is open. If it's closed, he can't see this part of the house and he won't hear you moving in the hallway because of the soundproofing. It's excellent."

From the glare she shot my way, I got the impression she was tired of hearing about the soundproofing. "Give me the keys," she said. I twisted the master off my key ring and held it out toward her. She reached across her body with her right hand and belted the radio, then snatched the key from me. The shotgun, however, remained in her left hand the whole time.

She retrieved the radio from the carrier on her belt and mumbled into it. Listened. Argued. And finally said to the two cops by the door, "Move into position in the hall outside this office"—she poked at the diagram on the wall with the antenna on her handset—"and wait for orders or to be relieved by the SWAT commander." She raised the radio to her lips. "Is the door clear?" she asked. She listened to a reply and apparently understood it. She turned to the two patrolmen. "Go," she said flatly.

They tried to go, but the door was still locked. They looked at her expectantly. She meandered over and unlocked it as though that had been her plan all along. As the cops hurried into position down the hall, I could see past them to Diane's office door, still closed.

Charlie had reclipped the radio on her belt and had a cellular phone in her hand when I turned my attention back to the waiting room. "Suspect's not answering," she said to herself. She probably wasn't eager to hear my supposition that Diane had turned off the bell of the phone to avoid being disturbed during her session, so I kept it to myself. After again exchanging the phone for the radio, Charlie repeated over the air that the suspect wasn't answering.

Between radio squawks she ordered me to "get over there," indicating the farthest corner of the waiting room, using the shotgun as a pointer. She wanted me out of the way. "The hostage negotiator's on his way. He'll take over in here any minute. I'm sure he'll want to talk with you. He'll be fascinated about the soundproofing."

Fewer than thirty seconds later she said, "Detective," greeting the hostage negotiator as he entered the room. I recognized his big gray overcoat before I recognized him. The hostage negotiator was Detective Samuel Purdy, M.A.

"Whatta we got, Charlie?" he said calmly. Then he saw me. "Oh, shit, I shoulda known," he moaned in greeting.

Detective Sam Purdy and I went back a ways. Two Thanksgivings before, he had interviewed me after a patient of mine committed suicide. "Routine," he'd called it at the time. Turned out it was anything but.

Later, another patient of mine died in a traffic accident. Still another was murdered, strangled in her bed. In the midst of it all I became a malignant minor celebrity, accused of sexually exploiting a patient. The only thing that kept me from being a suspect in the murder was the fact that a deputy DA and I were vacationing in Mexico at the time of the assault.

Before it was over, Detective Purdy and I spent a weekend in the mountains chasing a murderer. It hadn't been a holiday for either of us.

The detective tended to treat me as a cat treats a cornered roach, fully confident that any decision about ultimate squashing was his. Underneath it all, he liked me. I was pretty sure.

I was listening to Charlie recite her rendition of the events of the morning for Purdy when the muffled pop of a gun going off escaped the excellent soundproofing.

Everyone became still.

Then Charlie's radio crackled and a voice belched, "*Oh, shit!* He shot one!"

2

Purdy snatched the uniformed cop's radio. "Are you in place out there? Is the SWAT commander here yet? Can anybody take this asshole out?" he snapped staccato at whoever was on the other end.

An eternal pause, maybe five seconds, and then, "No clear shot from here, Detective. Taker's shielded by a hostage. First sharpshooter's just arriving, going up on the roof of the garage right now. Commander's arriving now, too."

Purdy said, "No time. Hold your fire, we're gonna go in from this side."

Purdy shrugged himself from his big coat, grabbed the shotgun, and gestured for Charlie to accompany him as he rushed down the hall. The officers who had previously moved into position stood on each side of Diane's office door, their service revolvers drawn. I trailed silently after Purdy and Charlie, my presence now an afterthought to them, and stopped halfway down the narrow corridor, trying my best to blend into the paint.

Another muted pop rumbled like a clap of thunder from the closed door in front of us.

The radio cackled immediately, "He shot her again. Jesus, he's just executing 'em." There was disbelief in the electronic voice.

Into the radio Purdy said, "At the count of five, create a disturbance outside the back door. Keep clear of fire from my side."

"Affirmative. On your count, Detective."

"One, two, three—"

Officer Charlie caught sight of me just as Purdy called

out "three." She had just parted her lips to order me away when another shot exploded from the closed office.

"*Five,*" screamed Purdy.

Charlie frantically waved at me to get down as she turned back toward the office, her revolver drawn and pointed at the ceiling.

I fell to a prone position, my eyes fixed in the direction of Diane's office. Purdy turned the knob on the door, releasing the latch, looked surprised to find it was unlocked, took a step back, and nudged it with his foot.

Too hard. The door flew back fast and immediately bounced off the rubber doorstop, reclosing like an immense high-speed shutter. The instant image that froze on my retinae was of the tall man's back, of a stained body on the sofa, one on the floor.

Oh, Diane, please be okay. Please.

As Purdy's toe caught the swinging door and then prodded it back open in a more gentle sweep, the room returned to view with the drama of a curtain rising in a theater. Everything seemed to move slowly, as if we were passengers in an immense vehicle sliding on ice, waiting for an inevitable crash. In the middle of the room the executioner was paralyzed by his ambivalence, attending first to the ruckus outside the back window, then focusing on the novel sounds behind him—the door crashing open and a voice, Purdy's, yelling, "Police!"

Finally making his reluctant choice, the gunman rotated, his right arm extended, the silver pistol establishing the radius of his turn toward the open door. Toward us.

Purdy didn't deliberate any longer than it took him to inspect his flash field for hostages and comrades. From my belly-down position in the hall I watched Purdy's finger squeeze the crescent of the trigger, and I recoiled as an earsplitting blast erupted from the shotgun. The tall man's chest and neck were instantly obliterated in a wash of red and orange. The gunman flew backward from the horror as though he were being sucked away from us, and he came to rest on the sofa, on Claire.

His body clung to Claire's for a moment before it began to slide down, so unhurried at first, as though even in death the man needed to stay tethered to his wife. The gunman's body then slipped faster, the grim path lubricated by his spilled fluids mingling with hers, his lanky, limp form finally stopping, contorted, on the floor. The back of his neck rested on the curve of his wife's foot. He didn't even look surprised.

Detective Purdy's shotgun barrel followed him every inch of the way.

I was in the office just after Charlie, even before the two patrolmen who had been flanking the door. I didn't hear the glass shatter on the back doors or windows or the snow-covered troops enter the room from outside. I wasn't aware of hearing the moans or pleas of Patricia Tobin, Claire Draper's divorce lawyer, sounds that would invade my dreams for weeks after the shooting. I didn't see, then, Claire's lifeless face or the wounds, one in her chest, one in her neck, from the silver handgun.

I saw only my friend, Diane Estevez, sprayed with blood, bending over Claire's inert body. I was joyous when I saw Diane's hands shaking, and her arms reaching, and then her lips, quivering. Finally her head turned to the room, to the police, to me, and I heard her say, her voice totally empty and without hope, "Please help Claire. She's hurt. She's hurt."

I started to cry. At first that Diane was okay. Soon that everybody else wasn't.

3

Diane Estevez was one of the scrappiest people I had ever known. I had never seen her even slowed, let alone immobilized, in the face of crisis. In the minutes after the shooting I expected her to be struggling to contain retaliatory urges that could surface within her with enough thrust to launch an interplanetary probe.

So I didn't know what it meant when she said blandly, "He didn't say much," in reply to a question from Purdy about what the gunman had talked about inside her office.

Diane was sitting on the leather chair at my desk. I sat behind her, perched on the edge of my filing cabinet, my hand on her shoulder. My presence was her only victory of the day thus far. As she had been led from the carnage in her office to the relative tranquillity of mine to be interviewed by Purdy, she had begged him to let me stay with her. The detective had hesitated, apparently reluctant to expose us to each other's versions of events. Diane said she was absolutely not going to answer any questions unless either her husband or I was present. Purdy offered a representative from Victim Services as an alternative.

Diane said, "No. Alan or Raoul."

Purdy spent two quick minutes grilling me in the hallway outside the office, ascertaining what I had witnessed, and then was almost genteel to Diane in his manner as he acquiesced to her request to have me present. Pointedly, he told me to keep my mouth shut unless a question was directed my way.

After Diane's initially circumspect response to his question about what the gunman had said, Purdy waited patiently for her to continue. As if he knew she was just finding her place.

He was good.

Diane twisted her lips, first north, then south, making some decision. "He told Claire that she must've known he'd find her. That safe houses are only safe if you never leave 'em." Now Diane was chewing on her lips. She gazed outside, where it all started, maybe rewinding her memory to before the butchery. "He said the gun wasn't fully loaded, that he only had six bullets. Two for each of us. Said he didn't have enough for the cops. Anyway, he said, he liked cops. It was women he hated. He didn't say 'women'; he said 'cunts.' " Diane's usually perfect posture was vanquished by the gravity of her grief. Her elbows rested on the desk, her fingers were entwined around a mug of water. The mug was decorated with ducks.

Briefly her eyes flashed fire. "I was third, he told me, because shrinks are a higher form of life than lawyers. But not much higher. If there was a rabid raccoon in here carryin' plague and foamin' at the mouth, he'd shoot him last. That's what he said. He laughed when he said that."

Diane closed her eyes and exhaled softly through her nose. I couldn't tell whether the closed eyes helped her visualize what she was being asked to remember or helped her block out what she wouldn't be able to forget.

"Claire moved a little after the first shot. It—the bullet—went in her neck." Diane touched the hollow of her throat, letting her fingers linger there for a few seconds before removing them. "After he shot the gun the first time, her eyes were so scared and she didn't move anything but her head. I remember thinking that he must've hit her spinal cord. Spit and blood dribbled from her mouth, like she couldn't control it. I asked him if I could wipe it away, help her. He laughed again. I think she was trying to talk to him. He waited, just watching Claire's face for a while, and then he shot her again. Between shots the rage left his face. He looked calm, and crazy—crazy calm."

Diane lifted the mug off the desk as if to take a drink. The mug never reached her lips. "Patricia was next. She was still on the floor when he shot her. He'd pushed her down when they busted in. He told her he was about to fire the shot heard in every fucking divorce court in America. The rage came back in his face. He called her a 'man-eatin' cunt' and a 'fuckin' dyke.' Asked her if she knew who'd get custody of her corpse. Like he actually expected her to answer. Patricia was trembling, whimpering. He laughed at her. Then he shot her. Easy. Like she was a fly he swatted.

"When you guys came in"—she didn't bother to shift her gaze to the assembled cops—"I just wondered where the hell you'd been while he was killing these women. In my head, I was already dead, too."

Diane became silent then. Nobody knew what to say.

"You can't go in there. *Stop!*" came an order from the hall. Raoul Estevez, Diane's husband, whom I had called in the chaos after the shooting, yelled something back at the cop in Spanish. Raoul spoke Spanish whenever he didn't like what some governmental authority was telling him in English. The last word from his mouth was "*mujer.*"

I said to Purdy, "It's her husband."

Purdy said conversationally to Charlie, by the door, "Let him in. Let's all take ten."

Diane stood and let Raoul hold her. Raoul's back was to us, his voice sonorous. "All of you. Leave."

All of us did.

I left last, closing the door behind me.

In a gesture I found poignant, Officer Charlene Manning, "Charlie," introduced herself to me in the hall. "Your patient, Eric whatever, left, said he'd call you. When we brought him back in to get his coat, he took a look in there." She pointed at Diane's bloodied office. "I'd pay not to have to see what's in there, and he goes over like it's a tourist attraction. Maybe that's why he's your patient, huh?"

I didn't reply immediately. Eric wasn't my patient. Sometimes you see somebody for supervision and you get a feel for them as if you were seeing them for psychotherapy. Sometimes after half a dozen meetings consulting on another therapist's clinical work, you're still unsure about them. After two meetings I was still unsure about Eric Petrosian.

Finally I asked, "Where is he now?" Through my shock and fury I tried to muster some concern for his well-being.

"He was giving a statement outside in one of the vehicles. Asked not to stay in here any longer. He's probably gone by now. Like I said, he said he'd call you."

Purdy had been cornered by some supervisory types from the department, I assumed to investigate the discharge of a firearm by an officer. The paramedics had sped Patricia Tobin away to the ER at the local hospital. The care of the two lifeless bodies required no such hurried attention and they were ignored by everyone on the scene with the exception of someone from the coroner's office.

The office suite I shared with Diane Estevez was overrun by a squadron of mud-and-snow-footed officers and blue-jumpsuited SWAT team members. They had no trouble looking important but couldn't quite manage to seem busy.

My office door remained closed, protecting what little privacy Diane and Raoul had left.

Elliot Bellhaven, a deputy in the DA's office, arrived with his generously cut wide-wale cords tucked into knee-high leather boots. His sweater was deep blue with blacks and browns and looked as if it weighed five pounds. He winked a greeting at me while he spoke to somebody from SWAT.

I knew Elliot through my romance with Lauren Crowder, one of his colleagues in the DA's office. In our seven months of dating, Lauren and I had experienced more ups and downs than a carousel horse. It had already crossed my mind that Lauren might be the deputy DA on call that day. Never feeling quite certain that the horse I was riding was up for long, I was relieved to see Elliot.

Elliot Bellhaven was free-spirited, brilliant, and barely a year and a half away from a top-ten-percent finish at Harvard Law. I had once asked Lauren how the Boulder DA had managed to snare someone of Elliot's stature. She had replied, "He comes from around here. And the truth is *he* chose us. I think he plans to run this town before he's thirty."

Once, at a party, a mildly drunken Elliot had confided in me that half the office wondered if he was gay. I asked what that was like for him. He said, "It's fine with me that they wonder." I wondered if he was gay, too.

I moved over to stand behind the SWAT lieutenant who was talking with Elliot, continuing to edge over until Elliot couldn't miss me.

A minute later, done with the preliminaries with the SWAT supervisor, Elliot caught my eye and walked over.

"Alan, you're all right?" he said, arm outstretched.

I shook his hand and nodded. "Diane Estevez, my partner, is not. She was in there"—I pointed to her blood-spattered office—"the whole time. She's in my office now. Can you get these guys to cut her some slack on the interrogation? Maybe interview her at home later today? Or tomorrow. She could use a break from all this."

He thought for a moment. "Did they get a preliminary statement from her?"

"Yeah. It sounded pretty thorough to me, actually."

"Somebody from Victim Services with her now?"

"No. Her husband."

"Let me check with the detective about her initial statement. I'll see what we can do." Elliot smiled at me, touched a hand to my shoulder, and moved off, gingerly, toward Diane's bloody office. "I do hope, ladies and gentlemen, that everybody in here's a crime scene investigator," he called out pleasantly at the door, effortlessly donning the cape of the guardian of the chain of evidence.

A taciturn man from SWAT cornered me in the waiting room and asked me questions for about fifteen minutes before he dismissed me. I parked myself upstairs in front of our architect-tenant Dana Beal's phone until I managed to reach most of Diane's patients and most of my patients, canceling their appointments for the remainder of the day. I enlisted Diane's answering service to persist in searching for the remaining few. Then I called Eric Petrosian's number and left a brief message on his answering machine tape that I would try to reach him again that evening.

By the time I was back downstairs the crowd of authorities had started to thin. I made coffee in the small kitchen, letting my mug catch the first ten ounces as it dripped from the filter nest. The coffee tasted almost as black as the day.

Elliot found me in the hall. "Ms. Estevez is on her way home. We'll be seeing her tomorrow morning, nine-thirty, at the Public Safety Building. Don't worry about her. I'll be there with Sam Purdy."

"Thanks, Elliot. I appreciate it."

"Not at all. By the way, we'll see *you* this afternoon at four-thirty. Same place. Same illustrious cast."

4

The office was a shambles by the time everyone left. Police department seals adorned both doors of Diane's office. The rest of the place, apparently, was being returned to our custody.

It took me most of an hour to locate somebody at the police department who was willing to authorize me to get the windows and back door to Diane's office repaired. It took another hour to find a glazier and a locksmith to agree to do the work that day. The owner of one glass company told me, "No way—not in this blizzard. I ain't riskin' my twenty-thousand-dollar minivan for a two-pane job. No fuckin' way. Uh-huh." I thanked him for his consideration. The janitorial service that did routine cleaning of the building promised to send a "disaster" crew out that night to try to undo the damage done by the siege.

I called Diane's answering service and told them I would be taking calls for her until further notice. They reminded me that I had already given them that instruction. I tried Diane and Raoul's house and left a message on their machine, offering to do anything I could.

I felt helpless. *I should never have let the tall man leave my office.*

Nothing else.

Around two-thirty that afternoon Lauren phoned me on the private line into my office. Although she'd apparently heard about the kidnapping and slaughter late morning, she'd only just been told by Elliot Bellhaven that Diane and I were involved.

"How *are* you?" she asked as soon as I said "Hello."

"I'm okay, I think," I said, and then added mindlessly, "How are you?"

She ignored my social reflex. "Alan, God, is Diane gonna be okay?"

I didn't know what she knew, so I explained that Diane hadn't been hurt physically. I told her that Diane was on deck when the cops busted into the office.

"She was gonna be shot next?" Lauren's voice was a little breathless.

"Apparently."

"Why?"

There were too many whys. I asked, "Why what?"

"Why did he do it? Why did he shoot Patricia Tobin, why was he gonna kill Diane?"

"I can guess if you want me to."

"Please."

"They helped his wife get away from him. He blamed them—Diane for helping the wife, Claire, find the resolve to get out of the marriage, and the lawyer, the lawyer for doing whatever it is lawyers do during divorces. I'm guessing he was a dependent guy with absolutely no self-esteem, a classic batterer, and couldn't take it when his wife left him. She must have felt she was in some jeopardy because she was staying at Safehouse, apparently, and he somehow tracked her to Diane's office. His only plan was to kill these women. He never expected to leave the office alive."

Lauren was silent. She was a seasoned prosecutor. But in quasi-urban Boulder she spent most of her time in the company of unimaginative sociopaths and minor league felons who occasionally committed major league felonies. Hell-bent executioners weren't her usual adversaries. I think she was searching for a context. I think that mostly because *I* was.

"God." A long pause. "What can I do, honey?"

My reflexive response would have been "Nothing." But I said, "I'm sure Diane would appreciate a call tomorrow or the next day." I thought for a moment more and asked her if I could come over to her house for dinner. I could pick up some takeout or we could order a pizza.

She said, "Of course," without discernible hesitation.

And then, "But I'll take care of everything. Seven-thirty okay?"

"Great," I said, my voice subdued by the volume of the day.

My interview with the police was as perfunctory as a discussion of mass execution could be. The only mystery about the incident was how long the paperwork was going to take. I was on my way home by five-fifteen.

The snow had continued falling in bushels all day. The city of Boulder's strategy for snow removal involved heavy reliance on solar energy; the streets, therefore, were a disaster. Even with my Subaru wagon in four-wheel drive I barely managed to avoid additional calamity on the three-mile ride up to Spanish Hills in east Boulder.

My neighbor Adrienne's Land Cruiser was winding through the lanes in front of me. She slid down our shared driveway and pulled her big car into the warmth of her attached garage after activating her remote garage door opener. I, in contrast, parked in a foot of snow as close to my front door as I could manage. In three short steps I was totally enshrouded in snowflakes.

One look out the wall of windows on the west side of my odd little home and I was reconsidering my planned visit to Lauren's house. From the perch of my living room on a high ridge in the eastern hills of the Boulder valley I could usually see a hundred miles of the Front Range; that day all I saw was a flickering wall of white against a backdrop of somebody turning down the house lights. I flipped on the TV to see what the local weather wizards had to say.

"A classic winter upslope," the perky weather lady called it. Somehow I was never quite convinced that the moisture that was falling in icy form during these "up-slopes" was actually transported from the warm waters of the Gulf of Mexico or the Sea of Cortés. The weather reporter replayed the satellite image about six times as if repetition would somehow convince those of us in her audience skeptical about the incongruity of tropically generated blizzards.

Pirated previews from *Sports Illustrated*'s upcoming swimsuit edition yanked my attention back to the TV screen. To my dismay, skin and Spandex quickly gave way to dung and denim as some unfortunate reporter wearing the requisite flannel shirt, blue jeans, boots, and cowboy hat came on the air live from the National Western Stock Show in Denver.

The station I sat watching was where my soon-to-be ex-wife, Merideth, was once a producer. Merideth's abrupt decision to leave me had been the loss that tugged on me most before my dog Cicero was hit by the pickup the previous autumn. By then I had two losses. And now I had just dodged a third. I was having trouble generating much gratitude about the near miss. I kept replaying the events of the morning in an effort to allay an annoying blister of guilt, trying to decide what else I might have done. *I should never have let the tall man out of my office.*

Suddenly I was looking at an angled shot of the little office building that Diane Estevez and I owned. I punched the mute button on the remote control to retrieve the sound on the TV. During the mayhem and chaos of the day, I'd managed to avoid the reporters and camera crews. I'd assumed they had been around, though, and from the location of the shot I was watching, it appeared the police had been successful at keeping them well back from the building. The reporter lost her train of thought twice during her stand-up as snowflakes attacked her irises. Despite the fumbles, she had the story pretty straight.

The phone rang. I guessed that it would be my friend and neighbor, Adrienne, concerned about what she'd just seen on the five o'clock news.

I was wrong. The deep voice said, "Alan Gregory? Dr. Gregory?"

After following a trail of dead bodies to my door the previous year, Detective Sam Purdy's usual sardonic salutation for me was "Dr. Deadly," so I was at a bit of a loss to explain to myself why he was being so cordial.

"Hello, Detective."

He said, "I have a few more questions about today, if you don't mind."

The other times he wanted to question me, he chose to do it in my living room. "Are you coming over?"

"Given the atmospherics, I think we can handle this one by phone."

"Fine. Go ahead, then," I said.

He sighed. "The other witness, your patient, Dr. Petro . . . whatever—can you tell me a little about him? Parts of his statement don't quite jibe."

Patient? I thought. Had Eric told the police he was my patient? I sighed. "Detective, you know I can't tell you anything. Privilege, remember?" Purdy would probably have been uninterested in the distinction, but supervision of therapists in training was governed by the same rules of confidentiality as was psychotherapy.

"It was worth a try, right?" His voice was light, with no evidence of animosity.

"Sure, it was worth a try."

"Dr. Gregory . . . you all right?"

Given the fabric of our previous relationship, Sam Purdy inquiring about my well-being was an event about as likely as Patton worrying about whether Rommel was too warm in the desert. "Please call me Alan. And, yeah, I'll be okay. I'm worried about Diane, but I'll be okay."

"Don't sweat about tomorrow's interview for her. The investigation is routine at this point. Our perpetrator is quite dead. We've got witnesses. We've got motive. We'll be real gentle with your friend. Just routine stuff."

"I appreciate that. I really do. Thank you." I hesitated a moment, then asked, "What about you? Are you all right? About the shooting, I mean." I could only guess what kind of mixed emotions would accompany shooting somebody in that morning's circumstances.

The syllabic extensions that accompanied his Iron Range accent grew more pronounced as he replied, "It's funny, but mostly what I feel bad about is that I didn't get in the room sooner. I don't have trouble with the shooting." In northern Minnesota, words like "sooner" and "shooting" came out sounding like "soooooner" and "shooooting." He continued, "There was no choice about firing; the guy was gonna die, he chose that. What bugs me is—this is nuts

—what bugs me is that I stopped to take a leak after I caught the call for the hostage negotiator. I lost, what— two minutes, and *blam blam*, two victims. I keep telling myself I shouldn't have stopped to piss. The things you think about, huh?"

I didn't know what to say. "Are you on administrative leave, or whatever they call it, for the shooting?"

"Officially? Yes."

I made a quick decision. I asked, "I have a question for you, too, Detective. What doesn't jibe about Eric's statement? Is it important?"

"I doubt it. But you know me, no stone unturned, right? Anyway, shit, even if it was important, if I can't drop my bucket into your well, I'm not about to let you drop yours into mine any time you want, now, am I?"

Fair's fair. "I guess not."

"Listen—anything you or your partner need, call me, okay? Victim Services might be of some help. I'll run interference for you. Okay?"

"I'll pass that along to Diane. Thanks. A lot."

"Change your mind about this Eric guy, don't hesitate to call about that, either."

"Don't hold your breath."

I heard him chuckle. "I never do."

As I hung up the phone I recalled Sam Purdy telling me, after I became a reluctant bleeding hero at the conclusion of the case where we met, that he owed me one. I guessed then that he'd meant it.

I fielded two calls from reporters before I grew tired of saying I didn't have any comment to make and having the reporters act as though they were hard of hearing. I phoned Eric Petrosian and left another taped message before I turned on my answering machine and began to get dressed for the blizzard outside.

My trusty Subaru wagon and I made it crosstown to Lauren's house in record slow time. Being in love with Lauren Crowder explained why I put up with her pitched internal battle about getting too close to me. It explained why I put up with it. It didn't excuse it. I still wasn't convinced she was good for me.

She hadn't cut her hair since I'd met her the previous July. When she opened the door her hair was down, plunging like a single curved sheet of black glass to the round of her shoulder blades. A washable silk warm-up suit hung fluidly on her, and when she moved, the flimsy fabric found its way to the separation between her breasts. The silk was pale blue and drew bright tints from her chameleon eyes. Her left hand held a pool cue, tip up, rubber bulb on the floor. There was pink chalk on the narrow bridge of skin that stretched between the thumb and forefinger of her left hand and some on her nose where she must have scratched.

"I thought you'd never get here," she said. "I was getting worried."

"The roads are—"

"I'm sure they are. Come on in. Hurry. You're covered with snow." She brushed me off quickly and then looked me over, counting limbs, looking for evidence of injury. I slithered out of my jacket and tugged off my boots.

She took my hand and led me down the hallway toward her study. "Wait here a second," she said, excusing herself into the bathroom. A moment later, backlit by diffuse yellow light, she appeared like an apparition in the doorway opposite me and beckoned me into her bedroom. Although I was accustomed by then to her penchant for the dramatic naked entrance, I somehow always managed to be ambushed.

While she stood before me plucking at the buttons on my shirt, tugging on my belt, she stopped to kiss me, covering my mouth with hers, whispering, "Shhh. We'll talk later," and then, on her knees, on the floor, yanking on my socks, "If you think there's any chance this will last fewer than thirty minutes, I'll take a few seconds and call Domino's now." I draped my arms over her naked shoulders and laughed for the first time since I'd seen the gun that morning.

I had doubts that she would ever get enough distance from her fears to read my needs with any accuracy. Or respond to them with any sensitivity. But she read this one perfectly even before I was aware I had it.

As she raised herself from the floor to her knees, her fingernails skated fine lines up my legs and she brushed me here and there with her hardened nipples. She ran her fingers through my pubic hair and around to my ass and slowly up my back, long, probing stokes against my taut muscles. My eyes closed and I lost all memory of the day. Her hands moved around to my chest, and then suddenly she pushed me gently back among the mound of pillows on her bed and crawled slowly up the linens to join me, climbing only halfway up.

5

I woke once at Lauren's house during the night. What woke me was the light.

Sometimes, as the final throes of a Front Range snowstorm lingered in the predawn hours, a pale tangerine glow invaded the darkness and infiltrated bedrooms, sneaking around curtains and window shades or illuminating the tiny horizontal slits of miniblinds. During our marriage, Merideth would wake me during decaying blizzards to sit with her and marvel at what she called the "Dreamsicle lights," all vanilla and citrus and coming from nowhere at all.

I didn't wake Lauren to share the lights. I felt selfish and I felt generous. The lights were mine; but sleep was hers.

The second time I awoke the phone was ringing. Lauren's side of the bed was empty and cold. I ignored the phone; Lauren would not welcome the presumption implied by my answering her phone.

Her machine picked up the call after four rings. I heard her familiar taped greeting. Then I heard her call out, "Alan, wake up."

I grabbed the extension by the bed. "Good morning. I think I'm in love," I said.

"Good morning, Alan," she said cryptically before announcing that there had been a new development in the previous day's shooting. Claire Draper, it turned out, had been a witness scheduled before a grand jury the following week.

"You guys don't do grand juries very often, do you? What's it looking into?"

"No, we don't. And you know I can't tell you what they're up to, honey."

"So there are occasional reasons for discretion in communication?"

"Yeah," she said evenly. She wasn't biting at my provocation. The boundaries of confidential communication were a point of ongoing philosophical debate between us.

"Was her testimony important?"

"Crucial, I'm afraid. I hear she was the star."

"You *hear* she was the star? What does that mean?"

"The grand jury isn't mine. And the slaughter at your office yesterday is Elliot's. I'm just a draftee on this campaign."

I said, "So what are the good guys going to do?"

"Don't know. There's a big meeting at noon today to rearrange our cards. Who knows what'll be decided."

I posed the obvious question. "Any chance that Claire's husband didn't want her to testify?"

"Obviously, it's being considered. But there's no connection we can find. The testimony she was scheduled to give is apparently about stuff she knows—knew—from her job. Her husband wasn't part of any of it. Yesterday just looks like a domestic quarrel."

Quarrel? "You know my thoughts about coincidence," I said.

"Yeah, I know. But you can be excused that—it's in your blood. Anyway, most of that stuff's just psychobabble. If you weren't so adorable, nobody would listen to you about any of it."

I suddenly realized there was another reason for this call.

"You're gonna go after Diane about this, aren't you? See what she knows?"

"We're not gonna go after anybody. But we do need to know what she knows. She was part of all this. She was treating the grand jury witness. And she witnessed the murder."

I couldn't argue with any of that. But I felt a twinge for Diane anyway.

"She won't talk to you."

"We'll see."

"You gonna sit in on the interview with her this morning?"

"Probably not. But maybe they'll put out a call for a token female. Who knows? This is police business. But knowing Elliot, he'll be there for sure."

"Be nice?"

"Girl Scout's honor," she said. "By the way, the mechanics who are kind enough to let me drive my cantankerous little Peugeot occasionally say that my period of uninterrupted tenancy is over for a while. Something about valves. Is that serious?"

"Kind of like your pool table having a problem with cushions."

"Really? Damn. In that case, how would you like to buy me dinner and take me home after work?"

"Love to. I'll even take an option on sticking around and taking you back to the office tomorrow morning."

"I'll give that some consideration. Five-fifteen, then?"

"Is five-thirty okay?"

"Yes. See ya. I want Chinese," she said.

I reached Diane late morning on an unlisted second line. Her main number was being screened by Panasonic.

Raoul answered the phone, and he and I spoke for a few minutes about the events of the previous day. He told me that he thought he and Diane would try to get out of town for a while. When Diane got on the line she told me she didn't want to talk about yesterday, "I've only just stopped crying and my eyes feel freeze-dried. Okay?"

I said, "Of course," but I was a little concerned. Diane was a talker. She processed everything. Her reticence was an anomaly.

"How are you?" I asked.

"Pissed."

"And?"

"You know what else? I'm fucking grateful. And I'm even more pissed that I'm fucking grateful. Grateful? Can you believe it? Some *asshole* busts into *my* office and shoots two good, decent women and gets interrupted just before he gets to me and I'm *grateful?* Grateful? God."

I said, "I'm glad you're alive, Diane. I can't imagine how bad it would be if he'd shot you."

Tears in her voice, she said, "You're grateful, too. Wonderful. Listen, enough of this. My eyes, remember?"

I risked another question. "How's Patricia Tobin? Have you heard?"

"Yeah. Raoul talked to her husband this morning. She had a rough night—touch and go. She's out of danger now, but there's a lot of damage. The doctors think that the final step she took into my office yesterday might be the last step she'll ever take."

What was there to say? "I'm so sorry. I'm so sorry I couldn't keep him out of your office."

"Me too, hon. But I had my own chance talking to this guy, too. He wasn't especially open to persuasion. Though you know it's pretty pitiful that being grateful and being sorry are all you and I seem to be able to muster."

She coughed. I think it covered a sob or a sigh.

"You okay with the interview downtown? With the police?" I said.

"Other than being a little fearful that I'll act on my impulse to strangle them for taking so long to get into my office, I'm not much worried about it. That Claire and her husband were separated, that she was battered, that she was living at Safehouse, that he was an asshole—that's all in the public record. Do you know he'd been arrested twice for assaulting her before she left him? Do you know she had a restraining order against him and that he violated it more times than I can count? Do you know he publicly threatened to kill her? I don't need to tell them anything confidential. If the system is looking to indict somebody for failure in all this, they should find some big institutional mirror and just stare into it."

"I guessed there was a history like that."

"Typical. Tragic," she said. I would not have been surprised to hear her growl.

"Any idea how he found out she was with you? Her appointment time?"

"No. This was one frightened lady, Alan. She wouldn't use her car in town. Afraid he'd see it and follow her. She took the bus or borrowed cars from friends. The man had promised her he'd find her and kill her. She never went straight to Safehouse after work—she always stopped someplace or had a friend with her. I don't know how he found out her appointment time. We only kept the same time for three or four sessions. But everything he did seemed planned, you know? I mean, he stopped and kidnapped Patricia Tobin first. Maybe he scared Pat into revealing something. Maybe Claire had told Patricia her appointment time with me for some reason. I don't know. I just don't know."

"What can I do?"

"Actually there is something. I'm not feeling very chatty and I'm scheduled to host the monthly case conference group at my office tonight. You know, the one I started with Paul Weinman?"

"Yeah."

"Can you call everybody and cancel? I'm not up to convincing everybody that I'm fine. Especially since I'm not. Since Paul died the group's been having trouble anyway. I'd probably have to play momma to them all, and I don't want to. Last month it was my turn to present a case. I presented Claire, so I'm sure that everybody in the group will have some exaggerated feelings about all this. Shit, I don't need to explain this to you. Call them, please?"

"Of course, Diane. Who's in the group these days?"

Diane rattled off the names of a couple of local psychiatrists, three social workers, and two other psychologists, most of whom I knew fairly well. "Call Clancy Coates first," she suggested. "He's in Paul's suite and can reach some of these people real easily. And don't forget that new Ph.D. Paul was supervising. The one I begged you to cover until he could line up a new supervisor. Unlicensed, young—rented space in Paul's suite. Eric, uh, Petrosian. You seen him yet?"

"Yeah. I've seen him twice. He was in the office yesterday. I was meeting with him when all this . . . came down."

"Shit." She paused for a couple of seconds. "I'm glad that's your problem and not mine. All the more reason to cancel the supervision group tonight." She gave me phone numbers for the two group members I didn't know well. We talked a little more, Diane's denial in tidal conflict with her rage.

Eric Petrosian wasn't my problem for long. After Diane and I hung up I called my Voicemail to retrieve some messages. One was from Eric saying thanks for my help, but that he had found somebody who would act as a permanent supervisory replacement for Dr. Paul Weinman, his recently deceased supervisor. He closed by saying that our work together had "certainly been memorable."

I was instantly relieved not to be supervising him any longer.

I shouldn't have been surprised that the shooting had caused Diane to dwell, again, on Paul Weinman's death. Paul had been one of her best friends, and she'd eulogized him only a couple of weeks earlier.

I'd known Paul Weinman for years and had shared a couple of cases with him. His clinical skills were exemplary. But he and I had not been close. Diane, though, had been one of his good friends and one of his closest professional colleagues outside the cadre of his office suite. In fact, years before, she and Paul had been the founders of an ongoing clinical case conference group.

Despite the professional distance of our relationship, Paul's simple funeral had made an unexpected impression on me. His casket had been closed and was constructed of unfinished pine. I remembered thinking the humble box didn't seem wide enough to contain Paul's portly body.

Before the service, Diane and I had mingled on the sidewalk in front of the mortuary for ten minutes, talking with colleagues—psychologists, psychiatrists, and social workers—about Paul's accident the previous Friday. Paul had been skiing at Breckenridge, had somehow lost a ski, and had crashed into a tree. He'd been pronounced dead before the Flight for Life helicopter could whisk him to Denver for emergency care.

Some of the sidewalk conversation had to do with speculation about failed bindings and snow-crusted antiskid plates. But more had to do with shock and grief, with finding words of condolence for Paul's family, or words of support for the colleagues who knew Paul well or shared office space with him, or whispers of empathy for Cybil Malone, a therapist, one of us, Paul's steady companion since his separation from his wife the previous year.

Paul Weinman had been no better prepared for death than the rest of us.

At first his will couldn't be located. His lawyer was somewhere in Cancún. Some of Paul's patients stumbled across news of his death in the local paper or on the evening news. One of his colleagues in his office suite, apparently wanting to spare Paul's patients the anonymous announcement of their therapist's death in the media, had searched files for numbers and over the weekend telephoned many of his patients to let them know that he had died. There was some brief sidewalk discussion about how Paul should have designated somebody as custodian of his files in the event of his death. We all promised ourselves we would get our affairs in order. Few of us would.

I held Diane's cold hand as Paul's funeral service began. My grief wasn't severe; I was attending to display my respect for Paul and to support Diane. Raoul, Diane's husband, was out of town or he would have been in my seat.

As the rabbi concluded his perfunctory remarks about Paul, Diane let go of my hand and walked to the podium to deliver a eulogy.

"Those of us who know Paul well," she began, "know what a unique day this is for him." She paused and opened her dark eyes wide to create more surface for her tears to evaporate.

"Because if you know Paul Weinman at all, you know —that not since he stretched his poor mother's belly and her pregnancy to ten months plus, not since he took nine years of graduate school to get his doctorate, not since he filed for an extension with the Internal Revenue Service *every* year for the past twenty-five—you know that one thing dear Paul Weinman has never been is *on time*. For anything. Ever. If Paul and I agreed to meet for lunch at twelve, I didn't even start looking around for him until twenty after. If tennis was scheduled at ten-thirty, I didn't think of reserving a court before eleven.

"And today, look"—she turned and held out a hand toward the pine box, her voice almost admonishing—"God bless him, he was the first one here."

The congregated mourners laughed until Diane's voice brought them back.

"And that's how I know he's really gone."

When the dust all settled, Paul's will instructed Diane to take custody of his records. Nobody was surprised.

Lauren was only five minutes late joining me in the Subaru for sesame scallops and a ride home.

She put her hand on my leg just above my knee, received my welcoming kiss graciously, scrunched up her face, and said, "Can we run one little errand before dinner?"

I sighed. "Such as?"

"We've been recontacting witnesses scheduled to go before this grand jury. You know the one that Claire Draper was going to star in? Anyway, this storm has the phones out in the part of town where one of them lives, and I just need to stop by and ask him a couple of questions. You can stay in the car and listen to 'All Things Considered.' " She smiled. "Please? I promised Elliot I'd do this for him."

"What part of town?"

"Not far. Off Canyon, by the creek, east of Seventeenth."

Our destination was only a mile away. Her directions were flawless, and five minutes later we pulled in front of a Frank Lloyd Wright–inspired design of native sandstone with lots of horizontal windows and long planes of flat roof. The whole row of spacious houses backed up to the Boulder Creek bike path. I'd ridden past the back of the house on my bike many times and had admired it from the rear. I couldn't recall seeing the front before, though.

I parked the car on the street in front of the house. Lauren got out and dodged snow until she made it to the well-shoveled sidewalk. She bounded up three concrete steps and knocked on the front door. I watched her check her wristwatch, knock again, wait for a moment, and then move around to the side of the house, down the driveway, and into the backyard.

A couple of minutes later she reemerged and raised her palms to the sky in exasperation. Just as she was getting back into the Subaru with me, a Volvo station wagon raced down the street at high speed, turned recklessly into the long drive, and pulled from sight behind the house.

"That's our guy," she said. "Though I think I may need to have a little chat with him about his driving. But don't worry. This will just take a minute." She dawdled, searching her briefcase for something, allowing him time to get into the house, then she headed back toward the front door. On her way she exaggerated the sway of her excellent hips for my benefit.

I was smiling in appreciation and she was halfway to the steps when the house exploded.

6

Concussion rocked the car. Lauren flew straight back down the walk as though she were a player on a videotape that had been reversed. Distinctly, after a delay, the sound track started—rumble and roar, not crisp like the gunshots I'd recently heard, but drawn out long and low. The walls of the house near the ground burst out sideways, as if shoved aside by a giant wall of water. But there was no water. And then with a thunderous crash the heavy roof settled on the rubble. The last notes were high and sharp, the sound of glass shattering.

The neighboring houses stood intact, their erect posture mocking the adjacent destruction. Dust and debris fluttered to the heavy blanket of snow on the ground around the demolition.

Lauren was crawling back toward the house.

I jumped out of the car and stopped her. She protested momentarily, not quite digesting what had happened, and then allowed me to support her and guide her back to the car as I scanned her body for blood or missing pieces.

"We need to call somebody, get some help," she said.

"Lauren, are you all right? Do you know where you are?"

She ignored me, her gaze transfixed by the day's waning light, the settling dust, and the echoes of explosion.

"I think it was a bomb," she said.

"Maybe," I said distractedly. But my concern was only about her. Was she all right?

A minute passed, and sirens filled the air. In moments police cars, rescue vehicles, and fire trucks surrounded us. Lauren and I leaned against the Subaru, dazed, and watched the assembly multiply until a paramedic guided us into an ambulance. Inside the ambulance it was warm.

We were treated to free physicals. The paramedics were unswayed by our assertions that we weren't hurt. Lauren's protests were more vocal than mine, as was her style. Her shock was abating, and she wanted to get back outside and play DA. The examinations we received in the ambulance were quite thorough.

I followed her back to the scene. I was confused by my first perception of the explosion. The images that were frozen in my mind were all horizontal. Explosions should go up, I thought, not out. But everything had looked lateral. I didn't know what to make of it.

The chaos control accoutrements were being set in place. Yellow ribbons identified a wide perimeter around the collapsed house. Uniformed Boulder police officers eased back a well-behaved, curious crowd. A patrol car–mounted loudspeaker urged everyone in the neighborhood out of their houses and into the street. Nearby Boulder High School was identified as the closest evacuation center.

Masked fire fighters were crawling over and into the debris. A cop wearing a bomb squad jacket recognized Lauren. She quickly told him what had happened and told him that there was probably only one person inside. He asked if she knew who it was. She said, "Yes," and told him the homeowner's name was Lawrence Templeton.

She turned to me. "This is murder," she said crisply.

I put an arm around her, which she removed immediately.

"Where's my briefcase?"

"You left it in the car. It's safe."

"Is the car locked?"

"I don't know. I don't think so."

"Go lock it," she ordered me. "Make sure the briefcase is there first. No—bring it to me." Her tone convinced me that our date was over before it began and that I was now a civilian fortunate enough to be permitted to assist the authorities.

As I was locking the car a voice said, "Go-oin' somewhere?"

Detective Sam Purdy was shaking his big head. "Hi, Sam," I said. "Here we go again, huh?"

He just nodded.

I pointed at the briefcase. "Lauren's waiting for this." Purdy called over a patrolwoman and told her to sit me in a patrol car until he was free for a chat. Purdy reached for the briefcase, and I handed it over to him. He suggested I should go get warm.

He broke away to find Lauren striding toward him.

The policewoman put me in a black-and-white Chevrolet and closed the door. She stood outside, arms crossed over her chest, observing the mayhem.

Purdy came back about twenty minutes later.

"They found the guy. Dead. Crushed bad." He popped something, a candy or maybe an antacid, into his mouth. "What did you see?" he asked.

I described the explosion to Purdy. He tried a few questions to which I answered, "I don't know." He seemed mildly disappointed that I had been mere audience, that I didn't have a few sticks of dynamite poking out of my pocket.

"Sam, was it a bomb? Why did the blast seem to go out, not up?"

"Who knows? The bomb guys say it doesn't smell like a bomb at this point. They're guessin' gas. A heavy gas."

"Like natural gas?"

"That's what I asked. He tells me they're all natural, then he laughs. Bomb disposal guys have this strange view of the world. Anyway, says it could be natural gas or propane, or methane, or this 'ane or that 'ane. Some are heavy—they settle. Some are light—they rise. He doubts it's natural gas, though, because the guy should've smelled it. Or maybe Lauren would've smelled it when she was at the door. He said that if there was enough of a concentration to do this and she had rung the bell instead of knocking, she could be dead, too. Just a little spark will do it. He guesses the guy created a spark when he came in the house. Or maybe he switched on the furnace or started a kettle for a cuppa tea . . . whatever."

When Purdy was done with me he told me I could go.

"I'm Lauren's ride home."

"Not to worry. I'll get her home. *Safely,* I might add." His implication was that hitching a ride home with Charlie Manson would be safer than hanging around with me.

I searched for Lauren and found her huddled with Elliot Bellhaven. Lauren's forehead was pink and her lips were pursed forward. She gestured forcefully with her left hand, something she did only when angry. Elliot was unruffled, as always.

Lauren's breath was visible and shallow when I interrupted to say good-bye. Elliot's greeting and smile were natural and warm.

"Lauren, may I talk to you for just a minute?" I said.

"Alan, please, I'm busy," she said, distracted.

"I know. Please, it won't take long."

She walked a few feet away from Elliot Bellhaven and Sam Purdy, who began conferring about something. I didn't have much of her attention.

I touched one of my cold hands to her cheek, captured her gaze, and said, "Lauren, don't shut me out. I just need to know you're okay. If you're too busy to be nice to me, just say so. I'll understand. But don't ignore me. I won't tolerate it again. I didn't blow the guy's house up, lady." She stared at me impassively. I waited, then said, "I guess I'm going to go. Sam Purdy said he'd get you a ride home."

She touched me lightly on the shoulder as I turned away. "Alan, you're right," she said. "You're right." Then, in a softer voice, "I'm not being fair to you. But I'm really all right. And I'm sorry if I've been . . . rude."

I nodded an acknowledgment, said, "Thank you," kissed her gently, and threaded the Subaru home through the maze of rescue vehicles.

I watched the local news for their report of the explosion and then surfed the black pads of the remote control, looking for more coverage. All the network affiliates had live crews at the scene, and ABC and CNN picked up local feeds and took the coverage national. The newscasts played some tape of the scene shortly after the explosion; I saw myself sitting in the ambulance with Lauren. As the voice-over reported that the police were not willing to discuss possible causes or suspects, the video image shifted to me sitting bored in the back of the black-and-white, a policewoman blocking my escape.

"This is great," I said aloud, to no one. I had to laugh.

7

Going to work the next morning seemed irreverent considering the litany of tragedy I had stumbled upon over the previous forty-eight hours.

My first patient that day was tall. I found her height disconcerting. Over my years of practice I had discovered that my patients tended to get taller as their psychological scars healed. Men who had shown up for their first session short and stocky would say good-bye at termination looking me level in the eye. Women who were frail and bent somehow stood straight and average in height by the time their work was done.

The woman on the chair across the room from me was going to cause major problems with my hypothesis. If Elaine Casselman got much taller, she wouldn't fit through my door. As I pondered this predicament she paused from the story she was telling and turned to me for a reply. She made eye contact for only a second, as much as she ever tolerated.

I waited. Her anxiety accelerated. Silence did that. Finally I said, "Well, now there's one thing you know. And there's one thing you don't know."

She acted as though she hadn't heard me. It was possible that she was chewing on the ambiguity of my confrontation. More likely she had retreated to some place where a comforter of hysterical denial insulated her from the chill of words like mine.

Elaine Casselman's body had been made for someone else. Despite having had twenty-nine years to get comfortable with its striking proportions, six feet three, maybe one hundred thirty-five pounds, she still tucked her sharp elbows in close to her prominent ribs, bowed her prodigious shoulders, and sat at such an angle in her chair that she could hope to disguise the dramatic length of her legs. When she entered my office for the first time a month before and I saw her walking, so uncomfortable with herself, I wondered if she simply wanted to be smaller. I knew now, after half a dozen sessions with her, that she would have preferred to be invisible.

Elaine swept sandy hair away from her mouth. The cut of her hair was sharp and close to her face, as if to caricature her angularity. She made no attempt to enhance or soften any feature. Her clothes, she had once confessed, were all catalog bought, never altered, never returned. Even her shoes didn't seem to fit.

Within minutes of beginning her first appointment she told me she was "a voluntary virgin, not a real one." After a moment waiting for an elucidation, I told her I wasn't sure I understood. "I was sort of raped in Australia," she explained, and smiled. I paused, again looking to let her take the lead. "It was my only time. You know." She blushed. "So I've never done it voluntarily. I'm a voluntary virgin."

It disheartened me even more over the next few minutes to learn that the purpose of her recounting these facts seemed to be to frame the desperation she was feeling about her loneliness. She yearned for what she didn't have: a relationship with a man. The rape seemed as unimportant as dust in some corner of her life. I was saddened.

"You were 'sort of raped'?" I was ambivalent about pursuing the rape so early in treatment; maybe I should have dropped it.

But she nodded matter-of-factly, as if I had asked her if she was an engineer at IBM, which she was. And she went on to something else.

A pathetic tone marked the next few meetings. Then she met Max.

"You said something about knowing things. Didn't you? I was thinking about Max. Sorry." Her smile was conspiratorial and illicit.

Max was her lover of "sixteen days and sixteen hours" and had her spinning like a whirlpool. She had been telling me the things that they had in common, of the fun they had, of the food they ate, of the sex they had—great for him, he apparently kept telling her; dry and dead for her, she told me—and of the time he had almost strangled her when she got more playful in bed than he wanted. "It was my fault. I should've known when to stop. We talked about it. He apologized even though I told him it was my fault. Isn't that great? I mean, of him? That he said he's sorry. I told him not to worry about it."

That was when I said, "Well, now there's one thing you know. And there's one thing you don't know." At her acknowledgment that she hadn't heard me, I repeated myself for her. She looked at me then with a face that defied interpretation and tugged some more errant hairs from her mouth.

"So what is it that I know?" she asked. The defensiveness was so clear, I could almost picture a barbed-wire fence in front of the words.

I said, "You know that this dog bites."

She interrupted her inhale for an instant, then breathed deeper than she would have. She crinkled her nose. "What dog?"

I allowed her to find an answer to her own question and then nodded my head while I said, "Max."

I found some encouragement in the defiance I saw in her face. "And what is it that I don't know?"

"Any guesses?"

She shrugged, annoyed.

"You don't know when he'll bite again."

A pause. "He won't. He promised."

"This dog bites. Whether you like knowing it or not, you know that now."

"He won't," she countered without conviction.

"And the man in Australia said you were friends, that you could trust him."

She glared at me.

Elaine always asked permission. "May I change the subject?"

I didn't respond. She waited, then said, "Well?"

"I'm not here to tell you what to do. I doubt I even need to point out what your diversion is about."

The mild confrontation glanced off her like bullets off Wonder Woman's bracelets. "I," she said, puffing out her chest, "am on jury duty. *Grand* jury duty, no less."

Much of psychotherapy is permitting the obvious. "You're pleased."

"I think it's exciting. Don't you?"

She couldn't stand my not approving of her feelings.

I didn't reply.

"The prosecutor said everything's confidential. He said we couldn't tell anyone about what we hear. That doesn't include you, does it? Since you can't tell anyone anyway."

I was always a little uncomfortable hearing information in psychotherapy that was legally privileged in another arena. But my discomfort was my problem. It certainly wasn't my role to tell Elaine what she could and couldn't talk about.

Anyway, given the events of the past two days, I was more than a little curious.

My next appointment was with Randy Navens.

Randy, now seventeen, had been in psychotherapy with me since about six months after his parents and sister were killed in the crash of United Airlines Flight 232 in Sioux City, Iowa. He'd been referred to me by Diane, who had been treating his sister prior to her death. Randy arrived in my office for his initial appointment tormented by memory-bleached nightmares and feelings of anguished loneliness, helplessness, and failure. He was ashamed of his accidental wealth, and he was guilty about being the sole member of his immediate family to survive the crash.

His father's younger sister and her husband had moved into the Navenses' home and assumed guardianship of then fifteen-year-old Randy. Their nephew was in constant conflict with them about many things. According to Randy, his guardians blamed the chronic conflict in the household on him and, obliquely, on the crash. Randy thought they were angry primarily because the terms of Randy's parents' will gave him—Randy—the money and his aunt and uncle all the responsibility. Randy said their indifference to him was simple—they didn't want him around; their real baby was their new restaurant, Pain Perdu, outside of town. Randy's uncle wanted the freedom to spend some of his nephew's considerable inheritance—a combination of life insurance proceeds and settlement dollars from the crash —and constantly reminded Randy what a mess his father and mother had created by designating someone else trustee of the money. The house, the uncle argued, desperately needed central air, and Randy's aunt couldn't figure out how Randy's mother had managed in her hopelessly outdated kitchen. In defiance Randy lived like an ascetic, his millions in abeyance, in trust, insisting to his trustee that he needed the house to stay exactly as it was.

" 'In trust.' Odd term, don't you think?" Randy didn't wait for my reply. "If they trusted me, they'd let me have it so I could do what I want with it. If I trusted them . . ." His own words puzzled him. "It's like saying 'If I could fly.' No way I'll trust 'em."

He looked at me as if he wanted to tell me something. Randy had been a good student, mostly B's, a few A's, before the DC-10 crashed in the corn field in Iowa. He was straight A's now. I suspected he was smoking some dope, but I had gone no further than voicing my suspicions, only to be met with his silent stares.

He raised his hands to his face and rubbed his eyes with the backs of his hands, his fingers spread to the sky. As he lowered his arms he said, "I spent some money. I bought a new car."

"And?"

"Isn't that what everybody wants? Aren't you thrilled?"

"Is it what you wanted to do?"

Silence. He was disinterested in "things."

He raised the stakes. "I've got a gun, too."

Great. Now I'm thrilled. Not too provocative, kid. "You've got a gun?"

He reached into his day pack and pulled it out. "See?"

The gun was chrome. Stocky and square. Large.

"Please put it down, Randy."

"Why? You scared?"

"Yes. I'm scared of the gun."

My candor apparently surprised him. He put the weapon on the table to the left of his chair, between us.

I repeated, "So. You have a gun."

"You gonna tell anybody?"

So that's what this is about, I thought. Trust was on the table right there next to the pistol.

"Depends."

He looked at me askance and asked, "On what?"

"Your plans."

In an instant his reticence disappeared. He jumped in. "I got it to kill myself, I think. And then, once I had it, I went back and forth. I had it last week when I was here. I was gonna tell you. Didn't. Once I had it with me there didn't seem to be any hurry."

"So it gives you a sense of control?"

"I guess. At least of my death. That's something."

"It is. It's more than you had over the other deaths."

He rocked a little bit at my interpretation but didn't acknowledge any impact. "I'm still afraid you're gonna tell me I need to be in the fucking psych hospital."

"Do you?"

"Do I what?"

"Do you need to be in the hospital?"

He thought for a moment. "No. Don't think so."

"Still thinking about killing yourself?"

"I think about it. I'm not gonna do it today." He laughed a little, as if I should be amused and reassured.

"Where did you get it?" I looked down at the gun.

"It was my dad's. He liked guns. Not hunting. Got my mom interested. They would go to the range and target shoot. They have a few pairs of pistols in the house. He's always kept 'em locked up. I found the keys."

"You want to leave it here?" Over the years I'd taken custody of prescription medicines, packages of single-edge razor blades, a hunting knife, and even a set of car keys —all to retard the suicidal impulses of various patients. However, I'd never before been the custodian of a gun.

"You mean the gun?" He knew I meant the gun.

I nodded. "But I think I mean the keys, too."

"Leave 'em with you? What are you gonna do with them?"

I smiled a tiny bit. "Exactly what your dad always did. Lock them up until you're ready to be responsible with them."

"You almost trust me, don't you?" he asked.

"I do trust you, Randy. I even trust the fear you have that you're going to hurt somebody with that. Especially yourself. I'm willing to help until we can do whatever work we need to do to make that impulse pass."

"I almost trust you," he told me.

"I'm glad about that," I said. "It will help you understand why I need to tell your uncle and aunt about this."

He was nonplussed. "That's no big deal, they won't care," he said. I feared that he was right.

He left the gun and a couple of keys on a ring with a leather fob. I slid everything into a manila envelope and locked it into a cabinet full of my old files.

That night I left a message for Randy's guardians to call me. At around nine-thirty his uncle finally returned my call. I heard restaurant noises in the background.

I told him what Randy had done. What I had done in response.

He said, "Kids, huh?"

I said, "Excuse me?"

Geoff Tobias said, "Kids today. It's always something, huh?"

"Yes," I said, and wasted a few minutes trying to explain to Geoff what my concerns were about his nephew and what he should be on the lookout for.

"Glad to help. Glad to help. Anything else?" he said.

I couldn't think of a thing.

8

"Alan?"

"Yes."

"It's Me."

Me who?

"Hi. Hello," I said, trying to keep the befuddlement from my voice.

"Me. Merideth. Remember? Me."

Oh. *That* Me.

Me. As in MErideth. My wife.

It was probably the first of our intimate names for each other. I would playfully call Merideth by the first two letters of her name. As in, "Me, I'm home." It was a fun game, eventually spoiled by one of Diane's more dour shrink friends who overheard us using it. "Sounds borderline to me," said Diane's friend, commenting on the ego boundary–blurring implications and employing the pejorative shrink vernacular that was roughly the mental health equivalent of calling someone a communist during Joe McCarthy's days in Washington.

Merideth's use of the pet name now was an anachronism. And one I suspected was not without meaning. After Diane's friend poisoned our fun, Merideth and I pulled the name out rarely, reserving its use for moments requiring special intimacy. Intimacy for which "sweetheart" and "honey" were inadequate.

"Hi, hello. How are you?" I said to Merideth while I took inventory of my potential energy stocks, judging whether there was enough on reserve to sustain a protracted "Let's take one final look at our marriage" conversation. Or, even worse, an "I'm having second thoughts about the settlement we signed" confrontation.

"Okay, I guess. Considering," she said. I assumed she meant considering that our dissolution would be final sometime in the next few days.

Even though she was the one who had left me, my bruises had healed enough that I could again empathize with her sadness about ending our marriage. She had made the choice to be free of me and didn't seem to regret it. But the milestone act of wrenching free was a painful one. In divorce court, Colorado style, one could plan the legal slaughter of a marriage months or even years in advance with the assurance that the marital cow could actually be sacrificed in the relative anonymity of some clerk's or referee's office downtown. That's how our divorce was planned. This dissolution would happen by proxy. But we both knew when the blood would be let.

"Yeah. I know. Even though you've been gone a year and a half, I still get sad thinking it's almost over. I mean, for real, legally."

Her next words followed so rapidly that she must have been waiting for me to finish speaking. "I want to see you one more time before it's final."

I said nothing for half a minute, wondering after a few of the seconds passed if there was anything noisier than a silent telephone connection.

"You do?" I managed.

"You're surprised."

"Sure. Yes, I am. I haven't heard from you since you called to chastise me about my greediness over wanting to keep the rug in the bedroom. That was, what, couple weeks before Christmas?"

"It was a difficult time. I'm sorry if I was a bitch."

"So what's up? Why now?"

Merideth sighed. "I need to see you one more time. Why? Maybe it's like flipping through a book you've read before you return it to the library. I don't know. Maybe that's not it, maybe it's just like your coming out to see me last November." She paused, and we both remembered. "I was hoping you'd want to do this, too. I guess you don't."

I was ambivalent. "It's not that, it's—"

"Alan, I didn't want to have to say please. But I will. Please. May I come out to see you?"

More trenchant silence.

I'd said good-bye to Merideth, for good, I thought, during that visit the previous November. I'd given her up reluctantly. And now, even after a year and a half of separation, I feared that I was still doomed to crave her. That's why I didn't want to have to say good-bye again.

I wouldn't tell her that, now, though.

I said, "If it's that important, all right."

"I can get a flight out Friday. Will that work for you?"

"Fine. Call my Voicemail and leave a flight number and arrival time. I'll pick you up."

"Thanks, Alan. I mean it. I'm grateful. I'm not dense enough to think you want to do this. Thank you." She hung up.

Merideth's plane was right on time. The world worked according to her schedule. Always had. I fantasized that before each flight she'd call the airline, suggest that she was producing a news feature on flight tardiness, and imply there would be a crew on such and such a flight. I could think of no other way she always managed to have her flights arrive on time. Especially in Denver.

When she first emerged from the jetway, little about her looked familiar. Her clothes were coast smart, and her blond hair was long and loosely ponytailed. She'd left me short-coiffed and dressed like a captain of industry. And the expensive carry-on suitcase and matching garment bag she carried were certainly not detritus of our relationship.

As she approached I saw more I recognized. Her walk, as always, was confident and hinted at arrogance. The skin of her face was soft and pale, her lips fresh with lipstick, her cheekbones highlighted with just a little powdered color. Her violet eyes focused, then jumped, searching for me, I guess, darting discreetly from one face in the crowd to another. Merideth never, ever, looked out of place.

I stayed half-obscured by a pillar I was holding up. I was searching her visible demeanor for clues about the purpose of her visit.

When I finally stepped forward she located me instantly and moved in with a fluidity that unnerved me. She led with her shiny lips. I hesitated, offered a cheek, and realized late that I needed to shave.

I took the garment bag from her shoulder and reported the obvious. "You look great. California still agrees with you."

Her eyes were the almost purple of a perfect plum, entreating, maybe a little moist. They were eyes in which I'd proven a propensity to lose myself. "You look good, too," she said, "and I have to admit I'm glad the beard's not back."

With a hand on the small of her back, I accompanied her down the concourse. She turned to me and asked, quickly, as if she had intended to ask right away and almost forgotten, "How's your shoulder?"

I'd been knifed by a maniac ex-patient the previous autumn, and Merideth had last seen me when I was still stiff and sore, just out of my sling.

I waved the arm in the air like a fool and said, "All better. See?"

Under a black leather jacket she wore a rayon blouse of blues and striking reds. With the tug of the weight of her suitcase on her right shoulder, the fabric of the shirt sagged enough to offer a view of the swell of the top of one breast and of the pale skin stretched over the hard protrusion of her sternum. It was terrain I knew well.

Distracted, I asked, "How was your flight?"

"Fine. First-class upgrade. You know me, the frequent flyer." Merideth was a producer for the San Francisco–based West Coast bureau of one of the networks, and searching out features took her far and wide. She'd more than hinted that she traveled an amount she was sure I would have found intolerable. Apparently another good reason we were divorcing.

Reason number one, and the deal killer, was Merideth changing her mind about having children. I woke one

morning suddenly assured that the time had come for us
to have a baby. She shared my excitement for two months,
maybe three, until I confronted her about the foil of birth
control pills that spilled out of her dropped purse one night
in the car.

"I've changed my mind," she had said.

It was the first line of the play that led us to this anti-
climax.

"Have you eaten?" I wondered, knowing the response
already. She'd say, "I had a bite on the plane."

"I had a bite on the plane," she said. "But I'm still
hungry." She hesitated a couple of seconds and said, "How
about Dario's. Just for a nosh?" Dario's was an Italian-
Swiss trattoria-bistro where Merideth and I had frequently
rendezvoused for romantic, homey meals during better
times, times when she was still producing features at one
of the Denver TV stations. I'd drive in to interrupt one of
her twelve-hour days. We'd have an early dinner and once
or twice even screwed in the car in the parking lot of the
television station before she headed back to work.

"Sure," I said, "if that's what you want." I hadn't been
back to Dario's since she'd left me.

I headed west out of the airport on Martin Luther King
Boulevard and parked on the street in front of the restaurant after just a few turns.

Merideth and I spent the next two hours reminiscing. I
was reminiscing, anyway. I found it comforting yet sad to
talk about our years together, our home, our dog, our
fights. Our sex. Merideth was more upbeat. Maybe it was
a reflection of her year in a professional suburb of Hol-
lywood, but her recounting of memories of our past
sounded like the few minutes of recaps of "previous episodes" that precede the finale in televised miniseries. I
kept having the disconcerting sensation that there was to
be another installment.

After leaving the restaurant and heading northwest toward Boulder, I asked, "Where are you staying?"

She replied without turning toward me in the car.
"You're not making this easy, honey. I'd like to stay in

our house. Well, as of next week, your house. It's important to me."

I made up the guest room bed for her when we got back to the house. I half expected, half wanted her to sneak into my bed during the night.

She didn't. I was seven-eighths relieved.

We spent Saturday together and that night had dinner at Peter and Adrienne's house up the hill. Adrienne was witty and Peter distracting. But the melancholy of the impending divorce seeped in frequently during the evening.

Throughout Merideth's visit I found myself tearing off and on at our failures and changes, and puzzled about the true purpose of her visit.

I drove her back to the airport on Sunday morning, and we sat in the No Parking zone at curbside to say goodbye. My prescience that something had gone unsaid all weekend proved accurate.

I turned to kiss her, I thought, a last time. She interrupted my momentum and held my face in both her hands and kissed me soft once and then again, hard, on the mouth. She held me there, freezing me in place, searching my eyes for something. Her lips were two inches from mine when she spoke.

What she said was, "I'm pregnant."

I didn't know whether to say "Congratulations" or "I'm sorry." I was flustered that I didn't know. Finally I managed the truth: "I don't know what to say."

She sat back on the seat. "And I don't know what to do." She sighed. "I wanted to talk to you about it all weekend, but you seemed so guarded around me. I'm sorry. I need you to be my friend now. And maybe it's just too soon. I want your advice. I want you to tell me what to do. And then"—she smiled here—"just like old times, I want the absolute freedom to ignore your suggestions. But instead, I just feel out of place, like an ex-wife, I guess. I don't know. I don't know. I suppose I should have told you on the phone before I came out. Maybe I shouldn't have come at all."

I was reeling. O. Henry would have loved this.

I said, "What does the, um—"

"Father think?"

"Yeah."

"I haven't told him. I'm not sure I want to give him a vote about all this."

I had some strong feelings about that stand but kept them to myself. "You don't love him?" I said.

She shook her head and started to cry just a little. "No. No. I don't love him."

"How pregnant?"

"One hundred percent, unfortunately." Then, "Six weeks and two days. But who's counting, right?"

I caught her eyes in mine. "You've always been real clear about this, Me. You don't want kids. You've got a choice. Hell, for all I know you're still a board member in NARAL. If you don't want this baby, why not an abortion, honey?" I was aware of pulses of anger stirring my blood. The irony of all this was grating. A few days before this woman finally divorces me because of her discomfort with my desire for a child, she announces she's pregnant.

"You're right, I have a choice. But I'm not sure abortion's the right solution for me this time, Alan." The other time she was alluding to was an abortion she'd had during her junior year in college.

"Neither, in the not-so-distant past, was pregnancy," I said. I would have liked to be above a well-placed dig; I wasn't.

She whispered, "Ouch." Suddenly hurried, she hugged me tightly and hopped out of the Subaru. She stared at me the whole time she was opening the back door and grabbing her bags. Looking for something, waiting. She bent down a last time and said, " 'Bye love."

She was crying.

And I couldn't tell whether I was more angry or more sad.

9

Adrienne asked me up the hill for coffee.

My dog Cicero and I had made the short trek a few hundred times before she was hit by a pickup the previous autumn. Often I still felt her presence beside me as I walked. Cicero was always serene and well behaved when she looked in on me in those months after she died, never too exuberant, never ornery. Death and the bleach of memories had tamed her. I was comforted and saddened by it each time.

Adrienne screamed, "In here," after I cracked open her front door and called her name. I found her in the kitchen, recently installed as a permanent gallery for her husband's woodworking talents. The cabinets and island were all handmade from South American hardwoods and were devoid of right angles. At the time of the construction of his kitchen cabinets, Peter, like most of the rest of us, had been ignorant about rain forest annihilation.

Adrienne was fussing with a coffee maker that had spouts for drip coffee, espresso, and steamed milk and digital readouts for time, temperature, and days till the vernal equinox.

"You recovered?" she asked.

"From?"

"Don't be a complete putz. From Merideth. The prodigal wife."

"Yeah. Despite my initial dread about her visit, I'm actually glad she came. I think it was good to have a little time together before the divorce is final. But it wasn't my idea of a fun weekend, if that's what you're wondering." I hesitated before I continued, sipping from the mug that

Adrienne shoved my way down the counter. In my heart I knew that saying—to Adrienne—what I was about to say next was the equivalent of making a shovel the tool of choice for getting myself out of a hole.

I said, "She's pregnant, Ren."

Adrienne's dark eyes opened wide. "Merideth? Seriously?"

I nodded.

"Of course, of course." She gently tapped herself on the forehead with the heel of her right hand. "So she wants you back. That's it, right?"

I'd thought of that already, too. Instead of acknowledging it, though, I said, "Don't be absurd. She just wanted some advice. Wanted to say good-bye."

"Bullshit," said my friend with a smile that looked reptilian. "Wake up. She somehow managed to find an accidental sperm donor. Now she's looking for a surrogate daddy. That's you, Mr. Rogers."

"She talk to you about this?"

"No. But it does make some sense of the way she was treating you over the weekend. She was like, examining you, you know. It seemed like a weekend test drive. It all makes sense now."

"I think you're decompensating," I said. Despite the fact that I, too, had been ruminating about the possibilities, I nonetheless decided to press my argument. Adrienne was *too* certain already, and she would feed on any equivocation on my part like a shark on fresh chum.

"Whatever," she said. My protests had been dismissed. "You seem to forget—fertility is one of my subspecialties; I know about this shit. And the doctor has spoken. Merideth Gregory was here on a recruitment visit—you know, like a coach coming in before the draft or the national letter of intent day or whatever athletic servitude is referred to as during these enlightened times. God! The irony of it all. When's the divorce supposed to be final?"

"By the end of the week."

Adrienne's speech became clipped and rapid when she was excited. She was zipping along way above fifty-five. "I predict a postponement." She read doubt in my face.

"You wait. I'm right about this. Wanna bet?" She held out one of her tiny hands. "Dinner at Pain Perdu? For four. I'm right, which I am, you and the prosecutor and me and Geppetto go to dinner and you buy." Geppetto was her occasional sobriquet for her carpenter husband, Peter.

I shook her hand and nodded. "You're on," I said, falsely confident, quite conscious that Adrienne's instincts were rarely fallible.

She fumbled around trying to rip open a packaged Pop-Tart, finally resorting to taking a cleaver to its center, extracting half the ersatz pastry from each end of the divided bag, and offering me one. I declined.

"You know, I envy you and I don't," she said.

I watched in amazement as she began eating the Pop-Tart untoasted. Her mouth was momentarily too full to continue the speech she was contemplating. I gave her a moment, savoring her abundant energy. She sat on a tall stool that Peter had made out of twigs and branches. It didn't look as if it would maintain its balance and didn't appear capable of supporting weight. Like much about Peter, it was deceiving. With Adrienne as passenger, however, the stool wasn't required to support much weight. She was small and dark and elfin.

"Yes?" I said with some ambivalence about encouraging her to go on.

She took another bite of Pop-Tart before proceeding. The astringent quality of the barely cooked dough was making it difficult for her to find enough moisture to lubricate her mouth for speech. She persevered. "I picked Peter during my first year in med school. He was like an antidote to everything I hated about medicine. Doctors sprint. He ambles. Doctors examine and diagnose. He ponders. Doctors are sophisticated. He still listens to Grand Funk Railroad, for God's sake. I make more money in a morning doing TURPs than he does in a month in his studio. And you know what?" She looked around her stunning kitchen. "As good as I am, and I'm a damn good urologist, he does better work than me.

"I love him, Alan. But he's not all I need. Probably

won't ever be. I respect him—I *admire* him—but reality eludes him sometimes. You know. It tends to drift in his mind like so much snow, piled too high here, absent over there. Early on, before things got weird and she began deciding you were too dull for words and left you—you and Merideth were best friends. I envied that so much." I started to protest, but she waved me off. "Honey, we're great friends, you and I, but that's because she's gone and nobody else has moved in with you. Soon it'll be that junior DA or maybe Merideth cum child again or somebody else and, then, well, we'll fade. It's like being in the sun too long, it'll bleach us."

I opened my mouth to speak. Adrienne interrupted, "Don't argue with me, Alan. I'm not done. I'll tell you when I'm done. Anyway, I watch you dating now, I watch this weekend's samba with Merideth and the slow waltz with Lauren, and before with those others . . . oy"—the little Jew crossed herself, always covering her bases, and glanced up toward the heavens—"and I envy you. What I envy is that now, now that you're a little smarter and hopefully know a little more, I envy you that you get to do it again. You know, pick again.

"And then I look at how hard it seems to be to pick right, and I'm so glad I have Peter and that I don't have to do it again. But then, all I have is Peter, and sometimes that seems like a universe full and sometimes, bless him, it doesn't. So, *boychik,* I envy you that you get to do it again. And I pity you that you have to."

She watched me for a reaction, stuffed the last corner of Pop-Tart into her mouth, and said, "Weird shit, huh?"

"Are you done now?" I said.

"Completely," she replied.

I had as much chance of winning my bet with Adrienne as I did of winning the Colorado lottery.

Our reservations at Pain Perdu were for eight on Friday night. The fact that the neglectful guardians of one of my patients owned the restaurant briefly tempted me to try to talk Peter and Adrienne into an alternative restaurant in town. But Adrienne wouldn't pass by an opportunity to accuse me of trying to renege on our bet. And Peter would be silently troubled that I had asked him to miss an opportunity to visit some of his woodwork. So—a little bit more than slightly ambivalent—I kept my mouth shut.

We were going to arrive late at the restaurant because Adrienne got stuck at the hospital with a psychotic stockbroker named Raymond who thought he had a vagina. "The damn internist is smart enough to know he needs a specialist, so how come he's not smart enough to know that imaginary genitals are the sole province of psychiatry? I dictated him a letter suggesting that he should have called an imaginary urologist," she complained to Peter and me from the backseat as we blasted up the big hill heading south out of Boulder.

I looked over at Peter, who was smiling. "I love this stuff she does sometimes, don't you?" he asked.

Adrienne growled from the backseat.

Pain Perdu was built on the infamous ruins of a restaurant that had burned down in a suspicious fire almost twenty-five years before. At the time the city of Boulder was dry. The unincorporated county was wet. The previous restaurant on the site thrived, at least in part, because it was just outside the city limits and thus permitted to serve alcohol. When the city voted itself out of its pretense of prohibition, the motivation for the populace to drive a few extra miles out of the city for a drink faded rapidly. The old restaurant declined. And then one night it burned.

The site was spectacular, on the crest of a ridge that intercepted the thrusting peaks of the Front Range south of Boulder. The city spread out to the north, the wilderness of the steep foothills dominated to the west, and to the south, well, to the south was Rocky Flats Nuclear Weapons Facility.

From the outside the new restaurant was part farmhouse and part spaceship—the Jetsons meet the Waltons. Pain Perdu's bar was nicknamed Stonehenge, and the huge vaulted space enclosed selected remains of the previous establishment's landmark stone pillars. Inside, a burntwood post-and-beam frame composed stunning views to the north and west. Peter had spent much of six months creating cabinetry and sweeping curved staircases that cascaded from level to level in the single expansive dining room.

The big room was noisy and vibrant, somehow simultaneously infused with elegance and irreverence. From its opening night four months before, Pain Perdu had been packed. Everyone had scoffed at Geoff and Erica Tobias's plan to raise an expensive restaurant on the abandoned ruins too far outside of town. Rumors were that investors had avoided the prospectus as if it were printed on plutonium-enriched paper. Somehow Geoff and Erica had raised the money, and nobody was laughing anymore. The restaurant drew customers from a hundred miles away, and weekend reservations were booked at least a month in advance.

Unless you happened to make them in the name of the resident woodworking guru.

On forty-eight hours' notice we got Friday-night primetime reservations. Because of Raymond's imaginary vulva we arrived thirty-five minutes late and yet were treated as though our tardiness were particularly fashionable. Erica Tobias greeted us warmly, ushering us past dozens of less fortunate souls to a corner table with moonlit views of the prologue hills of the Rocky Mountains. Ms. Tobias whispered something to Peter that caused him to blush and then excused herself to return to "my kitchen."

I was virtually certain she didn't know who I was. What was even more sobering was that I suspected she wouldn't have cared if she had known.

After our napkins had been ceremoniously snapped into our laps, our water glasses had been filled with bottled mineral water—this close to the Rocky Flats Nuclear Weapons Facility nobody really wanted to think they were drinking something that came from a well—and a waiter had placed an immense platter of varied shellfish dressed in carved carrot flowers on purple kale upholstery in the center of the table, I said to Peter, "So. I take it they like your work."

He smiled and nodded, quite distracted watching people walking up and down his stairs.

Adrienne was beaming.

Lauren had chosen not to join us. She had been polite and gracious about Merideth's visit the previous weekend, saying she understood Merideth's need to see me before the divorce. Lauren had even revealed that she and her ex-husband, Jacob, had rendezvoused at his house in Aspen before theirs. Still, there was some petulance and bitterness in her refusal to come with us to Pain Perdu. "I don't like the postponement," was all she offered in explanation, "and I don't like that you're not more upset about it."

The postponement. My lawyer had called on Wednesday to inform me that Merideth's lawyer was requesting a delay of final orders at his client's request. My lawyer said her lawyer didn't know the reason. Merideth hadn't returned my calls seeking an explanation.

When I told Adrienne about the delay, she acted like the Amazing Kreskin, told me she'd been so confident that she'd presumed to call in our reservation that morning, and reminded me that Pain Perdu didn't take American Express or any other plastic.

Pain Perdu offered three entrée choices each night. Our waiter, who looked like a young David Niven, asked whether we preferred the long or short rendition of the evening's choices. We opted short.

"Meat. Poultry. Fish," he pronounced, deadpan.

We ordered one of each and extra forks. Peter ordered a bottle of red wine with an impossibly long name. The waiter was back with the wine in moments and immediately entered into an intense discussion with Peter about the relative merits of decanting.

I watched Adrienne attack the shellfish.

"There are times," she said, digging into a stone crab claw, "that I thank God She's not too fussy about the *trayf* rules."

The waiter disappeared and then reappeared to place

flutes of champagne in front of each of us. "Erica thought you might enjoy these with your appetizer," he said.

Erica was right. I offered a toast to friendship. Adrienne insisted we drink to clairvoyance as well. I felt disloyal to Randy Navens with my first sip. But I got over it.

Adrienne sat facing the dining room and waved with barely masked disdain to medical colleagues at less desirable tables. Peter indulged himself in attention and praise from the staff and the owners. The only person I recognized in the whole place was Eric Petrosian, Paul Weinman's young protégé. I hadn't seen him since our last supervision session during the shoot-out in Diane's office. He sat three tables away at a round four-top with a man and a woman who looked old enough to be his parents. Eric was speaking forcefully to the man while the woman ignored her food and sipped insistently from a glass of white wine.

As our waiter delivered our dessert, I watched a man who I guessed to be Randy Navens's uncle, Geoff Tobias, circle the adjoining table of six with a steaming tureen of soup, offering seconds, working the crowd. He seemed to hesitate when his eyes caught Eric Petrosian's. He took two steps in a direction away from Eric, apparently changed his mind, and walked back over to Eric Petrosian's table. Eric refused to acknowledge Geoff's approach. Finally, Geoff leaned over and said something into Eric's ear in a voice that failed to carry to our table.

Geoff Tobias was round and balding. His generous forehead was boxed on the sides of his head by scraggly tufts of wavy white-blond hair dotted with flecks of peppery gray. From crown to thick eyebrows his uneven cranium sparkled like a moguled double-diamond run in need of attention from a Sno-Cat. A phrenologist's treasure.

Eric Petrosian apparently didn't like whatever Geoff Tobias had to say to him. He touched his napkin to his lips, slid back his chair, buttoned his double-breasted jacket with admirable patience, and then shot up suddenly out of his chair. He towered over Geoff Tobias. Eric Petrosian was a little taller than I, maybe six-two or -three, and a good half foot taller than Geoff.

Eric was dressed in a pale gray suit of medium-weight wool that hung flawlessly over his athletic body. Geoff wore cotton corduroys and a sweater that stretched over his ample abdomen like a plastic grocery sack straining to contain a watermelon.

Geoff Tobias looked nervous, and although Eric's visible demeanor was placid, Geoff's quick retreat and frightened eyes relayed a different impression—that Eric was speaking with some intensity and that he wasn't complimenting Geoff on the cuisine. Eric leaned over so that his mouth was inches from Geoff's copious forehead. Geoff tried twice to retreat from the intrusive closeness, but Eric stayed right with him, as if Geoff were leading him in some new Brazilian two-step. In comic desperation Geoff raised the soup tureen to force Eric either to back off half a step or risk creamed shiitake mushrooms sprouting on his fancy suit. Eric laughed at the maneuver just loudly enough to draw the attention of the two or three people in the dining room not already glued to this production.

Eric's laugh was directed right at Geoff's face, where his eyeglasses had clouded from the billowing soup steam. Geoff Tobias looked to the world like a short dumpy guy with wire-rimmed cataracts.

Whether from humiliation or steam, Geoff's face reddened. Finding himself at the top of one of Peter's staircases, Geoff Tobias turned abruptly and walked away, leaving Eric Petrosian smiling and straightening his perfect tie.

Peter, Adrienne, and I polished off the champagne, the bottle of wine, and a round of after-dinner drinks before we considered which of us should be the designated driver.

We drew straws and Yellow Cab won.

10

Diane stayed away from the office for two full weeks after the shooting.

Either the answering machine or her husband, Raoul, intercepted calls for most of the first week. They spent the second week at a resort in St. Croix.

She and I finally talked a few nights before she planned to return to work. She hadn't been back to the building since the assault, and her curiosity about what she would find had a desperate quality. I told her that the physical damage had been largely repaired. The walls had been remudded and repainted, the bloodstains in the oak floors sanded and polyurethaned away, the glass replaced. Her sofa had been cleaned, but telltale outlines demarcated the shadows where blood and other fluids had spilled from wounded bodies. I told her the sofa was in storage in the old garage behind the house. The decorator who had done Diane's office had offered Diane a loaner couch that I'd accepted by proxy. The Indian rug that had been in the center of the bloodbath was in Denver; the rug cleaners weren't hopeful. I'd lugged in a replacement from my house that she could use for as long as she wanted.

"So it's like it never happened," Diane said wistfully.

"I wish, Diane. If I could erase what happened, I would. All I did was wash the blood away. I hope it's okay."

"Yeah," she said with some hesitation, "it's okay, more than okay. I appreciate it. I don't know what I would do if it was all still there. You know, like it was that morning."

"And you know we can always sell the building, find another place for our offices." From the moment my own shock at the shooting began to ebb, I'd thought that Diane might need to move away from the memories of the carnage.

I could hear her swallow. "I've thought about that. Thanks. I may need to. Let's see how it goes."

Two mornings later, each of us between appointments, I found her sunk into the abundant stuffing of her beige loaner couch. She was quiet and pensive. I guessed she was searching for evidence of the old house's newest ghosts. I sat down next to her, put an arm around her shoulder, and placed my left hand over one of hers. She leaned into me and let me hold her for a few minutes. Light danced in the moisture that formed and faded in her eyes.

"It's not as bad as I feared it would be," she told me finally.

"In what way?"

"I don't know, I kind of expected the revulsion I felt about coming here to increase as I got closer. You know how cancer patients develop anticipatory nausea in their chemotherapy, how they start to get queasy on the way to the hospital and puke in the elevator even before they get to the clinic for their IV? That's what I thought it'd be like coming here, that the closer I got the worse I'd feel. But it wasn't that way. In a funny way it feels like a memorial, someplace almost sacred.

"I'm not scared being here, and I thought I would be. I still think I'll be petrified when I'm seeing another battered woman in here. God. God. I'll be furious all over again if what that asshole did in here interferes with my ability to help these women."

Diane's voice was steady and void of inflection. What mental health types call "flat."

"At some point you and I will talk about what happened. Not now," she said. I nodded.

I said, "Anything I can do?"

"No, Alan. I appreciate all you've done, all your help with my office. Well, almost all your help. This sofa"— she jabbed at the overstuffed, overpillowed, overflowered rowboat of a couch on which we sat—"has got to go."

Her brown eyes clouded over for an instant, a snapshot of violence intruding, unbidden. "You know, Raoul's going to be rigging a panic alarm in here for me. You want one? It'll work like a home alarm, will summon the cops, set off bells and whistles. The whole shmear."

"I'll think on it," I said. I touched my watch and told her that I had a 9:45.

She squeezed my hand and said, "Me too."

"You want this open or closed?" I asked as I reached her door.

"Open," she said.

"You'll let me know if there's anything I can do?"

She smiled and then resumed her quest to acquaint herself with the newest spirits inhabiting the room.

My 9:45 was an intake.

She'd called late the previous week, seeking an appointment. On the phone her voice had been proper and somewhere in the vicinity of arrogant.

In person, well . . . "Nice," she said, looking around at my office decor after I showed her in. "You do this yourself?"

"How can I be of help, Ms. Hughes?"

She raised her eyebrows at my overt failure to respond to her direct question. "I wasn't quite honest with you on the phone."

Silence from me. I was generally skeptical of relationships that started with lies.

She fussed a lot with her clothing and accessories. Her clutch was trim and fashioned from leather and a beige fabric embellished with a logo I was probably supposed to recognize. She moved it from her left side to her right, then stopped to pick at imaginary lint on her green wool skirt. Her hazel eyes avoided me while she rearranged her little piece of the room. A thread on the sleeve of her tailored black waistcoat caught her eye. She twirled it into a little ball and dropped it over the arm of the chair.

I wondered, watching the display of her obsessiveness, about the obvious run in her hose in front of her right ankle, about the missing black button on her left sleeve, and about the scuff marks on her shoes.

She smelled of cigarette smoke and fidgeted as if she wanted to light up.

"I told you I got your name from an acquaintance. That's not true. I got it from the newspapers. The attention"— she cleared her throat—"you received last year . . . interested me."

Great, I thought. The "attention" was a series of front-page newspaper articles about an investigation into an accusation that I had been sleeping with one of my patients who had subsequently killed herself. My eventual exoneration had received significantly less attention from the press than had my indictment. During the nine-month period of infamy, my practice had suffered a seventy percent decline. In the ensuing months I had managed to recoup about a third of what I had lost. Now, finally, my referrals were up, people choosing to come to me for psychotherapy despite the previous year's accusations.

This, however, was my first intake with somebody who had chosen me *because* of the accusations.

"Go on," I said.

She wet her thin lips and raised the corners of her mouth in an almost smile. Lynn Hughes was, guessing, mid-forties. Her clothes were exquisite but not new, and recently not well cared for. The diamond on her wedding ring was somewhere over a carat, but her fingernails were painted unprofessionally and unskillfully. I guessed this was a woman who had relied on hairdressers and manicurists for years and was now without that support system for her vanity.

"I think I want some advice." She looked at me as though it were my turn to talk.

I just waited.

"I've been seeing another therapist," she began to explain, "and, I'm not sure it's going, well, right."

A certain rhythm was developing and she would have continued, but I interrupted. "Does your therapist know you've come to see me?"

"No. God, no." Her face said "Are you nuts?"

"And you've come to see me for . . . ?"

"Like I said, advice." Her eyes focused on mine, and she held on to the stare while she said, "What you were accused of last year, that's what my therapist is doing with me."

"Your therapist is sexually involved with you?"

"Yes," she said, "we're screwing, among other activities. I'm not sure he's still my therapist, though. I haven't actually paid him for a while." She was fingering some slow tune on her thigh with her left hand. "When they wrote all those things about you last year, I wondered what the fuss was about. I mean, we'd been doing it for months by then, and I couldn't see what was wrong with it. My therapist keeps telling me it's exactly what I need, and to be candid, Doctor, I kind of agree with him. He told me I'd feel less worthless if I could feel a man respond to me. You know, if I felt desired. I do. Or at least I did. I liked it a lot at first. And now, now I'm not sure what's really going on.

"So, given what you went through—you know, last year—I want you to tell me—is it wrong?" The question was not posed naively; her words were benign, but there was spice of provocation in the tone.

"Yes," I said without hesitation. "Wrong. Unethical. Illegal. And most of all a tremendous mistreatment of you."

She exhaled slowly. "I thought you'd say that. I'm not sure I want to change anything, though. Can you understand that?"

I could, of course, understand. She must have been getting some need met through the relationship. But she wouldn't be confessing to me if that was the side of her ambivalence she wanted nurtured.

"No matter what reluctance you have about ending your relationship with him, you're being hurt by his betrayal."

"It was my idea at first," she countered. "The sex. He kept telling me how worthless I was to everybody. Once he asked me what good I was to anybody. I said I could screw pretty well. That's sort of how it started."

I spent a few moments composing some words that

would translate my outrage into something she might be able to hear. "And it was his responsibility to allow you the idea, to help you understand the impulse you were having, and most of all, to not cross the line by encouraging you to act out the urge."

"So what would you have me do now?"

"What did you mean when you said you weren't sure he was still your therapist?"

"Well, we don't actually *talk* much anymore. And like I said, I don't actually pay him—"

"But you did once? Talk to him about your problems? And pay him for his treatment?" *Treatment?*

"Yes."

"I'm not usually in the advice business, Ms. Hughes. But I will explain some options for you. First, your therapist is engaging in illegal and unethical behavior and should be reported to the Mental Health Occupations Grievance Board for investigation of his behavior. With your permission, I will do that. Even better, I will be thrilled to provide you with directions on how to do it yourself. Second, it's imperative that you immediately terminate any treatment that's harmful to you. In my opinion, the treatment you describe is harmful to you. Very harmful to you."

"I'm not interested in causing him any, uh, problems."

"He's hurt you. And it's his own behavior that's causing his problems, not you."

"This board. What will they do?"

"They can and probably will launch an investigation of his behavior, and make decisions about whether he has breached professional ethics and whether he has broken any laws. What you have described is, in this state, a felony. If they find violations, they can apply administrative penalties—revocation of his license, for instance—or request that the district attorney investigate for criminal charges. Or all of the above."

"Will my therapist know who filed the complaint?"

"Yes."

She shifted on her chair. "That won't do. That just won't do. This is more complicated than I let on. And I just can't, uh—afford?—to have my therapist angry with me. Especially right now." She pondered something for a moment, then continued. "No, that can't happen."

"Would you like to tell me about the complications?"

"Love to, honey." She sighed. "My husband"—she elevated her left hand and pointed at the rock on her ring finger as though his portrait were engraved on the stone —"is, well, prominent— May I smoke?"

I shook my head. I'd developed plenty of therapeutic rationales for the prohibition, but they all sufficed merely to protect a simple aesthetic: I hated the smell.

"Another nicotine Nazi, huh?"

I didn't respond. I did note, again, the ooze of provocation and hostility that seemed to seep incessantly from her.

She looked at her watch, timing her next fix. After a silent calculation in her head, I wondered if she was going to ask for a brief recess to replenish her diminishing nicotine levels.

"I'll tell you my story," she said, suddenly affecting a practiced southern drawl as she resumed speaking, "but I'm not going to tell you who the villain is yet, 'cause, you see, sugar, I just don't know if I can trust you, either."

I guessed that the histrionics were some precomposed support for her otherwise ineffective defenses. About her not trusting me, I said simply, "That's fair."

"Yes. It is." At this moment the script called for her to snap open a small painted fan and send the still air astir. She didn't. Lynn Hughes swiveled her hips a little, hunkering down to a comfortable place in the saddle. She was softening. The Dixie charade she was assuming felt like an odd entreaty, which I hoped might ultimately permit a diminishing of her initial distance.

"Do you want to fuck me, Doctor?"

I was Rhett now, clearly.

Her spicy words were pure query, not offer. I saw nothing coquettish about the question. Other than the affected drawl, there was nothing in her tone or manner to suggest that the question was intended to be any more enticing than "Do you take Blue Cross?"

"Would you like me to want to?"

"Ooooh. *En garde*. Good answer," she said, raising her eyebrows and lowering her chin in appreciation. She stared at me for most of a minute. When she finally continued, she said, "What the hell? Oh, what the hell? Honey, here goes. One more question first. If my therapist were to get financially involved with me, would that be right? Like legal, I mean?"

"What do you mean by 'financially involved'?"

"Investments, like that."

"No. Neither ethical nor legal," I said. "Is that a problem now, too?"

Her face grew thoughtful, but she ignored my question. After dropping the drawl, Lynn Hughes proceeded to tell me the vague outlines of a story I didn't quite believe and listened again to my suggestions about what she could do.

As she and I talked I felt tremendous frustration at my failure to convince her to act and at my inability to act without her permission. Her right to confidentiality prohibited me from reporting her therapist to the state grievance board without her permission. And anyway, she hadn't disclosed his name.

"Some people," a valued supervisor had reassured me once as I bemoaned my lack of success with a patient during my training, "are better at being crazy than you are at being therapeutic." As I repeated the words to myself after Lynn Hughes departed, I took mild consolation in the refrain, but my instincts were insisting that my new patient was paralyzed as much by psychological blackmail as by pathology.

The story she told was too simple. Her husband was a prominent local professional, and she couldn't afford to risk participating in a public scandal. "My husband thought the yellow brick road was really paved with penny stocks, and we're a bit squeezed financially right now," she explained. She seemed to think carefully about my advice not to go back to see her therapist before rejecting it with, "I don't think he'd appreciate that very much."

I asked what that meant.

"It means I'd better find another way out," she said.

"Who knows? You may have helped." She collected her purse and stood to leave. After handing me crumpled bills to cover my fee, she asked me not to send a statement. She declined my offer of another appointment and returned, I guessed, to her psychotherapeutic abuse.

11

Randy Navens had been silent for a few moments before he scrunched his eyes closed tight, touched them lightly with the backs of his hands, and opened them wide and said, "My memories are gone, you know."

I knew he didn't remember much about the plane crash. But I didn't know exactly what he meant that day, so I waited.

"When the plane went down, everybody died. I lost my father, my mother, my sister, and my memories. I never thought much about any of them before the crash. They were all just there. And then Creamed Corn—and they weren't. I walk around the house when my aunt and uncle are at the restaurant, which is mostly, and I can see the spot on the stairs where my sister used to sit to talk on the phone, and I can go into the kitchen where my mother would always be cooking, and I can go and sit in the chair in the living room where my father would always be reading a book, but there's no place where I can go and see all the things I *don't* remember.

"I never knew it, but one of things my parents did was keep all the memories. Like it wasn't my job—it was theirs. My mom would say, 'Randy, remember when you were six and we were camping in Guanella and you fell off the rock into the creek?' or, 'Do you remember the Christmas where the tree fell over just as we were sitting down to Christmas dinner?' Now I don't have anybody to tell me what I don't remember. It's like all my memories died during Creamed Corn."

"Creamed Corn" was Randy's ironic diminutive for the

crash of United Airlines Flight 232 into a corn field outside Sioux City, Iowa.

"All of your memories?" I asked softly.

"No," he said, "only the ones I don't know that I've forgotten." He paused. "I listen to you. I don't act like I do sometimes. But I do. One of my first times here you said that my family was dead and that nothing would change that, but that no one can take the memories away. And that's how my family can always be with me.

"But I think you're wrong. If I can't remember, then nobody has to take the memories away. It's like the memories are in the trust with the money. Everybody says the money's mine, but I can't have it. The memories are mine, too, but I can't have them, either. The difference is the older I get the more money they'll let me have, but the older I get the less I'll be able to remember."

DSM-IIIR, the *Diagnostic and Statistical Manual of Psychiatric Disorders,* version 3 (revised), called Randy's problem "post-traumatic stress disorder, chronic." Psychotherapists called it PTSD.

PTSD is how psychotherapists explained soldiers not adjusting after battle, battered wives not recovering from an abusive marriage, and an adolescent's prolonged suffering after his family perishes in a flaming DC-10 in a corn field in Iowa.

Randy Navens had plenty of memories. Of course he had seen the video clip of the crash—that vision through a chain-link fence first of desperate hope and then of a huge jet somersaulting into horror. He didn't remember the crash itself, though; of that he remembered nothing. He remembered being told while he was in the hospital that his mother was alive, then, hours later, dead. He remembered that his sister's body was so mangled and burned they wouldn't let him see it. He remembered that his father's body was so free of visible trauma that Randy refused to believe he was dead. The funerals. The cemetery. He remembered.

He remembered.

These memories exploded in Technicolor to disturb his

dreams, to poison his infrequent dates, to foul his daily hikes above Chautauqua to the base of the Flatirons.

This was the first time he'd talked about wanting to remember anything more. Up until then he had just begged to be able to forget.

"I'm still having those feelings sometimes."

"Which ones, Randy?"

"About killing myself." He paused to see what I'd say or do. He looked over at the filing cabinet.

I did nothing. It wasn't exactly calculated. Sometimes I waited just to buy time.

"Also, there's this new thing that happened. In the restaurant—you know, my aunt and uncle's restaurant?— I was there waiting to get my aunt to sign something for school before it got busy last Thursday night, and I get" —he swallowed and focused his eyes sharply—"I get like real scared and real pissed off all at once. My heart starts pounding in my chest, and I feel like just running out of there. I also feel like I want to go scream at my uncle, who's sitting at a table in the dining room talking to a waitress or somebody."

Randy's breaths were short and rapid. He raised his hands, palms out, in front of his face and lowered them quickly.

"I grabbed the paper away from my aunt and ran out to my car. I drove home real fast. When I got in the house, I ran downstairs to this little storage closet in the basement, next to the furnace room, and sat on this little stepstool that was mine when I was a kid. And after a while I felt okay, and I went to school to watch the basketball game."

Time was short. I contemplated doing some exploration about the memories that were surfacing—once forbidden associations opening vulnerable flanks for guerrilla strikes into Randy's consciousness. But today's session was almost over; the exploration would have to wait.

We did accomplish the prescribed litany about his suicidal thoughts. Was he having impulses? Did he have a plan? How intrusive were the thoughts?

I listened carefully. Randy, I decided, was frightened, but not suicidal.

As he was prone to do, he sat quietly for a few moments. He broke the silence by asking me if I still had the gun.

I said, "Yes," and tilted my head in the general direction of my filing cabinet.

Then I said, "Our time is up for today."

It's starting, I thought as he stood to leave. The memories are coming, the memories are coming.

God help him.

12

"Ugh. You need to shave your legs."

"I just did."

"When?"

"Last weekend."

"Uh-huh, that may be good enough for your bicycling buddies, but it doesn't cut it for somebody you want to crawl all over naked."

I'd been crawling all over Lauren naked for the better part of an early evening. We were at my house, in the bedroom.

"If you're going to shave your legs, you've got to do something about that stubble. I'm kind of accustomed to having one end of a man feel like sandpaper. Both ends, I'm not ready for."

Some of my bicycling friends had begun shaving their legs a few years before. I'd resisted joining them out of vanity and out of a chronic impatience with any repetitive grooming activity, like shaving. I did mostly road work anyway, didn't do city races, and didn't fall as much as my friends. The theory of leg shaving was that you lost less skin from falling if you didn't have leg hair. Therefore you healed quicker. If I didn't fall, I rationalized, I didn't need to shave. But a month back I'd gone down on a patch of winter sand out near Berthoud and had lost a rather amazing amount of skin off the hairy surface of my left calf.

And then there was the peer pressure. "Serious" riders shaved. "Casual" riders didn't. Which was I? I was a sucker for peer pressure. I shaved.

I told Lauren, "For you, dearest, I'll shave prior to all future anticipated naked encounters."

Lauren smiled at me. Then her pretty face turned serious. She said, "You *are* a good man, Alan. Better than most, anyway." I might have searched anyone else's tone for sarcasm. But Lauren spoke evenly, her words an apparent prelude to something.

My eyes said, Yes, go on.

Hers filled with tears. She waited until they were almost dry before deciding to continue. She was sitting up against the headboard, the comforter above her breasts, tucked under her arms.

"When you leave me," she said, "I'm afraid I won't know whether you're leaving me or the MS. I hate that—the not knowing." I started to protest; she waved me off. The comforter drifted down and exposed one breast, her skin textured with gooseflesh, the nipple firm. I noticed, then returned my gaze to meet hers. She went on. "I've tried—I'm trying—to be available to you. It may not feel that way to you, but I am. And I appreciate that you're trying to be patient with me. I think you think you usually succeed. You don't. Still, I like that you try. I hope you appreciate my effort, too. What you and I have is already better than my marriage ever was, better than what I had with any of my so-called serious lovers, but—damn you, Alan—it doesn't seem like it's enough for you. I feel myself failing you, and at times I'm furious at you for wanting things from me that are still elusive. Maybe they'll always be elusive. Sometimes I think you want me to be able to fly and silently criticize me because I can't."

As Lauren's speech grew longer so did the pauses between sentences. Each new sentence cracked into territory a little less charted.

"I don't like the part of this relationship that leaves me doubting me," she said. "At first, I was sure that was all my shit. But now, I think I know that it's your shit, too. Part of you wants me to doubt me. I don't pretend to know why. But I know it's true." Lauren looked at me again, saw me about to speak, and said, "Shut up, I'm not done yet."

She found her place and continued. "I'm not deaf, I hear the echoes as I talk. The echoes say that when you leave, you'll be leaving me, not my MS, not my disease. He's too decent, too valiant, to leave a woman because she's sick, I say. But in the next breath I say, So maybe that's why he keeps encouraging doubt in me, in my role in this, this, *relationship.* So that when you leave, you can tell yourself that it wasn't the MS—it was Lauren, poor kid, she couldn't cut it with me, intimacy problems, you know, too distant, not affectionate enough. Boundary issues. Yes, that's it, *boundary problems,* the ultimate psychological trump card. You know the drill, sweetie." She looked at my eyes. "Yeah, you know the drill.

"Other times I'm afraid that maybe I've picked a man who *can* accept my disease, but can't accept me. It's not fair. God, God, it's not fair. But, when you leave, when you go back to your beautiful Merideth, I think I'll be okay. I'm doing well in this relationship. I'm not perfect. I don't always scratch your back right on the itch. That's okay. I'm growing into all this. If you can't appreciate it, fine, I can. Maybe in time someone else will, maybe not."

For a moment I thought she was done. Her generous upper lip was set flat, her eyes were beginning to focus again.

She continued. "I can't leave the MS. I envy you that you can leave it. Every day it seems there's a little burn or a band of numbness someplace on my skin"—absently she touched the palm of her left hand with the tips of its fingers—"or a little visual weirdness, a little weakness, a numbing fatigue—something. Most days I note it and I move on. But other days there's big stuff. You've seen it. The blindness—remember that?—or falling over from vertigo, or dropping everything I touch." At tense times Lauren looked skyward, stretching the pale skin on her neck tight. She did that now. "Or having a man I love judging me, this disease an unwelcome factor in his judgment, like the car I drive or like the size of my boobs, but the whole time denying it's important to him—denying, denying. I know you'll disagree—you'll say the size of my breasts isn't important and my disease doesn't make any difference. But you . . . you like my breasts and you hate my disease. I fear sometimes that the choice you get to make is that simple."

Her words, oddly, weren't sad, though I perceived some pity in her inflection. But the pity, I think, was for me, not her. The solid mattress beneath me suddenly felt like a water bed. She rocked it just a little more, saying, "I so much don't want it to be—but I fear it's that simple."

Swaying, all I said was, "So you think it's *when* I leave you?"

She touched me on the skin beside my left eye. Her head moved up and down. She said, "When."

"No doubts, huh?"

"Not enough to change 'when' to 'if.' "

I did like her breasts. I was still sorting out how I felt about her illness. She'd say that was denial. Maybe she was right.

It was Lauren's multiple sclerosis. But it felt like ours.

In a few months shy of a year with her I had been learning more about her disease than the books and articles I read ever taught me. For now she had relapsing-remitting disease. Comes and goes. Comes and, hopefully, goes. I'd seen her temporarily blind, off and on off-balance with vertigo, in real pain from burns the product of some neural imagination, limping one day from a foot drop. I'd seen her so tired she didn't have to slow down to take naps. "Naps take me," she'd said.

And I'd seen her look better, healthier, more beautiful, than I felt anybody had a right to look. I'd seen her play second base, ski double-diamond runs, shoot pocket billiards like a champion, give stirring prosecutorial speeches in court, and make love as though she invented it.

I'd seen her try to hide the pain, the annoyance, the frustration, and I'd seen her succumb to the reality and retire to her room, for sleep, or rest, or sometimes just to hide. She'd canceled more than a few dates to pay homage to the MS god's demands.

And she did it all without complaint. Not saintly; I could sense her outrage. Not even always gracefully. But the word she used most when I got her to talk about her illness was "fortunate." Never fortunate that she had MS. She never condescended to consider her illness a blessing in disguise or part of God's plan. But fortunate that she had a life that was enviable even for somebody without MS.

I asked her once if she ever wondered, "Why me?"

She looked at me, sincerely puzzled, and said, "No." And then, "Alan, why not me? I've been eligible for many blessings in my life. I've been fortunate in so many ways. I think it would be remarkably arrogant to rule myself ineligible for any hardship that might come along.

"Honey, I'm not crippled yet. If my neurologist is as good a soothsayer as he is a human being, I will never be. This disease won't kill me. I was the beneficiary of wonderful advice about disability insurance, so I'm well insured if and when I can't work. This disease won't throw me into poverty. I'm bright. I have some wonderful friends. I love my work. I have you—sort of.

"Indeed, why not me? I'd like to think I'm as well prepared as anybody for living with this illness. Don't pity me, honey. Just know me. This illness, multiple sclerosis, is one of the constellations in my sky. It's there. Like the Little Dipper. Sometimes it's obscured, sometimes it's the brightest light in the sky. But it's always there. I don't think about it all the time. When I do look up, it's there. That's all, it's just there. Part of my sky."

An hour or so later I finally fell asleep next to Lauren. My sleep was restless and I had troublesome dreams that I couldn't remember, but I woke thinking they were about the shooting and about Randy Navens.

And about how easy it is to make bad choices.

13

Lauren was preoccupied with work.

The grand jury investigation had been postponed while the special prosecutor decided how to proceed despite the sequential deaths of her two most important witnesses.

I found myself amazed by how difficult it turned out to be for the experts to ascertain what had caused Lawrence Templeton's creekside home to blow up. The local paper interviewed chemists about light gases and heavy gases and explosions up and explosions out. Geologists and anthropologists and local historians recounted the history of dairy farming and urban dumping along the banks of Boulder Creek at the turn of the century. Methane was suspected, propane was suspected, dynamite was suspected, plastique was suspected. Test holes were dug, neighbors' homes were monitored constantly. A gas station a few blocks away was checked for leaking tanks.

The Bureau of Alcohol, Tobacco, and Firearms came to town in a converted RV. Investigators from the Department of Energy checked out links to Rocky Flats. Everybody assumed the FBI was helping, too. Swarms of scientists from CU and the School of Mines in nearby Golden offered free help and free hypotheses.

Larry Templeton's widow and children made their grief public on local television. They were sure he had no enemies. Maybe it was terrorists, they said. He was an executive at Rocky Flats, after all.

His daughter, pinprick diamond in her nose, speculated in a monotone that maybe the local antinuke lobby decided to show everybody what bombs could do. It was disconcerting that how she felt about the possibility wasn't readily apparent.

I watched all the interviews and read all the articles and discovered after a week that nobody had any answers. Mostly, after digesting all the profiles of Larry Templeton, I wondered what this nice guy in a Volvo station wagon who hunted and fished and windsurfed at the reservoir was planning on telling the grand jury.

And I wondered if Lauren was right in asserting that Larry Templeton's death was murder.

Lauren was closemouthed about it all. About most office matters, she tended to be. But some new distance was developing. Her announcement that she was certain I was preparing to leave her had made things even more awkward.

We had a couple of conversations that she began with, "Hi, honey. Are you divorced yet?"

During the most recent one we were walking on the Downtown Boulder Mall on a Thursday afternoon, dodging slush puddles and shaded ice patches on a blustery day that teased us with the distant spring. We missed the light at Broadway. I finally told Lauren that Merideth was pregnant.

"Oh, fuck," she said mildly, almost swallowing the profanity, "so *that's* what's going on."

"It's not what you think," I said without a clue to what she was thinking.

She ignored me for a moment, then turned her head away from me and asked, "Is it yours?" The light turned green. Our fellow strollers pushed across the street. We stayed put.

I was boggled by the question. Not that the thought hadn't crossed my mind. And back. A few times.

I said, "Of course not," as I replayed the mathematical date games in my head. When was I in California to say good-bye to Merideth? How far along in her pregnancy was she now? And try as I might, I had no memory of condoms or diaphragms or gels or foams or caps.

"I don't believe you," Lauren said.

"There's not much I can do about that." Irony seemed to be the order of the day. At that moment I was angry that Lauren could actually suspect me of having slept with Merideth a couple of months before. My anger wasn't the least bit impeded by the fact that her suspicions were true.

"You're getting your baby, Alan. Your precious baby is coming and you want to be there. Right?"

What had Merideth said about not wanting to give the father a vote?

Was that me she was talking about?

Lauren made up an excuse to return to her office before our scheduled lunch. We both knew it was an excuse.

I went home and got my bicycle out for the first time in a couple of weeks. I put on winter cycling gear, checked the air pressure in the tires, and took off for a workout. I started easy but soon had my spin up. I was moving north and vaguely east, riding without destination. I skirted Longmont and headed toward Berthoud before dropping over to Lyons and then back along the foothills to Boulder. Maybe thirty-five miles. Back home I was covered in slush muck and was tingling from sand pebbles flung at me from passing vehicles. Road riding in winter was a little like time-elapsed sandblasting. Still, it felt good.

The red light on my answering machine signaled a call. The message was from Merideth. I hadn't heard from her since her visit to Boulder ten days earlier. She hadn't returned any of the calls I'd made trying to find out her reasons for the postponement. This message was cryptic, "Hi, it's Merideth, please call me at . . ." and she left a mountain exchange.

While I showered, I wondered what she was doing back in Colorado. Work, probably, although the Rockies were out of her production responsibility.

The number, it turned out, was the Denver number of the Hyatt Regency Hotel in Beaver Creek, an isolated, upscale ski village that was part of the Vail empire. I'd skied there only once, early in my marriage to Merideth, when the area was just open, Hyatt-less, virtually hotelless, the base lodge a huge inflated bubble in a sea of frozen mud. I remembered enjoying the mountain and appreciating the planning that compelled skiers to park at the bottom of the mountain and take shuttles a couple of miles up to the ski area base. To be honest, I liked the shuttle idea more in theory than in practice since I had been one of the commuters standing in line waiting for the shuttle.

I asked the hotel operator for Merideth Gregory, was told that there wasn't one registered, and shyly asked for Merideth Murrow. The phone started ringing, and Merideth Gregory, née Merideth Murrow, answered on the fifth ring.

"Yes," she said in her office voice.

"Hi, honey," I replied, surprising myself at the use of the endearment.

"Alan," she said, her voice belying some disbelief that I had returned her call.

"You're in Colorado," I said.

"Yeah, a little R and R on skis unfortunately contaminated by some strategic planning meetings for the network. I wondered—if you're still taking Fridays off—if you'd like to ski with me tomorrow?"

I wasn't as surprised as I should have been. "That sounds very nice," I said.

She gave me a second or two to continue on my own and then said, "That sounds very nice, yes—or that sounds very nice, no?"

"Same Merideth, cut right to the chase."

"Well?"

"No" was easy and probably smart. I could claim that I had an appointment or two scheduled the next day. But I said, "Yes, I'd like to ski with you tomorrow," while doing some arithmetic in my head. Ski traffic on Friday shouldn't be too bad, although I hadn't been paying enough attention to the recent weather reports to be able to guess how snowpacked the roads were likely to be. Vail was a couple of hours' drive on dry roads, Beaver Creek ten minutes farther.

"How are the roads?" I asked.

"Don't know. We flew into the Eagle airport from L.A., skipped Denver."

I wondered about the "we" but said, "I can probably be up there by ten, I guess. Where should I meet you?"

Merideth was silent for a moment, then said, "Ten tonight or ten tomorrow morning?"

This was one of those conversations where talking to Merideth was like playing tennis with Chris Evert in her prime, the rallies were eternal, the ground strokes devastating. I said, "I was thinking tomorrow—"

"Listen, love, please think 'tonight' and call me back. I'll leave you a key. But I can't talk now. I just got out of the shower, I'm standing here naked and cold, and I have to get ready for a dinner meeting. Please come. Okay? Please? 'Bye."

" 'Bye," I said to the dead line, remembering in some salacious detail the image of her naked body covered with gooseflesh.

"Tonight," I said to myself, already rationalizing. Already having decided, without wasting any neurotransmitters on the process, that I probably wasn't going to tell Lauren.

The drive up wasn't too bad. The chain law was in effect on the approaches to the Eisenhower Tunnel and again over Vail pass. In four-wheel drive the Subaru had little trouble with the snowpack, and the extra aggravation was a small price to pay for the compensation of a few inches of fresh snow in the Vail Valley.

The canyon that fractures from the Sawatch Range into the boom town of Avon is narrow and steep. The village of Avon straddles the narrow strip between I-70 and the mouth of the canyon. The town is three blocks wide and is replete with all the amenities and liabilities of boom—time-shares, condos, ski shops, fast food, a trailer park, a Wal-Mart. That's about it.

After crossing the Eagle River, I made my way to the entrance of the canyon road up to Beaver Creek, stopping at a small guardhouse attended by a young woman all-American enough to have been a hostess at the Magic

Kingdom. Her deeply tanned face suggested how she spent her days. I said I was on my way to the Hyatt. She smiled, told me the conditions on the mountain were the best of the season so far, gave me a parking pass, and told me where to turn.

The road up to the ski area hangs on the western side of the canyon, looking down over a golf course, over Beaver Creek itself, and over numerous condominiums and fairway homes. Upslope from the road were vacation homes that seemed to start in size at five thousand square feet. Dozens of these holiday palaces surrounded the groves of aspen and lodgepole pine that dotted the hillsides on the eastern-facing slope. Near the high, cul-de-sac end of the canyon, lodges, huge condominium hotels, shops, restaurants, and the Hyatt Regency crowded around the base of the ski area. Uniformed ski bums with brown skin and white teeth were everywhere. One dressed in a one-piece ski suit took the Subaru from me at the entrance to the lobby, another scurried away with my skis, boots, and poles. Another, dressed for indoors, carried my single bag to registration. I waited on line a moment and when my turn came asked if Ms. Murrow had left a key for me, retrieved a magnetic card instead, and had a polite discussion with the bellman about whether it was acceptable for me to carry ten or fifteen pounds all the way to her room. Two dollars convinced him I could manage.

I knocked. No answer. I used the plastic card and walked in and smelled my wife. Her perfume, her soap, her musk. Few of her things were in sight. Her clothes would be hung or folded away neatly in drawers. A hardcover novel sat by the nightstand on the side of the big bed farthest from the window. I didn't need to look to know that the dust jacket would be in the top drawer of the nightstand. Merideth's briefcase was centered on the small round table by the window. Her fountain pen stood upright in a water glass next to the telephone. Her leather appointment calendar was aligned aside the glass.

The room was on the fourth floor with an exposure to the ski slopes. The moonlight was filtered by broken clouds, and the snow glowed with fluorescence. The headlights of Sno-Cats flared at odd angles high up the mountain.

For a moment I thought of looking around Merideth's hotel room. I didn't.

Unpacking consisted of dropping my bag next to an immense wooden bureau that held the TV and minibar. I pulled the door closed behind me and strode off to find a bar. By that time of night the lobby lounge was a crowded pit of après, après-ski revelers. A single place at the bar next to the waitress's station seemed my only choice for a seat. I ordered a drink and signed a tab, which I hoped would send the bill to the network. The two women sitting on the stools next to me at the bar were, judging from their accents, South American. From their furry boots to their leather-adorned cashmere sweaters they were picture-perfect, postslope partyers. One turned to me and smiled, first with some interest and then with some cocktail of pity and disdain as she took in my old leather boots, worn corduroys, and fleece sweatshirt.

I sipped my drink in silence, then had a brief conversation with a cocktail waitress about the conditions on the mountain. "Primo," she said. "But you really should go over to Vail. The back bowls are incredible, powder all the way up to my—um, ribs." She briefly held one hand just a little bit higher than the lower part of her rib cage and then dropped it a few inches.

I smiled and mumbled something about my bowl days being behind me. She looked at me as though she suddenly realized how old I was. She offered me a well-trained smile and took off carting a tray full of alcohol to a room full of people who didn't seem to need any more.

I asked the bartender for an icewater, and he obliged. He was at least twenty-five, and that made him an elder among this crew. "The skiing's great here," he said. "Ignore her. Don't go to Vail. You'd have to get back in your car or take a bus and schlepp all your stuff down the valley. And the lift lines to the gondola in Lionshead are a bitch. Stay here—we'll warm your boots, cart your skis out the door to the snow, and if you want, even give you a little push over to the quad chair. At the end of the day we'll help you out of your skis, give you some hot cider, and show you the way to the hot tub. Why would you want to go to Vail?"

This guy was management material. His name tag read "Chuck" and informed me he was from Bend, Oregon. I said, "For the life of me, I can't imagine, Chuck." At that moment I saw Merideth emerge from the door to the restaurant that was just to my right. She was dressed in deftly patterned red wool leggings and a white sweater that reached down to her thighs. I'd given her the sweater, the diamond studs in her ears, and the chunky sterling chain around her neck. Chuck turned to see what I was staring at. After one look at Merideth he nodded his approval, as if he'd seen me hold up a card with a 9.5 on it and he was concurring.

I waited and watched while her party reassembled. Chuck said, "You're reaching for the stars tonight, cowboy." I nodded, dropped a dollar on the bar for Chuck, and walked over to greet Merideth.

Catching Merideth off-guard was a rarity and often an illusion. I walked up behind her as she chatted with two men and a woman. I said, "Hi, my name's Alan."

She turned casually, a little mischief in her eyes as she saw me. We stood a foot apart, arms down, lips unpuckered. "Hi," she said.

"Hi," I said.

Between us we had fourteen, sixteen years of college and graduate school. It was frightening to think about what our conversation would have been like without the advanced education.

14

We rode up to the room in an elevator crowded with Merideth's colleagues and a gaggle of strangers. My tendency was to adhere to international elevator etiquette, certainly in crowded elevators, anyway. Face the doors, stare at the numbers, don't fart, don't talk. Merideth, on the other hand, treated elevators the way she treated any place else. If she was there, then she was at home.

She spoke to two strangers, Texans, as if they were new neighbors she had just invited into her kitchen for coffee. Had the hotel been a high rise, we probably would have discovered their prairie roots before debarking on the thirtieth floor. As it was, by our fourth-floor destination Merideth had learned everyone's name, made flawless introductions, and already divined that the visiting Texans owned a restaurant in Austin and that they recommended trying the wood-oven pizza and the Caesar salad from room service.

The walk down the corridor was long. As we entered her room, she said, "Oh. You've been here a while," spying my bag next to the colossal piece of furniture across from the bed.

"Roads weren't bad. I made good time. You weren't here, so I went and had a drink in the bar."

She nodded.

"You didn't want me to come in your room without you here?"

"I didn't know I didn't want you to. But I guess I didn't."

"Well, I'm sorry."

"It's okay."

I moved toward the window, past the bed. The maid

had turned down the linens, left a single piece of foil-wrapped chocolate and a room service breakfast menu. The sheer curtain liner was pulled across the windows. I slid it open and watched the Sno-Cats slither across the glowing ski runs.

"So," I said, "I'm here."

From behind me Merideth said softly, without any discernible defiance in her voice, "I'm going to keep the baby."

I nodded. "Is it mine?" I asked, turning back to face her.

She teared a little. "I don't know," she said. "I wish I did."

"But possibly."

"Yes. Possibly."

I was fighting an antediluvian instinct of unrefined paternalistic contempt—great, this is wonderful, you're pregnant and you've been slutting around so much you don't even know whose it is. Certain instincts are best left hidden. This was one.

"Go on."

"I was seeing a guy when you came out in November. You must remember. The guy I was with in Big Sur." I remembered. I'd interrupted their romantic weekend with some persistent phone calls about Merideth being on the hit list of one of my patients.

"I remember."

"Well. He's the only other one."

"He's the one you don't love?"

"Mm-hmm." Merideth didn't show hurt easily or often. Standing across the room from me, she looked soft and delicate and vulnerable.

"I still love you," I said, and immediately regretted the impulse to tell her that.

"I know."

Damn her.

"Are we getting divorced?" I asked.

"It only takes one."

"Are you gonna be that one?"

"Well, you're the one who signed the dissolution. I didn't sign; I postponed the final orders."

Yeah, I'd heard.

"Alan, I could be pregnant with your baby."

"Yes," I said, "and you're only a signature away from divorcing me because I wanted to have one. Anyway, for all you know right now, you could be pregnant with the baby of the weekend sports anchor of KRON."

She laughed. "You're closer to the truth than you think. Adam is actually weekday sports—though you've got the wrong station. But hey—let's face it, what you say is true. What a puzzle we have, huh?" She lay down on the bed, her fingers entwined on top of her head. She looked away and said, "You're seeing somebody?"

"Yes," I said.

"Is it serious?" She was unwrapping the chocolate now.

"Serious enough that I didn't tell her I was coming up here to see you."

"What does that mean?"

I paused. "I'm not sure what it means. But it's serious between us. She's important to me."

"Do you love her?" She popped the whole candy in her mouth. I had wanted a bite.

"Yes."

"So, why are you here?"

"I love you, too."

"You're in a quandary as well, then."

I lay down next to her and said, "Yeah. What a puzzle."

My usually untamable lust for Merideth was strangely tempered by the possible mitotic consequences of our last coupling. She seemed unburdened by the same forces. But then she wasn't one inclined toward burden. I'd always been her emotional sherpa.

We talked in bed for an hour or so, at first holding hands across the big bed, later with her curled against me, her head on my chest, then finally with my head cushioned by her right breast. We slipped into these postures with the security and familiarity of the married.

Our talk was catching-up talk, checking-the-weather talk. The shoot-out, the exploding house. Her work, my lack of work. What's this friend up to. Her lawyer, my lawyer. A couple of references to the "current situation."

Shortly before midnight I stood. She looked up at me and immediately began to pull the white sweater over her head, mistaking my standing as a prelude to disrobing.

Underneath she wore a sheer body stocking. Gazing down at her, I said, "God, it's tempting," in an inadvertent attempt to get into Guinness in the "Understatement" category, "but not tonight, Me. I'm going to get my own room. If I can't get one—if the hotel's full—I think I'll head back home."

"I'm sorry you feel that way. I was hoping, you know—"

"Yeah, I know," I said. "Who knows, honey, maybe sometime. But not tonight. I'm more than a little confused."

She said, "Welcome to the club."

"I have to tell you this. I don't want to. But I should. I'm having a hard time trusting you."

"I'm not happy to hear it, Alan. But I'm not surprised. I haven't been very consistent with you."

"No. You haven't been that." I paused and continued. "For a while before we separated I was worried that your decision to have a kid was at best an abdication, at worst a gift—that you didn't really want it. You were doing it for me. It felt like a rotten reason to have a child, but I was touched by your generosity, your caring. Now"—I pointed at the sheer fabric stretched over her flat belly— "it's more like old times, it's like I'm the one who's expected again to do the giving, make the sacrifices, swallow the humiliation. Where's the evidence of your love? For me? All I see is your request for evidence of mine. That doesn't feel good, Me. It's too familiar. It's not good enough."

"I'm kinda selfish sometimes," she said quietly.

"Yes," I said. "So what's changed?"

"I've been thinking about that a lot. I still don't know. Something, maybe. But I'll have to think on it some more." She looked up and made eye contact with me for the first time in a while. A warm smile. "Alan, I would like you to think about the possibility that I made an awful mistake about us and that maybe I might deserve the graciousness of a second chance." She rolled over on her side, her hands together between the pillow and her cheek. "No matter what, though, thanks for coming up here. Thanks for not just telling me to get screwed. Because I probably deserve that, too."

We both smiled at the inadvertent allusion. I said, "If I'm here in the morning, I'll meet you in the lobby for breakfast at eight. I think it's the best I can do right now. Good night." I leaned down to kiss her good-bye. She reached up and wrapped her arms around my neck, part embrace, part vise. I fell on top of her and felt the richness of her body against mine. Quickly her tongue was in my mouth.

Like a saint, or a fool, I managed to pull myself away and walk from her room down to the lobby, where I sat thinking and warming myself for a while on an inviting chair in front of a fire that was dwindling to ash in a wonderful stone fireplace the size of a one-car garage. I declined an offer of a drink from a pleasant woman who said she was Carly from Wichita, exchanged some dollar bills for my skis, boots, and car, didn't ask about room availability at the desk, and drove down I-70 to Vail.

I got an expensive room in a cheap motel and the next morning skied the back bowls. Alone.

More snow had fallen overnight, and the powder *was* as high as the barmaid's bosom. And the back bowls were incredible.

I, on the other hand, needed some serious work.

15

On most winter days in the Colorado mountains you can point a camera just about anywhere, put the picture on your refrigerator back home, and know that your friends are going to ooh and aah every time. Temperature in the thirties, no wind, sun in your face. Snow that seems to fall only at night, blanketing everything. The ski resorts of the Colorado Rockies make a good living on it.

On the way back home from Vail that Friday evening, somewhere around Idaho Springs the picture-postcard paradise got out of control. The first clues came in the form of little snowflakes catching the paltry light and dancing around my windshield, flaunting gravity. Farther east, near Evergreen, snow flurries became snow, by Genesee snow became snowstorm, and by Golden the snowstorm evolved into a good, old-fashioned, eastern plains, upslope whiteout. My direct route back to Boulder, past Rocky Flats and Pain Perdu, was closed by crosswinds and drifts, and I spent a miserable hour and a half touring Denver's western suburbs on inadequately plowed boulevards before I finally made it home.

The tape on my answering machine was packed. Merideth had called. No message. Give her a call.

And Lauren had called Thursday night. Decided to go to her place in Aspen for the weekend, would I like to go? Another message, Friday morning, There's a storm coming in from the south, need to leave early Friday afternoon, please call. Finally, another one, Are you okay? I need to get going to beat the weather. Call me at Jake's.

"Jake's" was her wealthy ex-husband Jacob's vacation palace on the banks of the Roaring Fork above the Rio

Grande Trail just outside of Aspen. As part of her dissolution agreement Lauren got to use it just about whenever she wanted.

I phoned Jake's place but didn't get an answer. I read a novel until I fell asleep.

When I was awakened by the phone on Saturday morning my eyes were assaulted by the glare of six inches of shimmering powder and my ears by the echoing lilt of Detective Sam Purdy, who greeted me with, "Want a ride in a police car?"

My first thought was, What am I being arrested for?

I said, "Is this an official request?"

He laughed. "You mean like with a warrant?"

"Yes," I said.

"It's not my style to call first. I like to surprise people when I bust 'em. Works better. They tend not to run or load their guns or whatever they might think of to interfere with me doing my duty."

"So it's not official?"

"Official police business, sort of. But not so official that I can make you come if you don't want to. And not so official that you're gonna get to charge the city your normal hourly rate. Somewhere in between. I just want to show you something, ask you something. Hear what you might think about something."

I was hungry and I needed a shower. "I can be ready in an hour," I said.

"Great," said Purdy. "I'll see you in thirty minutes. Breakfast is on me."

A pot of coffee had just finished dripping when he pulled down the driveway in an unmarked four-wheel-drive Tempo. "City gets 'em used from Hertz and Avis," he explained at the door when I asked if that was the police car I was getting my ride in. "No more driving around in white Plymouths with spotlights and black tires. Bad guys can't spot us so easily."

"You want coffee?"

"Sure. To go. We gotta hustle."

I poured two cups into cardboard cups, and we walked through the snow to the Ford.

Purdy drove the speed limit back into town. At first I thought we were heading to police headquarters for doughnuts, but instead he stayed on Arapahoe to Folsom and made a couple of quick turns into the parking lot of the Village Cafe.

I'd hung out there a lot in the 1970s but hadn't been there for years. It seemed like nothing had changed. Okay, everybody, including me, was older. But the coffee in the stained white stoneware mugs was the same bitter blend and was on the table before we were sure we had asked for it. The owner's hair had grayed, but he still worked the burners and the griddle with a confidence and dexterity that would have made him a fortune in the operating room. The service was friendly and curt simultaneously, and I could still order a number five over medium with wheat toast without looking at the menu. The waitress looked at me as though she thought she knew me and didn't even bother to ask Purdy what he wanted.

The Village Cafe was immune to trends. An oddity in Boulder, where everybody, local skeptics argued, was an individual, just like everybody else. The stability at the Village Cafe was comforting; even once reliably dingy Tom's Tavern had carved windows into its brick walls and added sidewalk seating.

"Home away from home?" I asked Purdy.

"I come here sometimes," he said. "You a little curious about my wanting to see you?" He was settling onto his seat.

"A little."

He made a whimsical noise as he met his too full mug of coffee halfway up from the tabletop. We sat silently and drank coffee for most of a minute. I was in no hurry.

Purdy broke the silence. "You ever wonder why people keep dying in your vicinity?"

"The question's certainly crossed my mind. I would, however, like to assure you that the trend is recent."

"Good to hear. But the question's crossed my mind, too," he said. I watched as across the room the cook cracked six eggs simultaneously without breaking a yolk. The waitresses zoomed across the dining room like blurs of light. "I'm just wondering if maybe your presence is a common denominator."

"You serious?"

"Yeah."

"I don't see it, Detective."

"Couple of weeks ago, I was Sam."

"I don't see it, *Sam*. If there's any similarity between the shooting and the bombing, it seems to be the grand jury investigation. And I hope you know more about that than I do. All I know is the speculation in the paper that 'a public official' is involved."

The detective's coffee mug sat empty for six or seven seconds before it was refilled. As the waitress finished topping off his mug, she set down a huge platter of food to fill the space in front of his folded arms and, simultaneously, slid my eggs, hash browns, and toast in front of me. I looked at my plate and couldn't remember the last time I'd had a fried egg.

"Guys need anything else?" asked the waitress. Then she looked at me and nodded knowingly. "You're the shrink, right? Alvin? You used to have English muffins with your five." She didn't wait for an answer to her question and moved off. She was right: I used to have English muffins with my five. I'd forgotten.

"You've been made," said Purdy, blending runny eggs into his hash browns. "I'm not suspicious of you," he continued a moment later, his mouth full of sausage and egg. "I'm more curious whether you might know something that you don't know you know."

"I've thought about this, Sam, I have," I said, savoring a forkful of the perfect hash browns, "and I don't see what I might know."

"Whattya make of this?" He handed me a sheet of three-ring notebook paper enclosed in a plastic sleeve.

The writing was immature and southeast of literate. "Kimber," it read, "I'm goin to get your mother and bring her hear. For good and for ever. If it dont work you can blame it on the lawwer or that guy from work. I love you. Always know that."

It was signed "Daddy."

As I lifted my eyes from the paper Purdy said, "Daddy is Harlan Draper."

I'd guessed as much. The man with the silver gun. Claire Draper's husband.

"We just got this a couple of days ago. Kimberly, the Drapers' kid, had found it and stashed it with her stuff. Never told us about it. Her foster parents saw her looking at it and gave it to us."

"Maybe I'm missing something, but if I were going to kidnap my estranged wife and maybe kill her, it might be the kind of note I'd write."

"Yeah, well. What about the blame part?"

So this is what Purdy wanted, some free consultation. Why not?

"Batterers aren't renowned for taking responsibility for their abusiveness, Sam. They tend to shed blame like a snake molts. I'd expect him to lay the blame on somebody else. You know as well as I do that there are numerous cases of divorce attorneys being hurt by aggrieved spouses. It's much easier to take the batterer out of the belligerence than it is to coax the belligerence from the batterer. It's nothing novel that Draper did. Merely horrifying."

Purdy's mouth was full and his plate already empty. Fifteen seconds later his plate was gone and his coffee cup was refilled. I pushed aside my half-finished breakfast and sipped coffee. He looked at me, past me, back at me, the whole time twisting his face while trying to dislodge some errant food from a front tooth with the tip of his tongue.

"So you think the 'lawwer' in question is Patricia Tobin, the one Harlan shot?"

"You don't? His animosity towards her is kind of un-questioned at this point."

"Claire Draper worked for a 'lawwer.' "

"So?"

"Could be him."

"Could be Perry Mason, too."

He ignored my sarcasm. "The firm she worked for is

the one founded by our ex-mayor, current county commissioner, Russell London."

"Makes it interesting, Sam. Don't see how it makes it likely."

He was still massaging his incisors with his tongue. "I'm supposed to be outta the loop on this, and you didn't hear it from me, but I kinda suspect that he's the 'public official' that the grand jury is suspicious about. Remember, Claire Draper was the first witness due to testify."

Made some sense. "So what is it he's supposed to have done?"

"I don't know," he said with a look on his face that said that maybe he did but he wasn't about to tell me. He asked the circulating waitress for a toothpick. She had one in her pocket, wrapped in cellophane, and dropped it on the table.

Purdy plucked the plastic-covered notebook paper from the side of the table, folded it once, then unfolded it, and said, " 'Or that guy from work.' It says 'or that guy from work.' "

I was confused. "Why would he say the lawyer *or* the guy from work if they were the same guy? It doesn't make sense."

"I agree. See, the real interesting part might be where Harlan Draper worked. Maybe he was talking about where he worked. Not where she worked."

"Okay. So where did he work?"

"At Rocky Flats." He ran his tongue over his cleanly picked teeth, first the uppers, then the lowers, and said, "Which is where Larry Templeton worked. You know, the guy whose house blew up. Grand jury witness *número dos*."

"And you don't think it's coincidence?"

He was sitting back in his chair. "Where a meteorite hits the ground, maybe that's chance. How much damn snow we get each winter, maybe that's chance. That two people who are scheduled to testify before the same grand jury *and* maybe know each other die violent deaths in our quiet little slice of paradise within a few hours of each other—that's not chance. That's suspicious."

"Wait a second, Sam. You suggesting Harlan Draper didn't kill Claire Draper? We were both there. Remember?"

"Nope. I'm not suggesting that."

"You suggesting that Larry Templeton's house blowing up was murder?"

"That one nobody seems to agree. You know the 'experts' haven't decided on a cause."

"So what are you suggesting?"

"I'm not sure. If I was sure, I wouldn't be here picking your brain. I was there both times. I saw the shooting in your partner's office. Or at least I heard it. I saw Larry Templeton's body pulled from his house. Both times I walk away I feel funny, you know, something smells. You know how sometimes you get in your car and something smells, and you sniff a little while, then look down and turn up the soles of your shoes and sure enough—dogshit. Well, this smells like dogshit. So I'm out looking for the dog.

"I'm thinkin' since you were there both times, maybe you smelled dogshit, too. Anyway, that's why I bought you breakfast." He struggled to pull a fat wallet out of his hip pocket. "Now, now I'm thinking maybe you don't."

I could have admitted that I had a strong urge to look at the soles of my shoes. But I didn't.

16

Back home I tried unsuccessfully to reach Lauren in Aspen.

While I was searching fruitlessly for the scrap of paper on which I had written down Merideth's number in Beaver Creek to return her call from the day before, she saved me the trouble and phoned again.

"Alan, oh good, I was afraid I wasn't going to find you home. Listen, I want to thank you for coming up—and I want to tell you I'm real sorry you didn't stay. The skiing is, well, fabulous, and the truth is I could've used a few more hours with you."

My truth was I didn't have a few more hours of willpower. I didn't tell her I'd skied Vail. I did repeat that I was confused.

A pause. "Honey, there's something I didn't get a chance to ask you about. Is there a story in what's going on with these deaths in Boulder? You know, with the shooting in Diane's office, the bombing, the grand jury? People here at the meetings are wondering if there might be some national interest."

"What people?"

"People like me. Story people. Producers."

"Isn't this out of your jurisdiction, or territory, or whatever you call it? Aren't you just West Coast?"

"Yes. You're right, it is, and I am. But I'm also the network's resident Boulder expert. I speak the native tongue. Anyway, I know you, I know Diane, and despite what you always tell me, I know a little about psychotherapy. So if there's something going on, I'm a natural. Anyway, I've already got a source that's telling me some things that make me think this isn't just mundane tragedy."

I was fighting an instantaneous, and surprising, awareness that I didn't want Merideth in Boulder doing this "story." I needed her to be a thousand miles away in San Francisco while I sorted all this out. What I ended up saying about the "story" possibilities in Boulder was, "I don't know what your source is telling you. I can tell you that I don't see how this has any national interest. Looks like a domestic homicide and a natural-gas explosion of some sort."

"My source tells me Russ London is involved in all this. That makes it intriguing. I mean, Alan, I used to campaign for the guy. What's the *Daily* saying? Catch me up a bit."

I did, a bit. I didn't tell her about the suspicions that Purdy had revealed during breakfast. The whole time I was wondering who her source was.

"Maybe I'll make some calls, check with my old friends at the station in Denver, see if they're interested—you know, sniff around. I'm looking for a good excuse to spend some time in Boulder."

"That's up to you," I said. "I've never pretended to understand how you people choose your stories."

"Well, I'll think about it. And I'll call you in a few days to talk more about . . . our . . . circumstances."

"Okay. But please don't get your hopes up and expect any fast answers from me. I doubt that I'll have any that soon."

We said good-bye. It was easier than I would have expected. I found myself barely surprised that Merideth had a more accurate reading on the political pulse of Boulder from a thousand miles away than I did right in the thick of things.

When I called Aspen around six that evening, Lauren was back at Jake's place.

She told me she'd skied a half day at Snowmass and was tired and a bit concerned that maybe she had pushed herself too hard. Despite her fatigue, she was eager to talk about what it was like to be back in the house in Aspen for the first time since she'd been assaulted there the previous Halloween. I found myself surprised at her openness, and I encouraged her to keep talking.

She seemed genuinely disappointed that I hadn't been able to join her for the weekend. I felt certain she somehow knew I'd been in touch with Merideth. She made no mention of it, though.

I missed Lauren as soon as we hung up.

The night was the dense black of a new moon. The fresh snow on the face of the Flatirons captured a mere trace of the city lights. If I'd had some company for dinner, I probably would have discovered enough motivation to cook something that was worthy of eating in the dining room with a bottle of wine and candlelight. Instead I scrounged around the kitchen for fuel, rejecting and discarding most of the once fresh food from my refrigerator. Five minutes later I carried a bowl of ramen noodles and a chunk of stale wheat bread into the living room and ate alone facing the night, drinking a beer.

The fact that I'd been invited to spend the weekend with two different beautiful women in two different gorgeous ski resorts wasn't lost on me. Nor was the reality that despite my prospects I was somehow managing to spend my Saturday night dining alone, would soon be watching television alone, and ultimately would be sleeping alone.

It wasn't lost on me, either, that I wasn't doing something right.

Diane Estevez was sitting on the steps of the small cedar deck outside the rear door to her office when I drove up on Monday morning. The day was postblizzard temperate. Slush was everywhere on the driveway. Streaks from dried tears lined the makeup on Diane's face.

"Somebody broke in over the weekend," she said, jerking her head back in the direction of our offices. "It's a mess," she said.

Surprisingly calm, I sat down next to her. "You all right?" I said.

She laughed. "Yeah. Just great. And how was your weekend?"

"Two beautiful women invited me to go skiing and possibly screw my brains out, and I somehow managed to ski by myself and sleep alone all weekend. And you?"

"Raoul's in Alabama talking about rockets. I just hung out at home. Couldn't get the damn snowblower to work."

"Cops know about this?" I hooked a thumb at the building.

"Yep. I called. They told me not to touch anything. So I came out here to sit. Hoped you'd show up."

"They gonna stop by?"

"So they say."

"How bad is it?"

"Inside?"

I nodded.

"In terms of disorder, it's worse than the backseat of your car, not as bad as Raoul's study."

"File cabinets?"

"Open."

"Both offices."

"*Sí.*"

"Dana's studio?"

"I didn't go up there."

"Did the new alarm work?"

"Raoul's in Huntsville. It's not done. You know Raoul." I nodded. "Not a great January, huh?"

She rested her head on my shoulder and said, "No shit."

Two cops came and went. They were polite, filled out a report; their demeanor suggested we had as much chance of catching our felon as we did of intercepting Santa Claus next Christmas Eve. Diane asked about dusting for prints. One of them said, "For a burglary?"

They told us to make a list of what was missing. The quieter of the two warned us to take our time doing it. "Most people don't realize what's missing right away," he said. His partner scoffed at the suggestion and said, "I find I'm always amazed how many victims discover what's actually missing shortly after they rediscover the terms of their insurance policies."

The French doors from my office had been used for entry. The dominant cop shook his head in derision when he saw how easy it had been.

"When you put a deadbolt in a glass door," he said, "you gotta key it on both sides. Otherwise the perp just busts out a pane, reaches in, turns the latch, and walks in the door." He reached through the absent pane and showed me how it was done.

I was pretty appreciative. I got to feel invaded upon and stupid simultaneously.

After a few moments of awkward silence the police officers left Diane and me standing in her office, all of us recognizing the futility of their mandatory visit. I suggested calling Sam Purdy. Diane scoffed at the idea. "I'm tired," she said, "of cops showing up after it's too late for them to help."

Silently Diane and I surveyed the damage.

I hadn't recently seen Raoul's study. But if it was in worse order than our offices were that morning, it probably could be used as a laboratory for the study of chaos.

Diane suggested we work together to clean up, do the rooms one at a time. I didn't want to be by myself, either, and readily agreed. We started with the waiting room, which required only minor straightening. The kitchen was even neater still, and the amplifier and CD changer that sat on shelves in the small closet were suspiciously untouched. The medicine cabinet and the vanity doors in the bathroom were open. Otherwise that room was unmussed.

Diane's first appointment arrived for a session while we were standing useless in the kitchen. Diane went out to explain our predicament while I made some coffee.

The intruders had saved most of their hostility for our offices. Diane's stacked oak bookcases were empty of their books, which had been scattered across the room. In her office she kept only one small two-drawer filing cabinet for her current cases. Her closed files were stored someplace else. The sole filing cabinet had been pried open, a handful of files dumped unceremoniously on the floor. Her prize old cherry desk was covered with the contents of its many drawers. The drawers had been thrown haphazardly in a pile against the wall.

I poured us each a mug of coffee and then reshelved books while she sorted her files to see if anything was missing. No files appeared to be. Her business checkbook was. Uncharacteristically she said, "Fuck me," to that news.

My office was in disarray similar to hers. I stored more old files in my office than she did in hers. It was fitting, then, that more of my files had been dumped, fewer of my books scattered. But some of my furniture had been tipped over.

In my office we reversed roles. Diane reshelved; I sorted files.

"I think," Diane said, "that our visitor was a little frustrated at the slimness of the pickin's, ended up taking out his frustration on our stuff."

"I wonder if he or she was looking for drugs."

"Ah-ha! Fools. Must've mistaken us for *real* doctors or something."

The heavy envelope with Randy's father's pistol was lying on its side on the bottom of the drawer of one of my two file cabinets, largely covered by the file frame and remaining hanging files. I pulled the envelope back to vertical and leaned it against the back of the drawer where it had been.

"Anything missing?" Diane asked.

"Doesn't look like it. No missing files that I can see. I've got a gun that a suicidal patient left with me. I was afraid it'd be gone. But it's still here, too."

"A gun? Really? With bullets?"

"Yeah. Don't you hold things for impulsive patients sometimes?"

"Sure. I've done it. Drugs mostly. A gun, though, I think, I'd give to the police."

"Can you do that? And why would you?"

"Sure you can, for safekeeping. If you explain the circumstances, they don't make you tell them whom it belongs to, and they'll hold on to it until you ask for it back."

"I didn't know that."

"Now you do."

I snapped my fingers. "Just my luck these days. Find out I need a cop five minutes after they finish a house call."

The door to Dana Beal's studio/office upstairs was locked. Diane trudged back down to her office to look for her master key; I followed. As Dana's landlords we each had one. Diane found her key ring aside the pile of crap from her drawers that sat unsorted on the middle of her desk. We trudged back up the stairs and opened the door to Dana's little suite with some trepidation, as if the burglars might have locked themselves in accidentally or something. Dana's studio was unmussed. Her houseplants needed water, though.

"You seen her lately?" I asked.

Diane shook her head. "She's probably in Bora-Bora."

"I'll get some water," I said.

"We need to call a glass person and a lock person," she said.

I held out the tiny water pitcher I had plucked from a windowsill in Dana's studio. I said, "I'll do that. They know me. You get the water."

I spent the rest of the day at the office, squeezing a few therapy appointments into a calendar crammed mostly with tradespeople. Diane managed to see half a dozen patients after her office was made habitable just before noon.

Lauren was back in her office at the Justice Center by eleven. I called and spoke with her for about thirty seconds while she packed her briefcase before rushing over to court to plead something or other. I always had trouble with that image. Other lawyers might plead; Lauren, never. I did manage to tell her about the burglary and invite her over for dinner. She was curious and empathic about the break-in and discouraging about the meal.

Tired of dining alone, and feeling sorry for myself because my office had been burglarized and my nose had started to run, I got myself invited up the hill for dinner, where Adrienne and Peter were making chili and corn-bread. Purdy called as I was getting dressed to go up the hill. He wanted to talk about the burglary. I wasn't sur-prised.

And he wanted to offer me a job. I was surprised.

17

I woke with the embers of a campfire in my throat and a plug of cement in my sinuses. I tried to swallow and winced with the futility. I tried to breathe through my nose and managed only to create more vacuum pressure in my brain. What I needed was a Roto-Rooter for my sinuses and a thick coat of Teflon for my throat. What I had was Sudafed and ibuprofen, and I gulped three of each; they were about as effective as a tissue on an oil slick.

Purdy met me at the coroner's office at nine-thirty. When he glanced up at me from the copy of *National Geographic* he was reading in the small waiting area, he boosted my confidence by telling me I looked like crap. I said I knew. A few minutes later the receptionist led us down the hall so Purdy could introduce me to Scott Truscott, the chief medical investigator.

Colorado's coroner system was antiquated but constitutionally mandated and thus difficult to amend. There were no requirements that the elected coroner in any Colorado county be a forensic pathologist, a pathologist, a physician, or even a reasonably intelligent human being. In fact, the only requirements were those for any other general office—meet minimum age and residency criteria and get enough votes. In recent years Boulder County residents had demonstrated the foresight to elect a forensic pathologist to the post and were blessed in return with a professional coroner and a competently run coroner's office.

The man Purdy wanted me to meet was the chief medical investigator, the second in command in the office of the Boulder County Coroner. He performed the actual administrative duties of the office, and was responsible, among other things, for supervising the three staff medical investigators who did the field investigations on unattended and suspicious deaths.

Scott Truscott greeted us at the door to his small, neat office. He was dressed in heavy brown wool slacks and wore a nice crew-neck sweater over a white shirt and tie. His sandy hair was full. I had a vague recollection of seeing him stooped over Claire Draper's body inside Diane Estevez's office in the chaos after the shooting.

Purdy started things off. Pointing to me, he said, "Scott Truscott, Dr. Alan Gregory. This is the guy I told you about, Scott. He is, singlehandedly, responsible for bringing more work your way than anybody in town. There are gerontologists in town who see fewer dead bodies in a year than can be found at this guy's feet in a fortnight."

I held out my hand and said, "Hello, nice to meet you." The voice I heard didn't sound like mine; congestion had somehow rendered it much more proficient with vowels than with consonants.

Scott Truscott took one look at the wadded tissue in the hand I wasn't extending to him, another look at my red nose and porous eyes, and said, "I think I'll pass on the handshake."

I said, "Probably wise."

"There's something going around," he said, backing off a step. "Most viruses get transmitted by touch, you know."

I nodded, thinking, It's just a cold and a runny nose, Scott, not HIV and an open wound.

Purdy was sitting on the edge of Scott Truscott's desk. "Anyway. Scott here's short a couple of investigators— What? One quit? The other—death in the family? Something like that. Is that ironic or what? Anyway. I tell him I got this psychologist whose practice is on the skids through no fault of his own, maybe might like a little contract work on the side. I tell him you know how to interview people. I say, You got any suspicious suicides, well, who's better at doing a psychological autopsy than a psychologist? I tell him you're naturally too nosy for your own good. I tell him, hey, you're his best referral source in town, he owes you one."

Purdy turned back my way. In my face he may have seen the bewilderment that I was experiencing over his carnival barker sales job to the chief medical investigator. To me he said, "Scott says he'll meet you, see what he thinks." He waited for some sign of animation on my part. Nothing. So he returned his attention to Scott Truscott. "So, Scott, whattya think?"

Scott gazed at me with obvious and—given that I was dabbing prophylactically at my nostrils with a tissue wad —understandable distaste. "Why you want to do this?" he asked.

God knows, Scott. It's either this or find a bus to walk in front of.

"Like the detective, says, I've got the time. I like challenges. It sounds kind of interesting." I sighed; this had all the hallmarks of developing into one of my more eloquent job interviews.

I unfolded a new tissue and tried to blow. Nothing moved but the membranes in my eardrums.

Scott Truscott opened a file on his desk and appeared to study something for a moment. "You're a Ph.D., right?"

I nodded. My brain sloshed around in my skull.

"Know anything about medicine? This work involves a lot of interface with docs—interviews, chart reviews, etcetera, etcetera. Some kind of familiarity with medicine is essential—it's something the coroner insists on with all the investigators." The tone of his voice told me he was hoping I'd say I found the medical profession in general and dead bodies in particular pretty revolting and wanted nothing to do with any of it.

I held up an index finger in an attempt to communicate that if I could ward off an impending sneeze, I had an answer for him. Willing the sneeze away didn't work. I honked rather offensively.

If I hadn't felt so miserable, I am sure I would have been humiliated.

Finally I said, "Yes, I have a medical background. I did

my internship at County in Denver. And then I worked inpatient PLD—Psychiatric Liaison Division—doing consultation to the medical floors for a year right after I got my Ph.D. I still do consults here in town for a couple of internists and a urologist. I can read charts without any problem. I'm familiar with most medications. I get along with physicians, most of them, anyway, just fine."

Scott Truscott looked at me with some new respect. He said, "Mmm," and bobbed his head up and down once or twice. "Can you give me eight to ten hours a week until I hire and train a couple of new investigators?"

I nodded, wondering why my brain no longer felt anchored to my cranium.

Scott seemed ambivalent. "I can't pay you much. Certainly not what you're accustomed to."

"How much isn't much?"

He told me.

I said, "Let's just say we're both fortunate I'm not doing it for the money."

Purdy laughed. "So. We got a deal here or what?"

I said, "Sure."

Scott said, "Yes." And then, to me, "Call me this afternoon—no, make that tomorrow morning. I'll get the paperwork ready and we'll talk some more."

Purdy said, "He'll call, don't worry, Scott."

Back out in the hall I told Purdy I didn't know what his buffoon act was all about, that I felt as though I were watching his premature reincarnation as a used-car salesman.

He exhaled deeply and said, "Look, I really want you to have this job. I want your help with this explosion case. Scott's a bright guy, and a good administrator, but he's kind of straight, know what I mean? I wasn't sure he'd go for somebody like you. I mean, today of all days, you show up looking like something I should be dragging to detox. Anyway, the thing I like about you—well, maybe not exactly 'like,' maybe more like have come to appreciate, see—is that you've demonstrated a certain, well, creativeness, about developing investigatory strategies. Scott wouldn't be too thrilled with that particular part of your character, so I thought I'd take some of the heat off you in there—distract him, you know." He paused for a moment and shook his big head, looking befuddled. "Anyway, how the hell was I supposed to know you'd actually be qualified for this job?"

My day didn't get any better. My tissue use far exceeded that of my half dozen patients. And after work I made the mistake of visiting my neighbors in search of sympathy.

"The prosecutor and I did lunch today, buckaroo."

"What?" I said.

"This little virus affecting your hearing?" Dr. Adrienne shivered in mock disgust. "I am soooo glad I don't have to deal with that gooey, sticky end of people. Phlegm. Snot. That green stuff that looks like mildewed gray matter dripping down their throats. Ugh."

"Adrienne, there is plenty of goo at your end of people, too."

"You don't understand. Nobody ever understands about urology. Pay attention, you might learn something: People tend to go see internists and family practitioners when they're leakin' a lot. Like you. Or like people who are puking or got the runs or, God help us, both at the same time." She stuck out her tongue. "People come to see me when they're not leakin' enough. I fix 'em up and then they have the good manners to return to the privacy of their bedrooms and bathrooms before they start gooin' again. Except for those times when I have to deal with those occasional valves that are stuck in the 'on' position, urology is like a perfect part of the universe. People come to see me when their plumbing is plugged or their plumbing needs some design changes. You, on the other hand, are gushing foul fluids like an outhouse at Woodstock. And that—thank our Lord—is the territory of internists."

I'd had enough. "You saw Lauren for lunch?" I asked. Adrienne and Lauren were cordial with each other, but always wary. Not buddies.

"Yeah. We talked about you, mostly." She was smiling a smile now that told me there was some truth in what she was saying. It was going to be up to me, however, to assay the extent of the hyperbole.

"You did?"

"Yep."

"Adrienne, please. I'm dying here. I can't match wits with you tonight. I couldn't match wits with Dan Quayle tonight. You have something to tell me?"

She was buzzing around the kitchen in quest of dinner, opening and closing cabinets, rummaging around in the freezer and the refrigerator. "It started out as a prosecutor/doctor rap—you know, a working lunch. See, I was on call at the ER when this rape victim came in a few weeks ago. She was torn up. Some asshole had really worked her over. They couldn't get the catheter in. They called me to work magic. I worked magic. Your girlfriend's the prosecutor. She wanted to talk. Invited me to lunch.

"We went over the case. I didn't have much to say. The forensic stuff had already been done by the ER docs by the time I got to the hospital. I told Ms. DA what I thought the asshole might have done to mess this kid up so badly. She takes some notes, nods, and then your girlfriend asks me how well I know Merideth."

Adrienne actually tried to look sheepish when she said Lauren was asking about Merideth. But Adrienne wasn't skilled at looking sheepish; I was reminded more of the wolf than I was of the lamb.

Although I wasn't sure I ever heard the thing ring, Adrienne zoomed across the room to answer the phone. She listened for about ten seconds, nodding her head impatiently, making circular motions in front of her with the hand not holding the receiver. She said, "Fine. Change the antibiotics. Give her Cipro, 500, *p.o.*, *b.i.d.* Give one now—not at nine o'clock tonight with the bedtime meds, now. Okay? Good." She listened for a moment. "Fine, fine, fine. Go ahead and give her some Restoril. . . . Mmhmm, that's right. Then maybe we can all get some rest." She listened some more, said, "Yes, no problem. I will." Some more hand signals encouraging the nurse to accelerate to the end of the conversation. "Tomorrow, yes. Thank you," she said, hanging up.

Adrienne returned to my romantic triangle without missing a beat. "So me and Lauren did some *bonding*. You were the glue. Mostly she wanted to know about Merideth. Is she 'real,' you know—God, I hate what the eighties did to our language—like 'present' or 'connected' or 'intimate.' You know, I've been thinking maybe I'll take some lessons and start speaking to everybody in French. I can't imagine the French would let this happen to the way they talk. They have language police, don't they? Like word cops?" Without sufficient warning, Adrienne began to speak like Jerry Lewis impersonating Maurice Chevalier. " 'I am so sorry, madame, but that will be a one-hundred-franc fine for being feloniously trendy.' "

I wanted to scream. "And you said?" My sinuses were so occluded, I was starting to lisp.

She dropped the French accent and, intent on irritating me even more, for a few words tried to mimic my viral intonation. "I said that Merideth was my friend, and that I missed her. But I also said she was a princess. I said she took advantage of the fact that you're a sap where women are concerned. I said that as far as I can tell, you profess to want more intimacy than you can really handle. I told her that, for you, I think it's an occupational hazard. I hope I don't need to remind you that I'm being generous here calling what you do an occupation. I told her that in your soul you're probably most content with garden-variety intimacy."

"And Merideth?"

"She prefers the canned variety." She smiled at me and asked if I wanted some antibiotics.

"I thought this was a virus."

"It is. An adenovirus to be precise, if my buddies in infectious disease are on top of their game."

"So antibiotics won't help."

"Nope."

"So why are you offering them to me?"

"Sometimes I do what works, love. Sometimes I just do what I can."

Peter walked in from his shop. He carried an empty picture frame that he placed in the corner of the room.

After kissing Adrienne and affectionately squeezing her left breast through her sweater, he pulled a beer from the refrigerator, offered me one, and headed off, I guessed, to shower away some of the sawdust and grime.

I pulled the pop-top on the can of beer he'd given me. I pleaded with Adrienne, "Sweetheart, you're trying to tell me something. I can't read between the lines tonight. What am I supposed to be hearing?"

She looked at me intensely, then walked over to the sink to rinse her hands. Drying them, she said, "Merideth was never what you made her out to be, Alan. You always made allowances for her as naturally as you pump the pedals on your stupid bike. Lauren, I doubt, is what you make her out to be, either. But for some reason you don't seem to want to cut her any slack."

"And I'm making her out to be what?"

"Honey, I see some symptoms. But I haven't seen the X rays. I'll defer my diagnosis. But you probably already know what disease you have."

I tried hard to think about what she was saying. At least until she continued talking.

"By the by, me and Geppetto are pregnant. Mostly me. The in utero name for the little tyke is Pinocchio, and yours truly gets to be the whale."

18

After a night drowning in a histamine sea, I kept my ten
A.M. appointment with Scott Truscott. Alone. Purdy had
acted a bit like a flight instructor who thought it was premature for his student to attempt his first solo, but I prevailed by telling him I was going by myself or I wasn't
going at all.

This time Scott made no big deal about not shaking my
hand and was accommodating enough to have a mug of
herbal tea waiting for me on my side of his big desk. He
asked if I was feeling better.

I lied, saying, "Yes, thanks."

He sipped from his mug of herbal tea and said, "You
know Sam Purdy well?"

I nodded my head yes and said, "No, not really."

"He's a good cop. He plays by most of the rules. He's
been fair with this office over the years, has treated my
investigators professionally, shared investigatory data as
well as anybody at the department, and when he's had to
tell my crew that they are in over their heads, he's done
it in a way that didn't splash acid onto their dignity." He
paused and took another sip. "I owe him a few. Okay?"

"Fine."

"When I agreed to meet with you I thought I'd found
a cheap way of repaying a favor. Say hi, hear your dis-
qualifications, then tell Sam that I didn't think you would
work out, even temporarily. But with your background—
and some supervision—you might actually be able to help
me out." Scott smiled for the first time. "So I go into this
thinking I'm repaying a favor and it turns out that the big

midwesterner may have done me another one. And Lord knows what he'll ask for in return next time."

"I'll do my best, Scott, to put you further in his debt."

"I hope you do. I know he wants you on the house explosion death investigation. I haven't made up my mind on that, yet. The investigator who quit last week was handling that case and kind of dropped the ball on it. I'm going to spend a couple of hours reviewing his work till now, and then I'll decide whether you can be of any help."

"You're the boss," I said, aware that I didn't have an illustrious history of doing well with bosses.

"Remember it," Scott said. "Especially when Sam Purdy is encouraging you to develop temporary amnesia." He shuffled through a few files on his desk and handed me a manila folder. "Your first case."

I started reading, and he started talking. "What we have is a two-and-a-half-year-old kid dead from overwhelming sepsis. He died at The Children's Hospital in Denver, but he's a Boulder County kid, so he's ours. Death was six days ago. Autopsy was performed by the coroner here in Boulder. Our boss. His report's in there." He reached over and flipped a few pages in the file until the autopsy findings were in front of me. He poked at the bottom of the last page and said, "Manner of death was left pending."

I read through the findings and understood very little of what I read. To my untrained eye the gross findings on autopsy seemed to describe a toddler whose body had for some reason lost a fight to massive infection.

The vague details of my first case weren't promoting in me a tremendous amount of confidence about my new job. If an experienced forensic pathologist and all the docs at a big regional children's hospital were unable to determine manner of death, I didn't see how I was going to be of much help.

Scott Truscott said, "Parents are beside themselves. Father is furious at the hospital. Mother is numb. Like a zombie."

"Where do I come in, Scott?"

"You come in—we come in—because of this. It came by messenger late yesterday." He handed me a computer-generated lab sheet from The Children's Hospital. "Those are the results of cultures done during the post—the autopsy. Look at the circled ones."

I did. I could tell by looking at the normal range markers in the last column that the values that had been assigned to this child's cultures were almost off the scale.

I said, "Okay, I see the abnormal values. But I don't know what they're supposed to be telling me."

"Well," Scott Truscott said, "what those numbers say, the docs tell me, is that this little guy's blood and bone marrow and sundry other tissues were packed full of bacteria that are generally only found in one place."

He waited. I waited.

He continued, "They're found in human feces."

"The kid was eating his feces?" Unusual for a toddler, but not unheard of. Often considered a sign of psychological problems. Now I could guess where I came in.

Scott thrust a letter on hospital stationery into my view. "No, he wasn't eating his stools. What the infectious disease people at Children's think is that somebody was injecting fecal material into this kid's blood."

I had a vague memory of reading about what Scott was proposing. One of those academically fascinating psychopathologies that are so rare that most clinicians would never see a case in their careers. I had never seen one in mine.

"Munchausen by proxy," I said.

Scott nodded.

"Momma?"

"Usually is Momma."

"You ever seen this before?"

"Nope. Never. You?"

"Munchausen's, yeah, a few times. But not somebody making their kid sick on purpose. Never."

"Well," Scott said, "in this case, it's not just making a kid sick, it looks like we're talking about making a kid dead."

"God."

"Yeah," he said. "The police are going to be executing a search warrant on the house today. I want you to go and see the parents at the same time. I'd go myself, but I have a budget conference with the county commissioners that I really can't miss. Social Services will probably either be there at the house or be half a step behind you." He paused and offered a small smile. "Welcome to the coroner's office, Dr. Gregory."

"Thanks," was all I could think to say.

At that Scott reached into a drawer and handed me a laminated card identifying me as a consultant with the Boulder County Coroner's Office. He told me that if I were an actual staff investigator, I would be a Class III law enforcement officer. He suggested I call the detective on the case at the police department to coordinate things, and he told me good luck.

He reminded me I was a consultant, not a free agent. He didn't have to tell me I was on probation. We both knew that.

The detective, Georgie Montoya, told me about his phone interviews with all the players at the hospital in Denver. Medical history of the dead child was long and complex and absolutely consistent with the pattern of intentional parental malice. The kid had been sick for so long with so many illnesses requiring infusion treatments that an indwelling catheter had been placed into a vein in his chest to reduce the trauma of his frequent need for intravenous fluids and therapy.

That morning Montoya had been to the hospice where the mother was a volunteer. The hospice had suffered minor supply pilferage over the months she had been working there and told him what was missing. What was missing included supplies for injecting medicine into IV lines.

My psychotherapy practice required some attention from me prior to shifting any more of my focus to my new job with the county. I had four appointments clustered around midday and saw my patients back to back before heading away from downtown to a cedar ranch-style house in a subdivision in north Boulder. The house sat in the middle of what appeared to be a creek wash, and its location suggested that it might have been built to be employed as a sacrifice to the gods who controlled the spring runoff and the fifty-year floods.

I parked my car on the street a few doors down from the suspect residence and sat waiting for Georgie Montoya to arrive, luxuriating in the experience of having air migrate through my nasal passages for the first time in a couple of days.

After the police arrived and I accompanied them into the house, I spent much of an hour with the dead child's parents and got nowhere. The child's mother was mute with grief and denial. Her husband was shocked by the presence of the police and was acting as perplexed as I was. I don't know why this all doesn't add up, either, he said. I want to bury my son and go on, he told me. He seemed sincere. The only explanation that made any sense to him was that the hospital had screwed up.

When my turn came to interview the mother alone, she sat crossways on an oak captain's chair aside the kitchen table. I sat across from her and waited, silently.

"What do you want to know?" she asked.

I paused long enough to force her to look my way. In a compassionate voice I said, "You didn't want him to die, did you? That wasn't the idea at all. You just liked how everybody treated you when he was sick. People paid a lot of attention."

She didn't move, not a muscle.

"What'd you use? His feces? Yours?" My voice was soft, sad.

Did I see a nod?

"You didn't know he could die from this, did you?"

She stayed immobile. Then her lips barely cracked open.

"What was it at first? Viruses, colds, rashes? Just normal developmental things. And you loved the attention you got when he was sick." I opened the file folder I brought with me and pretended to examine a page from it. "The record says he had chronic otitis media—chronic ear infections. Did you actually give him the antibiotics for those? Or did you just throw them away? Down the sink, a few teaspoons at a time. Nobody noticed."

She exhaled so deeply that I feared she would deflate.

Then she swallowed and asked me not to tell her husband. In a moment—almost too quickly, I thought—she recovered her composure, glared at me with abject rage, and said, "I want a lawyer."

I figured that was my cue to turn things over to the professionals and called her husband in to sit with her while I searched for Georgie Montoya so he could do whatever he had to do to inform her of her rights.

I stayed another thirty minutes with the child's baffled father, gave him the names of three good therapists for continuing help for him and his wife, went home, called my boss and told him what happened, ate an apple, and slept fourteen hours.

This new job was going to be great.

19

Scott Truscott introduced me to the black hole of public service paperwork the next morning. He also told me I had done a good job on the Munchausen-by-proxy case and handed me the Lawrence Templeton death file as a reward. He dismissed me from his office with a smile and suggested, once again, that it would be good protocol to check in with the investigating officer over at the police department.

Like I really had a choice on this case.

So I called Sam Purdy. He had already heard from Georgie Montoya about my acing the case the day before and was thrilled that Scott Truscott had let me pick up on Larry Templeton's death.

He suggested a late breakfast at Dot's to discuss our collaboration.

Purdy, I was discovering, loved breakfast. He seemed to be enamored of saturated fat, and he announced over grits, eggs, sausage, and biscuits that his serum cholesterol was 146. I savored a wedge of Texas grapefruit and told him that I was happy for him.

It seemed Purdy was known at Dot's Diner. I surmised that he was known at every breakfast restaurant in town on speaking terms with a chicken. Dot's was, well, unpretentious. About twenty seats were sardined into the windward side of an aging filling station on the west end of Pearl Street. Customers, mostly regulars, sat on chairs, drank from cups, and ate from plates that had been, or should have been, donated to the Goodwill long before the discovery of the transistor.

The waitress stood expectantly beside our table, her

pencil still perched above her pad despite the fact that I had ordered a half grapefruit and a cup of coffee and handed her my menu. Her confusion wasn't her fault; light dining wasn't Dot's specialty. Silky grits, sausage gravy, eggs, and eggs—that was Dot's. When she realized that grapefruit and coffee was going to be my entire breakfast, she looked at Sam Purdy with a sympathetic face that seemed to wonder if he knew he was dining with a wuss. Purdy's ample order cheered her up before she trotted off toward the kitchen.

"We don't know much more about the explosion than the papers have reported," Sam Purdy told me a little later as he blended basted eggs into a sea of grits. "They're still arguing about this gas and that gas, whether he could smell it or whether he couldn't, whether it was a natural buildup or an accidental leak. Me—like I told you the other morning—I'm not convinced this explosion isn't a tad more nefarious than all that. The autopsy—you probably know this by now—shows the guy died a traumatic death. Either the concussion from the explosion, and/or the house falling on his head, killed him. That gives us cause of death. Manner of death is something else."

"Scott went over this once with me, Sam. Pretend it didn't take; explain the difference again, okay?"

"You really should already know this," he said, and signaled for more coffee before he continued. " 'Cause of death' is a medical determination. We almost always get a clear picture of cause from the autopsy. Unless there's been serious decomposition, the guys you work for can almost always tell us what happened to the body to cause it to expire. But 'manner of death' is more about the why than the how." The waitress walked over with the pot of coffee for Purdy, and I nodded when she pointed it my way. "If a guy gets shot in the heart, *cause* of death is listed as 'gunshot wound of chest' or some such jargon. That's how he died. *Manner* of death is homicide or accident or suicide or whatever, depending on who was holding the gun that was pointed at the guy's chest and what their motivation was when they pulled the trigger. That's why he died. Our job with Mr. Templeton—yours and mine—has to do with manner of death. And there's lots more questions to answer about manner than about cause with our Mr. Templeton.

"I should probably tell you, too, that this isn't the highest of priorities right now with either the city or the county, which is why Scott can assign an absolute novice like you to the case and not raise a single eyebrow."

I interrupted. "I was wondering about that."

Purdy looked around to signal for more coffee and asked offhandedly, "What?"

"Why you really wanted my help with all this. What you're saying is you plan to get me to do the things that your bosses don't really want you to spend the time—or should I say 'waste the time'?— to do."

For a few seconds I thought Sam Purdy was actually going to respond to my speculation. I was wrong.

When he continued he said, "The conventional wisdom at the police department says accidental death, and whether or not more questions get asked depends on the final report from ATF, which nobody expects to see before the leaves start falling again."

"What's ATF?"

"Feds, Treasury Department. Alcohol, Tobacco, and Firearms. They investigate explosions and bombings in cooperation with the FBI. Especially when the deceased is an employee of the division of the Department of Energy that makes nuclear warheads."

"Triggers," I said, "and they're shutting down."

"Whatever."

I said, "And the feds, they're slow?"

"No. In a murder investigation 'slow' is the end of the week. What these guys are is more like paleontologists."

"Is there a deputy DA assigned to this?" I asked.

"There is. At least was. Elliot Bellhaven. You must know him from hanging around with Ms. Crowder."

"Yeah, I know Elliot. He seems pretty sharp."

"He is that." Purdy's tone lifted wistfully as he spoke.

"And?"

"And I don't know. He seems all done with this case. Has convinced himself and a lot of other people that there's nothing criminal to pursue. I asked him how he could keep from being curious about two grand jury witnesses dying in twenty-four hours. He says, 'Shit happens, Sam. Even on your shift, Sam, shit happens.' So to get back to your original question—yeah, there's a deputy DA on the case, but he doesn't think we have anything to investigate. My supervisors don't really think we have much to investigate. They all may be right. Who knows? That's where we come in, Dr. Coroner's Investigator. My job is to develop a case to present to Mr. Bellhaven to convince him we have evidence to warrant a charge against somebody for something, which for some reason nobody in his office or my department seems to really want me to do. Your job is to find whatever you need to find to convince Scott Truscott and the coroner to move Mr. Templeton's manner of death from the 'pending' category to something a little more gutsy and definitive, which nobody really believes you'll be able to do. But, let's say you get lucky, and you find something that lets the coroner rule that the bombing was homicide—well then, I'm back in business."

"And where do you suggest I start?"

"The family. They're motivated. Larry Templeton's survived by a grieving wife and two kids. She works part-time; has got to be worried about money. His life insurance has a suicide exclusion, so they haven't been paid his death benefits yet. They would love a determination of manner of death from the coroner that says 'accident' or 'homicide.' Then they can get this big chunk of money, start themselves a new life. So I think they'll help you out. I'd start there."

I nodded and asked a related question. "What's going on with the grand jury this guy was supposed to talk to?"

Sam Purdy said, "I'm still out of the loop on that. The investigation was apparently Elliot Bellhaven's baby early on, but it's been in the hands of a special prosecutor for a while. Rumor is they think they're gonna have trouble getting a bill voted with Larry Templeton dead and Claire Draper dead. But they aren't sharing their strategy with me. Who knows, maybe you'll stumble over something that can breathe some life into that investigation, too."

"I wouldn't even know what that something might look like."

He sat back in his chair and looked at me in a manner I interpreted as pensive and professorial. "The beauty of it is you don't need to know what you're looking for. The procedure involved is a basic investigative technique. You plod along until you trip and fall on your face. Then you look behind you and see what you tripped over. Piece of cake. We pros do it all the time."

Purdy sat back in his chair, removing his impressive forearms from the table.

I said, "You're still smelling that smell, aren't you, Sam?"

His eyes were warm as he smiled at the waitress and asked for the check.

Elaine Casselman was wearing high heels when she walked into my office for her regular one o'clock that afternoon. She was at least five inches taller than I that day and seemed to relish the advantage.

She told me that the grand jury she was on was on hold for now and wondered if I would be able to reschedule her appointment when they were called back into session. We spent a couple of minutes checking our schedules for an alternate time.

Boulder County rarely employed grand juries, most indictments simply being handed down directly from the district attorney's office. The grand juries that were seated were usually reserved for investigations of a political nature. Elaine's grand jury knew the broad outlines of the case in question from a presentation by one of the prosecutors. Elaine seemed to take some hostile joy in being circumspect with me about what she knew. She said it involved an ex–office holder for Boulder. She didn't specify city or county of Boulder, and she didn't let on whether the office was citywide, countywide, statewide, or federal. It could be anyone, I assumed, from our recently resigned mayor to ex-Senator Gary Hart.

Elaine was still seeing Max, who hadn't hurt her in the weeks since his original attempt at strangling her. She said she thought I disapproved of Max, that I was as much against her happiness as her mother was, and that "one little incident" doesn't say anything about what Max was like. I thought of Claire Draper dead in Diane's office and wondered about the future consequences of Elaine Casselman's denial. I hoped I was wrong.

I also suspected that she was sensing my curiosity about the grand jury and was being deliberately vague to get even with me for my insinuations about Max.

Lynn Hughes left an urgent message on my Voicemail just as I was leaving the house that evening to pick up Lauren to see a movie. I had to search my memory to recall who Lynn was. Finally I did, and my curiosity was piqued as I dialed the number she left for me; I hadn't heard from Lynn Hughes since our sole psychotherapy session when she'd revealed her conflicts about having a sexual relationship with her therapist. She'd given me no reason to think I'd ever hear from her again.

As she answered the phone Lynn Hughes was trying hard not to be frantic.

"You told them, didn't you?" she said.

"Told who?"

"The damn state hearing board whatever-you-call-it. About—you know about what. He knows. I'm sure he knows I told you. Why? Why did you have to tell them? Do all of you play God? You promised not to tell. Now what's going to happen? Oh, God."

Calmly I said, "I didn't tell anyone anything about you."

Quiet for an instant; then her restrained voice said, "I don't believe you."

"What makes you think he knows?"

"Before . . . before he used to tell me that others—like you—wouldn't understand what was happening between us. That if anybody else knew how worthless I was, they would lock me up and throw away the key. That's why I couldn't tell anybody about him and me. Not my girl-friends—nobody. This afternoon he said if he ever found out I told anybody about us sleeping together, he'd use some things I told him about my husband—he said, he'd use them to, he said, 'to bury us.' "

"What kinds of things?"

A high-pitched laugh. "Sorry, hon." She sighed. "I've made that mistake with one of you. I'm not gonna make it again. Let's just say some things that could force me to live in a manner in which I'm not eager to be accustomed."

"What, like divorced?"

"Boy, for some reason I keep pretending that you know me. But you don't, do you?" I listened as she fumbled with a lighter and heard her suck hard on a cigarette. "My husband is a fool. For years he was an upper-middle-class fool. Lately he's been on the verge of being a bankrupt fool. I can suffer rich fools. I won't suffer a broke one. See, I'm much more concerned about poverty than I am about divorce. And my therapist knows some things that, let's say, might affect my financial security."

"What can your therapist do to affect your finances? I don't get it."

"You're not evil enough, honey. My therapist—nice name for what he is—my 'therapist' and I are birds of a feather. We're users. Pure and simple. He's on top right now. Not for long, though."

She hung up.

Before getting dressed for the movie, I'd showered and shaved my legs. I wasn't sure how Lauren would feel about physical intimacy with someone with the dregs of an upper-respiratory infection, but I did know how she felt about it with somebody with stubble.

It turns out she and I had a lot to talk about. We never made it to the movie. We never made it to bed, either.

20

Lauren was pushing a run of about forty balls when I knocked on her door. She swung the door open, pecked me quickly on the lips, and tugged me into her living room so she could continue to *thwack* the ivory balls into the leather pockets. I counted another dozen successes before the eleven ball failed to drop. Lauren's back arched up and she looked momentarily like an angry feline. The eleven didn't seem to care; it hung spitefully on the lip of the side pocket closest to the Rockies.

She boxed her cue and asked me what movie I wanted to see.

I said, "Something mindless. Just about anything mindless."

"Arnold Schwarzenegger mindless or Goldie Hawn mindless?"

"Given my new career, something where nobody dies. Romantic comedy."

She had the local paper open to the movie section. She folded it in half with a sharp movement, handed it to me, and stabbed at a big ad for a new release. I shrugged my shoulders and said, "Sounds fine."

"It doesn't start till eight," she said. "We've got some time. You eaten?"

"No. What about you?"

"Yeah. I had a salad."

"Want to get a beer someplace? I can grab a bite to eat."

"Sure," she said, seeming distracted.

I watched her disappear down the hall toward her office and bedroom, and I grabbed the ski parka I'd worn to repel January's cold. She emerged from the bedroom end of the house, struggling to locate one of the sleeves of a long black wool coat. I stepped over and raised the elusive sleeve to help her.

She said, "Thank you," and then, "Okay if I drive?" Immediately she stumbled across the room as though she'd been pushed, finally catching herself on the rail of the pool table.

The look on her face warned me against saying anything. I said, "You all right?"

"Fine. I'm having some balance problems."

"Apparently. Maybe I should drive?"

"I'm fine when I'm sitting. I'll drive."

The Peugeot didn't want to start. Lauren mumbled a couple of obscenities and pounded the steering wheel with the heel of her hand. After a deep sigh she asked me if I minded passing on the beer.

"No, not at all. Do you have something else in mind?"

"Yeah. You'll see," she hissed, and then cranked the starter until it reluctantly sputtered the engine to life. She pointed the Peugeot east on Arapahoe in the general direction of my little house before pulling into an auto plaza that contained dealerships selling the cars of half a dozen different nameplates.

"I'm thinking of buying a new car," she whispered.

"Why are you whispering?" I whispered back.

"I don't want to upset the Peugeot. It causes me serious aggravation when it's upset."

"Oh."

I wasn't sure of my role as I watched Lauren wrestle with a succession of salespeople. I may have been there as moral support, or audience, or maybe foil—I couldn't tell which. Eight o'clock came and went sometime during Lauren's protracted bout with one of the luxury-car salesmen. I didn't care about missing the movie. There was little chance the film we'd selected would be more entertaining than watching the deft moves that Lauren used to avoid sitting at one of the little desks where the car pros tried to establish their advantage.

She started every conversation with every salesperson

by asking them about passenger-side air bags. She abruptly nailed the sales manager at one dealership for selling cars that didn't even have air bags on the driver's side. At another, to an asthenic salesman with hair coming out of his nose in bushels, she said, "Let me get this straight. If I want my passenger to survive a head-on crash, I have to buy the model with the leather seats?"

The salesman said, "Well, we, um, have excellent passenger restraints in all our models."

"You mean seat belts?" she said. He nodded. She was just getting warmed up. "Is the leather seats–air bag connection a technological limitation? You know, air bags don't work in the presence of synthetic fibers or something?"

He was smart enough not to try to answer that one.

"Or is it that if I'm so cheap that I won't spring for leather seats, my passenger doesn't deserve to live?"

It was a short walk to the last of the dealerships. I put my arm around her as we ambled over. "You're enjoying this, aren't you?"

She smiled up at me warmly and said, "I guess. You're not upset about the movie?"

"No. I'm enjoying this much more than I would a movie. I could use some air, though. Mind if we walk for a minute or two?"

"Sounds good to me, too," she said. We crossed Arapahoe, gloved hand in gloved hand, and strolled down a side street toward a brick-fenced enclave of houses pretending to be from a wealthy part of rural England. The evening was cold but not awful. Probably hovering near freezing.

"You gonna buy one?" I asked.

"Yeah, I'll probably buy something. I'm tired of the Peugeot breaking down all the time. And I want air bags and antilock brakes."

"You're good with those guys, much better than I am."

"I spend half my professional life with sociopaths. These guys are amateurs compared to them. It's like what Mark Twain said about school boards and idiots."

"And he said what?"

"He said something like 'First God invented idiots. That was just for practice. Then he invented school boards.' In this case: First God invented car salesmen. That was just for practice. Then he invented sociopaths."

I laughed.

She asked me about my consulting job with the coroner's office. I told her about the dead toddler and my collaboration with Purdy on the Larry Templeton case. When I was through she said she had caught the Munchausen-by-proxy case and that the mother would probably be charged with child abuse resulting in death and would probably plead not guilty by reason of insanity.

Then she warned me to be careful.

She said she had stuck her neck out to generate some prosecutorial curiosity in the DA's office about the explosion at Larry Templeton's house and discovered that there was some serious political pressure to let the Draper and Templeton deaths just go away. I asked her if she knew anything that could be helpful to me in my pursuit of manner of death.

She said, "No." I was tempted to believe her.

"I take it that there are some people who won't be too pleased if I find something that suggests anything but an accident?"

She paused for a moment before answering. "I don't think they'd be too upset about suicide."

" 'They' being?"

"They being whoever has enough influence to get my boss, Royal Peterson, and his current favorite son, Elliot Bellhaven, to climb up on soapboxes to encourage the rest of us in the office to accept the circumstances of fate."

"You remain unconvinced?"

"That's a good word. I'm unconvinced. Look, common things happen commonly. Rare things happen rarely. The easy explanations for the two deaths are the common ones. Abusive husbands murder wives. Gas leaks cause houses to blow up. None of us have any, I mean *any*, evidence anything else might have happened. Anything *rare*." She looked at me askance. "And given your vast investigatory experience and skill, I seriously doubt if you'll find any, either."

Walking back to the auto plaza, she gripped my arm tightly. I could feel her sway and knew she was using me for balance. She buried her face in my arm and told me she was flying to New York on Friday.

"What for?"

She sighed. "There's this doctor at Albert Einstein College of Medicine in New York City who's been doing some research trials with a drug called Copolymer I. In initial trials it's shown some real promise at reducing the incidence and severity of MS exacerbations. They're gearing up to start phase-two trials, and I'm flying out to see if I can get into the sample. One of my old law school professors is on the board at Einstein. He got me the eligibility interview. I've got a good chance. From everything I've been able to find out, I think I meet criteria."

"Would this doctor really take people from out of state? Wouldn't it be hard for him to follow you?"

"If I get accepted for the Cop I trials, I'll see—I might even have to move there for a while. If the stuff works— if it could help me slow down the progress of this disease—it'd be worth it. Alan, I've had three exacerbations in the past ten months. I need to do something." An echo of desperation resonated in her voice. She must have felt, too, my stiffening silence at the prospect of her leaving. "And maybe it'll give you some time to sort out what you want to do about Merideth and the baby. And about me and multiple sclerosis."

I was quiet. While we waited for the light to change, she said, "You were wonderfully patient with me last year, Alan, when I was hot and cold with you. I can be patient with you now. I feel I owe you, and us, that. But I owe it to myself not to be stupid about all this, either. If you can't sort this out in some reasonable amount of time, I'm going to start protecting myself."

She leaned up and kissed me.

Back across Arapahoe, exhaustion grabbed her like a vise. She asked if I would mind driving her home. I noted the rare admission of infirmity, the vulnerability she was willing to risk. I did drive us home, then supported her into the house and watched her get ready for bed, tucked her in, and then drove to the commercial strip that bisected the town to find some fast food.

A string of unlit storefronts limited my choices until I discovered an unoccupied polyurethaned oak bench in the garishly lit dining room of Taco Bell. Within minutes I'd apparently eaten two grilled chicken soft taco things but didn't remember tasting or swallowing them. Though it seemed I did have taco breath.

After being dumped by a wife I thought I loved and being jacked around for much of a year by a woman I'd grown to love, it seemed I was finally in a position to get to make a choice. If these ladies were to be believed, I could have either of them.

I couldn't go wrong. Right?

Adrienne's admonishment to me about Merideth and Lauren kept reverberating in my head. What didn't I want to face about Merideth? That she was self-centered and lacking in some of the more refined notes on the scales of empathy? I knew those things. For a long time I had loved her anyway.

Loving her, I'd decided long ago, was like climbing mountains on my bike. The climb was painful and endless, but the vistas at the top made up for the agony. There was the reality that with Merideth, I never got to stay long at the top. I spent a lot of my time climbing. I sometimes assured myself all the exercise made me stronger.

Lauren was more of an enigma. For a long time, when I wanted to be close I wasn't able to find her. Now she professed to be available, and she actually seemed to be. I feared, though, that if I went to embrace her, she would vanish. Again.

And what was Adrienne trying to tell me?

What had she said about me and intimacy? That I really just wanted the "garden variety"? If Lauren was truly available now, why was I hesitating? Trust? Sure, a possibility. Her illness? Another possibility. Or maybe I just liked running protracted expeditions in search of women

I never really hoped to capture. Maybe I feared Lauren *would* be there when I went to embrace her?

No. It was the baby.

Merideth might be carrying my baby.

Then again, she might not be.

The interior of the Subaru was ice cold after my protracted reverie in Taco Bell. But rather than head directly home, I drove back toward the west and took a few turns to Larry Templeton's pile of once well-designed rubble. I parked in front and just stared at it for a while, engine running, heater blaring, hoping for inspiration. Warning signs and yellow tape continued to pronounce that the site of the explosion was off limits to the public. After a few minutes the Templetons' next-door neighbor's porch lights flashed on, and I noticed a shadow move across the picture window of their living room.

It was time to go.

I drove home slowly, full of Merideth maybe coming and Lauren maybe leaving and Larry Templeton dead by his own hand, or God's hand, or another's hand, and Adrienne's reproof about where I cut slack and where I didn't and her insinuation that my slack cutting was neither particularly objective nor often in my best interest.

Full of concern for Diane, whose wounds were deep and exposed and seemed to be festering, and for Randy Navens, whose wounds were immense and buried below strata that rendered them unreachable. Full of grief for the small child dead at his mother's hand. Full of fear for color-blind Elaine Casselman, whose Max was showing his true colors, and for Lynn Hughes, who had to look no further for abuse than the next visit to her therapist.

And for the Peugeot, whose days, apparently, were numbered.

21

Another problem, I'd realized as I'd driven away from the wreckage of the Templeton home the night before, was that I didn't have any idea where the surviving Templetons might be residing. I hoped they'd stayed in town.

Purdy wasn't in when I called the police department before nine the next morning. He was probably inhaling breakfast someplace. I left a message asking him if he knew where I could find the Templetons, gave the receptionist my pager number, and drove to my office. I arrived shortly after nine to discover my office door wide open and six-foot-two Raoul Estevez standing on a three-point ladder just inside my French doors. Diane's office door was closed.

"Good morning, Raoul."

He turned a quarter turn and said, "Alan," in a warm greeting. When he said my name it invariably came out *Alain,* sounding French and sophisticated. I liked it.

"What are you up to, my friend?" I asked.

"My wife, you know, she doesn't feel too safe after the bullets, the burglars."

"But this isn't Diane's office."

"Yes," Raoul replied, "she said you might take notice of that." He turned back to his work on the top of the doorjamb and squeezed the trigger on a cordless drill, hoping, I think, to shut me up and make me go away. I couldn't see his face, but I imagined a wry smile.

Raoul and Diane had met before I knew either of them. At that time he was a recent electrical engineering graduate from Cal Tech who had come to town to help a little computer memory company called Storage Technology;

Diane was struggling to finish the dissertation for her Ph.D. After Raoul left Storage Technology, he'd signed on sequentially with just about every fledgling Cinderella high-tech start-up in town and had always managed to get out just at the apogee of their success. His résumé read Storage Tech, NBI, Miniscribe, McData, Exabyte, and now a little company called TelSat that was planning to use satellites to do something rural America apparently couldn't wait to have done.

I'd met Diane and Raoul when he was at NBI and she and I were on internship together in Denver. I'd bought a little stock in NBI at his suggestion and sold it when he left the company. He never told me when to sell. I just trusted his instincts. If Diane and Raoul and I were going hiking and he carried a poncho on a bright sunny day, I did, too. I'd successfully followed his investment example in the stock market at Miniscribe, McData, and Exabyte. I now owned five thousand shares of TelSat. Largely because of Raoul, I had a lot of money in the bank. Even after the divorce I would have at least half of a lot of money in the bank. Which was still a lot of money. And who could tell what profits investing in the celestial future of rural America might bring?

"The alarm?"

He said, "*Sí.*" I worried he was about to go foreigner on me. It was something he did at his convenience.

"I didn't ask for one."

The drill whined, and I watched the back of his head.

"So?" I said, hoping for an explanation, rather sure what it would be.

"You know Diane. It is hard to say no to her. No?"

"Yes," I acknowledged.

"Well. She tells me. So what if she's safe? If you are not. Both times, the men come in your office, not hers. So if you are not safe, she is not safe. Anyway, she says your judgment is"—he turned to face me now—"and I'm quoting here, my friend, 'some of the time poor like piss.' "

"You mean piss poor."

"*Sí,*" he said absently while turning his attention back

to the door frame. "She says if I ask can I wire your office, you might say no. She says I don't ask, just do it, you will shrug your shoulders and be kind and gracious to me. To her you will say something snide and that will be that. So, I'm wiring. That way, you get to have the argument with her. I don't have to."

"What if I ask you to stop?"

He turned in mock horror. "Alain, after all we've been through. You would do that to me?"

I laughed and asked him when he'd be done. He told me he and a friend of his had worked the entire previous evening, and he would be out of my office in twenty minutes, maybe an hour. I glanced around and saw a plastic pad with push buttons and little lights by the entry door, a recessed plate with a switch on it on the floor by my consulting chair, and a recessed infrared device in one corner of the room.

"The doors are wired, the window screens are all wired, the hallway has an infrared monitor, the staircase has sensors. An automatic dialer will call my friend who owns an alarm company and who gave me all this stuff at cost and then will, in sequence, dial Diane's pager, your pager, her portable phone, our home, your home, my office. Maybe your girlfriend's home, too?"

"Don't think so, Raoul."

"You change your mind, well, you let me know."

"I have a ten o'clock."

"You stop chatting with me, I'll be done by ten."

"Raoul?"

"*Sí.*" His back was turned again.

"Thank you."

"*De nada.*"

True to form, if not to his word, he was done by about twenty after. While Raoul was packing up, I asked him— if he wasn't busy later—maybe he would like to come with me for a drive up in the mountains? Purdy had called with the location of the Templetons' temporary residence. They were staying way up Coal Creek Canyon in a place that I'd never heard of called Mirabelle.

I told Raoul I didn't think my visit with the Templetons

would last long and that I'd enjoy his company. He said he would love to come with me and told me when I was done with my patient I could find him at Lucille's having lunch. He wanted to drive.

My moderately paranoid ten o'clock allayed my guilt about the delay in starting his appointment by being openly conciliatory about my being late; he even offered that, given recent events, he thought the alarm was a pretty good idea. I took his endorsement in stride; on his overtly paranoid days he even thought concealed weapons were a pretty good idea.

By late morning I'd reached Larry Templeton's widow by phone and had scheduled a meeting over the noon hour. My walk down the sunny side of the mall to Fourteenth Street to track down Raoul was pleasant and winter warm. Raoul was drinking coffee and reading the local paper at a sun-washed table at Lucille's. He encouraged me to order something to eat, but I told him the family was expecting me around twelve-thirty and that, unfortunately, we needed to get going. We each ordered a cup of chicory coffee to take with us and climbed into his new 4 × 4. There was a computer-generated parking ticket on the windshield. He climbed back out of the truck and removed it with remarkable aplomb.

"In some towns, you know, you must worry about getting tickets for parking too long. In Boulder, there is no worry. You *always* get parking tickets. Boulder has more parking ticket people than Spain has closet fascists. I'm tempted, you know, to sneak down one night and take one of these meters apart. I suspect that they emit a radio signal when time is expired that summons one of those parking ticket people."

"How many do you get, Raoul?"

"Many."

"Do you pay them?"

He looked hurt. "*Sí*. I budget for them."

Raoul drove with an equanimity and patience that exasperated his wife. She was born to change lanes. He needed a compelling reason. The ride south out of Boulder was relaxing.

Just outside of town past the cutoff to Eldorado Springs, we passed the empty parking lot of Pain Perdu. Raoul said that he and Diane hadn't eaten there yet. I praised it and suggested we make a visit together soon.

"It will be good for Diane," he said. "She is morose. You will bring someone, yes?" he asked.

"Sure."

"Date or wife?"

"Lauren," I said with surprisingly little hesitation.

We talked about our mutual concern about Diane's numb reaction to the recent assaults and intrusions. By then we were approaching the western entrance to the Rocky Flats Nuclear Weapons Facility. We passed the huge complex silently. Moments later Raoul turned up Colorado 72 into Coal Creek Canyon.

I despised trying to follow directions that said things like "Two dirt roads past the cluster of mailboxes on the right that are 2.2 miles from the fire department, take a left." Such were Purdy's directions to Mirabelle. Colorado 72 hugged Coal Creek deep into the carved canyon. Ice patches slicked the blacktop in the perennial winter shadows despite the recent moderate temperatures. We drove through the village of Coal Creek and climbed toward Wondervu past the dirt roads that cut up to Gross Reservoir. Frustrated by Purdy's directions, I tried to get some assistance from an AAA map I found in the glove box. No Mirabelle.

Myriad unpaved roads in varied states of repair sneaked off toward rustic cabins and modern chateaux hidden in the thin forests that butted Coal Creek. The warm downslope winds of winter were blowing hard at Wondervu and rocked Raoul's big vehicle. The Continental Divide was an ominous wall of stark white peaks stretching as far as the eye could see both north and south. I couldn't help imagining the despair of the pioneers as they climbed three thousand feet into these craggy foothills to reach this apparent precipice we call Wondervu, only to find a fourteen-thousand-foot-high wall twenty miles ahead.

The pioneer name for Wondervu was probably something like "Oh, Shit."

Raoul had taken the paper with Purdy's directions from me and read them silently between hairpin turns descending into a narrow valley. He nodded his head assuredly and told me not to worry, he'd find Mirabelle.

In the next ten minutes he took two wrong turns on his own, and another one with my assistance, until, almost by default, we stumbled onto the left-hand turn that led the half mile to Mirabelle.

Sometime just after the turn of the century, I would learn later, the Rio Grande Railroad had decided to build some tunnels on the route through the Continental Divide to Winter Park. Some expansive functionary at the railroad named them Tunnels 18 through 22. Nonexistent transportation to and from the Front Range population centers prohibited the use of a commuting labor force for the project, so the railroad set up an itinerant camp for workers on about five hundred acres in the valley below the divide. When the work on the tunnels was completed, seven Front Range families saw a golden opportunity for a predeveloped site for their vacation cabins and bought the land and the crumbling cabins from the railroad for an amount of money that would make a modern developer weep.

The families named their Valhalla Mirabelle and over the next half century built new "cabins," a caretaker's residence, and a holiday life-style of secluded leisure only a half hour from the contemporary chaos of the Front Range. There were seven "cabins" in all, although only a few were winterized. The caretaker's cabin had a wood stove but no plumbing.

Rita Templeton was the granddaughter of one of the original seven, and she and her son were staying in one of the winterized cabins. For some psychotic reason I expected to find the Volvo station wagon I'd seen Larry Templeton drive behind his house just before it exploded. Instead, parked in front of the only cabin with smoke coming from a chimney was a white minivan. The Volvo was probably crushed. Although they may be legendary for surviving accidents, they probably had trouble surviving houses exploding over them.

Raoul said he was going to hike around and do some exploring while I conducted my meeting. I told him to check back with me in about forty-five minutes. Rita Templeton was waiting at the door of her cabin as I walked up. She looked over my shoulder as I approached, and her eyes followed Raoul heading down a dirt road that wound behind the cabins farther into the valley.

"Who's that?" Her face was young-looking and unwrinkled. She wore tight stone-washed jeans and a thick turtleneck in a shade of coral that was perfect for her skin and her rouge.

"A friend. He drove up with me. He's just going to walk around while we talk."

"There're abandoned mine shafts out there," she warned.

"He lives in the mountains, too. He knows how to take care of himself." I didn't want to have an argument about Raoul's presence; if his safety wandering around the mountains was an issue, I was even prepared to present him as a visiting Basque if I thought it would help mollify her.

Rita Templeton asked to see my identification and invited me in to a big house of exposed wood and inadequate insulation. The chill was permeating my flatland clothing everywhere but in front of the big wood stove in the kitchen. We sat there and she poured me tea from a ceramic pot.

"I'm tired of this," she said after examining my identification once again and handing it back to me.

Her voice said she was expecting an argument. Maybe even wanted one. I decided not to cooperate. "I can only imagine how drawn out this must feel after suffering such a tragedy. My hope is that taking a little of your time today may help bring this process to a close."

She eyed me suspiciously and said, "Well. I certainly hope so," her tone an octave softer. "You know about the insurance mess?"

I nodded, looking first at her exquisite hands and then

at her sculpted eyebrows. It wasn't fair of me, but I decided she was Junior League.

"Unless my work uncovers some new information, the coroner is prepared to declare the manner of death 'undetermined,' Ms. Templeton. The claims evaluator for the part of your husband's life insurance that provides a death benefit may or may not have trouble with that categorization. The coroner's office has no influence—"

"How the hell can it be 'undetermined'? Our goddamned house fell on top of him!"

"We know," I said in my therapy voice, trying to sound expert about something that I had learned over the past seventy-two hours, "that the explosion and the house collapsing did indeed kill your husband. The injuries he suffered as a result helped us ascertain what we call 'cause' of death. Cause of death is not at issue. But we are still unclear what caused the explosion that resulted in the house collapsing. When we ascertain that, we will know 'manner' of death."

"It was a gas leak. Everyone, *everyone,* says it was a gas leak."

"But there is no agreement on the type of gas, the source of the gas, the manner in which it was leaked into the house, or even the nature of ignition of the explosion."

She sighed deeply and sank back onto the chair, momentarily permitting her squared shoulders to round. She recovered her posture quickly.

"Okay, okay, okay. I'll go over it again. What do you wish to know?"

I had reviewed the cursory interview done by my predecessor and went over the basic facts again quickly. Lawrence Templeton was a wonderful father, good provider, only problem he seemed to have was how hard he was working, was gone a lot of evenings. Loved to windsurf and ski and sail and hunt. No enemies. Didn't do anything classified at Rocky Flats that she knew about.

The kids were typical kids. The daughter, Erin, was quasi-punk, the son, Brian, quasi-jock. Larry was closer to his son than to his daughter; Larry and Brian did a lot of athletic activities together. Rita worked part time in a dress store a friend of hers owned near the Downtown Boulder Mall.

Just to keep her talking, I asked her about Mirabelle, and she eagerly told me the history. The families who owned the area had been together for three generations, sharing vacations, Fourth of July celebrations, weddings, projects, and occasional tragedies. The Templetons spent frequent weekends at the cabin and tried to carve out at least one two-week stay a year. Other families spent about the same amount of time, except those that owned winterized cabins would occasionally have a family member take up extended residence. The current caretaker for the compound was a young woman whose boyfriend lived twenty minutes away in an old log cabin on the grounds of an ancient hunting lodge on the Peak to Peak Highway near Rollinsville. She apparently spent more time with him than she did at Mirabelle. Rita didn't sound fond of the caretaker.

Rita offered me more tea and began to talk about how frightened she was. The kids were overwhelming her. Erin was in town staying with a friend, refusing to tolerate the commute to high school from Mirabelle. Rita talked as if she barely knew her son and couldn't begin to help him find an outlet for his grief. I silently reviewed the symptoms she described and decided that Brian's grief was not pathologic but made a mental note to call her in a short while to check on how he was doing. She was oddly flat about her own loss and resisted my gentle suggestions to talk about her marriage, preferring to focus on practical things she could still influence. She wanted to search through the wreckage of the house for the family album and for a few heirlooms. "When are they going to let me look for my memories?" she asked, and for an instant I thought about Randy Navens. Rita Templeton seemed more troubled about losing her wedding album than she was about losing her husband. But psychological distraction was readily available to her, and she focused her attention on the kids, on having enough money to manage, on finding a new place to live, on replacing everything the family owned.

I thought about referring her for psychotherapy but decided her grief fell somewhere in the normal range and decided now wasn't the time.

She gave me the address and phone number where her daughter was staying in town and said she'd phone and prepare Erin for my call. She suggested that her son wouldn't be of any help but that if I could come back some afternoon after four o'clock, he'd probably be home.

I thanked her for the tea and told her I would do everything I could to put the investigation to rest.

Raoul was still wandering when I emerged from the cabin. I walked over to the crest of a northwest-facing ridge and watched him make a leisurely ascent up an old mining road to the cluster of cabins.

22

"Ever been to Rocky Flats?" I asked Raoul as he guided us skillfully back down Coal Creek Canyon.

He stole his eyes from the road for an instant and shook his head at me.

"Wanna go now?" I asked.

Raoul examined his watch with affected care. "Why?" he said.

"It turns out that this guy whose death I'm investigating—he worked there. Thought I'd do a little fishing."

"What did he do there?"

"A manager in an environmental department of some kind. Don't really have a clue what he actually did." I felt stupid that I hadn't asked Rita Templeton more about her husband's position at the nuclear weapons plant.

"So?" Raoul wasn't convinced about the need for the detour.

"The guy who busted into Diane's office and shot everybody, Harlan Draper—he worked at the Flats, too."

Raoul said, "I got nothing better to do."

Getting past the armed security force wasn't easy. My identification as a consultant to the coroner didn't impress anyone at the main gate. One guard indicated where we should park the truck while our request to enter was being considered. His demeanor suggested he'd be happier if we just left. Raoul had an inborn petulance in the face of authority that put my own to shame; we waited. Raoul and I talked more about our mutual concern for Diane and listened to the Cowboy Junkies on his forty-seven speaker sound system while the uniformed security people called, first, Detective Purdy and then Chief Medical Investigator Scott Truscott to find out who the hell I was and what the hell did I want. Twice I was called to the phone. Everybody I spoke to wondered out loud why I hadn't made an appointment. One guard said, "People just don't drop in here."

"Next time," I promised, "I'll call."

Just when I was acknowledging to Raoul that popping into Rocky Flats unannounced hadn't been one of my more inspired ideas, a female guard whose button-popping khakis revealed not only a few unappealing triangles of white abdominal flesh, but also her apparent refusal to admit that she had gained a couple of cheesecakes' worth of weight since her uniform had been issued, waddled over to where the truck was parked, handed Raoul a couple of clip-on visitor badges, and gave us directions to the building where Mr. Templeton's office had been. She also suggested that taking detours inside the compound might not be advantageous to our health.

We, of course, got lost. Raoul and I both decided that given the armaments we had already observed, driving around looking for the correct turn was probably not the best problem-solving strategy. So we stopped. A four-wheel-drive security vehicle came to our rescue within a minute, and we followed the two guards inside to a small parking area in the midst of a complex of industrial-looking buildings. The woman who had been Lawrence Templeton's supervisor was waiting for us near the entrance to a building called Building 24. She shook our hands with a firm, guy-type grip. She didn't ask for my identification when we walked up, assuming, I guess, that if I was inside the gate with a badge, I'd been well vetted.

Larry Templeton, it turns out, was a senior-level manager in the department at Rocky Flats that was coordinating the environmental aspects of the long process of going-out-of-the-nuclear-trigger business. Administering environmental cleanup didn't sound like one of the more sinister things that might occur in a place like Rocky Flats, but then the technology of nuclear triggers had not been one of my more complete studies.

The department head introduced herself as Sylvia Torenson. She was a pleasant-looking woman in her forties wearing a forest green suit of worsted wool. Her shoes matched her suit, and she'd even managed to adorn herself with dark green earrings. Her hair was, appropriately, the color of weathered bark. She led us down a long hallway past numerous closed doors in a manner that told me she was someone accustomed to being followed.

Raoul and I allowed ourselves to be escorted into a ten-by-ten office without windows. The three of us filled all the available chairs. Ms. Torenson didn't wait for me to ask any questions. "Larry was my chief deputy, really. I take care of the politics and the budget. He managed the staff and oversaw project schedules." The look on Ms. Torenson's face said "I'm sure that about covers it, anything else?" Her cryptic speech to us reminded me a little bit of watching televised briefings from the Pentagon during the Gulf War.

Not willing to be dismissed so adroitly, I said, "Did his responsibilities include doing anything that might make him a target for a terrorist?"

"No." Ms. Torenson was apparently, by nature, not effusive.

"A target for blackmail?"

"No."

"Did he have access to nuclear material?"

"Absolutely not." See, I knew I could get her talking.

While she and I got to know each other, Raoul twisted on his chair to look around. From my own cursory examination, I knew there wasn't much to see. Raoul turned back to us and sat with his hands in his lap, looking bemused.

"Did your department have any interaction with another employee named Harlan Draper? He was in the—"

"The first time I ever heard Mr. Draper's name was after that awful episode in Boulder." She said "Boulder" with a leer that implied that such a thing wouldn't have happened in one of Denver's more sedate bedroom communities.

"Was Larry's office around here?"

"Right next door." Ms. Torenson hooked her thumb to her left.

"May I look?"

"His personal things have been boxed. We're waiting for Rita to tell us what she wants done with them. She asked us to hold on to them until she gets a new house."

"May I see what's there?"

She sighed. "Yes. I have a meeting in"—she looked at her watch—"eight minutes. I assume that will be a sufficient amount of time."

She pointed us to the adjoining office. It looked unoccupied. Two corrugated boxes on top of a locked file cabinet held Larry's things. One once held toilet paper, the other Coors beer. The desk top was clear, the computer monitor dark. Eight minutes was going to be about seven too many.

Larry Templeton's personal effects consisted of pictures of Rita and the kids, a gym bag with some jogging clothes, a toilet kit, his appointment book, and a couple of framed pictures of sailboats. Raoul looked silently over my shoulder as I picked through the toilet kit, looking for prescription drugs, and flipped through the appointment book, looking for I didn't know what.

While I was engrossed Raoul sat down at Larry's desk and flicked on the computer.

"Raoul!" I said in a loud whisper.

"Shh," he replied, and I was sure we were about to be arrested.

Ten seconds later he flicked off the machine and said if he had enough time, he could probably figure out Larry's password.

I didn't realize he was looking over my shoulder, but when I was about to close the appointment calendar he said, "There's a couple of pages of phone numbers in the back."

The edges of the pages were creased. I unfolded the

crimps and separated the sheets. I didn't recognize any of the names and assumed that the numbers were for people related to Larry Templeton's work.

Raoul said, "There's a copy machine right out in the hall." He took the book from me, walked out to the machine, and tried to make copies of the pages of phone numbers. My extensive experience as a coroner's consultant failed to provide the ethical or proprietary compass necessary to determine whether what Raoul was doing was legal or nice. Nobody in the office said a word to him, but his mission was a failure.

"You need one of those counting things," he said upon his return.

I started to repack the boxes and said to Raoul, "Another dead end, I guess."

He nodded and said, "Yes. But then two times today you and I have been lost, Alain. Each 'dead end' teaches us something about our ultimate destination. No?" I didn't know what he was talking about. But that happened a lot with Raoul.

I finished packing up. Sylvia Torenson was happy to accompany us back to the building entrance. Raoul stopped at the gatehouse, and we returned our passes. As he completed the right turn back toward Boulder, he dumped Larry Templeton's black appointment book in my lap.

"I think you're going to need this."

Immediately I recognized what he had done. "Oh, shit, Raoul."

He smiled at me. "Nobody knows you have it. If anybody misses it, nobody will be sure he didn't have it with him when the house exploded. Don't worry. You need it, I think."

"Why?"

"Look at the calendar. The day before the explosion."

I opened the book to the appropriate page. Raoul said, "What do you see?"

"He had a busy day planned."

"Sometimes, Alain, I think you are thick."

"Look at his lunch," said Raoul.

"It says 'M.' "

"Anywhere else is there just a letter, an initial? Anyplace else is there ninety minutes blocked off?"

I examined the rest of that day, then turned back to the previous week and to the one before that. All of Larry Templeton's appointments were with people whose names were spelled out. There were no initials in the book but the occasional M's. At least two M's were penciled in each week. Once at lunch, once after work, almost always sixty or ninety minutes.

"Diane always tells me you are pure of mind, Alain. I do not always believe her. But apparently it is true. Alain, your Mr. Templeton was scheduling assignations. With this M. So maybe M knows something to help you with your puzzle. No?"

Raoul was an international chameleon and had just managed another seamless transformation from ignorant peasant to continental sophisticate. His tone encouraged me to acknowledge that he was much more experienced than I in the world of assignations.

I said, "Maybe."

"Alain. Even if she doesn't know anything that helps, talking with this 'M' is certainly going to be more interesting than interviewing that woman who was dressed like a pine tree."

Raoul admitted that there *was* the problem of finding out who M was. A thorough examination of the phone numbers in the back of the appointment book yielded two possibles: one, a Martha Capwell, turned out to be the assistant director of Human Services at Rocky Flats and a sixty-one-year-old grandmother of five; the other, an Elizabeth Morisot, was Lawrence Templeton's married sister who lived in Fort Collins.

Neither Martha nor Elizabeth seemed to consider my phone call the highlight of her day. I placed the calls from my office desk while Raoul wandered around the building, checking his handiwork on the new security system, looking forward to Diane's being done with her last patient so that he could "arm" the whole system for the first time.

Diane finished at five-fifteen, and while we sat in her office I filled her in on my escapades with her husband that day. A deafening siren interrupted us twice, both times followed rapidly by Raoul racing by the office door toward the disarm button near the master panel he'd installed in our kitchen. Diane smiled maternally both times. "He really enjoys this. Are you angry I told him to put the alarm in your office, too?"

"No. I understand."

"I thought you would."

"One of us is going to have to learn how to work it, you know."

She sighed. "Yeah. I vote for you."

"Diane, I can't set the clock on my microwave. And *you* even know how to work a cellular phone. How difficult can this be?"

Just then the siren blew for a third time, and Raoul again raced past us down the hall. We both laughed.

"How about we both learn?" she asked.

"Agreed," I said. Diane seemed more animated and more at ease than at any time since the assault in her office.

"How are you?" I asked. The appearance of the question in the middle of a conversation required that it be considered more than perfunctory.

"How am I?" Her eyes reviewed the places in the room where the women had been shot. Some stains can't be sanded away. "Poor to fair, working on fair to good."

"The burglary didn't help."

"No, the burglary didn't help. Neither did Paul Weinman's death." She paused, sighed. "He was a really good friend, Alan. I don't have to tell you that. But after his separation last year we became even closer. He was more open, more vulnerable somehow. I've thought since that Paul's dying felt almost as devastating as if it had been you who had skied into that tree." Her eyes glistened. "And I'd barely begun to find my grief about his death when that asshole came in here with the gun."

"And now it's not just grief."

"No. It's not just grief. It's rage, violation, vulnerability. It's funny, but I'm sorry that Harlan Draper's dead. There's nobody left to be furious at. Part of me wants him to be suffering still. If death is okay for Paul and for Claire and for Larry, then it's too good for Harlan Draper. He doesn't deserve that peace."

"You knew Larry Templeton."

"I knew of him. Through this whole Claire Draper thing." The sweep of her arm encompassed the geography of the tragedy. Diane smiled. "I really can't talk about it, you know?"

I'd momentarily forgotten that Larry and Claire were both scheduled to testify in front of the grand jury. I shouldn't have been surprised that they knew each other. And that, by proxy, Diane knew about Larry Templeton. Nonetheless, I went through the mental exercise of comparing Claire Draper's initials. "She have any nicknames? Claire?"

"Not that I know of."

"Are you in a position to tell me if she was romantically involved with anybody?"

"No. I'm not." Annoyance flickered in her voice. Then her usually quick brain caught up with my suspicious one. She smiled again. "Oh, shit, honey, I see what you're getting at. She's not your M. Don't worry, all right?"

Raoul paused in the doorway long enough to tell us he almost had the system up and running. The siren mocked him by shrieking again during an affectionate, or lustful, glance at his wife.

He rocketed away. Diane asked, "So, what are you doing about your sudden cornucopia of romantic riches?"

"Merideth and Lauren?"

"Yes."

"Don't know. Got any advice?"

"Follow your heart. Then do what your brain tells you is safe."

"Cynicism doesn't fit you well, Diane."

"I'm a little distrustful about romance right now."

"That's what I told Merideth. That I didn't trust her."

"Yes, there is that. But then there's also the question of whose gametes participated in the current conspiracy in her womb."

I didn't want to talk about my mess right then. "Speaking of wombs," I said, "Adrienne and Peter are pregnant."

Diane came alive. "That's wonderful. Oh, God, I'm so happy for them. Were they trying? Did it take them long?"

"They seem real happy. But I'll let her share the motivational and operational details." Diane seemed to be fighting an impulse to go straight for the phone to call Adrienne.

"Lauren might be moving away," I said.

Diane's attention came right back to me. "Really?"

I told her about Cop I and the clinical trials and New York and Lauren's understandable chagrin about the limbo of my divorce and the open question of the identity of the donor of the sperm participating in Merideth's fertilization. And about how generous she seemed to be considering how confused I was. And about my fear that she could come close to me now only because I'd backed off a bit. And about Adrienne's judgment that I only wanted garden-variety intimacy.

Diane was pensive for part of a minute. "You probably don't want to hear this."

"Hear what?"

"Alan, my dear friend. You've grown a lot. Now—*now*—I think Adrienne's right. *Now* I think you're ready for garden-variety intimacy. Before, you weren't even ready for that. If you'd wanted serious intimacy when you got married, you wouldn't have chosen Merideth. Honey. Be wise. She's a talented, beautiful woman, Alan, and has been a decent friend to me, but she isn't comfortable with 'close.' She never has been. You know that. And you knew that when you married her. Wanting intimacy and choosing to marry Merideth is like wanting to buy a lawn mower and shopping for it at a bookstore."

Diane leaned over and kissed me on the cheek before she continued, "Ever notice how we get older so much faster than we grow up? I worried about you so much last year—all the stress you were under, all the losses you endured. Now I know what it feels like, too. I hope I'm as resilient as you've been, I hope I can seem to have grown up a little more when this shit I'm going through finally stops. You've grown, honey; don't knock it.

"Anyway, there's nothing wrong with garden-variety intimacy. Please don't be offended."

23

The ten o'clock news proclaimed that the next day would be a high-pollution day in the Denver metropolitan area, which for purposes of bad air included the city of Boulder. No woodburning. Please curtail your driving. Thank the politicians for ethanol.

But the sun mocked the prognosticators and rose to reveal a crystalline morning of exquisite beauty. The pollution alert would be quietly revoked sometime during the morning, only to be squirreled away for redemption on another day of anticipated inversion. I spent the better part of an hour at my dining room table, trading my attention between the banality of the morning paper and the scraggy demarcation on the horizon, where white-tipped peaks jostled against a sky the blue of water dreams. Puffs of clouds dotted the sky.

I sipped coffee and ate toast and tried not to think about dead people.

An hour later, after a shower and shave, I went out to the Subaru and headed down the hill to town. When I got to the office I called Scott Truscott and reviewed the previous day's developments with him. Given my failure to develop anything new—and my decision not to tell him about the appointment book Raoul had hoisted—he wondered aloud if the case deserved the resources he was investing in it. I was certain he was still feeling some pressure from Purdy to march on, but I didn't know him well enough to judge how susceptible he was. Anyway, he didn't pull the plug. But he made it clear his hand was on the chain.

* * *

I saw four patients and then didn't see Randy Navens.

He was a no-show.

In the time I'd been seeing Randy, he'd never missed an appointment, had rarely even been late. I called his home, trying first the line into his room, then his aunt and uncle's phone. No answer on either. I called the high school to see if he'd attended classes. He hadn't.

I called Pain Perdu, and after I'd convinced a charming hostess that she really couldn't help me and that I absolutely needed to talk to either Erica or Geoff Tobias immediately, she reluctantly went off to track down one of Randy's guardians.

The conversation with Randy's aunt was dismaying. I introduced myself as Alan Gregory and realized soon enough that Erica Tobias didn't recognize my name. I clarified, calling myself "Dr. Alan Gregory" and identifying myself as Randy's therapist.

On two different occasions shortly after I'd begun treating Randy Navens, I'd tried to interest the Tobiases in their nephew's treatment. On both occasions they had gone to great lengths to elude me. Randy had given me only narrow permission to speak with them. I couldn't reveal anything he said to me—and really had no interest or desire in doing so—but did have his permission to hear their general concerns and impressions and respond with nonspecific counsel. Neither Erica nor Geoff ever heeded my request for appointments. Erica had finally agreed to speak with me over the phone. The conversation had been an unfortunate parody of concern.

She'd told me how gratified she and Geoff were that Randy was keeping his grades up, that he wasn't using drugs "like so many of them are these days." At that time I was estimating that Randy was stoned about ten percent of his waking hours. Erica also told me that it was "wonderful" that he was getting the help he needed to get over that "awful tragedy." I'd fished for specific concerns she and her husband might have about Randy and even resorted to asking about delineated symptoms of post-traumatic stress. Nothing. She was just "so grateful" for my help. Randy seemed to like me. I was being paid, wasn't I?

I told her that Randy's trust paid my bills regularly.

"Fine, then," she said, "thanks so much for calling. And don't hesitate to call if there's anything we can do to help."

The day Randy seemed to be missing, Erica Tobias finally responded to my identifying myself as her nephew's psychologist by saying, "Of course you are." I felt greatly reassured.

"What can I do for you, Doctor?"

"Randy missed his appointment today. He apparently never made it to school. Is he home ill?"

A pause. "Well. I don't think so. Let me ask Geoffrey."

I was put on hold and listened to a recitation of the day's menu along with a plea for my patience, assuring me that someone would be with me shortly. The menu sounded great.

It sounded more wonderful the first time than it did the second. And by the third time I was wondering why someone would want to do what they were doing with mascarpone cheese and free-range chickens anyway.

Geoff Tobias's voice, tinny and tentative, came back on the line instead of Erica's. "Hello, Alan." As if we were old friends.

"Mr. Tobias, hello. I'm a little worried about Randy missing school and his appointment today. I was wondering if he was home ill and perhaps just not answering his phone."

"No. No, he's not at home. I heard him drive away a little after eight as always. Excuse me. . . ." His voice became muffled as he said, "Absolutely not—no more at eight-fifteen. I don't care. No." Then back to me, his trebled voice back at regular volume, "I hope he's all right." I made a judgment born of my irritation with these two "guardians." My judgment was that Geoff Tobias hoping Randy Navens was "all right" was more the product of concern for what an inconvenience it would be if something had happened to Randy than it was the product of any intrinsic compassion or concern for his welfare.

"As do I," I said, knowing that being cryptic was one

of the tools I used to thwart my propensity toward sarcasm.

"Have you called the hospital?" he asked.

I thought, No, Geoff, I think that's your job. I said, "No, I haven't," pausing poignantly.

"Well then, that's the first step. I guess I'll do it. This isn't a good time for this. We open in forty-five minutes. The house is full tonight."

I'd had enough. "How nice for you, Mr. Tobias. But I don't think this happened solely in order to inconvenience you. It sounds like Randy has been unaccounted for most of the day."

"I'll look into this, Dr. Gregory. Thanks for your concern." Click.

I could be real charming.

While I was shaving my legs for a date with Lauren I couldn't stop thinking about the cavalier manner in which I'd handled Randy's description of the apparent dissociative episode he'd had at his guardian's restaurant not too long before. In his therapy I had been anticipating a time when buried memories about the crash would begin to surface, when physical sensations of the nightmare would be reborn as physical symptoms, when brand names of fear would replace the generic ones assaulting his ego, when his grief would redouble. I considered the brief period of panic and rage Randy had experienced watching his uncle talk to the waitress and then his reflexive return to a childhood hideout to have been a sign that the process had begun. I'd told Randy as much, had told him to expect that more memories might surface, and had reminded him that he could call me whenever he needed.

But the day he disappeared I feared I might have underestimated the impact of what lurked on Randy's horizon.

Lauren knew the vague outlines of my psychotherapy with Randy. I had never mentioned his name, but she knew I was seeing someone who was a survivor of the crash of Flight 232. Randy suffered from local notoriety, and a feature story on him in the local paper on the two-year anniversary of the crash had brought Lauren to quiet tears one night. She revealed to me then for the first time how her drunken father had driven his pickup truck, with her and her older brother in it, into a utility pole. Lauren had been knocked unconscious and had broken an ankle and a wrist. Her brother was hospitalized for weeks with internal injuries and facial wounds. Her father was un-scathed.

"Momma called us her 'miracles' after that. She'd say, 'Here're my survivors,' when my brother and I would walk in the door together. I never felt like a survivor, though. I felt like maybe a 'near' survivor. Survive has to mean more than just staying alive. It has to."

Lauren was sitting at her kitchen table while she told me this story. She paused to brush at imaginary crumbs with the edge of her hand before she continued, "A neigh-bor's child, one of my little brother's friends, almost drowned in an irrigation ditch once. It was before the accident; I was about eleven then. She was rescued, but she'd been underwater too long. They got her heart work-ing and they got her lungs working, but they never really got her brain working again. Alan, she had been such a bright, sweet child." Lauren looked at me quickly, then away as she continued. "And suddenly she was a pitiful, twisted, foul-smelling monument to emergency medicine. And how she scared me. The family would say, when they needed to explain about her, they'd say, 'She nearly drowned.'

"I used to baby-sit for the family sometimes, and I hated to care for her after that—her name was Molly—those empty eyes, that odor—and I'd say to myself, Nope. Molly didn't nearly drown. She definitely drowned. What Molly did was nearly survive."

Lauren spent the next few minutes fumbling with tea bags, setting out mugs, and lighting a flame beneath an enamel kettle. I waited. "When I came to after the accident in the pickup, my first conscious thought was that I was going to be just like Molly. Foul-smelling and almost alive. I knew in my heart that all that was left of Molly was the frame. The picture was gone. After the accident I would go off by myself and check my body for odor sometimes, smell my underarms and my crotch, sure that if I started to smell, then I would be like her forever. See, when I was little I thought Molly was decomposing—that's why she smelled. I was so afraid I was going to be like Molly. But then, like magic, at some point I forgot all about Molly and forgot all about decomposing.

"And then my marriage failed, and I got MS, and there were times I was sure I was someone who had only nearly survived, too. And that if anybody got too close to me, they'd smell me decomposing and back away and see only my empty frame. That's why I was so frightened of you, Alan. That's why now I think that, in a way, you saved my life. You and Rebecca. You two saved my life."

Rebecca Washburn was Lauren's therapist.

Lauren was thrilled to help when I explained my fears about my anonymous patient the night he was missing. She called Purdy and asked if he could check and see if there were any reports of accidents, injuries, or crimes involving someone of his age and description. While we waited for a return call she distracted me by giving me a pocket billiards lesson.

She winced as I failed to sink a two-foot shot, and was saying, "You know, you don't have much of a touch," when the phone rang.

Purdy told her that he had found out "zip" but that he'd instructed the dispatcher to find him if anything came in. She thanked him for his help. She and I got ready for bed.

When the tart chirping startled us awake in the middle of the night, Lauren and I both fumbled for our beepers. Mine was on the belt of my pants, which were half under her bed. She located her beeper first and was wide-eyed in the dim blue glow of the clock radio light when she pushed the button to illuminate the message screen and said to me, "It's not mine, honey." The clock read 3:37.

I finally tugged my pager off my belt and saw the gray lines that read ONE PAGE. I involuntarily took a deep breath and pulled on my pants and shirt. Lauren had already pushed the phone to the middle of the bed for me and was pulling on a dark green robe.

I called my Voicemail service.

"One call," announced the computer-generated voice. A pause.

"Hi, it's Randy. I'm, I'm in the mountains. I'm okay, I think. But you said to call. It's pretty late. I'll stay here for a few minutes." He recited a phone number and hung up.

The computer voice said, "Ready."

I punched the number eight. The voice said, "Calls replayed." I made a writing motion with my hand, and Lauren scrambled after a pencil. She found one just in time for me to dictate the phone number to her.

Randy picked up the phone after half a ring.

"Dr. Gregory?"

I exhaled and calmed my voice. "Yes, Randy, it's Alan Gregory."

"I think I missed my appointment."

"Don't worry about that, Randy. Where are you?"

"I'm in the mountains. I think near Central City. But I'm not sure. This place feels real familiar, but I can't remember when I've been here. Maybe when I was a kid. My mom'll know."

I decided not to remind him, right then, that his mom was dead. "Are you at a pay phone?"

"No, I'm in a cabin, a house. I'm real confused."

"Do you know how you got there?"

"No. But my car's here, too." Some panic crept into his voice.

"Are you alone?"

"Yeah. I think so."

"Do you know whose house it is?"

"I've been here before. I'm sure I have. But I don't know. I don't remember. I'm scared."

Oh, shit. Fugue?

"Can you tell me what you did today, Randy? You didn't go to school, did you?"

"I don't know what I did. I'm getting more scared. I don't know how I got here."

"Can you give me directions? I'll come get you."

"I don't think so. I don't know where I am. And I don't think there's time. I don't think I can stay here that long.

I see headlights. There's a road close by. I'm going to drive to another phone."

"Randy, *don't hang up*. What do you mean, you don't think there's time? I'll get the police to trace the location of the number and come get you."

"No. I can't stay here!"

He hung up.

The next call came over an hour later. I had dressed. Lauren had made coffee while I showered, and afterward we sat in her kitchen and waited.

After Randy hung up on me she had tried to explain to me why the telephone company couldn't be of any help in identifying the location of the phone that Randy had used to call. At the conclusion of her explanation I wasn't sure whether the issue at hand was civil liberties or some function of limitations in RAM or ROM as a result of their failure to achieve everything they wanted from their last rate request to the PUC. I didn't buy it. I was one of those people who believed that the phone company could do anything. I didn't believe that in awe. It was a belief born exclusively of paranoia.

Before he hung up I hadn't had an opportunity to give Lauren's phone number to Randy, so his call near five in the morning was filtered through the same cumbersome screen of Voicemail computers, uplinks, downlinks and landlines. Finally I heard his voice say, "I'm okay. Are you mad?"

"No. I'm worried." Of course I'm mad.

"I'm on the Peak to Peak Highway now, I think close to Nederland. I'm going to my parents' house." Randy never referred to his residence as "home."

"Randy, I'd like to come and get you. Drive you there, myself."

"No."

"Randy—"

"Dr. Gregory, I don't want you to. I'm okay, now. I'm tired. I want to sleep. I do want you to call my aunt and uncle. If you can get them to lay off about this, I'd really appreciate it. Tell my aunt to call the school. Okay?"

Randy's voice was sluggish and weary. I considered pressing him about waiting for me to pick him up but decided against it. He seemed oriented. I needed to check on his impulsiveness.

"Randy, of course I'll call your aunt and uncle and I'll try and get them to back off until you and I get a chance to sort this out. In the meantime, I need to run something by you. We've talked some lately about your wanting to hurt yourself or somebody else. Are you having any of those feelings now?"

"No. I'm just tired."

"You're not suicidal?"

"No. I promise." The edge in his voice screamed that I was pressing him toward exasperation.

I manufactured a casual tone to decrease the suggestion of pressure. "So can we do a makeup appointment this afternoon? Four-fifteen?"

"Sure. I'm sorry to bother you, Dr. Gregory. 'Bye."

As I hung up the phone, Lauren embraced me from behind and said into my ear, "If I was struggling to keep from drowning, sweetheart, I'd want you at the other end of the rope." Her hand dropped to my lap. She leaned over me, and I reached up through the gap in her robe and weighed one of her dangling breasts. It felt heavy and warm.

24

Sam Purdy had dropped by my office around nine, uninvited, just before my first patient. He wanted to know about my visit to Mirabelle and Rocky Flats. After I filled him in on the afternoon of futility I had spent searching for Larry Templeton's manner of death, I thanked him for his help the previous evening in checking for reports on "that adolescent patient of mine who was missing."

"So did you find the kid?"

"Yeah. He showed up this morning around five. As you can probably tell, I didn't get much sleep."

"Kids pull this shit all the time, you know."

"I know about acting out, Sam. I know about separation and individuation. This little episode wasn't about either, unfortunately."

"What do you mean?"

"Do you know what a fugue is?"

"I can provide some literary references." When Purdy didn't provide oblique reminders of his master's degree in English, I had a tendency to forget. "But other than that, not really."

"Psychogenic fugue—the psychogenic means that it's not caused by an organic brain syndrome, a physical cause—is a pretty rare event psychologically. It falls under the category of what's known as dissociative disorders. During fugues, which in theory tend to follow serious trauma, people suddenly do things—especially travel—outside the context of the premorbid personality. The experience will often seem purposeful and will not look pathological to a stranger who runs into the individual in the fugue, though the person may seem isolative and may have uncharacteristic outbursts of anger or destructiveness. Afterward the person doesn't remember a thing. The fugue —the dissociation—is a defensive response to an underlying conflict, and is often associated with the surfacing of a previously repressed trauma. My fear is that my patient was in a fugue last night."

"You know, even though she didn't tell me his name I knew who the kid was when Lauren called me last night. His parents—no, I guess his guardians—had already called in a report that he was missing. He's the kid who survived that plane crash in Des Moines, isn't he?"

"Sioux City. And I can't say, Sam."

"Well, that would explain it, wouldn't it?"

"Yeah. If it was that kid, that kind of trauma would explain it." Purdy was more concerned and inquisitive about Randy than Geoff Tobias had been when I phoned him right after Randy's predawn call to me.

Geoff Tobias had simply said, "He's on his way home. Good." I'd suggested that Geoff forgo any in-depth exploration of what had happened and certainly not discipline Randy until Randy and I had a chance to take a look at what had occurred. "Fine," he'd said, and had hung up.

Sam Purdy had been standing since he arrived at my office. He moved over and sat on my consultation chair. His back was to me as I sat at my desk. He said, "I don't think Scott Truscott's going to invest much more time in the Templeton investigation. And I'm not sure I blame him."

I was a bit surprised. Purdy's tenacity had always struck me as comparable to that of a pit bull who'd been slighted. "You're ready to throw in the towel, Sam?"

I couldn't see his face, but he'd begun to rock on my chair a little bit.

"Life goes on. A lot of people think I should let all this just fade away. Maybe it *was* just a leak," he said.

"That's what Saddam Hussein said about the oil slick in the Persian Gulf. Sam—jeez, I don't need to tell you this—the fact that it was a gas leak doesn't mean somebody didn't screw with the valve."

Purdy turned and looked over the top of the chair. "My, my. I think I've created a convert. Want to go get some breakfast, be suspicious together, talk it over a little?"

I laughed. "No, Sam, no breakfast. I've got to earn a living. I may try and see the Templeton girl this afternoon after school gets out. Aside from that, it's a private practice day. The county will have to make do without my services until tomorrow."

"Suit yourself. I was thinkin' maybe the Bagel Bakery. Lox and eggs, my treat."

"Enjoy it, Sam."

He lifted his bulk out of my chair. "You know I will."

The instant Purdy was out the door I regretted not handing him Randy's gun for safekeeping. Given what had happened the night before, there was no chance I would be returning it to Randy any time soon, and I would feel much more comfortable having it out of my office in the interim. I made a mental note to give it to Purdy during our next meeting.

I had a break from three o'clock until my scheduled appointment with Randy at four-fifteen. I called the house of Erin Templeton's friend and was surprised to find that Erin was home, had been expecting to hear from me, and would talk to me right then on the phone. When she came on the line, I asked would she mind if I came by in person. She didn't and gave me directions to a house on Mapleton Hill.

Mapleton Hill rose to the north of downtown and looked down on the rest of Boulder. It was only a short drive from my office. The tree-rimmed, divided parkway was lined, both sides, with stately homes built around the turn of the century by Boulder's founding fathers. Erin Templeton was staying with a friend whose family owned a medium-size castle of only four or five thousand square feet. After a pleasant introduction to Erin's friend's mom, a declined offer of refreshments, and a careful perusal of my coroner's identification, Erin and I were led into a sun porch off the kitchen. The view was south and endless. If

Pikes Peak would move over and if I squinted, I was pretty
sure I could see New Mexico.

I settled onto a deeply cushioned wicker chair. Erin sat
as far from me as she could in the long, narrow room. I
could either shout out my questions to her or move closer.
I climbed out of the chair and resettled at a wrought-iron
table a few feet from Erin. Her hair was oily and hung
limply to her shoulders. I couldn't tell if it was fashionably
oily or merely the result of an adolescent lapse in hygiene.
Maybe both. The little prick of a diamond I'd seen on TV
still studded the side of her nostril.

"Know why I'm here?"

She shrugged.

"Would you like to know?"

She shrugged again. I took a deep breath and squelched
an internal scream.

"It's about your dad."

She looked me in the eyes for the first time and said,
"Really. Like I'm *totally* surprised." In the dialect of my
own adolescence, the translation would have been *"Duh."*

"I'm trying to find out what caused the gas leak that
destroyed your house."

A long fluttering breath escaped her pursed lips. Then
she said, "Whatever."

I was getting a headache. I was also feeling more than
a little frustrated with the ration of adolescent rebellion
foisted on me over the last twenty-four hours.

"I think you know something." I didn't know if she knew
anything, but I felt like being provocative.

Erin Templeton grunted, a noise that reminded me of
a dog choking on a chicken bone, and turned her head
toward Pikes Peak.

I kept my gaze on her. She was tiny, one of those kids
who would develop late, who might blossom just in time
for the senior prom. Or who might not.

She said, "Whattya think I know?"

"Answers."

"What questions?"

"You tell me."

"God, where'd they find you?" she said, then sniffed

sharply through her nostrils. "I don't know anything."
Pause. Then, maybe hoping I'd leave her alone if she acted
just a little more defiantly, she said, "He smoked. He blew
himself up when he lit a cigarette. Smoking's bad for you."

In my mind I calculated that at county wages this interview, thus far, had earned me about a dollar sixty. "How
come you're not staying up in Coal Creek with your mom
and brother?"

"A thousand reasons."

"Can I hear the top three?"

"My friends. It's cold. And Janet."

Janet? "Janet?"

"The caretaker," she sneered. "She's a bitch."

"Tell me."

"She's a *bitch*."

Oh. That clarifies it.

"I know lots of ways people can be bitchy. What's hers?"

"She gives me a hard time. Okay? I don't like her. She's
a bitch."

"What did she do?" I wanted a drink. Or a bed.

She exhaled as if she were blowing out birthday candles.
"She says my dad was screwing around."

"What do you think?"

"I think she's a bitch."

Yeah, we covered that.

"What do you think about what she said about your
dad?"

"What does it matter? I hope he practiced safe sex.
Anyway, he's dead." Her petulant voice had a hairline
crack.

I waited. Finally I said, "Well. It looks like maybe your
dad wasn't perfect."

She teared for the first time. "No." Then she sobbed,
"I don't know."

I waited for the tears to build and said, "Take your time,
Erin, take your time."

She did, crying for a good twenty minutes.

Before I left I got a little more information. Erin and Janet
had become pretty good friends over the previous summer.

Janet supplied Erin with condoms that she didn't use and alcohol that she did. On Labor Day weekend all the Mirabelle homesteaders had been up to their cabins to say good-bye to summer. She and Janet had hiked to a nearby lake by themselves, gotten drunk on wine coolers, and Janet had told her that her dad sometimes came up to the cabin with some woman for nooners. Erin didn't think her mom knew.

I told Erin it was too big a secret to carry by herself and broached the possibility of psychotherapy for her. After we went through the mandatory adolescent "I'm not crazy"/"I didn't say you were" routine, she said she might go once or twice. I wrote down a couple of names and phone numbers for her to call, told Erin's friend's mom —who was visibly dismayed that I'd brought her charge to tears—that Erin was a little upset and to call me if she needed anything.

Seeing Erin had taken longer than I had anticipated. Despite rushing, I was two minutes late for my appointment with Randy. The light indicating his arrival in my waiting room was already on when I ran in the French doors to my office.

We spent most of the session discovering how little Randy knew about what he'd been through the previous thirty-six hours. He thought he remembered leaving the house the previous morning and for some reason, although he knew it wasn't true, felt that the incident where he got furious at the restaurant had happened that day, too. He still couldn't place the cabin and wasn't even sure what road it was on, but he still felt it was on the road to Central City. He thought maybe it was close to the Peak to Peak Highway but wasn't sure.

He had an image of himself as a little boy hiding in some odd cabinet that opened to both the kitchen and the dining room in the cabin. I asked him if it was a memory. He said, "No. More like a snapshot I've seen." He said he was trying to climb into the cabinet when he realized how disoriented he was and called me.

"I kept seeing lace. Everywhere lace."

"What's your association to the lace?"

"Nothing."

"On the plane. Were your mother or sister wearing lace?"

He shook his head.

"Your dad?"

He looked up at me and laughed.

"Another passenger?"

"I don't think so." His voice was calm.

"It wasn't gauze?"

"No."

"Not like the hospital?"

His eyes flashed anger and fear. "No. Like a tablecloth. Lace like a tablecloth." His face grew calm; as quickly as the torment came, it was gone.

"Stay with it, Randy."

Nothing showed in his face. He said, "That's it."

"Were you in first class? In the crash." I'd never spent much time in front of the curtain in airplanes, but my impression was that they graced the tray tables with some sort of tablecloth. Lace, though? Doubtful.

"No. We flew coach on Creamed Corn."

We were both silent in the void of failed discovery.

"Will it happen again?"

"What?" I asked.

"What happened yesterday?"

"The fugue?"

"Yeah?"

"It might, Randy, there's no way to know."

"Can you do anything to keep it from happening?"

"What we're doing. Uncovering."

"I wonder what else I did?"

"It must be scary. Not knowing."

"Tell me about it," he said.

An Isuzu four-wheel drive with a cheap ski rack on top was parked on the dried weeds halfway between my house and Adrienne and Peter's place when I got home from work. The license plate started with a Z. That meant it was probably a rental. Adrienne and Peter had guests.

I pulled the Subaru close to the edge of the mud flats

by my front door so I could have a reasonable chance of exiting the car onto the meager remnants of my lawn rather than into a pool of muck. A glance up at the divide disclosed that Boulder's interlude of balmy weather was just about over. It was gonna snow tonight. At least the mud would freeze again.

The house was cold. I cranked up the furnace, hurried downstairs, and was halfway out of my work clothes when Adrienne phoned and asked me up to the big house for dessert with her and Peter. And my wife.

Peter had made an apple tart. I thought it insufficiently sweet but kept my criticism to myself. I was keeping most of my thoughts and feelings to myself. Given my day till then, Merideth's unannounced arrival was like frosting on a badly baked cake.

Merideth had already explained to Adrienne that she was in town to research a couple of stories. She repeated the rationale for Peter and me. The main purpose of her visit was a planned story on Nobel Prize–winner Thomas Cech's work at the University of Colorado on applications of RNA research in the development of antiviral pharmaceuticals. The secondary purpose was to look into the deaths of the grand jury witnesses to see if it was anything worth pursuing.

And the third reason—the real reason, the unspoken reason—was me.

Merideth announced to the third reason, me, while Adrienne and Peter absented themselves to the kitchen in a manner that seemed choreographed, that she had "begun therapy to sort all this out." She then described her therapist in San Francisco as somebody she'd heard wonderful things about from a girlfriend at the network. And she and the therapist had so much in common. The therapist, too, was divorced from a "mental health type" and knew exactly what being married to one could be like. For some reason that escaped me, Merideth had also learned that her therapist had herpes and that she knew exactly how difficult it was to meet good men who weren't gay. And —empathy abounds—the therapist had an abortion once, too. At the end of the first session the therapist and her new patient had cried together and hugged.

Merideth had felt ever so much better.

For a moment I actually considered keeping my mouth shut. But the hole was so big; the goal line so close. "Merideth," I said, " 'psychotherapy' is a word that needs to be used with a touch more discretion. What you're describing doesn't exactly sound like psychotherapy to me."

Merideth, despite living with me for many years, had managed to stay remarkably naive about psychotherapy. The experience she was describing, starting therapy, was a first for her.

"She seems very nice," Merideth insisted.

I felt as if she were begging me to climb up on one of my favorite soapboxes. I obliged. I immediately regretted it. But I obliged. "Honey," I said, "be careful with this. 'Nice' doesn't cut it. The fact that you find yourself sitting in a room, alone, talking with somebody about your life doesn't mean you're 'in therapy.' Anybody with a tongue and a beating heart can hang out a psychotherapy shingle. And in some states even those criteria get waived."

"She has a Ph.D. Just like you." Merideth's defensiveness only fueled my flames.

I sighed. I was being unreasonably judgmental, but there was no stopping me, especially given my day thus far. "The fact that the person sitting across from you has a Ph.D. or an M.D. or an M.S.W. after their name and is charging you upward of a hundred bucks for forty-five minutes doesn't mean that the service they are providing is 'therapy.' The Ph.D. could be an astrophysicist into personal growth; the M.D. could be an alcoholic rheumatologist who can't get privileges anymore. With your unwitting permission anybody can cut you with a sharp knife—the act doesn't make them a surgeon.

"And the fact that you feel better after leaving somebody's office doesn't mean that the salient process was 'therapeutic.' A whore makes people feel better—at least in theory—but it doesn't mean shit unless she can make you *get* better.

"Getting better takes time, honey, at least a little. It

rarely feels great, sometimes it feels awful. And it takes skill. Some of what therapists need to know is taught in school. And some of it isn't. The education is necessary; it's not sufficient. Don't be fooled into thinking that camaraderie and mutual disclosure and hugs and embraces equal therapeutics. Incompetent and malevolent people sometimes put their own needs in front of their patients' needs, and they aren't about to be moved by lectures on ethical treatment of patients."

Merideth listened to my polemic and said simply, "Maja isn't malevolent. And I thought you would be pleased." She stood and left the room to join the company of Adrienne and Peter, who probably wouldn't behave as if someone were chewing on their hemorrhoids.

"Maja?" I said to the empty room.

25

Merideth didn't stay at Adrienne and Peter's house much longer than it took to be polite and say good-bye. She jutted her passive face into the living room, where I sat watching the fire, and departed after a wave and a curt, "See you."

Her manners were better than I deserved.

After a few minutes I joined Peter and Adrienne in the kitchen, and we busied ourselves picking things up and putting things away.

"Meri says you have a stick up your ass," Adrienne said conversationally, her back to me.

I looked at Peter. He smiled, looking mischievous.

Suddenly, in a metallic voice, he belted out, "This is not a test. Progesterone alert—enhh, enhh, enhh. Watch it, Alan. Careful. Raging hormones present." As he finished his wailed warning, Peter ran out of the room, barely escaping being bonked by an oven mitt launched from Adrienne's left hand.

I turned to Adrienne. "Yeah, well. She shouldn't have dropped in like this."

Adrienne said, "She wants to mend fences. You acting like a jerk doesn't make things any easier for her."

"You're right. I was a jerk. But everything I said was true. And, you're right again, she probably does want to mend fences. Problem is I'm not sure she's any more eager than ever to share control of the gates."

Adrienne's eyes grew wide, and her grin covered half her face.

My face looked sheepish. "I'm trying not to be a sap," I said.

She shook her head, winced, closed her eyes tight and cupped her breasts in her hands, and said, "*Ohh, Mama. My boobs are soooo sore.*" Then she turned her attention back to me and resumed the earlier lesson. "Trying not to be a sap is great, *boychik*. The key here, however, is not to replace it with being an asshole." She looked around the kitchen. "Where's Geppetto? If he thinks I'm cleaning up his mess in here, he's got sawdust for brains."

Fresh flakes icy like frozen membranes were scattered on the dirt and hibernating grass on the way down the hill to my house. But no snow was falling as I picked a path to my door—an apparent interlude between blustery movements. My beeper vibrated as I shed my coat. After taking a moment to empty the meager remnants of a bottle of cognac into a water glass, I called my neighborhood Voice-mail computer, punched in my access code, and listened to Sam Purdy asking me what was I up to tomorrow? Give him a call. I replayed an earlier message from Scott Truscott. He had a new case to give me. He, too, wanted a call in the morning.

I called Purdy.

A lilting little voice answered the phone at the number Sam had left for me by saying definitively, "Hello, this is Simon." I remembered seeing a picture of a toddler in Purdy's office during a brief visit the previous year.

"Hello, Simon. Is your dad there?"

"Yes," he said.

I waited and listened to Simon breathing into the phone.

"May I talk with him?"

"Yes."

More breathing.

"Will you go get him now? Please?"

"Yes."

Simon hung up. I looked outside. The snow had resumed falling in earnest.

I redialed and heard Sam—not Simon—Purdy say, "Hello."

"Simon did great, Sam. A few wrinkles still to be worked out. But great."

"He's already better at this than half our dispatchers. Listen, thanks for calling. Got anything for me?"

I told him I had a lead on Larry Templeton's extracurricular activities. Told him about my interview with Erin Templeton and her story about Janet Lasker, the caretaker at Mirabelle. "Might be worth a drive, Sam."

"Glad you think so. See you at nine. Meet me at—"

"Scott's got a new case for me, Sam. You can handle this one by yourself."

"Scott's case is a nothing. You can take care of it after lunch. How about Mother's for breakfast? Nice folks at Mother's."

"How do you know about Scott's case?"

"I don't. That's the point. If I don't know about it, it's a nothing."

There was some logic lurking here, I was certain. I said, "You go ahead and eat, Sam. I'll come by about a quarter after."

"You sure? Great pancakes."

"I'm sure. Good night. And say good night to Simon for me. We didn't get a chance to say good-bye."

Either Purdy had arrived late at Mother's Cafe, or he had been served in a fashion more indolent than that to which he was accustomed. An obscene mixture of pancakes, eggs, and maple syrup was still being shoveled repetitively from his plate to his mouth. I was reminded of a PBS documentary on the wonders of robotics. I stood across the room watching him eat, read the paper, and gulp coffee. Just when I'd decided to stay where I was until he was through, he raised an arm and waved me over, never looking up.

Another gesture brought a cup of coffee and a menu for me. I said, "Just coffee, thanks," to the waitress, who dropped a few more ampules of half-and-half on the table and snapped my menu away.

Sam Purdy said, "Good morning."

"I've got some news. I did some detecting this morning that may save us some time."

"Yeah." Purdy looked amused at my allusion to his profession.

"I called Rita Templeton to see if this Janet Lasker was staying at Mirabelle right now. She said no, hadn't seen her in a few days. Which apparently isn't unusual. But she gave me the boyfriend's phone number and some directions to his house up in the mountains. I tried to call, just got a machine. But Rita said to expect that, says they're legendary for not answering the phone."

"Where's he live?"

"South of Rollinsville, on the Peak to Peak."

His plate was empty. He threw some money on the table and said, "Let's go." I dumped a dollar on the pile of bills to cover my coffee and followed him out to his car.

In the car he threw a bound book of maps in my lap. "Try to find out what county this guy's house is in. May be some jurisdictional toes waiting to be stepped on."

I turned pages for a few minutes and compared the directions I received from Rita Templeton with the lines on the map. Finally I said, "I'd say it's Gilpin."

"Shit. Why can't all these people stay in one county?"

Purdy drove slowly on the slick streets over to Canyon Boulevard and pointed the car up Boulder Canyon as he began a series of radio calls either to arrange permission to carry his investigation into Gilpin County by himself or to get a deputy from the local sheriff's office to meet us in Rollinsville. We were past Boulder Falls, heading into the narrows of Boulder Canyon, when he got word that we'd been cleared for a solo.

The canyon was beautifully dressed in its winter best. Deep carved gorges, the creek bed frozen solid, waterfalls frozen in place and time. But the road was awful. The sheet ice was so bad, I prayed for spots still packed with snow from last night's storm.

A dozen cars lined up behind the speed-limit-obeying Purdy. "They'd shit if they knew they were tailgating a cop," he said, smiling. Most of the trailing convoy either stopped off in Nederland or turned away a few miles later for the entrance to the ski area at Eldora. While he drove, Purdy chronicled a criminals' low-life tour of the mountain fringes of Boulder County. Drugs, murder, cults, and mayhem from Ward to Nederland to Rollinsville. "Sometimes I think people assume that laws don't apply at nine thousand feet. Like there's an altitude exclusion or something."

The road was familiar to me. The Peak to Peak Highway navigated ridge tops and clung to mountainsides in an uneven line south from Rocky Mountain National Park past Colorado's pioneer capital of Central City to Interstate 70. Almost the entire roadway lay above nine thousand feet in altitude, and the views challenged any driver's best intentions to keep his or her eyes on the road.

Intermittently along the Peak to Peak, and dramatically near Rollinsville, the western horizon was dominated by the ragged, glacier-sided, fourteen-thousand-foot behemoths of the Continental Divide. I knew the territory west of the highway well; Merideth and I had cross-country-skied many of the trails that departed from the wide dirt track that bisected the Peak to Peak at Rollinsville on its way to the Moffat Tunnel.

Purdy said, "You know, I think I know which place this is. Old stone place. Wagon wheels by the highway. Lotta old pioneer shit scattered all around." A minute later he slapped himself on the thigh and said, "What'd I tell you? Sure enough, wagon wheels, here we are."

He pulled the Ford onto some hard-packed snow just off the highway a dozen feet from stone gateposts adorned with the telltale red wagon wheels, and I followed him on foot as he lumbered with his hands in his pockets down a snowy lane to the largest of the old stone-and-log buildings dotting the dozen or so acres below us.

The woman who answered the door in the main house had so much red hair that, backlit, she risked being mistaken for a sunrise. Her face was pale and free of freckles, the lines of her cheekbones and jaw angular. The impression she gave was one of intensity and formidability. She was also quite pretty. She eyed Purdy suspiciously and failed to return my smile. After a long glance at Purdy's identification she said, "You're in the wrong county, Sheriff."

"It's 'Detective,' Miss . . . ?" She made no attempt to

fill in the blank. Purdy continued, "The Gilpin County sheriff is aware that we're here. You can call him if you want."

She ignored Purdy's offer. "And who are you?" The authority in her tone was now directed at me.

"Alan Gregory. Dr. Alan Gregory," I said. Purdy looked at me with a mixture of astonishment and disdain.

He sighed. "This isn't FAC. She doesn't want to know your sign. Give her your ID." *Asshole.*

Oh.

"I'm with the Boulder County Coroner's Office." I held out my ID, and she took the plastic card from me.

Purdy said, "May we come in?"

The lady at the door said, "No," in a tone that underlined her assessment of the absurdity of the request. "I don't even know what you want."

"Are you Janet Lasker?"

"And if I am?"

Purdy was on the verge of abandoning "polite" as a tactic. I could feel excess energy pour from him like water down a spillway as he answered, "We would like to speak with Ms. Lasker as a routine part of an investigation that does not otherwise concern her. She is under no suspicion whatsoever."

"This investigation involves homicide or manslaughter?" She nodded toward me and handed back my ID. "Or he wouldn't be here, right?"

I nodded. Purdy shifted his modified glare in my direction. It was becoming difficult to determine whether Purdy was more annoyed with me or with her.

The lady at the door seemed to reach some conclusion and said, "Janet Lasker is the girlfriend of one of my tenants. They live in the cabin at the north end of the drive behind the house." She closed the door in our faces. But she didn't slam it.

"Defense attorney," Purdy said as we walked off. "She's a goddamn defense attorney."

"You know her?"

"No."

"Then how do you know?"

"Cops know criminals. Criminals always know cops. Cops know defense attorneys. We just do. It's the law."

A single vehicle had already traveled up the long, narrow drive behind the house, leaving parallel tracks through the six inches of fresh powder. Purdy took the left track down the drive, I took the right. Fifty feet from the cabin, the most distant of three along the trail, Purdy said, "Damn, no one's home."

I couldn't tell how he knew that. The morning sun was reflecting off the southern windows, and the glare made it impossible to see inside. There was an old beat-up Toyota in front of the cabin.

"And how do you know *that?*" I asked.

"No smoke from the chimney. Would you sit inside without any heat? It's no warmer than ten degrees up here. I guarantee you that place doesn't have a high-efficiency Lennox."

"Maybe they're still in bed?"

"Possible, I guess. Let's go be their wake-up call."

Purdy pounded on the cabin door. We waited. Ours were the only footprints on the wooden porch outside the door. Nobody had been in or out of the cabin since the night's snow had stopped falling. The windows of the cabin were icy and were insulated with sheets of cloudy stretched plastic that obscured even further the already minimal clarity of the glass. Purdy tried to look inside, but the curtains were drawn over the windows facing the door. I bent down and looked through the keyhole and saw only an old wood stove and the corner of a bed covered with what appeared to be a pile of down sleeping bags.

"Anything?"

"Nope," I said.

He sifted a card out of his wallet and left it stuck in the door and told me to do the same.

I took a pen from Purdy's pocket and scrawled my office phone number onto the back of a generic card from the Boulder County Coroner's Office. As I slid the card into a crack in the jamb, a deep grunting noise shuddered above me. I looked up just in time to see a huge drift slide from the roof of the cabin, and with a sound like a paper bag exploding the snowslide buried me. I screamed. And flailed my arms as if I could startle the snow into jumping back off me.

Purdy had leaped back at the groan of snow moving on the slick roof and had been spared the avalanche. He stood with his arms folded, laughing at me.

"I'm not totally convinced you're cut out for this work," he said.

I shivered twice, once from evaporating terror, once from having my spine frosted.

"Let's go have another chat with Ms. Manners," he said, and marched me back up the drive to the stone house.

The landlady examined me carefully as she opened the door. "Snowball fight? Let me guess who lost."

Purdy held out his card. I searched for another one of the cards with information about the coroner's office but finally settled for one of my own business cards instead and held it out to her.

The woman with the red hair collected both of them.

"Let me save you some trouble. I haven't noticed them around for a day or two. Doesn't mean they haven't been here, though; I'm gone a lot. And when she shows back up, I'm to ask her to call, right?"

"Please," Purdy said with overdetermined civility, and turned away to leave, then turned back. He continued, "By the way, what county courts do you work in?"

She smiled for the first time. "Jeffco, Detective. Mostly Jeffco."

"Sam Purdy," he said, taking a glove off his right hand and holding it out. She shook his hand.

"Casey Sparrow," she said after she got her hand back.

Purdy nodded once, said, "Ms. Sparrow," and walked back toward the car. I said a quick good-bye to Casey Sparrow and was still fishing snow out of my collar as I followed Purdy back to the car.

The case that Scott Truscott wanted me to follow up on his secretary had called "routine." When I called in she passed along the assignment with a triteness that was understandable but disconcerting.

I suppose the death was "routine." The death in question was of a twenty-seven-year-old man who had died in the emergency room from injuries suffered in a one-car crash. No alcohol was involved, but a prescription for Prozac was found among items that had scattered from his briefcase in the car. A toxicology screen mandated for all vehicular deaths revealed that the man was indeed using the antidepressant. Scott Truscott wanted me to tie up a few loose ends from the preliminary investigation.

My afternoon-long inquiry involved an interview with his widow, who was a frightened twenty-four-year-old woman with two children, a telephone consultation with the psychiatrist who was treating him for depression, and discussions with his supervisor and co-workers at Public Service Company, his employer.

By phone I reviewed the findings of the Colorado State Patrol trooper who had written the report of the circumstances of the accident, which basically involved black ice, high speed, a bridge abutment, and failure to obey Colorado's seat belt law. The CSP trooper noted that the dead guy had averaged one moving violation a year since his arrival in Colorado three years before he died.

Just before five I called Scott Truscott and told him that the death was accidental, that the man was being treated for dysthymia, that the Prozac had been effective, that he was displaying no current signs or symptoms of depression, that he had not shown suicidal inclinations prior to the accident, and that he was renowned among friends, family, and acquaintances for driving too fast and not wearing his seat belt.

Scott said, "Great. Write it up. I'll pass it on to the coroner."

The light on my answering machine was beckoning as I walked in the door to my house. The message was from Merideth, who was inviting me to dinner so I could "apologize properly for last night." She left a number.

I called the number she had left and reached her in her room at the Harvest House. "Thanks for the invitation," I said, "but I can't tonight."

Merideth hesitated an instant. "Have a date?"

"No. I'm taking Lauren to the airport in an hour."

"Lauren is?" She knew who Lauren was.

It was my turn to hesitate. I was conscious of Adrienne's admonition about not being an asshole. "She's the woman I've been seeing."

"Oh," said Merideth, "then I suppose you'll have some free time this weekend. Since she'll be gone."

I was quiet.

"Dinner tomorrow, then? Please."

Shit, why not? "Okay. I'll come by the hotel around seven."

"Thanks, Alan."

"Yeah. See you tomorrow."

26

Saying good-bye to Lauren was more difficult than it should have been. On the drive to Denver's airport she sensed my discomfort and reassured me twice that she was only going to be gone for five days, but still I couldn't shake an apprehension that this temporary estrangement would generate repercussions of larger dimensions.

At the airline gate I wished her luck with her eligibility interview and kept to myself all of my considerable ambivalence about her leaving.

"You want to know my biggest concern?" she asked as she fumbled for her ticket.

I nodded, expecting she would say something about me and Merideth that I didn't want to hear. I had already confided to Lauren that my almost-ex and I would be having dinner together the next night. She'd reacted with an absence of jealousy that I'd found too many troubling ways to interpret.

"My biggest fear right now is that the good news is that I'll be accepted into the Cop I study and that the bad news is that after spending six months in New York, I'll find out I had been randomized into the control group."

Since Lauren's first mention of the Cop I clinical trials, I'd assumed that the study would be run as a standard double-blind design. In double-blind research trials neither the patients nor the doctors managing the study knew which patients had been randomly selected to be part of the experimental group that was receiving the drug being evaluated or which patients had been selected to receive a placebo. In theory, only when the study was over did everybody learn who was who.

"It's a big risk, isn't it?" I said, trying to sound empathetic.

She touched the side of my face with her cool fingers. "So's leaving you right now. Isn't it?" she said. She drew my face down to hers; her lips were soft. She walked down the jetway to the plane.

The next night I hoped I would dine well courtesy of the network. Merideth could write me off as a "reluctant source."

At seven-thirty she was sitting on a chair in the lobby of the Harvest House Hotel waiting for me. She was dressed in flowing black knits that made it difficult to ascertain where her tunic ended and her legs began. The knits hugged her body in a manner that also had the effect of engendering tremendous curiosity in me about ascertaining exactly where the tunic ended and her legs began. I was a perfect audience for her.

Merideth was more elegant than she was beautiful. Which was a bit like saying that the Pacific Ocean was wetter than it was big. She offered her cheek for a kiss and hugged me gently. My impression was that she seemed to want to underscore our established marital status. She asked if I would drive to the restaurant. I said yes, knowing that my Subaru would be an inadequate carriage for Merideth's gentility that night. As it always had been.

Dinner was to be upscale; she'd made reservations at the Flagstaff House. In the car on the winding road up Flagstaff Mountain, I apologized for the tone of my speech two nights earlier at Peter and Adrienne's house. She accepted. She also took advantage of the cover of mountain darkness to say that she had indeed made a mistake about us, and although she didn't want to pressure me she did want to say clearly that she would like for us to reconsider the divorce. I responded in the sudden glare of headlights from an oncoming car only by saying that I appreciated her not pressuring me.

In the restaurant we were seated at an ideal window deuce, and I had trouble concentrating on the menu. The lights of Boulder twinkled below us, but in the vague distance so did the lights of Denver's sprawl. I mentioned to Merideth that it was odd seeing this view from 180 degrees away from my house.

She smiled, said, "*Our* house," and asked me what I was thinking of getting for dinner.

Everything felt wrong, awkward, out of place. I even wanted to be sitting where Merideth had been seated.

The waitress came, and Merideth ordered a spinach salad and a steak. "This pregnancy—my 'crit's low," she said to me in explanation after the waitress had departed, "but the damn iron supplements make me constipated." I didn't really want to know the state of traffic flow in her intestines, but the forced marital intimacy of her disclosure wasn't lost on me. People on dates rarely talk about bowel function; those discussions tend to be reserved for the married.

I ordered shrimp. It was to be prepared with fennel and Pernod. Sounded like way too much licorice to me, but what did I know. Because of the pregnancy, Merideth wasn't drinking, but she picked a glass of wine for me from the wine list. I knew she would choose something that would be perfect for the shrimp and would somehow even manage to compensate for all the anise. It all felt just like old times.

Merideth was feeling well—"Great, as a matter of fact. I think pregnancy agrees with me." My eyes wandered the knits again, and I couldn't think of a reason to disagree. And her trip to Colorado was productive so far. "Tom Cech is a great story. He can almost make this RNA stuff understandable. He's got good camera presence. So far he's refused to sell out and move to the Ivy League. I think the story will go—we're calling it 'The Cowboy Scientist.' Unfortunately the correspondent on it is an airhead. He's a talented airhead, but he's pretty sure the double helix is a football formation."

"And the grand jury story?"

"I'm still hoping you can help me with that."

I told Merideth about my consulting position with the coroner's office. She was curious, so I told her a little more. She pressed me, but I insisted I still couldn't see any national or even regional interest in the story she was considering pursuing.

"In fact," I maintained, "there isn't even any current local interest."

After dinner, back at the hotel, Merideth looked and acted alluring but didn't invite me up to her room for a drink. I was grateful. I wasn't eager for another opportunity to display my sexual discipline. She did offer to buy me an after-dinner drink in the bar. I said yes.

As I sipped my drink I listened to her sing a litany of praises about living in the Bay Area. She was renting a condo in the marina, a newer condo that hadn't suffered serious damage in the big earthquake of 1989. She was raving on about the restaurants, and the ocean, and the art, and the museums, and the shopping, and I was barely hearing her because my attention was consumed watching Sam Purdy and, I guessed, his wife, skim over the dance floor adjacent to the lounge with a grace and camaraderie of spirit that moved me. The woman swinging aside Sam Purdy was blond and round. Not heavy, not fat, but generous and round of eye and face and breast and hip. Watching him gaze at her, and lead her, watching her move with him, and smile, I realized Sam Purdy wasn't anywhere near as large as I had always thought he was.

Merideth finally paused from her travelogue long enough to notice the moisture in my eyes and reached under the table to squeeze my hand. "I know how you love Boulder, honey. But living in the city is special," she said. "Don't worry, we'll work it out. You watch."

It was a swing and a miss. Though I didn't bother to call the strike.

It wouldn't have been fair. Merideth had never hit a curveball in her life.

Someone pounded on my door like a maniacal Fuller Brush man the next morning before eight. After my unconscious failed to force the harsh noise to conform to the quasi-erotic confines of my current dream, I woke slowly, then suddenly.

And as soon as I had eleven brain cells firing simultaneously, the pommeling jolted me out of bed.

My house is on a hill, the bedrooms downstairs on the slope. I grabbed cotton sweat pants and pulled them on, tugging on the drawstring as I raced up the stairs and yanked open my front door.

Sam Purdy said, "Geez. You sleep harder than Simon. I've been out here for ten minutes. Get dressed. We're going for a ride."

"I don't want to have breakfast with you again." I tried to sound justifiably irritated. Doing so was not difficult. Was it just last night I had seen this man dancing like Fred Astaire?

"No breakfast. It's more solemn than that. Think of it as church. Go get dressed. Be quick. Trust me on this."

I stormed back downstairs and peed, took an electric razor to my face, a brush to my hair, and a toothbrush to my mouth, ranting silently while I dressed about the abuse I had apparently volunteered to endure by becoming a contract employee to the county. What I thought was, I don't need this.

By the time I got back upstairs Purdy had settled onto the big leather chair in the living room and was talking on the phone. I waited until he hung up and said to him, "This better be good. What's up?"

"It's your friend. Diane. Somebody busted into her house last night, she came home, surprised them, and took a bad blow to the head. She's in the hospital."

My body went from standing to sitting without any conscious decision on my part to alter my posture. I blurted, "How is she, Sam?"

Purdy shrugged his shoulders. "You know doctors."

"Come on. Tell me! How the hell is she? Is she conscious?"

"Was. For a while. That was the hospital I just called. Somebody said something to the sheriff about some danger of her brain swelling, so they're inducing a coma with barbiturates and putting her on one of those machines, a ventilator, I guess, to breathe for her."

"Damn. Damn. Damn." I started to pace. "I want to see her."

"Can't."

"Then what good are you? Why the hell are you here?"

Purdy was serene. "I want you to come to her house with me."

"Why?"

"Because apparently all this jerk went after were her old files."

I followed him out to the car and had to ask him to wait while I ran back inside to find a jacket.

"Was Raoul home?"

"Is that her husband?"

"Yes."

"No. He's not around. You know how to reach him?"

"Maybe. He works for a little company that does business in Huntsville, Alabama. He's been spending a lot of time there." Purdy asked the name of the company. I told him.

He said, "I'll check it out."

Diane and Raoul lived on Lee Hill Drive, well up into the foothills north of Boulder. Purdy took the parkway across town, and I pressured him to use his siren or at least to drive faster.

"Be patient, Alan. At the moment it's just a big empty house surrounded by cops."

I looked over as a prelude to arguing with him and realized he was wearing the same clothes I had seen on him the night before at the Harvest House. He'd been up all night.

"If Raoul isn't home and Diane was knocked out, how did you guys find out about it? You've been up all night, haven't you?"

He said, "Yeah, I have." His shoulders sagged as he admitted it, as though he were just becoming aware of the fatigue himself. "Your friends have an alarm. The company that monitors the thing called the sheriff. I was out late last night and picked up the radio traffic on my way home. I remembered the break-in at your offices, so I called to fill them in. Got their permission to come up and look around. So I've been busy since."

Although the route he had chosen was as direct as any for getting across town, the ride took forever. An old Dodge Power Wagon in front of us on Lee Hill was overflowing with hay or alfalfa or straw or whatever it is horses eat, and it was going half the speed limit.

Raoul and Diane's house was invisible from the road. My patience was exhausted by the time Purdy completed the two switchbacks on the steep driveway and the cedar and glass of the two-story foyer emerged from the trees. Crime scene tapes disappeared into the surrounding pines. A single sheriff's deputy stood on the steps leading to the carved front doors. Purdy flashed his badge. I didn't know any better, so I pulled out my ID, too.

The deputy eyed my coroner's card and said, "She dead?"

Purdy looked at me and said, "No. He's with me," seemed to contemplate explaining further, didn't, and walked in the front door. I followed him into a house I'd been in a hundred times. The stunning glass tower of the entryway was a twice-repeated feature on the far side of the house, effectively carrying the view of the trees, rocks, and sky into both the living room and kitchen. Raoul and Diane each had an office on the north end of the main level; the master suite took up the entire second floor.

I kept waiting for Diane to appear and welcome me into her home.

A huge LeRoy Neiman acrylic I'd not seen before dominated the big wall above the fireplace. Raoul was a Neiman fanatic and unfortunately had the money to indulge his passion. Diane usually prevailed in keeping the paintings out of the house's most public spaces, but Raoul's messy office always looked like a sports bar after a tornado.

Purdy sensed my hesitation about being in the house and beckoned me to the kitchen. "I don't need to tell you not to touch anything, do I?"

I didn't respond.

"Guy came in here," Purdy said, pointing to the cracked

frame of the door leading from the breakfast nook to a cedar deck. "No finesse. Just busted in."

Purdy turned on his heel and walked out across the landing that spilled down to the living room toward the twin offices in the opposite wing of the house. "Just one guy. His feet were wet—big feet, man-size feet. We think he came straight down here. Like he knew what he was looking for. Straight to this room, looks like her study. Popped open the filing cabinet with a midget crowbar— which is downtown now—and started rifling files or reading or whatever.

"He hears the car drive up. Comes over, stands over here." Purdy did a little two-step over to a corner of the foyer. "Waits. She—your friend—unlocks the door, walks in." Purdy hesitated, forcing me to attend to his face. "He shoots once, misses." He saw the surprise in my eyes. "Yeah—he's got a gun. Then maybe it jams. Don't know. Or maybe he didn't really want to shoot her. But when she turns to run, to go back out the door, he catches her and whacks her once with the crowbar. The blow was hard but glancing. If he'd hit her straight on, he would have crushed her skull, probably killed her. And then he leaves. That's how we got it, so far."

"How do you know about the gun?"

He pointed up the wall behind where I stood. A big hole was ripped into the wall about seven feet from the floor. "That was a bullet hole before the crime scene guys carved it up to get the slug. Hit a stud. And she asked the doc in the ER if she was shot. Said there was a gun."

"You don't have the gun?"

He rolled his lower lip into the shade of his mustache and shook his head no.

Purdy wanted me to go through Diane's files to see if I could tell if anything was missing.

Despite sharing office space, friendship, and coverage, Diane and I ran separate businesses. I didn't know much about specific cases in her practice; she was similarly ignorant about mine. I tried to explain that to Purdy.

He said, "Just try."

I said, "This stuff is confidential, you know. I can't just go waltzing through her files."

"She's incapacitated, Alan. You're her partner." Don't be a jerk, Alan.

Aware of it or not, Purdy was making a valid point. Diane and I had agreed long ago, and had renewed our understanding after Paul Weinman's death over the holidays, that we would be custodians of each other's records in the event one of us died. Or was incapacitated.

I glanced quickly at the records in Diane's big file cabinet. Next to the patient name on the file tab was the year the record was open—"Smith, Jane (86)."

"These are all her old files, Sam. She keeps her current case files in the file cabinet in the office."

I was thumbing forward through the C's and D's when Purdy verbalized what I was thinking. He said, "Is Claire Draper's file there?"

Dougherty . . . Dogwood . . . Drew. "No Draper," I said.

Purdy was pensive.

I said, "It may still be at the office. She may not have gotten around to moving it here since the murder."

"Tonto," said Purdy, "how 'bout we go to town."

On the way back to the city I badgered Purdy into using his radio to check on Diane's condition at Community. He humored me. Nothing was new.

Our little office building on Walnut was locked up tight. After jiggling the doorknob on the carved oak front door, Purdy insisted that we take a look around anyway. We jiggled all the other doors and finally entered the building through the French doors to my office. Purdy insisted on walking in the door first. Part of me wanted to see him draw his gun and twist through doorways in search of perps. He didn't.

From the connecting hallway between the offices I used my master key to unlock Diane's office, and we peered in to an absence of disarray.

"You wouldn't want to have a look at her records while we're here, would you?" Purdy asked.

A little sarcastically I said, "And would I be doing this as her partner or as a coroner's investigator?"

He smiled as meekly as he was capable of smiling.

"Because her partner would probably require a subpoena from the authorities and would then ignore it. The coroner's investigator would tell you to shove the damn job up your ass."

"Really."

"Just so," I said.

Purdy had been eyeing Raoul's electronic handiwork. "How come I didn't see you disarm this thing when we came in?"

"Raoul—Diane's husband—just installed it. It still needs some . . . um, debugging. So we're not using it yet."

"I'd feel much better if you got it working, you know."

"And would you be saying this as a cop or as a friend?"

His tired eyes were at half-mast. Russet stubble dotted his face. He said, "Both."

I forced a smile his way. "Look, nobody has busted in here, Sam. Take me to the hospital, please. You go home and get some sleep. I'll take a cab home."

"Deal," he said.

Diane Estevez was in the ICU, the expensive care unit, and looked remarkably at peace for a person whose life was totally dependent on the reliability of public utilities.

From my days working at County in Denver after my internship, I had more than enough experience seeing people attached to ventilators and monitors and IV pumps and arterial lines. But the desensitization that comes with familiarity evaporates instantly when these machines and their plastic snakes are attached to somebody you love. I cried silently and held Diane's immobile hand for the fifteen minutes they allowed me to spend at her bedside.

Since I was on the affiliated staff at the hospital, I thought nothing of moving into the nursing station and using the phone to call Adrienne.

"It's Alan, Ren."

"Oh, shit," she said, hearing some emotion catch in my voice, "something's wrong."

"Diane was assaulted by a burglar last night. I'm in the ICU at the hospital with her. She's in an induced coma. They won't let me see her chart and I can't get a straight word from the docs who are here. Will you see what you can find out?"

"What happened?"

I told her.

"How are you, Alan?"

"Okay. Pissed. Worried."

"Cryptic?"

"Sorry, Ren. I don't know what's going on. I'm still kind of numb. I'm scared to death for Diane, and I need to track down Raoul in Huntsville and get him back here."

"Raoul's in Alabama? On satellite business?"

"Yes."

"Wow," said Adrienne, seemingly as amazed by the connection of Alabama and satellites as she would have been if Raoul had traveled to Calcutta to sell T-bones. "Got your pager on?" she asked.

"Yes," I said.

"Hang tight. I'll see what I can find out. I was gonna go in soon to do rounds anyway. I'm sure I can find out something. When I do, I'll call."

I didn't have my Day-Timer with its telephone directory, my car, or much patience. I wasted twenty minutes and five dollars' worth of quarters failing to find Raoul in Huntsville. When I walked out the hospital door a few minutes later, I saw Adrienne exiting her Land Cruiser in the parking lot.

She saw me approaching her car, and when she climbed down we walked into each other's outstretched arms. I asked to borrow her car. She gave me the keys and told me she should know something soon.

At those times when she was being particularly cognizant of her posture, Adrienne might have managed to stretch herself and seem five feet tall. So that she would have a prayer of seeing out the windshield of her Land Cruiser, the seat of the big four-wheel drive she drove was so far forward and so high up that there was not a chance I was going to have success squeezing between the seat and the wheel. I reached across to find the release handle and moved the seat back manually so that I could get in.

My pager went off.

Responding to my worst fears, I bolted back inside the hospital, tore up the stairs, and ran into the ICU. Adrienne sat at a low counter with a phone to her ear. When she saw me she reacted to the panic in my face by looking startled and worried, and I realized with relief that she wasn't the one who had just paged me.

I grabbed one of the vacant telephones in the nursing station and phoned the Voicemail computer and listened while it did its stretching exercises. Finally I heard my message. "Alan, Sam Purdy, I found Raoul Estevez in the Marriott in Huntsville. He'll be on the twelve-twenty Delta flight into Denver."

Adrienne and I hung up at the same time.

I spoke first. "The cops tracked down Raoul. He's on his way back."

Adrienne exhaled and allowed her shoulders to sink an inch or two before she nodded an acknowledgment.

Then it was her turn. "And I tracked down the neurologist and got the skinny on Diane." I waited. Adrienne's face was soft, and her speckled eyes encouraged me to suck some comfort from them. She said in a quiet, calm voice, "Our friend took an awful bad whack to her head, honey. She's one sick puppy. But so far her docs really don't have a guess on how she'll come out of it."

I tried to smile through the news. "Come on, Adrienne," I implored. "*Please* try to talk in layman's terms."

She walked over and gave me a hug.

After a while Adrienne went off to do rounds. I stayed in close proximity to Diane until Raoul arrived in the late afternoon. His proud face was composed, but his eyes were full of rage and resentment. In other circumstances I might have been amused at how he handled the nurses as they tried to explain the rules and schedules of the ICU. This time I just stood back and hoped they would graciously allow him the flexibility I had no doubt he'd end up with anyway.

When Raoul came back out after his first visit with his wife, he was immune to my condolences; he just wanted to know what I knew. So I told him everything. He shared the suspicion with Purdy and me that the break-in at the house had to be related to the earlier burglary at the office. Raoul also expressed concern about Diane's practice. I told him that I'd already put her answering service to work canceling her appointments that week and that I was covering emergencies. He thanked me and suggested I go home. I knew he wouldn't.

It was almost dark when I walked the mile or so to my office from the hospital. The clothes I'd grabbed at Purdy's insistence that morning weren't appropriate to the evening cold, and I was brittle and red upon my arrival at the office.

I picked up the phone to call Peter to ask him to feed Cicero. The phone was ringing before I remembered that my big dog was four months dead. During stress or times of absentmindedness I frequently behaved as though she still required my attention, some strange blend of guilt and wishful thinking at work.

I tried New York, and Lauren. With the time difference it was seven-thirty in the evening there. She wasn't in.

I called Merideth. She was.

She was mortified at the news about Diane and wanted to rush over to the hospital. And she wanted me to accompany her. I declined, suggesting she call the hospital instead of hurrying over. Raoul was there, I explained, and they only allowed one visitor at a time.

After declining her offer of company, I called Yellow Cab and ordered a taxi to take me back home.

Merideth's last words to me were, "Well, I think there'll be some local interest in all this now."

27

Somehow, I slept. But my conscious mind apparently wanted nothing to do with either horror or reverie because I woke with a certainty that the night's passage had been dreamless.

I called the hospital from the phone beside my bed and talked to a nurse who had been on during my vigil the previous day. She spoke to me openly and warmly and left me feeling assured that I was hearing an unsanitized version of the truth. The truth, apparently, was that the doctors still didn't know shit.

Adrienne answered her phone after half a ring and promised me she would let me know immediately if she learned anything about Diane's condition. She told me she would be in the OR all morning doing something sacred to somebody's kidneys and would keep checking on Diane in the ICU.

I couldn't figure out what day it was. After going into the bathroom to pee, I pulled on some clothes and trekked up the driveway to get the newspaper from the tube on the mailbox by the road.

Monday, the paper proclaimed. Still February, but barely.

The story on Diane's assault blared boldly from the front page of the second section, and as I read it I was pleased at how little the paper had learned. The reporter didn't even allude to the previous burglary at the office, to Claire Draper's murder in Diane's office, or to Raoul's local business prominence. They even got Diane's profession wrong, calling her an "established local psychiatrist."

I knew from personal experience that the local paper

deserved points for persistence despite a tendency to misplace the occasional fact, so I imagined they would have most of the pieces in place in a day or two. Which gave Merideth and her crew a head start that I was certain they would use to significant advantage.

Lauren had finally returned my call just as I was climbing into bed the previous night. She'd been out with her old law school professor, and they had eaten a late dinner at a Russian restaurant in Brighton Beach. She thought I'd called to chat and tell her how much I missed her.

I did miss her.

As I told her what had happened to Diane, I could feel my words jolt her. She wanted to know, of course, only things I couldn't tell her. Diane's prognosis. The direction of the investigation. The state of the evidence. Which one of her colleagues from the DA's office was on the case.

And then, "Would you like me to come back home, honey?"

I was touched. "No," I said. "You're wonderfully sweet to offer, but I can make it until the end of the week. You need to complete your evaluation there. It's important, too."

"Are you sure? I will come home, you know."

"Thanks, but I'm sure," I said, wishing that she and I could somehow be as good at receiving kindness as we both were at giving it.

Purdy wasn't available to take my call, and Raoul didn't answer at the home number. So I started a pot of coffee and showered and shaved while it brewed. Despite not having an appetite, I managed to eat a banana and a piece of toast with honey on it while I finished my first cup of coffee.

By eight-thirty I was dressed for work and was on my way downtown to the office. My first patient wasn't until eleven, but I wanted to return some phone calls to patients, put up a notice about Diane's absence for any of her patients whom her answering service had been unable to contact, and drop by Community Hospital to check on Diane—all before my initial appointment.

February was pretending to be April. Not an Academy Award performance, but certainly worthy of nomination. The night had apparently been so pyretic that the slush on my driveway hadn't frozen, and the day was already warming slowly and crossing its heart, promising to be in the sixties. The sky was soft blue with white horizontal streaks painted in feathery strokes above the mountains—like a logo for God by some astral graphic artist with a big brush and commercial inclinations.

I parked the Subaru in back of the building, in Diane's spot, which I coveted openly. Both parking spots were in front of the dilapidated old garage that hugged the rear boundary of the lot. But my spot was under an ancient cottonwood that mercilessly fouled the car beneath it with tree snot and bird droppings. Diane had been quite reasonable about parking place selection—she'd said if I insisted on having "her" spot, she would cut down the goddamn tree.

As was my practice, I entered my office from the backyard through the newly rekeyed French doors. The new key displayed a propensity to stick, and it took me a minute to enter. I plopped my old leather briefcase on top of the desk and walked out to go through the morning routine of turning up the heat, starting coffee, choosing some music for the waiting room, and collecting the mail that had accumulated inside the front door.

Halfway across the waiting room, I paused. Something wasn't right.

I couldn't tell what at first, so I reexamined the room. The furniture was where it usually was. The magazines were neatly arranged on the side tables, which meant Diane had straightened up before she'd left the office the previous Friday. The lights were off, as they should have been. The miniblinds were set in their ubiquitous angle. The switches that announced our patients' arrivals were in the "off" position.

This entire examination was accomplished from the far side of the waiting room, from the doorway that separated it from the offices in the back of the old house. I had just about convinced myself that my suspicion of anomaly was groundless and had edged another step into the room when I realized what it was.

The mail wasn't in the right place.

The bundle of mail, wrapped in a wide rubber band, was jammed against the shiny oak molding on the wall that jutted out at a right angle behind the door. On days that the front door was locked, our mail carrier just dropped our mail through the brass slot eighteen inches or so up from the bottom of the door. Gravity being what it was, the mail tended to fall straight down, give or take a millimeter or two. To get wedged over by the molding, one of three things would need to happen. First, the mail carrier could have stooped down, stuck her hand through the slot, and flipped the mail over by the wall. Seemed unlikely. Two, somebody could have kicked or pushed the bundle over to where it currently rested. Or, three, the mail would have skidded over there if somebody had opened the front door.

Two and three were worrisome. Number one seemed ludicrous. I immediately prayed that our itinerant tenant, architect Dana Beal, was the inadvertent culprit. I backed out of the waiting room and treaded gently up the stairs, hoping to find Dana bent over her drafting table designing an addition for some beach house in Antigua.

She wasn't there. After going back downstairs to the kitchen where we sorted mail to see if Diane had collected hers—she hadn't—I grabbed my keys and returned to the landing at the top of the stairs. What I discovered when I opened the door to Dana's studio was that, once again, her plants needed water. She hadn't been around for a while.

Back downstairs in my office, I picked up the phone, called Sam Purdy, explained what had happened, and told him that he'd better get over right away. I told him to come in around the back. He told me not to touch anything. While I waited for him I visually re-examined the open areas of the office for signs of an intruder. Nothing but the migrating mail caught my eye.

Ten minutes later Sam Purdy and I stood together in the doorway to the waiting room re-creating our moves on Sunday morning. Neither of us could remember going near the front door from the *inside*. We had checked that the front door was locked by jiggling the knob from the *outside*. Neither of us remembered noticing the position of the mail on our admittedly cursory examination of the waiting room.

After cursing quietly and engaging in a parody of foot stomping, Sam Purdy paraded down the hall like an infantry soldier off to battle and used my phone to call out the crime scene investigators.

While waiting for the forensic technicians to arrive, I called my four appointments scheduled for that day and rescheduled them for later in the week. I wrote out a note for the front door, announcing Diane's absence due to illness. And I called the ICU to discover that nothing was new with her medical condition.

Purdy told me to stay at my desk and draw a diagram of my movements in the yard and the building that morning, paying particular attention to anything I might have touched. While I obeyed, he sat on my consulting chair and sketched out his best memory of our visit the previous morning. Upon the arrival of the CSIs, Purdy conferred with them for a while, gave them our maps, and then walked me down the street to Nancy's for breakfast.

I told him I'd already eaten.

"So have I," he said.

"Oh," I said, mildly chastising myself for being surprised.

He ordered biscuits and coffee. That's all; I did the same. Jam with the biscuits for me. Lots of butter for Sam.

Purdy was all business and started walking me through a number of scenarios. That the mail got moved by an act of God. Where crime was concerned I imagined Purdy to be such an ardent believer in acts of God that that theory inspired a lot of credibility. Or, he suggested, somebody got into the office Saturday night after assaulting Diane and that we somehow missed the signs in our rapid perusal on Sunday. Purdy's tone left me no doubt how distasteful that particular oversight would be for him. Or, that somebody got into the office sometime Sunday after we had already checked the place for signs of disturbance.

I nodded a lot and pecked at my biscuit, which was the size and shape of a malignant hardball. But it tasted just fine.

Purdy was just starting to consider my question about why there didn't seem to be any signs of forcible entry when his radio squawked, startling me, and I almost choked on a big flake of crust.

Sam took his radio out of the folds of his coat and belched something back into it. A vaguely feminine voice said something that sounded ominous even to me, who wasn't fluent in any of the Motorola chicken scratch dialects. Purdy responded by saying, "Affirmative, I'm on my way," glancing immediately at his watch, then grabbed his little notebook from a side pocket of his jacket and wrote down the time and date. Then an address.

Finished, he stuck the radio back into his coat, repocketed his notebook, gulped the rest of his coffee, shook his head twice, and said to me, "Well, *Mister* Doctor Coroner's Consultant, it appears we have ourselves a fresh one. You're coming. Let's go. You pay."

I dropped some money on the table and followed Purdy out to the sidewalk. We almost jogged the two blocks back to my office and his car. Remembering his fluidity on the dance floor, I tried not to be surprised at the ease of his long stride as I struggled to keep up with him. Sam asked me to wait—no, told me to wait—while he ran into my little office building to confer with the crime scene people. He was out in less than a minute.

He pointed to his Ford and climbed in, having instantly reverted to a mode where we were barely colleagues, obviously expecting me to take orders from him. Taking orders with equanimity isn't something I do with noteworthy grace, but I was terribly curious and morbidly excited to see what would happen next. Scott Truscott had told me during my brief orientation that sometimes coroner's investigators go directly to crime scenes. Apparently I was going to get my chance.

My jaw dropped when Sam Purdy fastened his seat belt,

slammed the car door, and turned to me and said, "The deceased is apparently the wife of our ex-mayor and current county commissioner, Russell London." His face scrunched up, and he wrinkled his nose as if he had just discovered sabotage to the plumbing of a public toilet. "Smell any dogshit now, my friend?"

Purdy drove down to Ninth Street and then up the hill toward Chautauqua. I expected—okay, I hoped for—him to thrust his left hand out the window to affix a magnetic revolving light to the top of the car, switch on the siren, and blast at high speed to wherever we were headed. He didn't. Instead he proceeded as though we might've been heading to church and he intended to arrive well into the sermon. He asked me if I had ever read *Zen and the Art of Motorcycle Maintenance*, ignored my affirmative nod, and began a lecture about the Chautauqua movement and the string of Chautauquas around the United States, and did I know that Boulder's was one of the best-preserved facilities around? I surmised that he didn't want to be interrupted as he talked, the purpose having something to do with shutting me up so he could ponder the murder of Russell London's wife. Purdy was apparently adept at thinking about one thing while talking about another, a cognitive juggling act that was a prerequisite skill for psychotherapists as well as for detectives.

At Baseline he jagged a quarter of a block and then turned up Kinnikinnick into the grounds of Chautauqua. He slowed briefly as a patrolman guarding the entrance to the parking lot by the ranger station waved us farther up the road, past a string of streets with flower names, up behind the huge wood frame of the Chautauqua auditorium. Purdy stopped abruptly at the end of the street where it bordered a usually quiet knoll that stretched up toward the base of the immense vertical rock face of the first Flatiron. A large, curious crowd had preceded us to the crime scene, but apparently not by long. Uniformed Boulder police officers hadn't finished stretching yellow crime scene control tape around a base perimeter of an area that seemed to be at least a couple of acres in size. An ambulance was on the scene along with half a dozen patrol cars, two crime scene vans, and a couple of civilian-looking late-model sedans and wagons.

And an Isuzu four-wheel drive with a license plate that started with a Z.

Purdy shoved me in front of him as we reached a patrolman who held a clipboard while guarding the entrance to the roped-off area. "Show him your ID," Purdy hissed at me, and we waited while the patrolman scribbled down my name and coroner's ID number, looked at his watch, and wrote down the time. These police officers had certainly developed a sudden thing about wristwatches and note taking.

To Purdy the patrolman said simply, "Hello, Detective."

Sam grunted something and then asked the patrolman, "Who was first here?"

"Charlie," he said, and gestured up the knoll with the clipboard toward the patrolwoman who had accosted me during the hostage situation at my office.

Purdy wrote some things in his book, an act that took almost a minute, and then said to me, "Stay with me. Got it?"

I didn't think a reply was required.

Purdy did.

"I said, 'Got it?' " he growled, ensuring my attention by compressing my bicep into the diameter of a bratwurst.

"Yes," I said.

He released my arm, moderated his voice back to tenor, and said, "This is a murder scene. Walk only where I walk. Touch nothing. Say nothing."

"I understand."

"Good."

I noticed the press assembling and looked everywhere for Merideth, hoping not to find her.

Purdy walked up the meadow to Officer Charlene Manning. I traipsed alongside like a dog on heel. Officer Manning's hair was pure gold in contrast to the dusky yellow and brown of the surrounding grasses. I thought I detected a faint hint of eyeliner, but otherwise she was without makeup. She was more slender than I remembered her from the morning of the assault in my office. The heavy blue jacket she was bundled in seemed too warm for the day. Though not for the circumstances.

She and Purdy just nodded at each other. I wondered if I detected a level of familiarity in their mutual greeting that went beyond the merely collegial.

Charlene Manning raised a small pad about six inches farther from her eyes than should have been necessary and began to report to Purdy. "Body found by a jogger at approximately nine-fifteen A.M. this morning," she began, her anxiety under control except for the redundancy, "who apparently moved the body while checking to see if the victim was deceased. When he was certain she was—deceased, that is—he ran down to one of the houses"—she pointed toward the Chautauqua cabins—"and called in on nine-one-one. Wilson and I ran emergency, arriving at nine thirty-two A.M. this morning, confirmed by radio the need for ambulance, CSIs, detectives, coroner, and backup, briefly interviewed the witness, and began securing the scene. Wilson started a crime scene record while I established a perimeter. Next on the scene were the paramedics, who confirmed her dead—"

Purdy cut her off. "Tell me about the victim."

"Victim apparently is . . . a Marilyn London, according to the jogger who found the body and is acquainted with her because he is apparently a neighbor. Deceased's husband is apparently the mayor—no, the ex-mayor of Boulder. Or something."

"Or something," mumbled Purdy. "Cause of death? Weapons? Sexual assault?"

Purdy began walking up the knoll toward the crime scene. Two investigators held cameras, one a video camera, the other a 35 mm, both trained on the area around the deceased. A third investigator stretched a measuring tape and jotted numbers on a sketch he was making on an oversize clipboard.

Charlie stayed right with Purdy and continued her report. "Cause of death is apparently two gunshots, one to the upper right chest area, the other to the abdomen. A perimeter search is under way. No weapon has been located yet. Deceased is fully clothed. No apparent indication of sexual assault, pending autopsy, anyway." She looked up at me. I nodded as if I concurred. Mostly I felt out of place.

Purdy said, "Great," then, "Who talked to this witness?"

"I did, sir."

"Where is he now?"

"My patrol car."

"Good. I'll get back to talk to you and him in a minute. As soon as you can, get somebody to begin to canvass these houses for witnesses, people who heard gunshots—"

"Already begun, sir."

Purdy stuck his tongue into his cheek and sucked on his upper molars. "Good," he said, and seemed suddenly to remember that I was tagging along. "Come with me," he ordered.

The body was about two hundred yards up the hill from the trail head, approximately fifteen yards off the path that led farther up the knoll to the sparse forest at the base of the first Flatiron. About ten yards from the body, on the path, was my boss from the coroner's office, Scott Truscott. He didn't look pleased to see me.

Truscott turned immediately to Purdy. "Sam, the coroner's coming up here to do this one himself, I don't think it's—"

"Relax, Scott, he was with me on the Templeton thing when the call came in. Thought he could learn something by tagging along. Jesus, I know he won't catch this one."

Scott Truscott softened, let his shoulders down a little, and said, "Alan, why don't you stay with me. You might learn something."

I looked at Sam Purdy, hoping he wouldn't make me choose between my masters. He said, "Good idea, Scott. But I still need to talk to him about another matter, so" —he started sucking on his molars again—"so, don't go anywhere, Alan."

"Sure, Detective," I said, and took a step closer to Scott

Truscott, feeling a bit like a kid who was being transferred between baby-sitters.

Purdy moved gingerly as he edged closer to the body. He suddenly seemed fifty pounds lighter, and I recalled his grace as he danced.

Scott Truscott told me he wanted me to accompany him when he was given clearance from Purdy to move closer to the body to do whatever it was his job required him to do. From where I was on the trail I could see that the body lay facedown on a sparse bed of dried native grasses. Any residual morbid curiosity I had suddenly vanished. Increasing my intimacy with this savagery held absolutely no allure.

I decided to beg off. "Scott," I said, "look, I'm not going to make a career of this. I don't think I want to learn whatever I could possibly learn by getting any closer than I am to that body."

He eyed me suspiciously and then with some apparent relief. "Fine, Alan. Why don't you go back down the hill outside the perimeter."

"Good idea."

Truscott seemed to be coming to a welcome realization that I wasn't going to be lobbying him for a permanent job on his staff. I stuffed my hands in my pockets and followed the well-worn trail down the hill to the yellow tape, staring mostly at my feet.

After checking out with the patrolman with the clipboard, I looked around for Merideth, whom I didn't find. But Merideth's rental car was still on the scene, and one of the four or five video cameras that were set up undoubtedly belonged to her network crew. Merideth would be around somewhere; she could be pretty relentless about news. Today, no doubt, Tom Cech and his RNA would be on hold.

My car was parked at my office, a relatively pleasant downhill stroll twenty blocks down Ninth Street. I could be there in fewer than thirty minutes if I was willing to risk Purdy's wrath—he had told me in certain terms to stick around.

Not eager to have Purdy angry at me, I went over and

sat on the wide bumper of an unfortunately superfluous ambulance. That's where Merideth found me.

My gaze went immediately to her abdomen. Her hand, fingers spread, followed seconds later, extending over her long black sweater as if to demonstrate the continued flatness of her belly.

"Hi," I said.

She was smiling and leaned over to receive a kiss. "Any word on Diane?" she asked.

I shook my head, having a little trouble keeping all my active crises straight. I was wishing that no part of me wanted to see Merideth. But it wasn't true. I wanted to be through with her. But I wasn't.

"One of my sources," she said, pausing to ascertain that my attention was undivided, "told me that the grand jury thing has to do with Russell London. And, as you probably know, that's his wife dead up the hill." I was momentarily confused. I was tempted to nod, a man merely acknowledging his spouse as she talked about her job, then wondered if Merideth was using me as a second source who could confirm for her a fact that she had already learned from somebody else.

I said, "Yes, that is Ms. London up the hill. Apparently."

Offhandedly, as though my reply would mean nothing to her, she asked, "How'd she die? Was she raped?"

My pager vibrated against my hip. Merideth watched me fumble to find the buttons that would still it, and then she reached into the big leather bag that hung from her shoulder and retrieved a cellular phone in a fake leather pouch.

"Need a phone?" she said. I was surprised and shouldn't have been. The network wouldn't really insist she keep a pocket full of quarters and hunt for pay phones.

The pager vibrated again. I fumbled again.

"I don't know how those things work," I said, sweeping one hand toward the portable phone.

She slid the phone from its pouch, punched a single button, handed it to me, and said. "Pretty complicated, honey. Just punch the number. Then push Send."

I did, then punched in my Voicemail code and listened to Geoff Tobias inform me that Randy Navens had, once again, not shown up for school that morning.

Beep. Pause.

And to Rita Templeton's soft voice telling me that Randy Navens was in her kitchen in Mirabelle, wanting very much to speak with me.

28

"I have an emergency in my practice," I said to Merideth while fighting an impulse to scream "What next?" I held up the phone to her and asked, "May I make a couple more calls?"

She said, "Of course," and then seemed bent on following me as I walked away from her around the ambulance to get enough privacy to call Randy.

Rita Templeton sounded terribly relieved to hear from me. She told me Randy was fine—unhurt, anyway—but that he seemed confused. I spoke with Randy briefly, and he agreed to stay put until I could get to Mirabelle.

Next, I called Pain Perdu and was told Geoff Tobias was in a meeting and couldn't be disturbed. Too weary to argue or to beg, I told the young man on the phone to tell Geoff I'd just found Randy and that he seemed to be unhurt. As I tried to find the button to turn off the phone, I noticed that Merideth had edged to the corner of the ambulance in order to keep an eye on me.

I handed her the phone and explained that I had to go see a patient.

"Will you call me later, Alan?"

"Yes, I will. Right now I need to find a ride down to my office. I don't have my car."

She thought for a moment. "I'd give you ours, but I don't know what's going to happen here next. I'm sorry. I'd like to help. Let me see if I can find you a ride."

I said, "No, no, you're busy, I understand. It's fine. I'll find a ride." I was almost too distracted to notice that Merideth had indicated a desire to help. Merideth could,

Also by Ed McBain

THE MATTHEW HOPE NOVELS

Goldilocks (1978) Rumpelstiltskin (1981) Beauty and the Beast (1982) Jack and the Beanstalk (1984) Snow White and Rose Red (1985) Cinderella (1986) Puss in Boots (1987) The House That Jack Built (1988) Three Blind Mice (1990)

THE 87TH PRECINCT NOVELS

Cop Hater • The Mugger • The Pusher (1956) The Con Man • Killer's Choice (1957) Killer's Payoff • Killer's Wedge • Lady Killer (1958) 'Til Death • King's Ransom (1959) Give the Boys a Great Big Hand • The Heckler • See Them Die (1960) Lady, Lady, I Did It! (1961) The Empty Hours • Like Love (1962) Ten Plus One (1963) Ax (1964) He Who Hesitates • Doll (1965) Eighty Million Eyes (1966) Fuzz (1968) Shotgun (1969) Jigsaw (1970) Hail, Hail the Gang's All Here! (1971) Sadie When She Died • Let's Hear It for the Deaf Man (1972) Hail to the Chief (1973) Bread (1974) Blood Relatives (1975) So Long As You Both Shall Live (1976) Long Time No See (1977) Calypso (1979) Ghosts (1980) Heat (1981) Ice (1983) Lightning (1984) Eight Black Horses (1985) Poison • Tricks (1987) Lullaby (1989) Vespers (1990) Widows (1991) Kiss (1992) Romance (1995)

OTHER NOVELS

Where There's Smoke • Doors (1975) Guns (1976) Another Part of the City (1986) Downtown (1991)

on occasion, be generous, but the impulse was usually the result of some internal drive of hers and not necessarily responsive to someone else's actual need. Early in our relationship I'd had to adjust to her relative insensitivity to needs of mine that were less than overt and less than convenient for her to meet. In the present circumstances I was tempted to expend my shallow energy trying to allay Merideth's remorse at not being permitted to find me a ride. Instead I squeezed her shoulder and told her I would talk to her later.

When I tracked down Purdy a few minutes later, he was talking to the patrolman with the clipboard. I waited impatiently for almost two minutes before I blurted out, "I've got a patient in trouble. I need to go. Can you get me a ride back downtown?"

He seemed irritated. "What?"

"It's that kid. Remember? The one who was missing? It happened again. I need to go."

He nodded absently and turned back to the cop with the clipboard. I couldn't tell if Purdy had even processed what I told him. I turned on my heels to walk the twenty blocks back to my car.

"Hold it, damn it!" Purdy snapped.

I took three more steps before I stopped. I turned slowly to face him.

He said, his voice pretending calm, "I'll get you a ride. Give me a goddamn minute."

I had too many things going on to pretend calm myself. I said, "And you remember, Detective, I'm not on county time. I'm not on your time. I have a patient in trouble. Your 'problem' "—I swept an arm up the hill toward the body of the ex-mayor's wife—"I might remind you, isn't going anywhere. Mine needs some attention. Now!"

After my outburst forced his hand, Purdy raised the stakes by screaming up the hill at a young cop guarding the western part of the perimeter of the crime scene. The cop ran over. Purdy told him to drive me downtown. I turned and trailed after the young cop. Neither Purdy nor I bothered to say good-bye.

But I finally got my ride in a real cop car.

* * *

It took a little more than half an hour to retrieve my car and get to Mirabelle. Other than Rita Templeton's minivan there were no signs of habitation in the cluster of cabins. I wondered about the whereabouts of Randy's car.

By the time I lifted myself from the Subaru the front door to the Templeton cabin was open. Rita Templeton stood in the doorway, wearing tight cords and a rag sweater I thought I'd seen in the Eddie Bauer catalog.

Randy, behind her, looked awful.

His sparse stubble was long. His eyelids were rounded and heavy, the bags under them were full and hard like overpacked luggage. His pupils were pinpricks, and he seemed to be fighting to keep his eyes still.

"Randy," I said in a quiet voice, "it's Alan. You asked me to come."

"Hi," he said.

I kept my eyes on Randy and said to Rita, "Can you give us a few minutes? Maybe get us some coffee or tea, something without caffeine?"

She anxiously brushed her hands on her hips and said, "Sure. Of course. Right away. Use the living room, right here. Please."

I walked slowly to Randy and suggested we go in and sit down. In the living room I chose a chair about six feet from him, the distance he was accustomed to from sessions in my office. I said nothing, wanting to allow him some time to get comfortable with my being there.

The room was large and cold. The couches and chairs were wonderful round upholstered pieces from the thirties, dusty and not recently used. The side tables were familiar Sear's catalog oak pieces that dated from the early part of the century. A wagon wheel chandelier hung in the center of the room, and an alluring interlocking pastiche of elk racks framed the heavy stones above the fireplace.

Randy was bent on his chair, rocking ever so slightly. His hair was oily, his clothing filthy.

Finally he said, "It happened again."

"Yes. It appears so."

"This is where I came last time, too."

"I wondered about that."

More rocking.

"You know where you are?"

"Mountains," he said, smiling puckishly at the obviousness of his answer.

"Know what day it is?"

He looked at his watch. "It says Monday. I'll guess Monday." He smiled again. "Is this a test or something?"

"I'm checking to see how oriented you are."

"How'm I doin'?"

"So far so good. What's your birthday?"

He told me.

"Your name?"

"Randy Navens. Is that a trick question?"

He was starting to relax, his irreverent humor starting to emerge.

"Tell me about last night. This morning. Whatever."

Before he responded I noticed Rita Templeton hovering in the doorway, holding a tray with a teapot, mugs, and some aromatic muffins. There was a little vase of flowers on the tray, too.

"May I set this down and then get out of your way?"

"Certainly, Rita—Ms. Templeton. Thank you. The muffins smell wonderful. Cinnamon?"

"You're welcome. Yes, they are cinnamon. I love to bake, but Larry never cared for the things I made. He would have eaten sawdust if it was nourishing. Thank God for the kids. Anyway, enjoy." I waited for her to exit and poured Randy a mug of tea. He took it and held it in both his hands.

I poured another mug for myself and sipped and waited.

"I don't remember much. Story of my life these days, isn't it?" In a parody of a parrot he continued, *"I can't remember. I can't remember. I can't remember."* He moved the mug near enough to his face to smell the aroma of the peppermint and lemon from the tea. Steam rose in front of his eyes. "Same place as last time. I was in the same room, trying to get into that same damn cupboard. And lace again, the same lace again. And suddenly I was there—I mean back here, whatever. Like, you know," he said, mimicking a hip voice common among his peers, "back in the cosmic plane." He returned to his normal tone of voice and continued. "I knew who I was. I saw the car here and knocked on the door. This lady called you for me." He looked at me with a slight smile, raised the tea, and said, "Ta-dum."

"Scared?"

He finally took a sip from the mug and said, "Hell, yes."

"I bet. Me too, I'm scared for you. Any memories or images from the crash?"

"Nope."

"Sure?"

"Yep."

"It's easier if you can joke about it?"

"Not sure about that. I'm afraid maybe it'll be worse if I don't."

"Which cabin were you in?"

He stood from his chair and moved to the window facing the compound. I followed him. "That one," he said. He pointed to a two-story frame-and-log house that sat at a roughly right angle to the Templeton home. The house was stained a dirty red.

"Whose is it?"

"Somebody who's probably pretty pissed that some twerp keeps busting into their house trying to squeeze into their cabinets." He looked at me.

"But you don't know?"

"You know, I'm not sure. I think I've been there before. I mean when I was younger. But I don't know for sure."

Rita Templeton was in the living room doorway again. I was rather certain her makeup had been refreshed. Her spicy perfume preceded her into the room. "You doing all right in here? Need anything? More muffins?"

"Rita, we're fine. One question, though?"

She opened her eyes wide to encourage me to continue.

"Whose cabin is that?" I asked, pointing across the compound.

She walked over so she could see where I was pointing.

"Oh, that's the Tobias place. Most of them live in Arvada and Wheat Ridge. They don't really use it much."

Randy Navens was unmoved by the news. Unless you counted the fact that he dropped the mug of tea he was holding.

Randy had removed his filthy shoes at the front door to Rita Templeton's cabin, and when the mug of tea slipped from his hand it fell straight down to the big toe of his stockinged left foot. The mug didn't break, although it appeared, from the immediate amount of swelling on Randy's foot, that his toe might have.

Rita was much more upset about Randy's foot than were either Randy or I. She rushed out to the kitchen and then rushed back to the living room and supported Randy as he hopped with her into the only warm room in the big house. She sat him on a pressed-back chair and raised his foot onto the quilted cushion of another. She cracked open old metal ice-cube trays and tied the broken cubes into a deep green kitchen towel that she placed gently on his foot. After wiping her hands on the hips of her corduroys, she asked if we needed anything else.

Randy and I both declined.

I said to Randy, "I take it that these Tobiases include your aunt and uncle."

He nodded absentmindedly. He looked exhausted. As he was prone to do, he rubbed his eyes with the knuckles on the backs of his hands. I guessed that he was remembering something. And I imagined that the experience must have been like driving from a thick fog to a thin one.

Rita returned from the living room to the kitchen with the teapot. "You mean the restaurant people?" She said. "Isn't that place wonderful? They're your *relatives?* I've only eaten there once—Larry and I, on our anniversary . . ." And her voice instantly trailed off into a shadow place of mourning while she busied herself at the stove.

She wiped the already clean enamel for half a minute or so. Her eyes were moist when she turned back to face us. "The other kids—I mean, the other Tobias kids—use the cabin more than Geoff and his wife do. They must be so busy with that restaurant! There're three families, I think—I think all three Tobias kids are married. The parents are dead. I probably have some phone numbers somewhere if you want to call them. But nobody uses the cabin very much. To be honest, the place needs some attention."

Geoff's phone number wasn't my number one priority. I said, "No, Rita, thanks. I know how to reach Geoff Tobias."

At least, I thought, I know his phone number.

At my suggestion Rita brought Randy some ibuprofen and inexplicably added how helpful it was for her cramps. Randy looked uncomfortable at the allusion to menstruation. I explained to Rita and Randy that I wanted to walk over to the Tobias place to make certain it was locked up and would be back in a moment. Rita smiled an acknowledgment and offered Randy a can of Diet Pepsi.

Despite the time being around midday, I was chilled in the shadows outside. The Tobias place was isolated on one side of the Mirabelle compound. Compared with the other cabins, some of which were dormitory size, this one was on the small side. I tried the front door first. It was locked. I walked around the back and climbed up onto an expansive redwood deck that was decades newer than the house and tried some doors that led from the deck into the house.

Locked.

On the far side of the house, down a slight slope, a car—Randy's, I assumed—was parked at the entrance to a single-car garage that was terraced into the slope and attached to the house. The garage doors were ancient, maybe even original, and opened on big side hinges like barn doors. A smaller, people-size door was cut into the center of one of two large doors. An old rusted lock lay in the dust at the base of the smaller door.

Inside, the garage was dark and cold and seemed to have once been the final destination of a grand moraine that had swept away the inventory of a patio furniture museum. Deformed picnic tables, tattered canvas umbrellas, rusting metal lawn chairs, dewebbed aluminum chaises, cracked painted wrought-iron love seats, and modern enameled glass-topped tables with their matching cushioned chairs were piled haphazardly into the long, narrow room. I walked in far enough to see a small landing in the rear that led up a short staircase to the house. In the almost darkness the door at the top appeared to be closed.

I didn't want to walk into the house.

Yes, I did. Okay, I was ambivalent.

But I didn't go in. I decided that when I called Geoff Tobias to tell him what had happened with his nephew, I'd just tell him that he needed to arrange to get a new lock for the garage door.

I dropped Randy in the emergency room at the hospital in Boulder so somebody could look at his toe and gave the intake clerk his aunt and uncle's phone number so she could try to get appropriate authorizations and health insurance information. I left her with a wistful, "Good luck." Randy was calm and agreeable about waiting for me while I visited Diane.

Randy had been silent in the car on the way to town, unable or unwilling to talk about whatever images were filling his head. I broached the subject of his going to a psychiatric hospital for his own protection. Whatever was going on during these dissociative episodes might be dangerous, I explained. I had been surprised and reassured that his reaction to the idea of hospitalization was no more of a protest than, "Shit, I knew it."

About the Tobias cabin he said, "I guess I must have gone there as a kid. It seems familiar. But scary, you know, like a haunted house." I'd pressed for more memories or images without success.

Out of nowhere, while we were driving past Pain Perdu on the final leg back into town, he said, "I was sitting next to my sister on Creamed Corn. She was being nice to me. I've never remembered that before."

He said nothing more.

29

Diane Estevez was awake. Sort of. Raoul saw me trying to bluster my way past the nursing station and rushed over. Raoul wasn't much of a rusher; he actually sort of sauntered over. I knew he was hurrying, though.

"They're bringing her out of her coma," he began, then said, embracing me by grabbing my shoulders, "Alan, good to see you."

"Is she okay? Why are they—"

"These doctors, they are, uh, obscure. It's hard to say. I think they think it is safe to stop the drugs that are causing the coma. Her vital signs are—what's the word?—stable. Intracranial pressure is down. And that's good."

"Has Adrienne been up?"

"Doctor *Poquito*," he said warmly, smiling and holding his hand palm down, horizontal, at about his navel. "Yes. She went to find the other doctor, the *neurólogo*, said she would be back." He moved his large hand, fingers spread, to his chest. He said, "I think Diane will be fine." His dark eyes glistened with tears, thin, like a film of rain on asphalt.

I spent a few minutes watching Diane fight for consciousness and then retreated to the nursing station to phone Geoff and Erica Tobias. I listened attentively to a recording explaining Erica's plans for Colorado sea bass and pomegranates until Erica herself came on the line. Almost live.

"Yes?" she said.

"This is Dr. Gregory."

"Yes? You found him?"

"I did. He found me, anyway. He was up at Mirabelle. At the cabin that Geoff's family owns."

"Oh, that old place. Not my favorite. I'm not the woodsy type. I didn't know that Randy even knew about it. I didn't think he'd ever been up there. We don't use it much. We've got a new place in Vail," she said in an attempt at either explanation or pomposity.

"Geoff's going to need to get a new lock for the garage door on the cabin."

"I'll tell him to call the caretaker. I take it the boy's okay."

The *boy?* "Broken toe, I think."

"Yeah, we heard." Silence.

"I'd like to put him in the hospital."

"For a broken toe?"

God help me.

"No, the psychiatric unit," I said calmly, checking my tone for any residue of sarcasm, "for his dissociative periods. He may be placing himself in some danger while he is in the fugue states. He'll be safer in the hospital."

"You think it's necessary? What about school?"

"I do think it's necessary. And he'll continue school there."

"His insurance will cover this?"

"Most of it. The trust will make the co-payments."

"Whatever. Fine. Go ahead," she said.

"You'll need to assist in admitting him, Ms. Tobias. Sign some papers. Provide some history to the hospital staff. And he's going to need some clean clothes, toiletries, things like that."

Sigh. "Can't they mail me the papers and give him some hospital clothes? And you know his history. We're very busy." Her tone said, "Doing something much more important than this."

I was silent, mostly because I didn't know what to say.

I heard her muffle the mouthpiece and hiss something to someone standing close to her. The exchange continued for a moment, then she said, "Tell me where to go. Tell them I'll be there at five-fifteen and that I can only stay an hour. I feel a need to say, Doctor, that my assumption was that you were supposed to help Randy get *better*. That's not exactly happening, is it?" And, like a sinister version of Tinkerbell, in an instant she was gone.

When I looked up I saw that Adrienne had pulled Raoul into an unoccupied glass-walled isolation room and was explaining something to him that apparently required a lot of hand motion. I joined them in the room.

Raoul was smiling. So I smiled, too.

Adrienne looked over at me and said sharply, "What the hell are you smiling about?"

I tried to erase my grin and then started laughing. Fortunately they joined me.

I said hopefully, "She's gonna be okay?"

Raoul said, "It's looking better all the time, *boychik*." I laughed at his Yiddish and gave each of my friends a big hug. "But you know," Raoul continued through his laughter, "when she's finally awake, she's gonna be real pissed off."

If I'd been smart, I would have gotten up, gone home, and gone to bed, letting the day stop there, with its first good news.

But the day wasn't over. And I wasn't smart.

And, of course, Sam Purdy wasn't done with me.

I was just completing the paperwork to admit Randy to the adolescent psych unit when the ward clerk told me she had a call for me in the nursing station. I finished scribbling down the last details of an initial treatment plan, picked up the phone, and listened to him tell me to meet him at my office in ten minutes.

"Is that an order, Detective?"

"Don't be a douche bag, Alan, it's been a long day."

"On one condition. Buy me a beer when we're done."

"I'll buy you a fuckin' pitcher."

"Ten minutes."

I said good-bye to Randy, left a message for the psychiatrist who would be managing the medical aspects of the admission, did my best to prepare the staff of the adolescent psych unit for the likes of the Tobiases, ran downstairs and said good-bye to Raoul, kissed a sleeping Diane on the cheek, found my car in the hospital lot, and drove downtown to my office. Purdy's city sedan was in Diane's parking place, so I had to park beneath the effluent tree.

Sam was sitting in the hovering light, his back leaning against the rear door to Diane's office. His clothes were grimy, his eyes were red, and I thought I could hear his stomach grumble from twenty feet away.

I stood silently on the first step up to Diane's little deck, waiting until he finally removed his right hand from his brow and looked up at me.

"The CSIs say somebody was probably here. The knob on the front door and the knob on the connecting door from the waiting room and the knob on your office door have all been wiped. Just *your* office door, though. Not your buddy's. My question is how the hell did they get in? CSIs say maybe these pansy-ass doctors forgot to lock their door. I tell 'em to try again—like you're gonna leave three different doors unlocked and then a burglar is gonna go to the trouble of locking them behind him. There're no scratches or marks to indicate the locks have been picked. Their collective brains come up with nothing. Maybe tomorrow, they say. Need to look for matches for all these footprints and fingerprints. Takes time.

"Know what, Doc? I think our burglar has a key to your little kingdom. That's what I think."

I'd already had the same thought. But Purdy's speculation was much more interesting to me than my own, so I nodded some encouragement.

"What I want to know is everything you can tell me about your tenant, the one upstairs, the architect without any business."

It wasn't precisely true that Dana Beal, AIA, didn't have any business. She seemed always to have at least one consuming project going on at any one time. Somehow, though, she'd managed to develop a practice devoted almost entirely to the design of beach villas. This despite the fact that the sole location of her practice was the one large skylighted second-floor room of our little office building in the center of the absolutely landlocked high-desert state of Colorado. Dana was no dummy, always insisting that her clients permit her numerous site visits for pre-design this, construction supervision that, postconstruction . . .

I explained all this to Purdy, who sarcastically inquired if I knew what island she might be on at the moment. I didn't. I told him Diane probably did. He reminded me that Diane wasn't available for an interview. I told him about her progress. He seemed genuinely pleased.

He said he'd try to track down Ms. Dana Beal and then abruptly changed the subject and asked me if I was at all suspicious that yet another person related to the supposed grand jury investigation of Russell London was now the victim of a violent death.

"Yes," I said, although my head was too full of Diane Estevez and Randy Navens to invest much energy cooperating in Sam Purdy's expansion of his conspiracy theory so it would have enough room to include Marilyn London's murder in Chautauqua.

Sam seemed to sense my distraction and persisted in trying to reel me in. He said, "It makes it all the more important to figure out what happened to Larry Templeton when his house blew up, you know."

I looked over toward him. The western light had faded to the scruffy black of discarded old dress shoes. It was hard to see Purdy's expression in the dim glow.

"You convince your bosses of that yet, Sam?"

"Still working on it."

"Ah, so you still need little old me. What about Scott Truscott? Got his curiosity piqued yet?"

"Scott's a reasonable guy."

"Well, Scott's going to have another problem come morning. His consultant—yours truly—just admitted a patient to the hospital, and that will probably cut in half the number of hours I can give him for the time being. So, I imagine he's going to be even less likely to want to devote his meager staff time to what I'm pretty sure he thinks is a wild goose chase."

"The kid?" Sam asked.

I nodded.

"You take good care of him. Scott's my problem," said Sam.

Silence for a moment. I was getting cold. "So why did you want me to meet you here?"

"I want to know whether our latest intruder went after your files. I need you to take a look at what might be missing," he said, grunting himself from his slouching position to almost vertical.

"Inside?"

"Yeah. I was thinking inside."

He followed me over to the French doors; I unlocked them and said, "After you."

He preceded me into the room, switched on a lamp, and with significant understatement said, "The crime scene people are kind of messy."

He watched my jaw drop in exasperation as I examined the layer of talclike grime adhering to flat surfaces everywhere in the room. "Fingerprint powder and assorted chemicals, mostly. They're a bitch to clean up." He plopped down on my chair and said, "Take a look—no wait. First," he said, a smile on his face, a dramatically ominous shadow in his voice, "let me officially warn you that your fingerprints are everywhere in here."

I laughed.

"Anyway, we assume they're yours. We haven't matched 'em yet."

I walked over to the two-drawer filing cabinet behind my desk and fumbled for the key. The cabinet was a vertical design made of oak, with two wide drawers parallel to the wall. The cabinet lock had been replaced after it had been busted during the previous break-in. But it didn't look to me like the cabinet had been tampered with this time. I reminded myself that this burglar had apparently gone to a lot of trouble to keep his or her entry from being detected. And I knew from experience that a thin bladed screwdriver inserted between the drawer frame and cabinet would pop open the latch lock. I'd done it once or twice after my key stuck and wouldn't work. The fact that the drawer was intact didn't necessarily mean somebody hadn't been in my files.

I looked at the rows of files. The charts in both drawers were as orderly as I ever left them, and none seemed to be missing.

I made a mental checklist of my active patients and found all of their charts just where they belonged. I said, "The files haven't been trashed, Sam. I don't see anything missing. I'd have to read them with considerable care to know if any pages have been swiped, though."

He said, "I'd like you to do that. But maybe on your own time." Sam Purdy seemed tired and eager to move on to a meal and a pitcher of beer.

I finally remembered what I had forgotten to do every one of the many times I'd recently had the pleasure of having a police officer visit me at work. I said, "Wait a second, I want to give you something for safekeeping." I again unlocked the file cabinet behind my desk, reached to the back, behind the charts, and retrieved the heavy envelope with Randy Navens's father's gun in it. Every time I touched the envelope I was newly surprised at how much it weighed. I held the envelope out to Purdy and said, "Diane told me that you guys—the police—would take this off my hands, like take custody of it—until the patient who gave it to me is trustworthy enough to have it back."

Sam Purdy looked vaguely curious through the mist of fatigue that was generally flattening his expressiveness. "It's a gun," I said.

He finally reached out and took the envelope from me, hefted it once, opened it, peered in, and said, "It sure is."

"I don't want it in my office anymore. Especially since this place is like an internship for burglars. Will you hold on to it?"

"Sure. Gonna tell me whose it is?"

"Nope."

"Didn't think so. Suicidal somebody?"

"Yes. A suicidal somebody."

"You'll let me know when you want it back—right?" I nodded. He ran the pink tip of his tongue up under the bottom of his shrubby mustache. Then he asked, "Southern Exposure okay for dinner?"

"They don't have pitchers of beer, do they?"

"No. But they have great cornbread."

Realizing the drill was changing, I added, "And a more than adequate raspberry trifle."

"There's that, too," he said. "Shall we?"

"You're still buying me that beer, you know."

"Yeah, yeah," he said, almost whispering.

30

Again? I thought as I pulled the Subaru down the drive and spotted Merideth's four-wheel-drive rental parked in front of Adrienne and Peter's house. I didn't especially want to see Merideth. Dinner with Sam Purdy had been long and pleasant, and he had kept his word and bought me three beers. I'd drunk two and a half of them, and I was tired and I felt weak.

In the few minutes before the doorbell rang and shattered my denial, I deluded myself with the fantasy that Merideth's sole purpose for being in Spanish Hills was to visit Adrienne and Peter and not to lobby her almost ex-husband about terminating our divorce proceedings.

Although my big dog Cicero had been dead almost half a year, I was still unaccustomed to the impertinent whining chime of the doorbell. Cicero had always barked a warning seconds before the bell went off—as if she were saying, "Get ready, here comes that awful noise." Now, without her forewarning, the ringing of the bell always jolted me the same way the phone did when it rang in the middle of the night.

I opened the door. Merideth looked great. Whatever she had been doing since we'd parted at the scene of the ex-mayor's wife's murder that morning was apparently less taxing than what I had been doing. In contrast with her I looked like somebody who had been dealing with dead people, kids in crisis, injured friends, burgled offices, and recalcitrant cops.

"Isn't it great news about Diane?" she said, then, "Honey, you look . . . tired."

"Hello," I said, standing in the half-open door. "I am tired. I'm beat."

She walked right in, brushing past me, leaving me in the wake of her signature scent. It would never have crossed Merideth's mind that she might not be welcome.

She wore a coat that was an abstract mosaic of shearling and lamb leather. The collar was full and high, and she had tossed her hair back over it so that her long jawline was prominent and her sculpted perfect ears exposed. A two-inch spill of pink pearls sized in descending diameters hung from each earlobe.

"Come on in," I said to the empty doorway, and turned and helped Merideth shed her coat. Underneath it she wore a thin gray turtleneck sweater that felt like cashmere. It was tight across her chest. Her breasts looked fuller than I remembered. "Why don't you put on some music, get yourself something to drink. I'm going to take a quick shower," I said, and moved toward the stairs before she could suggest an alternative plan of action.

The phone started ringing just as I was stepping into the stall of the shower. Either the answering machine or Merideth caught the phone just after the third ring. I guessed that the worst was occurring and half walked, half ran naked into the bedroom, lifted the receiver and, hearing Merideth's voice on the upstairs extension, said, "I've got it."

There was a long pause, a click, and then Lauren said, "Hi, Alan. Hired someone to screen your calls?"

"God, Lauren, it's nice to hear your voice. You can't imagine what kind of day I've had."

"You don't sound too lonesome to me, darling."

"Merideth just showed up five minutes ago, uninvited. I was downstairs climbing into the shower when you phoned. She picked it up. Upstairs."

"You sound a little bit defensive."

"I don't want you to misinterpret this—her being here. I'm thrilled to hear from you. How's it going?"

"The interview went well, I think. Who really knows? I had a neurological exam that lasted over an hour this morning, and I spent the afternoon at the Whitney. They have some question about the films I brought with me, and there's talk of doing a repeat MRI. More appointments tomorrow. But I'm feeling confident about it. Are you sleeping with her?"

I exhaled. "No. I'm not." To bolster my contention I added, "I haven't even shaved my legs since you left."

"Good," she said quietly. "I don't think I could manage it if you were sleeping with her."

"I'm very aware that I'm not sleeping with you, either. When are you coming home?"

"Probably not before the end of the week. I may need to stay in town until they make their decision in case they want to run any tests, or examine me again, or do that MRI, or whatever."

"The end of the week is a long time," I said.

"Especially since my competition seems to have the run of your house while you're running around naked and probably pretty horny."

"Lauren . . ." The next words that my brain was sending to my mouth were "She's not your competition," but who was I kidding? So the words never made it out.

"I don't want to lose you, Alan."

"I don't want to lose you, Lauren." I paused. "I love you."

"Thanks. I needed to hear that. I love you, too."

I listened to footsteps on the stairs and was just a second late getting my hand over the mouthpiece before Merideth called out, "You out of the shower yet, sweetheart? I have a glass of wine for you."

Lauren said, "Listen, I'll let you go. You're obviously pretty busy."

"No, Lauren, please."

"Alan—oh, by the way, I spoke with Raoul at the hospital. He told me the wonderful news about Diane. He says I might even get to talk with her tomorrow. And you—please don't forget about me."

I was sitting naked on the bed, my stubbled legs drawn to my chest for warmth and cover. Merideth had moved into the bedroom doorway, a glass of wine in her left hand.

"Lauren, please, I need to—"

"Good night, Alan. I *do* love you," she said, her voice as plaintive as I'd ever heard. She hung up.

Merideth smiled. I tried to smile back. I wondered if my scrotum was exposed along with everything else.

"Glass of wine?" she asked.

My heart was racing. Her breasts *were* fuller than I remembered. I managed to say, "No. Not right now. I haven't showered yet. Give me ten more minutes. Okay?"

Her eyes drifted unselfconsciously down to where my butt and my balls touched the bed and then returned her gaze to lock on to my eyes.

"You're sure?" she said, her eyebrows arching momentarily.

I nodded and said, "I'm sure."

"Okay," she said, shaking her head just enough to register her disbelief.

Merideth's exit from my bedroom doorway was prolonged, offering me ample opportunity to change my mind. By the time I heard her footsteps on the stairs I realized I had been holding my breath for quite a while.

After a long, hot shower I threw on jeans and a sweatshirt and joined Merideth in the living room. With each step up the stairs I prayed she would do something absolutely abhorrent so my ambivalence would resolve.

"I've missed this view, the lights, the quiet," she said. I was surprised and wondered for a moment if she was being disingenuous. Merideth and I had joked frequently over the years that she was so oblivious of the view that if someone stole the mountains and moved them to Nebraska, she wouldn't notice for a week. I let her comment pass.

"How's your friend?" she asked.

"She's fine," I said. She nodded and took a tiny sip from a glass of water.

"Come sit, your glass is right here," she said, lightly patting the sofa next to her.

"I've been drinking beer, I think I'll pass on the wine."

I plopped onto my big leather chair and hung a leg over one of the arms.

She'd chosen an old album by Rita Coolidge. Rita was singing "Fever."

And Merideth was conducting this symphony with the theatrical flair of Bernstein in his prime.

My wife's shoes, black flats with a half-circle of playful golden dots on each, were on the floor next to the sofa. Stirrups from her stretch pants looped over the heels of stockings, which were mostly lace. One of her legs was tucked beneath her, the other extended onto the coffee table.

"We made a lot of plans here, didn't we?" she asked, looking for guidance or truth in the water she swirled around her glass.

What we had done here, I thought, was postpone a lot of plans. Remodeling, starting a family. "It seems like a long time ago," I said. "A lot has changed."

"Cicero's gone," she said.

I was quiet. Cicero's death still made me sad.

"I think you've changed, too, Alan." My immediate assumption was that she wasn't particularly thrilled about the progress of my development. "What you went through last year, it had to change you."

"I'm sure it did," I said, gazing out into the night, feeling tired and wanting to sleep, not wanting to reminisce about the last year.

"In what way?" she said. I recognized immediately that this was a difficult juncture for me. Merideth's questions often sounded like sincere interest, but the reality was that she was much better at interviewing than at conversing. She always seemed more interested in the information than in the informant. These were fresh insights at the time; I was trying them on. They appeared to fit, but I wasn't absolutely comfortable with the cut.

"It hasn't been that long, Merideth. I'm not sure I know yet. I'd like to think I'm smarter about people, more capable of compassion, more aware of what I want. I don't know. Time will tell." My words sounded trite and impersonal. The reality was that the events of the previous year had frightened me at a level more primal than I would have imagined. I had been beaten by my losses, stunned by my psychological and physical vulnerability, horrified by my capacity for rage and for violence. I'd been awestruck at the awareness I'd been forced to face of how reluctant I'd always been to get truly close to other people.

As I expected, however, Merideth seemed satisfied with my platitudes. She shifted on the couch, flicking her hair off her collar with the backs of her hands in a way that thrust her chest in my direction. She pulled a big red pillow from the corner of the sofa and stretched out on her abdomen, her arms around the pillow, looking at me. Her legs were bent at the knee, her ankles crossed in the air above her.

"Your detective friend has me convinced that there's something going on with all these deaths."

"You talk to him?"

"I called questions out to him from behind the crime scene tape. He harrumphed. No. I'm reading between the lines, based mostly on what you've told me and on rumors about the grand jury investigation that I picked up before today."

"So you've got a story?"

"It's probably more local than regional, but yes, I think I've stumbled across a second story right here in the People's Republic of Boulder. My boss will probably tell me to turn it over to the local affiliate. But maybe it'll give me an excuse to come back to Boulder. Who knows?"

I smiled at her use of a nickname for Boulder that I hadn't heard in years.

"We may be able to help each other," she said.

I wondered whether I was mixing up her two agendas for tonight's visit. But I was suspicious that the mutual benefit she was alluding to might be that I had this yearning for a child and she had a short-term need to locate a willing male parent, the biological fathering part having, conveniently, been previously resolved. But I wasn't ready to tackle that issue quite yet.

"I don't see how," I said.

"We could share information."

"Merideth, sweets, I think you have a greater professional interest in the outcome of this little drama than I do. My interest in playing coroner's consultant decreases logarithmically with each new dead body I see. I suggest you offer your trade to Purdy. Who knows, he may go for it. For me, right now, I want people to stop burglarizing our offices and Diane's house—"

"Wait! Hold it, Alan. What burglary in your office? There's been one besides the one at Diane's house?"

I hesitated and realized quickly that she could find out whatever she needed from police reports. So I told her the larger facts about the earlier break-in at our offices and the recent one over the weekend. I knew her quick mind was developing new strategies of investigatory attack as I spoke.

"Anything else you've forgotten to tell me?"

"Don't think so," I said.

"Can you get me an interview with this detective?"

"I doubt it. But I can ask." I wouldn't ask.

"You were saying about the burglaries?"

"Anyway, I was saying, I want the burglaries to stop, I want people to stop assaulting Diane, and I want to become, once again, a relatively obscure, relatively well-respected clinical psychologist with a relatively boring life and a couple of good bicycles."

"What about a wife and family?"

I made an embarrassing, involuntary guttural noise that started somewhere far down in my throat. When I recovered from the paroxysm I said, "Now available—for a short time only—in one convenient, premixed package?"

Merideth laughed and sat up. "But all of the above *is* what you want, isn't it? It's funny—early on, years ago, when we were first going out and I was complaining to everybody I knew about your preference for hanging out in your little fiefdom up here over doing just about anything else in the world—dancing, partying, skiing, whatever—Adrienne told me that when she first met you she thought you were 'splenetic.' I had to go home and look it up. Later, she said, when she got to know you, she discovered you were just dull. God! We're so different, you and I," Merideth said, suddenly animated, and looked at me with eyes that said that she wanted to fuck me.

And that said "And I know you want to fuck me, too."

I woke early and alone the next morning to the reappearance of chinook winds knifing with an intensity capable of sandblasting iron. The winds were downslope and, according to the morning TV weather person, gusting to 105 miles per hour in the "foothills near Boulder." Experience said I knew what it was like outside. During one serious chinook event shortly after I moved to Boulder, I was driving east out of town on Highway 36, the freeway to Denver, and was being encouraged up the first big hill by the insistent chinooks, the car going maybe sixty or sixty-five. I was passed on the right by an empty plastic thirty-gallon trash can going at least eighty.

By eight-fifteen I was seeing my first patient and struggling to figure out how I was going to explain the forensic slime that lingered over virtually every smooth surface of my office. By one o'clock I was thoroughly rattled by the way the buffeting chinooks made the windows hum, had seen four more patients, and was feeling renewed confidence about my work and justified about my growing inclination to resign from the county's slim ranks of coroner's investigators.

Elaine Casselman was one of my morning patients, and she talked for half her session about what she might have done to push Max away—he hadn't called her in five days—and the other half of the session about being excited and fearful after the apparent murder of Marilyn London.

She had plenty of momentum about Max, though she remained immune to my suggestions that Max's retreat had more to do with his own peculiar psychological infirmities than it did with her imagined social faux pas. When her enthusiasm for talking about Max subsided, I pressed her on the fear.

"Well, first this guy's shrink dies. Then the witnesses against this guy die. Now his wife dies. I thought this grand jury stuff was going to be fun. But the attrition rate of the participants is becoming a little worrisome." She tried to smile.

"Are you frightened for yourself?"

"Yes, I am. The man was mayor. Now he's a county commissioner. He must have a lot of friends. A lot of contacts. A lot of IOUs he can call in."

"You're fearful that he is killing witnesses, including his wife?" I was more than a little incredulous. I, too, had wondered if Russ London had a hand in his wife's death, but just couldn't see it.

"Not just witnesses. Participants. I mean, somebody definitely killed his wife and she wasn't even a threat—she couldn't have testified against him, could she?"

Elaine sat up straight, a prodigious sight, and continued, "When are the police gonna get the hint that if this guy has done this once he's likely to do it again? And maybe keep doing it."

She looked at me, waiting for I'm not sure what. Her question was intended rhetorically. But I had no plans to leave it there.

"Maybe the police will get the hint about Russell London when you get the hint about Max," I said.

Elaine Casselman folded herself over, again, compacting. And looked at me, glaring like a nine-year-old whose parents never approve of her friends.

I felt confident that I had left Elaine Casselman something to think about, having perhaps finally found a way to flank her denial about the love of her life—Battering Max. She had returned the favor, giving me something to think about, inadvertently providing me additional confirmation that the target of the grand jury was indeed Russell London and intriguing me further with the possibility that Mr. London had been in psychotherapy with Paul Weinman prior to Paul's death in the skiing accident.

I assumed that the therapist in question had to be Paul Weinman. I was sure the grapevine would have at least yielded rumors if another therapist had died recently. But I was mindful that my most reliable source of gossip, Diane Estevez, had spent the last month plus on injured reserve.

Maybe I had missed something. Shouldn't be too hard to find out.

On any other mild winter day with the temperature in the fifties I would have been tempted to walk the fifteen minutes to the hospital to visit Diane and see Randy Navens. But that day it meant bucking crosswinds and dodging airborne debris. So I drove.

Diane didn't remember a thing about the burglary or the assault. She said she had been to a friend's house in Niwot for dinner. Then she woke up in the hospital.

I teared as I hugged her gently and saw moisture glistening in her brown eyes, too.

"Welcome back," I said. "I missed you."

"Thanks. And I didn't even know I was gone."

I reassured her about her practice, told her that I was sharing coverage with a couple of colleagues from her supervision group and that everything was under control.

She looked suddenly pained. "Who's covering besides you, Alan?" she asked, struggling to sit up in her bed.

I said, "Diane, calm down. Lie down. What's the problem?" Her voice quivered, and her bright eyes were spoiled by anxiety.

She exhaled and said, "Please tell me who's covering."

I was baffled, but given her condition I wasn't about to argue with her even if she was contending the world was flat. "Besides me?" I asked. She nodded. "Mona," I said, "and Clancy Coates." Mona Lanier was a clinical social worker and an old friend. Clarence Coates was a psychiatrist Diane had used for medication consultations and someone I'd heard her say complimentary things about many times over the years. Mona and Clancy had both been eager to help cover Diane's practice after she was attacked; in fact, most of Diane's supervision group had called and offered to help.

"Oh, God," she said.

"What did I do wrong?"

"You? Nothing. There's no way you could have known." She stared up at the ceiling for about fifteen seconds before returning her gaze my way. "What I'm about to tell you is really confidential, okay?"

I nodded.

"Last week. Or whenever—I don't even know what day it is. Or maybe two weeks ago— Shit! It doesn't matter. One of my new female patients was once one of Clancy Coates's patients. She told me that he had touched her and tried to talk her into performing oral sex on him. I have no reason to think she was lying."

Wow. My feelings were mixed. I didn't know Clancy well. But I did know from personal experience what it was like to be publicly accused of sexual impropriety with a patient. For me it had been a slow descent into purgatory. When you heard the accusations about somebody else, though, there was always the possibility the charges were true. Immediately, I wondered if Lynn Hughes was on Clancy Coates's patient roster. I said, "I had no idea, Diane. About Clancy. Do you believe your patient?"

"At this point, I have no reason to doubt her. How would you have known, anyway? I didn't either," she said.

"I'll rearrange the coverage right away. I'm sorry. Has Clancy been reported for this?"

"At this point my patient is refusing to call the medical examiners. She doesn't want to deal with the repercussions of reporting him."

"I'm real sorry, Diane. I'm . . . real sorry if I put anybody at risk."

"I'm sure nothing happened. Why don't you call Jennifer Ekars? She'll give me a hand with coverage." Diane then indicated she was exhausted, thanked me, and asked me to come back later for a longer visit.

Raoul caught me in the hall to ask if I knew where the spare key was to Diane's Saab. He said he figured the police had picked up her keys after the break-in, and he couldn't find the spare. I told him that I was pretty sure she kept spare keys in an old Sucrets tin in the middle drawer of her desk at work, that I'd check when I got back to the office.

By the time I got upstairs to keep my appointment with Randy, I had thought twice about it and I couldn't wait to find a phone.

Purdy, to my surprise, was actually in his office.

"Sam, this is Alan Gregory. I think I may have stumbled on something. Did the crime scene people pick up Diane's keys—her house keys and car keys—at the house? You know, after she was beaten up."

Instantly he realized what I was getting at. "Hold on," he said.

Four or five minutes later he came back on the line. "No, the sheriff's people don't have them. They have lots of excuses, but they don't have any keys."

"Answers a lot of questions, doesn't it?"

"Maybe. Got an hour?"

"In an hour, I'll have an hour."

"Meet me at her house?"

"Two-thirty?"

"See you."

Raoul, too, grasped the importance of the missing keys immediately and insisted on coming along to the rendez-vous with Purdy. I thought that being on the same mountain with Raoul and Purdy would be wonderfully entertaining, and anyway, it was Raoul's house we were all heading to, so I said, "Great idea."

After an uneventful session with Randy, Raoul and I drove up Lee Hill. I suggested we take separate cars so I wouldn't be dependent on Purdy for another ride and he wouldn't have too easy a time hijacking me for the rest of the afternoon. Purdy was sitting on the front porch of the house when I pulled in. Raoul was seconds behind me.

Raoul exited his car and walked up to join us. "Detective Sam Purdy," I said, "remember Raoul Estevez?" They had met after the shooting in Diane's office.

Raoul reached out a hand and virtually without an accent said, "Detective, nice to see you again."

Purdy looked at me suspiciously, wondering, I think, whether I knew in advance that Raoul was joining us, and said to Raoul, "Same here. I wonder if you would mind if we searched around for your wife's keys."

"Sounds like an excellent idea to me, Detective. I think I would like to help."

Just then a Chevy Blazer from the sheriff's department

joined our growing congregation. Purdy said, "I called them. It's their case, after all. Jurisdiction and all that."

I examined the front porch, which angled away from the house in an exposure that was vaguely north and west. As if to insure even more winter shadows, it was shaded most of the day by big ponderosa pines. Two broad stairs led up to a painted cedar landing about twelve feet by eight feet in size. On each side of the landing were railings that matched the gray trim of the house. In the center of the area right in front of the door was a large inset metal grate for brushing and kicking snow off shoes and boots. The area beneath the grate was open so the slush and muck from shoes could fall out of the way. Off to each side of the porch were drifts of snow, crusted by the recent warmth and dusty from the dirt and debris carried by the chinooks.

Raoul said, "We push the snow from the walk and the porch over there." He pointed at the drifts. "It's why there's so much. It's almost always shady here. The snow doesn't melt all winter sometimes."

Purdy looked at Raoul and said, "Got some shovels, any loose screen or wire mesh or anything?"

Raoul nodded and shuffled off like a laborer toward the detached garage. The sheriff's deputy pulled Purdy aside and conferred with him—mostly, I guessed, about me and Raoul. The garage door jolted and clanked loudly in its tracks, and Raoul emerged with a couple of snow shovels, a couple of garden shovels, and some heavy galvanized wire fencing wound into a five-foot spool.

"This will work," he said definitively to Purdy. "In the summer Diane uses it to protect her vegetables from the rabbits and the deer. For some reason she prefers to have her crops die of neglect."

Raoul returned to the garage for a couple of sawhorses and a hammer and nails. As he gave me directions, he and I stretched the screen between the sawhorses and he nailed it in place. We grabbed shovels and started to scoop and sift snow. I attacked the pile to the left of the porch while Raoul lifted the grate in the deck and shoveled out the snow and crap from below. The deputy pulled a metal detector from the back of his big car and started scanning the ground in concentric arcs around the entryway. Purdy stood with his arms crossed and examined the wire mesh for the appearance of treasure. The whole scene felt vaguely archaeological.

After almost ten minutes a muted clank pulled everyone's eyes to the mesh. Purdy plunged his gloveless hands into the wet snow, his fat pink fingers already wrinkled and swollen from sifting. He raised a silver ballpoint pen from the screen with exaggerated aplomb, holding it up under its pocket clip by the edge of a key. Without a word Raoul climbed up from the pit below the porch and snatched it from him.

"Mine, thank you," Raoul said, slipped it into his jacket pocket, and hopped back down to root around more in the frozen muck under the deck.

The deputy complained that he seemed to get a reading just about everywhere he pointed his metal-detecting wand. Raoul informed Purdy that the roofer who had recently reshingled the house had dumped a full box of roofing nails off the front.

Purdy cursed and told the deputy to grab a shovel.

The whining winds were irritating, and everyone's eyes were watering from airborne dust when a few minutes later the vibrant ring of metal clanging on the chicken wire drew everyone's attention to the screen in front of Purdy.

Purdy cleaned the snow from around a sparse set of keys with his puffy hands and said, "Damn it," turning his head and spitting downwind. "I didn't think they'd be here. I really didn't. Nobody touch 'em."

31

"That's not all of them," Raoul said, bending his head down to examine the ring of keys resting on the galvanized mesh.

"How do you know?" asked Purdy.

"He's right," I said, "some are missing."

Purdy turned to me. "And how do *you* know that?"

"Captain," Raoul said, offering Purdy a pejorative battlefield promotion, "you are married? About your wife, you know certain things? It's like that."

"It's like *what*?" By character, Sam Purdy was long on perseverance but short on patience.

"Diane," I said in the hypnotic voice I tended to use on those occasions when patients started yelling at me, "kept her car keys on one ring, her building keys on another. They clipped together in the center with a little spring-loaded latch."

Purdy looked down to identify which half of the tandem was tangled in the chicken wire. The plastic-tipped key with the Saab insignia answered his question.

"So maybe her assailant has the other keys, maybe not. Who shoveled these up here?" he asked.

The deputy raised his spade proudly.

Purdy said, "Keep digging," and picked up the metal detector, focusing it on the mound of snow where the deputy had been digging. The detector beeped away like a wind chime in a chinook. "This thing's a lot of fucking good," he said to no one.

We manual laborers kept digging for another half hour, until all the nearby piles of snow were strained and sifted and the other half of Diane's missing keys remained undiscovered.

Raoul didn't get Diane's car keys back. Purdy slid them into a paper bag, wrote something on a tag, and gave the package to the deputy before they drove off in separate cars.

Before he drove off, Purdy told me he would call me later.

Raoul collected a big gray metal box full of tools, threw it in his truck, and followed me down the mountain to town. I'd called a locksmith from Raoul and Diane's kitchen, and shortly after Raoul began work on debugging the office burglar alarm, the locksmith arrived to begin, once again, rekeying all the locks in the building.

The locksmith said hello to me for the second time in a couple of weeks and said, "Working for you people is like having an annuity."

I smiled weakly and went off to gather cleaning supplies to begin to strip the black-and-gray crime scene slime from the offices.

The locksmith finished his work first. He gave me a bill. Raoul finished next, saying assuredly, "It works now." He insisted that I learn to arm and disarm the machinery and that it would only take a minute. He kept talking about security zones. I didn't get it. My lesson actually took about fourteen minutes longer than promised.

In gratitude to Raoul, I rifled his wife's desk for the Sucrets box and quickly located the spare key to her Saab. In the tin I also found half a dozen paper clips, a pink button, two safety pins, a spare key to the 280Z she had traded in on the Saab, two nickels, one twenty-two-cent stamp, and two small brass keys attached by kite string to a metal-rimmed white cardboard disk that read "Paul's files."

Raoul had asked me to attend Marilyn London's funeral with him. He wasn't eager to go alone but felt that, given his exalted position in the local business community, he was obliged to attend the funeral of the wife of the ex-mayor, current county commissioner.

The funeral was scheduled for eleven o'clock the next morning in one of the big old sandstone churches on Broadway near downtown. I squeezed in a ten o'clock patient, and by the time I met Raoul on the sidewalk in front of the church, the nave was packed with an odd assemblage of people, a mix of mourners who were sincerely grieving and constituents of the ex-mayor who were covering their political flanks. Raoul told me that he'd met the deceased at a number of social and political events over the years, but neither of us had any illusions about our status; we both knew we were part of the majority that day who were attending from obligation rather than any intense sorrow. Raoul's obligation was to the ex-mayor and his cronies; mine was to Raoul.

This was my second funeral in two months, my fifth in a year and a half, a rapid acceleration in my attendance of requiems that I was hoping did not portend a trend.

Marilyn London's funeral was as different from Paul Weinman's as it could have been. Paul's ceremony had been marked by a simple pine casket and by heartfelt eulogies from his close friends. Marilyn London's production was marked by a bronze casket that seemed to be lined with goose down and satin and by lots of inspirational music sung to solo guitar accompaniment. So many flowers carpeted the altar that one couldn't be sure a float from the Tournament of Roses Parade hadn't been hijacked and disassembled.

But the biggest difference was that Marilyn London's funeral was an open-casket affair. I could understand the needs of the family, and perhaps of a few close friends, to view Ms. London's remains one last time, but it seemed to me that the intimacy of a back room at the church would have been the ideal location for those final good-byes. Instead someone's dubious wisdom mandated that about three hundred curious and intrepid attendees line up on one side of the casket and chug slowly past Marilyn London's unmoving corpus.

The line moved sluggishly, it apparently not being proper to zip past an open coffin, and given that Raoul and I joined the procession at the back of the church, our march to the altar was tedious. Until Raoul and I made our final turn to the casket, I distracted myself by examining the workmanship on the stained glass and by critiquing the paucity of imagination used on the floral arrangements. Raoul was in front of me in line, and when he reached the spot for viewing he paused momentarily next to Marilyn's body, seemed to bow almost imperceptibly, then pursed his lips an amount that managed to comport his face into an expression that appeared perfectly respectful and somber. As my turn came I decided to attempt to acquit myself in a similar fashion. I lived under the illusion that Europeans in general and Raoul in particular were born with a sense of propriety that was worthy of plagiary.

As I moved next to the raised lid, I looked first at Marilyn London's neatly folded hands and carefully manicured nails and at the pink dress someone had chosen as her eternal wardrobe. I flashed briefly on the other time I had seen her, only—what?—two days before, when she had been lying facedown in the weeds above Chautauqua. Taking another measured step, I let my gaze move up to her placid, waxy face, already bowing my head slightly, preparing to purse my lips in choreographed respect.

Instead, much too loudly, I said, "Holy shit!" My solitary voice carried, I was certain, to every sacred corner of the sanctuary.

Once I registered my own shock at what I saw, and humiliation at what I had said, my next thought was: Adrienne would love this.

After the conclusion of my brief but dissilient seizure, the remainder of the service was blessedly uneventful. Raoul had managed to transform the black comedy of my fleeting soliloquy into bad soap opera; immediately after my outburst he placed his broad right arm over my shoulder and guided me back to our pew in the rear of the church—the whole time murmuring something unintelligible into my ear in Spanish as if I were overcome with grief and he were comforting me. Twice after we were seated I turned to him in order to explain my outcry over the open casket, and twice he lowered his eyelids to half-staff and raised a finger to his lips to hush me.

Seconds before the mourners would begin to file out to the sidewalk to assemble prior to climbing into their cars to form a headlights-on-in-the-daytime traffic-numbing procession to the cemetery, he guided me out the main doors of the church with a strong hand to my left elbow. The moment we exited the church a handsome young man with an expensive haircut who had apparently been patiently awaiting our appearance mounted an inverted plastic milk crate, brought his hands together in front of him to cradle a Bible, and said in a serene voice, "The good book says you *must* be born again in order to enter the Kingdom of Heaven." He nodded piously to us, apparently assured he had just preached a great truth.

I wondered if God was getting even with me.

Raoul seemed to read my thoughts. "Alain," he said to me, brushing past the sidewalk evangelist, "pay no attention. God is, this moment, having second thoughts about permitting your birth the first time. I suggest we keep walking."

My plan for the day had been to try to see Randy at the hospital after the funeral, over lunch hour. Raoul had been visiting Diane since early morning and had walked to the funeral from the hospital. After our hurried departures from the exequies, we strolled together down Broadway back toward the hospital.

Raoul released some of the pressure on my elbow as soon as we had crossed the street next to the church. But he didn't totally let go of my elbow for about a block.

We were waiting for a break in the traffic to cross Broadway when Raoul said, finally, "So Alain, first time with the lid up?"

"No . . . no," I said. I'd used the brief conversational void to continue to organize my thoughts about what I had seen in the church. "When I, um, saw her face, I realized that I already knew her," I said to Raoul. "It wasn't just some stranger's funeral anymore."

"You had met her somewhere before? And had forgotten?" he asked hopefully.

"Sort of. But not really. I'd met her, yes. But I hadn't forgotten."

Raoul was nothing if not polite. I was making no sense, and he was nodding as if I were Oppenheimer and the subject were introductory physics.

"See, when I met her she was using a different name."

Raoul thought for a moment and then, his face suddenly serene, said, "Ahh, you knew her before she was married! Maybe knew her— Ahhhh, I see." He was certain he finally had it.

I smiled at him. "No. You don't see, my friend. I may be as naive as you think, but I'm not quite so, shall we say, libertine. I met her only recently—and not romantically—but she introduced herself to me by a different name. So when I walked by the casket and saw her face, I was shocked to find out that the woman who was murdered was this woman I had met. And I was shocked to discover that she had misled me."

And I was shocked to realize that one of my esteemed colleagues might have had a motive to kill her. But I didn't tell Raoul that.

"What had she called herself?" he asked.

"Lynn. She called herself Lynn," I replied.

He nodded as if that made perfect sense to him.

So. What did I know? The ex-mayor's dead wife, Marilyn London, had introduced herself to me as Lynn Hughes, complaining about being trapped in a sexually exploitative relationship with one of my colleagues. In her subsequent frantic phone call to me a few weeks later, she had expressed terror that her therapist knew that she had revealed the nature of their relationship to me. And she said she was scared that her psychotherapist would do something that would severely impinge on her financial security.

Okay. I knew all that. I knew she had been murdered —shot twice on a hiking trail between Chautauqua and the base of the Flatirons. And I knew of at least one somebody with a motive to kill her—her therapist. I also guessed that since she was the wife of the target of a current grand jury investigation, there might be others with possible motives to kill her.

I also knew that somebody had been taking exceptional risks to discover something that was in either my files or Diane's files. Maybe it was Marilyn London's therapist trying to find out what I knew about his abusive treatment of her. But why would that person break into Diane's house?

This was headache material.

I tried to use ethical considerations to organize everything I knew. Even though Marilyn London had lied to me and had seen me only for a consultation, she was still entitled to the confidentiality of her communication with me. Which meant I couldn't release the details of my meeting with her without the permission of the personal representative named in her will. Which meant I couldn't make public the fact that I could surmise a motive and possibly a suspect for her murder. But her husband, if indeed her husband was in charge of running her estate, *could* authorize me to release what I knew to the police. So I had an out. Great. I would just go and talk to Russell London. This puzzle wasn't going to be so hard, after all.

Right.

Unless, of course, Russell London had reasons of his own for not wanting me to tell the police what I knew. Which I had a funny feeling he would.

Diane had been moved to a private room. She was perky and impatient for discharge. There was a pizza box on the windowsill. She asked about the funeral and watched as Raoul smirked, his dark eyes cuing me.

"I created a bit of a scene," I said.

She looked back and forth between Raoul and me, eager for details. If Diane were forced to choose between oxygen and gossip, she would choose gossip. It would be second on her list of essentials, though, just after food.

Raoul's face was mischievous; he was dying to tell her what I had done. To spare myself an instant replay of my recent humiliation at the church, I excused myself and walked up the stairs for my appointment with Randy.

"We were doing a crossword puzzle. Lily, my sister, and me. When the engine blew on Creamed Corn, we were doing a crossword puzzle." It was the first time I had heard him say his sister's name without being prompted. Randy and I were meeting in a small, windowless room on the adolescent psych unit. Each of us sat on a chrome-framed chair with molded orange plastic seats and backs. A broken clock radio sat on a chipped and scratched laminated coffee table next to a lamp that probably hadn't worked since Watergate.

"You're starting to remember more about the crash," I said softly, stating the obvious, wanting to stay with him without getting in his way. While I spoke, a piercing post-pubertal shriek flashed in from someone outside the door.

Randy nodded at my comment, ignoring the noise outside. "It's like I need to know, you know, what happened. But I don't really want to. The fear is going away about it. I mean, what could be worse than what actually happened?"

The nursing staff had reported no return of Randy's recent dissociative episodes since his admission, which did not surprise me. By all accounts, Randy was comfortable in the hospital; in fact, he seemed relieved to be there.

"These kids don't seem crazy," he said about his fellow patients, including, I imagined, the one in some distress outside the door.

"They're not, Randy. Neither are you." I knew that the odds were that one or two of the other kids *were* crazy, but Randy would discover that on his own time soon enough.

"I'm afraid I am sometimes."

"Yes, I believe that."

"My uncle thinks I'm batshit."

"Well . . . how do you feel about him?"

His eyes were subdued. "I'm kinda stuck with him, aren't I?"

He turned away from me and stared at his oversize feet

and his untied ankle-high pump sneakers. Then he said, "Maybe, I've been thinking, maybe the lace I've been seeing—maybe it was a word on the crossword puzzle that Lily and me were doing. You know, like *l-a-c-e*."

"Does that ring true?" I asked, trying to keep the skepticism from my voice.

"No. It just makes sense, it's easy. Lets me turn another page. I mean, let's face it, who's left to tell me what's real? My version of what happened is it." He looked up from his feet and smiled at me and said, "Shit. You know what? That's a laugh. All the family memories are stored right here." He pointed at his temple with his index finger. "But my hard drive has crashed."

32

For a few days it felt as if my life were returning to a semblance of normal.

Purdy was up to his big ears in the investigation of Marilyn London's murder. Scott Truscott had managed to woo an experienced forensic investigator away from Arapahoe County and said that if his office experienced only a typical number of unattended deaths that week, he might be able to spare me from having to pick up any new cases. Merideth had been summoned back to San Francisco to produce the network's coverage of the judicial escapades of California's latest mass killer. Diane was happy to be alive and was, therefore, bitching incessantly about her prolonged incarceration in the hospital.

I had an abundance of sympathy for Diane's neurologist and her nurses.

Russell London was, according to someone in the county commissioner's office, "unavailable for the time being." His secretary/assistant suggested that his grief over his wife's death was responsible and asked if someone else could help. I said no. Despite his own legal problems, I clung to my hope that once Russell London was out of seclusion he would have no reluctance to give me permission to talk to the police about his dead wife's fears about her therapist. So I decided to go ahead and give Purdy a little preview in a phone message.

In my message I told Purdy simply that I'd heard she was in psychotherapy, though I didn't know with whom, and he might want to track down her therapist—maybe he might know something. I felt guilty about the ethical lapse for about five minutes.

I had given a lot of thought to the discovery of the missing half of Diane's key chain. Ultimately I had concluded that sparse progress was likely to be made on that puzzle until Diane was out of the hospital and capable of doing an inventory of her home and office records to determine if anything was missing. I was actually doubtful that her search would help much. The possibility was real that the burglar was more interested in *reading* Diane's records than in usurping them. If so, and if he or she had been reasonably tidy, Diane would have little or no idea what might have been read.

Lauren, long distance from New York, was acting like a star athlete kept out of the big game by a nagging injury. Grand jury witnesses were falling like autumn leaves, the wife of one of Boulder's best-known politicians had been murdered, one of Lauren's own best friends had been assaulted during a suspicious burglary, Lauren's lover's office had been ransacked, Lauren's lover's almost ex-wife was back on the scene to no imagined good end—and Lauren was missing it all, trapped in New York City in a mid-priced hotel while suffering from severe museum fatigue.

She said she was coming back on Friday no matter what.

On Thursday I decided to take advantage of the lull in my storms to catch up on some delayed business. I called Rita Templeton after my last patient to thank her for her assistance with Randy Navens. Somehow I wasn't surprised that she was concerned mostly about his toe.

"They taped it. I think it will be fine," I told her.

"I'm so glad," she said.

"I'm calling about some other things as well."

"Yes, Doctor." She seemed pleased that the conversation wasn't over.

"I'm wondering how Erin and Brian are doing. I wanted to know if Erin followed through on the referral I made. And I wanted to see if Brian is feeling any better."

Rita paused momentarily. "I think they're both doing better. Brian's sleeping through the night now, and he's spending time with his friends again. Erin is, oh, Erin is —she's seeing someone, her name's Mona, I think, one of the names you gave her. Erin's real angry at her dad, right now. For dying I guess. I don't know about her," Rita said, her voice trailing off.

"And you, Rita, how are you?"

Her voice cracked. "It's hard," she said. "Very, very hard. And this insurance mess with Larry. It's so hard to piece together the financial records because so much was destroyed in the explosion. And you want to hear a good news–bad news story? His life insurance company decided to pay on the claim. And then they tell me Larry had borrowed away much of the value. And I don't know where the money is because I don't have his paperwork. And I'm lonely living up here. I think that's the worst part."

I was troubled by an uncomfortable sense that she might view me as a partial solution to her loneliness problem. I questioned her about somatic symptoms and ended up telling her that I didn't think she required psychotherapy but that if she thought it would be helpful, I would be happy to give her some names.

"Could I see you, Alan—Doctor?"

"No," I said a bit too quickly, "given our relationship, that wouldn't be appropriate."

"What *relationship?*" she asked.

"We know each other already. That precludes a psychotherapy relationship. But I will be happy to give you names of two or three very good therapists."

Too quickly she said, "I'll think about it. I'll let you know."

"Okay," I said softly, feeling the familiar pull I get from patients who would prefer I do something to make them feel better instead of doing something to help them *get* better. "By the way, Rita, have you seen Janet Lasker lately? The Mirabelle caretaker?"

"Well, it's funny you should ask. I had dinner with Russ London last night. He's up at the cabin for a while to try to recoup from his loss. We, Russ and I, seem to have a lot in common right now. Anyway, he asked me if I'd seen Janet, said he wanted to talk to her about being more considerate about where she was plowing the snow. I said, no, I hadn't seen her for a while, but I thought she was better with the plow than the last caretaker had been—he'd push the—"

What? "Russell London has a cabin up there?"

"Well, yes, the one with the black shutters across the way. I had such a crush on him when I was little. He's much older than me, but I thought he was the cutest—"

"Rita—I'm sorry to keep interrupting. Who owns the other cabins?"

"Well, there's ours. My maiden name was Holman, so it's the Holman cabin. And you know about Erica and Geoff Tobias. The cabin is the Tobias cabin. Her family name is Schleibman." I thought I detected just the slightest pause between "is" and "Schleibman." "And there's the Londons. And the Turners—they live in Arvada. And the Knorrs—Lydia Knorr and I were the best summer friends up here. And the Andersons' place. And the Bellhavens —the biggest place is the Bellhavens'. And I've always thought it has the best view. It was the doctor's house from the original camp."

"Bellhaven. Did you say Bellhaven?"

"Yes, the parents are Albert and Ruth. They have three children—"

"The Bellhavens, they're from . . . ?"

"Boulder. Do you know them?" I was afraid I *did* know them. Rita continued. "Nice family, and the kids are all so successful. I don't know how Al and Ruth did it—"

"The children, you were telling me their names."

"If you would stop interrupting, I could finish, Alan. Anyway—the Bellhaven kids, there's George, and Amanda, and the baby, Elliot."

I mouthed the word *Elliot* as Rita Templeton spoke it, wondering what it meant that the family of a deputy district attorney owned one of the Mirabelle cabins.

I had scribbled down the names of the proprietors of Mirabelle as Rita Templeton had recited them. I checked my list for any M's to match the initial in Larry Templeton's appointment book and came up with nothing. Since I had inelegantly chopped up Rita's recitation with my frequent interruptions, I had to call her back to find out the first names of all the rest of the owners, spouses, and children she could remember. On her list there were four first names beginning with M, but two of them were males and the other two were children. Before we hung up she asked me why I was so interested in Mirabelle's owners.

"Does it have something to do with Larry?"

"Rita," I equivocated, "at this point we don't know what might be important."

"But this has to do with my husband's death?"

Given the presence of Russell London's and Elliot Bellhaven's names on the list, I was no longer sure at all what I was dealing with. I said, "Maybe. I don't know, Rita. It's all getting pretty complicated."

She sighed and said, "I'll say."

After we hung up I immediately placed a call to Purdy. He wasn't in. I left him a message to call me back.

My beeper went off when I was in the produce department at Alfalfa's Market, looking at a little plastic bag of fresh basil, contemplating whether in the grand scheme of things it was worth thirty-one dollars a pound to taste fresh basil in the middle of winter. I rationalized that the bag actually held a small handful and weighed but an ounce. I threw it in my basket and went looking for a phone after checking to see what hothouse tomatoes were going to cost me.

Purdy came on the line and responded to my hello with an irritated harangue. "So whattya want? Gonna send me on another wild goose chase?"

"What?"

"This lady wasn't in therapy, Alan. We checked her checking account, her money market account, her husband's bank accounts. We ran a check on her health insurance. We went through her receipts and bills. Nobody knows a thing about her being in therapy with anybody. There's no notations on any of her calendars. Want to tell me a little bit about your source? I'd like to play around a little with him, maybe run the risk of a police brutality charge."

"Sorry it didn't pan out," I said meekly.

"Actually, I'm squeezing a bit here to make you squirm.

The insurance company records show that Russ was in counseling or whatever a few years ago. But nothing recently. We'll check it out. So whattya want now? I'm a busy man."

"I've been doing some more work on the Templeton thing."

"Yeah."

"I found out who owns the rest of the cabins up at that compound in Coal Creek Canyon I told you about. You know—where the Templetons have their vacation place?"

"I'm considering this conversation is like a tiny break from the more important task of solving a murder. So you can pretend you have my attention for, say, about thirty seconds. I'm counting, and I'm waiting to hear something worthwhile."

"Russell London owns one of those cabins, Sam."

"Shit." Dead air. "Really? Whattya know? Same place where Templeton has his?"

"Yes."

I heard him clap his hands together or pound once on his desk or something equally exclamatory. "So what do you fucking know?"

"And . . ."

"And there's more?"

"There's more all right."

"Tell me!"

"Another one, it seems, is owned by Elliot Bellhaven's family."

Sam Purdy was as silent as snow is white. When he finally spoke he said simply, "Oh boy," then, "Oh boy oh boy."

"Yeah," I said. "Oh boy, Sam. Dogshit."

"You know who owns the rest of them?" he asked.

"I have a list."

"When it's in my hands I'll forget who gave me that tip about the therapist."

"I'll drop it by your office on my way home."

"I won't be here. Give it to Madeleine at the desk. Good work, Doc."

I said, "Thanks, no problem," to the dead line.

After I hung up I wandered back into Alfalfa's, wondering why Marilyn London had told me so many lies. I reconsidered about the basil and put it back where I had found it. The number I took at the takeout counter was eighty-seven. When my turn came I ordered a pint of black bean chili.

My only stop on the way home was to drop off the list of Mirabelle's homesteaders with Madeleine at the police department.

A snowstorm bearing heavy, wet snow rushed in after dinner. I'd eaten the takeout chili with saltines and beer alone in my dining room while watching the corpulent clouds decide whether to spill over the divide and ruin everybody's rush hour the next day or stay up in the mountains and bless the ski areas with fresh powder. Once the storm had reached its decision to proceed into the plains, it wasted no time, shrouding the valley in minutes. My view was obscured by flakes and mist and darkness just as I finished my beer. I desperately wanted to eat something sweet but didn't have anything in the house. Adrienne could always be counted on to have a freezer stocked with frozen candy bars. But when I called nobody was home.

I tried Lauren in New York. No answer.

My beeper tolled. The Voicemail computer told me once that I didn't know my access code. I punched in the identical numbers once again to humor it and heard an unfamiliar female voice say, "I got your card. If you still want to talk with me about Larry Templeton, come on by my boyfriend's place on the Peak to Peak tomorrow morning. Don't bring the cop. I'm not fond of cops. I'll talk to you. I won't talk to him. Oh. This is Janet Lasker. You can't call me; the damn phone company shut off our phone."

Finally a break. Mirabelle's itinerant caretaker was willing to talk with me. Maybe I could finally clear up the question of the adulterous "M" in Larry Templeton's appointment calendar.

And suddenly I realized what was staring me in the face. "M" as in Marilyn. As in Marilyn London. As in the ex-mayor's dead wife. "M" as in murdered.

My craving to talk to Janet Lasker redoubled.

Lauren's flight was due in at two in the afternoon on Friday. The Denver airport was almost two hours' drive from Rollinsville. On dry roads. In the slushy mess developing outside, I probably had to allow two and a half or three hours. I decided to try to interview Janet Lasker at ten and be on my way to Denver to get Lauren by eleven.

I grabbed another beer and parked myself in front of the television. I was halfway through watching a commercially edited version of something starring Debra Winger when sizzling white noise on the screen indicated that the local cable TV company had fallen prey to the storm. I moved downstairs to my bedroom and read a novel until I fell asleep.

Four-wheel-drive cars have their advantages. During the summer and fall, having four-wheel drive opens hundreds of miles of jeep trails for exploration and abuse. In winter, unless snowdrifts are tickling the bottoms of their headlights, four-wheel-drive vehicles can usually find a way to smash along unimpeded. On winter roads carved into slush troughs filled with snow batter and muck, four-wheel drives provide a semblance of control not available to less dexterous vehicles.

And, on ice, having four-wheel drive greatly increases your measure of surprise when you spin out and slide into a utility pole.

But four-wheel-drive vehicles, like my Subaru wagon, have their disadvantages, too. The primary one is that because vehicles equipped like my Subaru *can* climb mountain roads in terrible weather, drivers like me develop the illusion that we *should* climb mountain roads in terrible weather. What might be prudent gets absolutely lost in the fog of what is possible.

So it was for me on my way to my rendezvous with Janet Lasker. By the time I was aside Barker Reservoir at the top of Boulder Canyon, I was edging along in an almost whiteout. Wind-whipped snow sheets that apparently hadn't even bothered to divide into flakes were confounding me into vertigo.

The Peak to Peak was in better shape than the Boulder

Canyon road had been. Snowplows had made at least one pass in each direction, and the blinding blankets of snow were less frequent than they had been in the canyon. I arrived at the driveway entrance to Janet Lasker's boyfriend's house about twenty minutes late for my ten o'clock appointment time.

My first problem was that I didn't know where to put the car when I arrived at the cluster of cabins. Waist-high hogbacks of snow pushed aside by the Highway Department plows lined both sides of the highway and blocked the entrance to the driveway, which was too steep to risk using in weather like this anyway. If I left the car next to one of the snow berms along the highway, the next snowplow to come along would bury my Subaru. Probably gleefully. I finally decided to pull the wagon up the hill a short way past the driveway where the road seemed wider and then back the Subaru through the lowest drift I could find, praying that the road crews would give me a break and not bury my car with their snowplows.

In preparation for this expedition I was dressed in knee-high fleece-lined leather boots, a down-filled coat with a hood, a sweater, and heavy corduroys. After pulling on my gloves, I headed out into the blizzard with the assurance that Boulder County was not paying me enough.

Using my newly perfected police investigatory techniques, I cheered myself and ascertained that someone was indeed home in the boyfriend's cabin. Smoke was definitely coming out of the chimney. I knocked on the door while keeping an eye on the twenty or so inches of snow piled precariously on the roof of the cabin. I assumed the snow on the roof was waiting to ambush me.

The cabin couldn't have been larger than twenty feet square, so I was perplexed why it was taking so long for Janet to answer the door.

"The *fuck* are you? . . . The *fuck* do you want?" finally said an unhappy, sleepy male voice through the unopened door.

"I have an appointment with Janet Lasker." My words sounded out of place as I said them. I'd spoken as if I were standing in front of a fashionable receptionist in a law firm or doctor's office, rather than speaking through a cracked wooden door to a profane mountain man.

"She's not here." I was rather sure I could hear anticipatory creaking on the roof.

"You don't understand. She called me and told me to meet her here this morning. I'm from the Boulder County Coroner's Office. My name is Alan Gregory."

"She's in Costa Rica."

"What? Will you open the door, please?"

"Are you kidding? It's too fucking cold."

"How long has she been in Costa Rica?"

"Two fucking weeks, at least."

"What's your name?"

"Fuck you."

I took two steps back from the door just in time to be spared the avalanche from the roof.

I cursed out loud as I trudged back up the long drive past the big house owned by the impolite defense attorney from Jefferson County, out the wagon wheel–adorned gates, and back up the steep hill to my Subaru. I had lots of questions. Had I gotten Janet Lasker's message wrong? Was she playing with me? Was it even really her message I'd received?

I had been away from the car a maximum of ten minutes, yet when I walked back up to it there were at least two inches of fresh snow on the windshield. While I brushed off the car a big orange snowplow emerged from the whiteness like an apparition. When I saw the light of the rotating blue beacon pulse through the snow, I feared the worst— that I was about to be buried by a tsunami from its plow. But when the truck drove slowly up to where the Subaru was parked, I could see that its big blade was up. The driver had slowed to drop some flares on the downhill slope of the road before continuing up the hill past me.

The decision to follow him wasn't an arduous one. With luck the snowplow driver would plow the road ahead of me the whole way to Interstate 70, which I could then catch east straight to the airport to pick up Lauren. The fact that something undoubtedly hazardous was causing him to lay flares back in the direction of Boulder Canyon reinforced my reluctance to use the road again in that direction anyway.

A minute later he disappeared up the steep hill to the south. I quickly decided to follow him.

But for some reason the big truck wasn't plowing. The road under me was thick with snow. Why didn't the jerk put his blade down? I was pretty sure that the plow part of the truck was designed to work best with the blade down.

Up ahead of me, at the edge of a thick stand of trees, I saw the blue light of the rotating beacon of the truck as the driver struggled to clear what appeared to be a five-foot-high drift of snow that stood like a roadblock across the highway. I stopped my car, switched on my hazard flashers, and waited gratefully for the snowplow to do its thing. For some reason the driver seemed intent on shoving the snow clear across the highway rather than just dumping it down the steep cliff that rose to the south of the old hunting lodge where I was supposed to have met Janet Lasker.

The big orange truck appeared and disappeared as the wind whipped shrouds of blinding snow aloft and then permitted them to quiet. After a period of a minute when the truck wasn't visible, I assumed it had completed its task and had moved on down the highway. Just then it startled me breathless as it rose up out of the frozen mist not five feet from my front bumper, stopped momentarily, and then moved forward, apparently clearing a lane for me to use along the shoulder of the highway. Catching my breath, I edged the wagon up into the newly cleared lane just as the immense orange truck mysteriously disappeared again across the highway.

Twenty-five or thirty feet into the newly carved lane I realized my advance had been premature. A pile of snow as high as my eyes blocked the highway in front of me, and another one rose almost as high on the driver's side. I looked around for an alternative route, found none, looked and listened in vain for the big orange plow, and had just thrust in the clutch to shove the gearshift into reverse when I heard a roar like thunder to my left.

A huge wall of white was coming straight at the side of the car.

I thought, Shit! Avalanche, and then I saw, as if in slow motion, the blade of the plow, ice-crusted and rusty and glistening and roaring and mean. I hit my horn to warn the driver that my car had moved into his path, and I fumbled to find reverse. I punched in the clutch just as the glacier of snow lifted the car as though it were being levitated and carried along on a great white wave. I heard the scrape of metal on metal and looked up and out the driver's side window and saw a dark face silhouetted in the cab of the plow.

He knew I was there.

In two seconds the blade and the wagon and I reached the edge of the cliff and the Subaru began to tilt and then, slowly, to fall. I fumbled frantically with the controls of the car, checking with my gloved fingers to see if it was still in four-wheel drive, as if driving skill were anything but immaterial when the car was sideways, going down a cliff, in a blizzard.

33

In the air everything was soft and white. The glare of the headlights reflected back at me as if off a screen. After one or two seconds in the air the hard concussion of hitting the ground was cushioned by the deep blanket of fresh snow. Still, my head bounced sharply off the glass of the driver's door.

Immediately the car hit something solid—a deep jolt that thrust me hard against the shoulder harness toward the center of the car—and the roar of crunching metal just preceded a snapshot image of an immense ice-crusted boulder crushing the passenger side door. The car spun off the rock, and in an instant I was moving again, upside-down now, sliding, not tumbling.

And then a rumble like thunder and another tumble, and the car sped up and my right foot fought to find a way to brake against the rapid acceleration. My body was confused at the richness of movement, and my eyes watched the white light fade but found no signals to tell me what was up and what was down and what was spinning and what was tumbling.

What had been white was suddenly black. So much black.

And then, in an instant, no more thunder, no more protesting metal. Quiet. Absolute quiet. And still.

I guess that I slept for a while, finally waking to feel something warm on my face near my right ear. I attended distractedly and felt the warmth migrate across my cheek and then above my lip into my mustache. And then out and away, the track no longer warm. My brain was reluctant to make sense of the migration of the fluid on my face. Finally I figured it out.

I had awakened on my side, left side down. And I was bleeding.

Everything was dark. Black dark, my eyes unaccustomed. I looked all around the car. Nothing but blackness. I felt for the switch and turned on the dome light and looked around again. The window glass was shattered in places, but not broken through. Some snow had edged in around the misshapen frame of the crushed passenger door. But the car was largely intact.

There was so much white. For a blessed moment that perplexed me.

And then I knew. I was buried. The Subaru had become a four-wheel-drive coffin.

Air. I gasped. I was going to suffocate.

Calm down, don't gasp. It will use up your air, stupid.

I tried to get calm. I wasted a minute trying to figure how many cubic feet of space were in the car so I could compute how many minutes of oxygen I might have left and then realized I had no idea how to figure any of it.

My head started to hurt.

I was dying.

How to get out?

Stay calm. Breathe slowly.

I unbuckled the seat belt and climbed onto the backseat. If I slid down the passenger window to check above me, snow would come in, air would go out, and I would die faster. But what if I was only buried in an inch or two or even a foot or two of snow?

I needed to know.

Trapped below the front passenger seat I found the accordion-shaped cardboard I used to shade the windshield from the summer sun, tore off two of the articulated sections, and then crouched, my feet on the glass of the back door on the driver's side, and slowly rotated the crank of the window on the passenger side until it was open about four inches. As it opened I slid a section of cardboard into the open space to keep the snow outside. At the back end I left an opening about four inches by four inches. I bent the other torn section of cardboard into a tube and pushed it up and out the opening, praying for a rush of light. In seconds the tube was out the window and my arm was mostly out the window and still there was no light.

I fought panic.

I took the rest of the cardboard window shade, opened it to its full length in the cramped car, and with frozen fingers began to roll it against the grain. It seemed to take hours to bend the thing into an almost four-foot-long tube. I began to shove it out the crack in the window up into the snow, but the resistance was strong and it didn't want to go. I put my shoulder into the cardboard pipe and managed to budge it a little farther and a little farther until, inch by inch, the tube was out the window. I peered up through as if it were the eyepiece of a telescope, and I thought I saw light, but what I saw I soon decided was nothing but fantasy and sunshine carved from wishes.

I was under at least four feet of snow.

The Subaru and I had triggered an avalanche. In my panic and incipient asphyxia I temporarily forgot how much assistance the snowplow had provided.

But, I reminded myself, at least I knew which way was up. And I knew I had to dig out or I was going to die.

It was my last deliberate thought before I lost track of time.

The dome light seemed to fade. As did I. How long had I been knocked out? I told myself my malaise was despair, but I had trouble staying focused. I heard waves crashing. Swish, crash. Swish, crash. Faraway voices, a dog barking. People playing on the sand. I thought I could feel the warmth of the sun upon my neck, but then it faded, too. Clouds covered the sky, everything was getting gray. I set down the book I was reading and decided to sleep. Just for a few minutes. Only for a few minutes.

A dog barked on the beach. My eyes wouldn't open to find it. Just a dog. And then a loud *thunk!* and my eyes wouldn't be bothered. And another *thunk!* and the voices, the people, were coming closer to where I lay. *Thunk! Thunk!* Swish, *thwop.* Swish, *thwop.* Glass broke. Shit, folks, be careful.

"Is he alive?" a woman asked in a frantic voice, and I realized someone must have drowned in the rough sea. Then I noticed that the sun had come back out, but that the air was cold and the surf must have been big because the spray was hitting my face. Something hard jostled my shoulder, and someone, the woman again, said, "He's alive! He's alive! Good girl! Good girl!"

I opened my eyes and said, "That's good, I'm glad," and looked up into what I was sure was the sun.

Casey Sparrow was stronger than she looked.

Despite the bitter chill and the falling snow, she was hatless, and the crown of flakes on her bright red hair gave her the appearance of a veiled Catholic schoolgirl on the way to Mass. Her skin was pale and pink but seemed rich and alive against the surrounding world of white.

Her dog was golden and happy and smaller than my dead dog, Cicero. Casey Sparrow was outfitted with snowshoes. The dog and I weren't, and as we trod alongside Casey, we kept sinking into the deep snow. Me to my thighs, the dog to its ears. Casey Sparrow was serene and athletic, and she easily supported my weight as she mundanely asked questions, appearing to be administering a mental status exam to me as we trudged the hundred yards to her house. She asked me my name and if I knew where I was and what day was it and could I add numbers. I answered all her questions and gratefully let her keep score.

The treeless slope above us fell at a fifty- or sixty-degree angle from the highway. I tried to imagine driving off the edge of the cliff and living. I couldn't do it.

If, as part of her mental status examination, Casey Sparrow had asked me how long it took to get to the warmth of her old log cabin, I would have said, "A month."

The house was made of aged logs and had big windows

facing the divide. The living room was full of chairs and sofas and looked as though it were lived in by a family of twelve with rather diverse interests and a good sense of compromise. The room was full of stuff—a lot of old western paraphernalia—saddles, wagon wheels, bony parts of dead animals—and Native American and Mexican Indian folk art, and antique globes and ancient maps, and Far Eastern rugs, and shelves and shelves full of books. The room was so welcoming and warm and lived in that on another day I could have been toasty there even without the hot fire in the big stone fireplace.

But that day I was grateful for my perch on the big overstuffed sofa in front of the fire. Casey Sparrow was even quieter in her house than she had been on the mountain. She pulled off my boots and told me to remove my wet corduroys and threw a blanket my way before she walked out of the room. She reappeared in moments with a brown plastic bottle of peroxide and some cotton balls and began working on my face. Her skin was inches from mine, and her eyes were green like early spring.

I winced at her touch and said, "Thank you."

She said, still intent on my bloody face, "I think you're gonna need stitches, maybe even a plastic surgeon." She darted her eyes over to catch mine for an instant and said, "And you're welcome. You know anybody in town who can stitch this up, check you for a concussion?"

I said, "I was knocked out for a while, I think. But I have a friend who's a urologist." As the words exited my mouth I thought that they alone were pretty convincing evidence of brain damage.

Without a change of expression she said, "Well, you can check the condition of those parts yourself." She stood up and left the room again.

A minute later she was back with some bandages. "I only have one butterfly. I'll put it on until we can get you to a doctor." She bent down with the bandage and said, "You're the psychologist, the coroner guy, aren't you?"

"Yes," I said, "Alan Gregory. You're Casey Sparrow."

"Yes."

"I came to talk with Janet Lasker. I had a meeting set with her this morning."

"You did? You sure? I haven't seen her car for a while. So what happened—you missed the driveway?" Despite the overt skepticism, I heard concern in her sweet voice.

"Somebody tried to kill me, I think."

She smiled at me for the first time. A sympathetic, barely patronizing smile. "You haven't had a good day, have you?" she said.

Casey hesitated a moment before she continued. "You know, when I saw the slide start—I was sitting at the table over there looking outside; we get slides on that slope every winter—when I saw the slide start I thought for a moment that I had hallucinated the car. It was there and then it was gone just like that." She snapped long fingers with short, unpainted nails. "But I decided to go check. So Toby and I went out to look around, and she went nuts at this place over the pond, digging and barking, so I went back and got a shovel and started to dig, and about two feet down I found this cardboard windshield thing all folded up and I thought it might have come from a car so I kept digging and Toby kept going nuts, and then I realized we were right on top of the pond and I was afraid if there was a car that it might have cracked the ice and I almost stopped digging."

I said, "I'm pretty glad you didn't."

"I turned the shovel upside-down and pushed down into the snow with the handle—you know, like you see the rescue people do when they look for avalanche victims on the news?—and I hit something hard a few times, so I kept going."

"Thank you."

"Yeah. Want some coffee? Tea?"

I nodded yes.

In a few minutes she returned with two mugs, gave me one, and then she sat on the floor a few feet from the fire. Toby, his heroics over, slept next to her. "So tell me what happened," she said.

I did.

She listened patiently and said, "In my line of work, I hear a lot of crazy stories."

"Yeah, me too," I said.

She sipped her coffee and asked, "Would *you* believe this one?"

"Casey—may I call you Casey?—let me put it this way. I'm beginning to believe that my judgment is, at times, kind of warped, and reluctantly I'll admit that my sense of self-preservation hasn't been particularly sharp lately, but I try to be pretty honest, especially with strangers who save my life."

She looked like she was considering what I said. "Then we need to call the sheriff. Should be a finite number of people out with big orange snowplows on days like this."

I took a drink of coffee and nodded. The nodding hurt. "Why aren't you at work?" I asked.

"In a storm like this? Only crazy people go out in weather like this." She smiled at me, amply communicating that she had residual questions about my sanity. But the room warmed a degree each time she smiled.

"How did you know to do that mental status stuff? After you pulled me out."

"I was a clinical social worker in a previous life," she said.

Then I remembered that I needed to meet Lauren and said, "Oh, shit, I was on my way to the airport. I need to pick someone up."

"You were on your way to the airport?" she said with undisguised disbelief. "If this is a new story you're fabricating, it needs some work—most people from Boulder tend to choose routes to Denver that don't involve any mountain driving."

"No, no. *After* my meeting with Janet Lasker I was going to go pick someone up at the airport. She was due in at two."

"It's twelve-thirty now. You're going to be late. Real late."

"I've got to leave."

Casey gazed at me, amused. She said, "You're in no shape to drive. And you don't exactly have a car."

Casey Sparrow was thinking a lot more clearly than me.

"Lauren," I said, "is going to kill me."

"Lauren?" she said.

I hadn't considered the possibility that Casey knew Lauren. I said, "Do you know Lauren Crowder? She's a lawyer, too, like you. Well, not exactly like you, she's a deputy DA in Boulder."

Casey Sparrow's smile kept getting warmer. "We've met," she said.

"In court?"

"No. No. I sat next to her at a bar association dinner last year." Casey looked away from me, remembering something. "I liked your Lauren Crowder a lot. She and I had a great time during dinner—some great conversation about some things I don't remember but that I think made me laugh a lot. She—your friend—is very bright, very sharp. We're both from Washington." Casey looked wistful, then continued, "We walked together to our cars after dinner. We got to her car first—she has an old Peugeot, doesn't she?"

Casey put the accent hard on the first syllable of Peugeot. "She sure does," I said.

"Anyway, I was feeling good and I asked her if she'd like to get together again sometime. She said that'd be great and gave me her business card. At first I couldn't find one to give her and I was looking around in my purse, and just out of the blue, I asked her if she would be upset if I told her that I was a lesbian.

"Lauren was so funny, she looked down at the card I was holding out to her like she expected it to say 'Casey Sparrow, Lesbian,' and then looked up and said to me, she said, 'No, Casey, I don't mind.' "

Casey watched me for a reaction. I tried not to swallow. But I swallowed.

"Then Lauren said to me—she was so sweet—she said, 'But, Casey, do you mind that I'm not?'

"And I smiled at her pretty face and told her that I thought the news was going to break my heart."

Casey Sparrow looked over my way and smiled that big warm smile at me. "And now, what do you know, it seems that I have her alternative sitting with his pants off in my living room in a blizzard.

"Life," she said, "is a scream."

34

Lauren Crowder received official news of the avalanche from Casey Sparrow via a white courtesy telephone. I assumed the experience was mildly disconcerting.

Lauren finally tracked me down in the emergency room at the hospital in Boulder, where Ms. Sparrow had delivered me to the medics in the comfort and safety of her 4×4 pickup in a storm that was abating as abruptly as it had arrived. At the hospital I spent quite a lot of time in "observation," which apparently consisted of being in a cold room by myself on a gurney.

By late afternoon I had finished giving a statement to the Gilpin County sheriff and a plastic surgeon handpicked by Adrienne was sewing up the gash on my temple. The neurologist who was treating Diane had already stopped by to examine me and confirm that I indeed had a mild concussion. He was altruistic enough, and cynical enough, to offer my partner and me group rates for future closed-head trauma.

Despite the fact that Lauren had been verbally abused on the drive to the airport in New York by a taxi driver whose name—she was embarrassed to report—she couldn't pronounce and whose country of origin—she was embarrassed to admit—she couldn't determine, had departed La Guardia half an hour late, had been seated on the crammed plane next to an obese person with a laptop and poor hygiene and behind someone whose seat back had never once approached the full upright position, and had landed in Denver in a blizzard to find that her ride home was on the way to the hospital, not the airport—

she looked beautiful. Her black hair shined, and her eyes were a soft blue gray. I was so happy to see her I could have cried.

She looked at me with a not unattractive blend of disapproval and compassion. The plastic surgeon had just finished embroidering my temple but had not yet come back in the room to bandage me. Lauren hugged me softly and kissed my forehead and my nose and finally my lips. I draped my arms around her neck.

"The night I left for New York you were off having dinner with a beautiful blonde. I come back and you're sitting half-naked in the mountain cabin of a bombshell redhead. I don't think you're to be trusted."

I said, "Lord, how I've missed you. You look gorgeous."

"Thanks. You don't. Does it hurt?"

"My head just a little, unless I move it. The cut is full of Xylocaine or whatever. But I'm starting to get a little sore from the ride down the mountain in the avalanche."

"Casey Sparrow said it was a snowplow that pushed you off the road and that you thought he did it on purpose?"

"Yes. Sound nuts?"

"Yes."

"Maybe I have brain damage. Did you get accepted into the medication trials?"

"They didn't say. I should hear something soon."

A deep voice overlapped with Lauren's from the doorway. "So-oh," Sam Purdy said, "it seems they found the snowplow. Guy who stole it left it on the Moffat Road near the Jenny Lind trail. The crime scene guys are going over it." He turned to Lauren and smiled warmly. "Welcome back, Counselor."

"Hello, Sam," said Lauren. "There really was a renegade snowplow?"

Purdy nodded and said, "Apparently he's not demented." He turned my way. "Not this time, anyway. You gonna live?"

"Well, thanks for getting around to asking, Sam. You almost lost your partner today. And I'm fine."

The detective leaned over and examined the stitching

on my temple. He scoffed, "You're not my partner. And you don't look fine. It looks like your doctor's name is Frankenstein and he's only half-done." Purdy scanned the treatment room for a chair but found only a small stainless-steel swivel stool. He spun the round seat up to a height more appropriate for his size and sat on the opposite side of the treatment table from Lauren.

"How much does she know?" he asked me, flicking a finger toward Lauren.

"The recent stuff, not much."

Purdy told Lauren edited versions of the break-ins at Diane's house and at the office and about Marilyn London's murder, about the multiple trails leading to Mirabelle, and about my being on my way to interview the Mirabelle caretaker about Larry Templeton's extramarital activities when I was the apparent victim of an attempted murder by snowplow. And about his suspicion that everything was somehow tied to the massacre in Diane's office and the explosion at Larry Templeton's house.

I suddenly realized that I hadn't divulged to Purdy my recent epiphany about Marilyn London and Larry Templeton and the initial "M" from Larry's appointment book, so I interrupted his lecture to Lauren. "Sam, Sam—wait. I forgot to tell you, but I think Marilyn London might be the 'M' we've been looking for. The Londons and the Templetons both had cabins up in Coal Creek, and now both Larry and Marilyn are dead. My hope this morning was that the caretaker had seen this mystery woman and could identify her for me."

"Yeah, makes sense. But, not surprisingly, I'm way ahead of you on all of this. So far we haven't been able to confirm that Marilyn is 'M,' either—but it's the best theory we've got. I've already started to track down the elusive Ms. Lasker so we can ask her a few things."

Lauren was following our conversation intently. She recognized a natural break and said, "Guys, is this little digression over? Sam, you were catching me up on this Mirabelle place and its connection to people in town."

"This last piece is sensitive. Okay?" He waited for an

almost imperceptible nod of acknowledgment from Lauren before he continued. "Elliot Bellhaven's family was one of the homesteaders at Mirabelle."

If Lauren was shocked by the news that one of her colleagues apparently shared a nest with suspected vipers, she didn't show it.

"I don't get it. Where does this Mirabelle place fit in this puzzle?" she asked.

"We're not sure yet," said Purdy. "So far all I've confirmed is that the Templetons, the Londons, the Tobiases, and the Bellhavens all have cabins up there."

I turned to Lauren. "Doesn't that pose a conflict for Elliot, Lauren? Ethically?"

"Maybe. Maybe not. It may just be the appearance of a conflict."

For some reason I thought of the savings and loan scandal and George Bush and his son Neil while simultaneously registering the slight change in timbre in Lauren's voice that indicated the blossom of defensiveness. And then with reckless abandon I ignored the warning.

I asked her, "How involved is Elliot with the grand jury that's investigating Russ London?"

Lauren glared at Purdy, assuming incorrectly that he had been the source of my knowing that Russ was the target of the grand jury inquiry. Since I wasn't about to reveal to Lauren or Purdy that I had a patient on the grand jury feeding me juicy morsels, if challenged by Lauren I planned to attribute my knowledge to speculation printed in the local paper.

Purdy simply shrugged his shoulders in response to Lauren's incriminating glare.

"Not much," Lauren finally said in response to my question about the propriety of Elliot's involvement in matters related to the grand jury. "None of us deputies are too involved at this point. Early on"—she seemed to hesitate and then decide to proceed—"we were just investigating some investment irregularities, some fraud involving the elderly. Back then, Russ London wasn't a target, wasn't even a focus. When we stumbled onto some questionable things that involved his old law firm, we immediately turned everything over to a special prosecutor appointed by the Court."

"Why did you do that?" I asked.

"It's customary. To avoid the appearance of impropriety or favoritism when a local bigwig is the focus of an investigation."

Purdy said, "So Elliot wasn't really involved in these investment probes?"

"He was early on. And lately he *has* been the most vocal campaigner in the office for calling the murder of Claire Draper a domestic dispute and for calling the death of Larry Templeton an accident."

"Well. Elliot's involved now," said Purdy.

"You mean because of this Mirabelle place?"

"Yeah, maybe, but more because he's the deputy DA working with me on Marilyn London's murder."

I turned back to Lauren. "Is that ethical? Can lawyers do that?"

"Do what?"

"Work on something that may be tied to them."

"It doesn't need to be a problem. There's no caveat against prosecuting the murderer of an acquaintance. Or against a lawyer representing a friend. But I'm surprised to hear it anyway because Elliot's really not senior enough to be assigned a case like that."

Sam smiled at Lauren and said, "Perhaps all the more qualified deputies were out of town."

She raised her eyebrows to concede the compliment.

I said, "We can't do that. Psychologists can't treat people we know socially or in business. We're required to avoid 'dual relationships' with patients. We're not allowed to wear two hats—friend and therapist, customer and therapist—with a patient."

"Lawyers do it all the time," Lauren said with a shrug.

Purdy wanted to get back to the matter at hand. "What do these investment irregularities involve?" he asked Lauren.

"Lately, I don't know where the investigation might have gone. Our office isn't kept informed of progress by the special prosecutor. At the beginning the investigation had to do with the questionable investment of assets of various retirement moneys."

Purdy said, "What? Buying drugs? Illegal arms sales?"

Lauren smiled at Purdy. "No, Sam. Just investing assets in ways not permitted by the fiduciary terms of the various plans. Mostly using plan assets as venture capital for start-ups. Pretty risky for retirement moneys. Some money was lost; some accusations made."

"Doesn't seem very serious."

"Wasn't. Isn't. Slap-on-the-wrist stuff if you say you're sorry and if you're not a politician who likes to be re-elected." Lauren stood up and faced me. "Now that I know you're gonna live for a few minutes, I need to run upstairs to see with my very own eyes that Diane's really all right. I'll be back down in a little while to take you home, Alan. So don't you go anywhere. 'Bye, Sam." She pecked a kiss to the air and walked off to find Diane's room.

Purdy's wave to Lauren was a dismissive gesture. He spun back to me on the stool. "So tell me about the snow-plow. From the beginning."

Purdy was gone and Lauren was upbeat after she returned from her visit with Diane. The plastic surgeon was standing over me, having just come back into the treatment room to give me a piece of paper covered with follow-up instructions intended to be so explicit that I couldn't sue him or the hospital even if my head fell off in the parking lot.

Lauren asked him, "Doctor, can your patient have sex?"

The plastic was wearing green scrubs. His mask hung around his neck. His thick, black-framed glasses were on top of his head.

He said, "Was he able to before his injury?"

Lauren smiled. "Sometimes."

He smiled back at her. "Then I suppose he can now. Hey, it's fine with me. As long as he doesn't use the side of his head. But I'm no expert about sex and concussions."

She smiled. "Well, he and I will just have to do some research and let you know. And I can assure you that I have no intention of using his head. Not the side of it, anyway."

I blushed.

I talked a nurse into pushing me in a wheelchair to the adolescent psych unit so I could check on Randy and explain why I wouldn't be meeting with him for our scheduled appointment that day. He listened to my avalanche tale with some fascination. He peppered me with questions about the snowplow, about crashing down the mountain, and about remembering and forgetting.

"Now you're like me," he said.

"What? You mean in the hospital like you?"

"No. You're a survivor. Like me."

"How does that feel?"

"Like I'm less alone." I recalled Lauren confessing that she feared for so many years that she was decomposing, and I thought I began to understand what she had meant.

"Why were you up there in this storm?" Randy asked.

I hesitated, unsure how much to reveal, and decided to tell him the truth.

"I went up there to interview a caretaker from the place where your aunt and uncle have their cabin. It's about some work I've been doing for the county. That's when the trouble with the snowplow started. I never talked to her, the caretaker. The police have begun to wonder if Mirabelle—the place where the cabins are—is somehow connected to some recent crimes in town, including that murder in Chautauqua—you know, that woman who was shot?"

He nodded, the backs of his hands now pressing against his eyes. He stood and looked at his feet, then at me. "I think that place is evil," he said. "May I please go back to my room?"

At my request a nurse wheeled me back downstairs to the ER, slowing long enough to complete a brief explanation that the emergency room was no longer a "room" but a "department" and that she would be transporting me back to the "ED," not the "ER." I tried to absorb the instruction but found that I was still distracted by Randy's words, and was finally beginning to recognize the extent of what I'd just been through and the unknown quality of what might lie ahead.

Diane Estevez and I were discharged late that afternoon.

Adrienne had just finished repairing the bladder of a pedestrian who had tried unsuccessfully to walk across an icy road faster than a minivan could fail to stop on it. The operation had gone well. And Adrienne was radiant not only from the gleam of her pregnancy, but also from the unlikely fact that both of her two brain-injured best friends were going home from the hospital with almost as many neurons as when they had arrived.

Raoul pulled his big truck under the canopy outside the ED, and we loaded Diane and three or four boxes of her yet uneaten get-well treats into the back. After hugs and kisses and good-byes, Lauren threw her luggage into Adrienne's Land Cruiser, and she and I piled in after it. Adrienne drove across the western edge of town and dropped Lauren off at her house so she could shower and get some fresh clothes. Then my little neighbor headed the big car across town to Spanish Hills, where we lived.

Adrienne insisted on being maternal when we got to my house. She supported me in the door, turned up the thermostat, asked if I wanted something to drink or eat, offered to bring more pillows up from the bedroom for the sofa, and wondered if she could run me a hot bath.

"Baby's getting to you, isn't it?" I said.

She looked annoyed. "Hey, can't a friend just be nice? Just act concerned without getting a ton of shit?"

"Adrienne, honey, you're a great friend. But nice? Adrienne, your mother wouldn't even call you 'nice.' Pay attention to what's going on here—you just offered *to bring me pillows and run me a hot bath*."

Her eyes widened. She laughed. "Oh, God," she said, her fingers clawing at her face in mock horror, "what's happening to me? Next thing you know I'll be baking cookies and delivering them to invalids."

"You can't bake."

"Or I'll become a Rotarian and raise money for burned kids."

"It's the Shriners, and I don't think they would have you."

"Maybe I'll suffer true estrogen poisoning and—"

"Change four million diapers and have the unidentified body fluids of a small relative spilled all over your best clothes."

"Yeah, that's it," she said, "that's the one. You're sure the prosecutor's coming over to check your plumbing, right? I don't have to do that? And the big cop is gonna keep an eye on you for a while?"

"I think I prefer Lauren's physical exams to yours."

"Ah, but you've never had mine."

I ignored that. "And Purdy promises I'll be protected from homicidal highway workers."

"You need anything, me and Geppetto and Pinocchio are right up the hill. But I'd feel better, you know, if Cicero was still here to eat the bad guys."

"Me too, Ren. Thanks."

She blew me a kiss and walked to the door. "If that DA of yours doesn't show up, you call us, hear?"

"Count on it," I said, and collapsed back on the sofa.

Lauren took a couple of hours to readjust to being home, which gave me some much needed time to myself. I took the hot bath that Adrienne had suggested, shaved my legs, took three generic painkillers, and spent the whole time wondering about the mess I seemed to be in. My bias from the start was to share Purdy's impressions that the deaths related to the grand jury were somehow also associated with the burglaries and the attempted homicides on Diane and me. But the only concrete bridges connecting any of the players were some half-century-old deeds and covenants to a renovated railroad camp in Coal Creek Canyon.

It wasn't much to go on.

I could argue that Diane had been sucked into the morass because of her treatment of Claire Draper and Harlan Draper's subsequent murderous madness. The burglaries at the office could have been staged to recover or at least take a look at Diane's files on Claire Draper. Someone in jeopardy of indictment could reasonably assume that Russell London or another suspect in the investigation might be wary of what Claire had revealed to Diane. If those suppositions were true, ransacking my office might have been just a diversion.

Or. Searching my office may have been the primary target of the break-ins—someone coming in looking for Lynn Hughes/Marilyn London's file. That would, of course, be her therapist—maybe Clancy Coates—checking to see what she might have told me about his abuse of her, or at least what I'd written down.

And then there was Deputy District Attorney Elliot Bellhaven. Did he own a piece of this puzzle, or was his appearance on the proprietor's list at Mirabelle just coincidence? Did he have some motive to try to thwart the investigation of the financial irregularities involving Russell London's law firm?

Suddenly, while I was studying the stitchwork on my temple, I remembered what Elaine Casselman had revealed about Russell London during her session the previous week. Russ London had been seeing Paul Weinman for psychotherapy; and Purdy had confirmed as much after he searched the Londons' health insurance records. I wondered for what malady Paul Weinman was treating Russ London. Those little brass keys in Diane's desk drawer, the keys to Paul Weinman's files, might hold some answers to that.

And, of course, the pounding in my head and the purple bruises emerging on my body insisted that I factor in the reality that someone had tried to kill me that morning with a snowplow. In my mind, nothing I knew or even conjectured made me dangerous enough to kill. Which meant one of three things. Either I knew something I didn't know I knew. Or I was about to discover something so important that it was worth killing me to keep me from my imminent discovery. Or the killer was wrong and I didn't know anything.

By the time Lauren knocked at my door with Chinese food in her hands and lust in her heart, I was almost too aggravated by the puzzle to think about either eating or sex.

But I didn't want to disappoint Lauren, so I managed to have a few bites.

I had switched on the answering machine before Lauren arrived that night. By the next morning I had a bunch of calls on the machine and on my Voicemail. In San Francisco Merideth had received word from the news director of the local affiliate about my joyride in the avalanche. On the tape Merideth's voice sounded irritated with my answering machine, sincerely concerned about me, and eager for story updates. Purdy said he had some news and invited me to breakfast. And Rita Templeton had called late the previous afternoon and left a message with my Voicemail asking that I give her a call. The local paper and the Denver dailies and some local TV people all wanted to talk to me, too.

Returning any of the calls to the media would have been a textbook example of victim-precipitated homicide. Merideth would've killed me if I spoke with anybody before I spoke with her.

Lauren and I took her Peugeot to meet Purdy for breakfast. Lauren ordered something called a breakfast salad. Purdy had burritos stuffed with scrambled eggs, beans, and green chili, and I had coffee and a bagel.

"The snowplow is telling us nothing," Purdy said. "It was missing from the county maintenance yard on the Peak to Peak about an hour before you and the car were pushed off the cliff. They didn't bother to report the plow missing, just figured one of the on-call drivers forgot to check it out. Paint on the plow blade matches the paint on your wagon. You know you went down like two hundred feet? You're a lucky fuck."

I knew that.

"And the boyfriend's phone works fine. Looks like you were set up by somebody like a tenpin." Purdy appeared to register sadistic joy at my naiveté.

Lauren said, "Off the record, Sam, what do you know about Marilyn London's murder?"

Purdy set down his fork and sat back in his chair. He reached for his coffee before he started. "Off the record, not enough. Shots were fired from below her on the hill from a semiautomatic handgun. We've got the casings. We have one mangled slug. The other one went right through her. We haven't found it. Ballistics are iffy so far. Time of death, evening. Residents nearby say they heard what could have been gunfire shortly after eight, which roughly corresponds to the estimate of time of death from the coroner. Her husband was out of town on business, so nobody reported her missing. No witnesses to the shooting. Yet, anyway. The body was dragged off the path. Fiber and trace evidence seems to be all hers, but the lab's still looking. There are eight million footprints on that trail. All in all, not much physical evidence to go on.

"Motive? Husband looks clean. Like I said, he has an alibi that's holding water without any leaks. Their marriage was shaky. But hey—whose marriage looks good under a microscope? Her life wasn't overinsured. So far there's no evidence he was stepping out on her or she on him. Friends describe them as typically and chronically estranged. There's the grand jury thing, but we don't have enough of the facts to know if any of it fits. Special prosecutor is going to brief me today but has warned me that I should expect to be disappointed.

"Friends say Ms. London often ran at night. A running buddy of hers says she carried ID and a can of mace in a little ass pack when she ran. If she did that night, it's missing, ass pack and all. So robbery's possible, but not likely. Trail's getting colder and colder. So to speak. And so's my burrito." He went back to work on his breakfast.

With his mouth full he asked Lauren, "Any thoughts on Elliot?"

Lauren swallowed a spoonful of yogurt and wiped her lips before she responded. "He was rookie of the year two years ago, Sam. And even though he's the youngest guy on the team, it seems—since he's managing this case we're all talking out of school about—it seems that now he's not only cracked the starting lineup, he's apparently batting cleanup."

Purdy looked from Lauren to me, back to her and back to me. I said, "She plays softball." He nodded his head slowly in one big sweep. Lauren shook her head in exasperation at his incredulity.

"Does Elliot play straight?" Purdy asked.

Lauren looked askance at Purdy and set down her spoon before answering him. "Sam, you know the rumors. Everybody is sure he's gay. Nobody I know actually *knows* that he's gay. And nobody really wants to know. He's smart, he works hard, he's always prepared in meetings and in court, and in the office it's clear he's got Roy's ear. And everybody in the office is willing to do almost anything to convince everybody else in the office that being gay in Boulder just isn't that big a deal anymore. Royal Peterson's probably only going to run for DA one more time. If you took a poll in our office, Elliot would probably get the nod as the guy most likely to succeed him, despite the fact he'll barely even be thirty."

Purdy murmured some acknowledgment and then looked forlornly at his plate, which was empty. I was surprised to find that Lauren was awed neither by the prodigiousness of Sam's appetite nor by his alimentary speed. She'd obviously dined with him before.

After breakfast Lauren took me to rent a car from an agency chosen by my auto insurer. The car I was given was a two-year-old subcompact that smelled like an ashtray fermented in pine deodorizer. After I was handed the keys I kissed Lauren warmly. She touched the side of my face with pronounced tenderness and her eyes glistened with tears as she said through a forced smile, "See you later." The parting felt oddly poignant, more as though she were saying good-bye to a lover she was never going to see again.

I followed her Peugeot back into town so each of us could go to work.

There was a note from Dana Beal on the side door of the building saying her key wouldn't work and what the hell were all the little stickers on the windows saying that there was an automatic alarm?

From my office I phoned her home and left a message on her machine that I would put her new keys and instructions about the alarm in the place in the old garage where we hid spare keys. Then I returned Rita Templeton's call.

She wanted me to explain why I wouldn't see her for psychotherapy. I told her about the prohibition concerning psychologists having "dual relationships" with patients. That since I was investigating her husband's death for the coroner's office, it was ethically inappropriate for me to offer her psychotherapy.

"I don't get it. Paul did it all the time. Half the people up here saw him at one time or another."

"Paul?"

"Paul Weinman. You didn't know him?"

Why did Paul Weinman keep popping up? I said, "I knew Paul. Are you saying he saw people from Mirabelle in psychotherapy?"

"Sure. He had a great reputation."

"You said he 'did it all the time.' Did what all the time?"

"Saw people he knew for counseling. The people up here."

"He knew all of you?"

"Alan, I thought you said you knew him?"

"Only professionally, Rita."

"He was separated from Lydia Weinman. Now Lydia Knorr. The Knorr cabin, remember?"

I was a little stunned. "So he knew all of you?"

"Of course. He and Lydia and the kids used the cabin a lot."

"And he saw some of the Mirabelle people in treatment?" I already knew that he had seen Russ London. Briefly, I had even considered that it was possible that Paul was the therapist abusing Marilyn London. The woman had misled me about everything else.

Rita answered my question with a tiny morsel of defiance in her voice. "Yes. He did. And if it was good enough for him, why isn't it good enough for you?"

I mumbled an explanation that I didn't think would be adequate to convince Rita Templeton of the validity of my ethical stance. And I wondered what the hell Paul Weinman had been up to. And with whom.

Diane would know. And if she didn't, she had custody of the files where she could look it up. But if Paul had been doing what I was beginning to fear he had been doing, he would have had to be crazy to write any of it down.

35

Diane arrived at work while I was making coffee. Raoul had driven her into town.

She walked into the kitchen and I said, "I'm not sure it's a good idea for you to be at work."

She had steeled herself for my paternalism and replied, "And who's talking? At least my bruises have had the time and good manners to yellow."

I made a face and said, "You're not planning to work all day, are you?"

"No. Just want to see a couple of patients who don't quite believe I didn't die. Coming in and showing them my face is easier than dealing with their daily phone calls. And what about you? I'm not convinced you should be here, either."

I shrugged my sore shoulders and poured her a cup of coffee, dumping in one heaping teaspoon of sugar. I left the plastic spoon in the cup. It took Diane longer to stir coffee than it took me to drink it. She had some theory about stirring and molecules in motion and how much energy it took to achieve true dispersal of sucrose.

"May I ask you a question about Paul Weinman?" I said.

She interrupted her stirring and said, "Should I sit? This sounds ominous."

"You're the custodian of his clinical records, aren't you?"

Diane nodded and resumed stirring.

"Is it possible," I asked, "that these burglaries have to do with someone wanting something that's in *his* files, not yours or mine?"

She finally took a sip from her mug, opened her eyes wide, and said, "You know, I never even considered that. But sure, it's possible, I guess."

"Where are they? Paul's records?"

"All over the place. Paul had been in practice a zillion years. The man had a ton of records. His antique records—the really old ones—are in three huge filing cabinets in the basement of Cybil's house on the Hill. You know, Cybil, his girlfriend? He was sort of living with her when he died. She told me I could leave them there. So I just went over with Raoul and he put new padlocks on the file cabinets.

"The records from Paul's closed cases from the last three years or so are in two file boxes in the closet of my office at home. I wanted to keep them kind of accessible; I figured they were the ones I would be more likely to get calls about. And the files of the patients he was seeing at the time of his death, who I assumed I would be most likely to get a lot of calls about, are here, in a file box, in the locked closet under the stairs."

I thought for a moment, then said, "Could you tell what files the burglar messed around with at your house? When you got home from the hospital last night—did you look?"

"Sure I checked. But I didn't see anything missing. The asshole did bust the lock open on my file cabinet. But I don't know what he looked at."

"Did he go into the closet after Paul's files?"

"Not unless he was real tidy. They didn't look disturbed."

I was still considering Paul Weinman's files and said, "I didn't think to check in the closet under the stairs here after the last burglary. But the master key opens that closet, doesn't it?" Diane nodded. I continued, "And our latest intruder apparently had the master key with him."

Diane turned and rushed down the hall ahead of me. She detoured into her office to get her key ring. She found the shiny new building master and moved down the hall to the side of the staircase, threaded in the key, and twisted open the lock. The closet was triangular and shelved. We kept office supplies and stationery in it. The corrugated file box was on the floor level. It was neatly marked "Case Files, Paul Weinman, Ph.D."

"Should I touch it?" she asked. "I don't want to screw up any evidence."

"I don't know. Maybe pull it out from the bottom," I suggested.

She did, then unwound the red strings that stretched around tabs to keep the box closed. She flicked the top open with her fingernails and gazed in at the files that, by my standards, at least, looked orderly and unmolested.

"Well?" I said.

"Don't know," she said.

"Have you been through these?" I asked.

"You mean like have I read them?"

"Yeah."

"No. There was no need."

The whole time we were having this little interchange I was reading the typed file labels that ran down the right side of each file. It was an inappropriate thing to do. But I was doing it. There were about forty files in the box. They were alphabetized. The second one read, "Bellhaven, Amanda." The second-to-the-last one read, "Templeton, Lawrence." For some reason the presence of neither of those files surprised me.

The last one did, however. It read, "Tobias, Geoffrey."

Diane caught me looking. "You shouldn't be doing that, you know."

I said, "I know."

"But you look like you've seen a ghost," she said.

"I think what's in this box may be why people have been trying to kill us," I said.

"Because of Paul?" Diane said, suddenly vigilant.

"You were his friend, Diane, and you're not going to want to hear this, but Paul Weinman apparently made some bad mistakes. And I think they've come home to roost."

She shook her head, prepared to disbelieve whatever I was about to tell her. I took her hand and led her back to her office. I retrieved our coffee mugs from the kitchen, returned to her office, and sat across from her before I began explaining the mess that Paul Weinman had bequeathed us.

"He's been seeing people in therapy he had no business seeing."

"What do you mean?" she said.

"He had patients who were friends of his, business acquaintances. He broke the rules against 'dual relationships.' "

"Paul wouldn't do that."

"He did."

"And how do you know?"

I explained about Rita Templeton and her stories about Mirabelle. About Paul and Lydia owning a cabin up there and about Paul apparently seeing other Mirabelle homeowners in psychotherapy. I explained that since Rita didn't ever mention it that I didn't even think that Rita knew that her husband, Larry, had been seeing Paul for psychotherapy. At least three people whose names were in the box were regular social acquaintances of Paul Weinman's. And at least one of the three, Larry Templeton, was already dead in suspicious circumstances, and another one, Amanda Bellhaven, had a brother Elliot who was the deputy DA investigating all this stuff, and that the third, Geoffrey Tobias, was the uncle and guardian of my patient who had survived the crash of United Flight 232 in Sioux City, Iowa.

Diane's resistance to believing me was waning. "Where does the last guy fit? What does this have to do with United Flight 232?"

"I'm not sure it does. I just know he has a cabin in Mirabelle, and so do Russ London, Larry Templeton, Elliot and Amanda Bellhaven, and Paul Weinman. And I know Geoff Tobias's name is in Paul's file box. But I don't know what any of it means."

"What does all this have to do with people trying to kill us?"

"I don't know. I just know it does. It has to."

Diane shivered and looked furtively around the room as though she were afraid she was trapped, again, in the room where it had all started with Harlan Draper's silver gun.

After half a minute she said, "I can't believe Paul would do that. See his friends in treatment."

"Maybe they weren't really friends. Just people he saw a few times each summer." The devil's advocate costume didn't fit, but I tried it on for Diane's benefit.

"Maybe," she said. "Still. If what you're saying is true, he owned property with them. Or at least Lydia did. It's definitely a violation of the 'dual relationship' principle. Definitely." Diane sighed and narrowed her big eyes. "He was my mentor, Alan. My guide. I always thought he was a perfect therapist. And he was one of the most ethical men I've ever known. I don't know why he did this."

"Well, there's gotta be a reason."

"What do we do now?"

"I'm open to suggestion," I said.

"We need to avoid jumping to the conclusion that this is all about Paul's records. We might miss something." Her usually crisp voice was liquid on the edges.

"Okay, that sounds prudent."

Diane scratched behind her right ear, near where she had been clobbered by the burglar, then said, "There's Claire Draper. I have her file. She's the only patient of mine that I can see any way might be linked to all of this."

"None of the other names in Paul's files have any ties to anybody you've treated?"

"Wait—no—well, maybe. You say this Tobias guy is the guardian for the kid who survived the plane crash?"

"Yes."

"You recall that I referred the Navens kid to you?"

"Yes."

"I probably mentioned it at the time, Alan, but the reason I didn't see him myself is that I had been treating his sister before the crash. So the link to whatever bomb might be ticking in Paul's files is pretty tangential, but—"

"What were you treating her for—Randy's sister?"

She thought for a moment and said, "Consultation, right?"

I said, "Right."

Diane exhaled. "Adolescent stuff, coming-of-age stuff, separation issues, some strange-eating pathology."

"Anything that would be worth breaking into your files to find out?"

"No. Not that I can recall. What about you? Do you have any records that someone might be interested in?"

"Well, I guess I share the same link you have to Geoff Tobias via the plane crash and the Navens children, but—"

"Wait, Alan. How do I know that name? Tobias?"

"They own Pain Perdu. He and his wife, Erica."

She nodded. "Oh. Still haven't eaten there. Too trendy for Raoul. Do you have any other patients who have any relationships to any of the names in the box of Paul's files?"

I raised an eyebrow and said, "Consultation, right?"

She smiled and said, "Sure."

"One odd one. A while back I saw a woman for a consultation who came to see me for advice about what to do about the fact that she was in a sexual relationship with her therapist. I gave her the advice. Never saw her again. But she called me once, in panic, accusing me of reporting her therapist to the state. Of course I wouldn't do that without her permission, which she had withheld. And I couldn't do it without knowing her therapist's name. And she never told me his name.

"Anyway, I think she lied to me, certainly about some of it, maybe about all of it. The next time I saw her she was using a name different from the one she had used with me. See, the next time I saw this woman she was supine in Marilyn London's casket."

"Ohhh. That was when you made a scene at the funeral."

"Yeah. And that was why."

Diane laughed. "God, I'm so sorry I missed that. It sounds like it was one of life's truly precious moments. Okay. So you have Marilyn London's chart, and think she might be related to this mess. That seems reasonable, given who her husband is. And it also adds another player to the roster: this therapist. You know what he is? Psychologist? Psychiatrist? Social worker? None of the above?"

"Don't know." I kept to myself my long-shot hypothesis about Paul Weinman being on the list of eligible perpetrators. Diane would never have considered it. Ever.

"Maybe it's Clancy Coates," Diane said, musing. Diane seemed terribly eager to believe that Clarence Coates, M.D., was guilty of the sexual transgression that he had been accused of by her patient.

"And maybe not," I said.

She ignored me. One of her specialties. "Any others?" she asked.

"I have a patient who is on the grand jury that's investigating Russ London."

She smiled a little. "Oh, you're full of information. So it *is* Russell London they're investigating? Our local daily guessed right."

"And I just remembered something else that I've been assuming you already know. But of course you don't. A number of years ago Paul Weinman treated him, too."

"The grand jury member?" Diane asked, puzzled.

"No. Paul treated Russell London."

"Really? For what?"

I shook my head and said, "Don't know."

Diane's puzzled expression belied the fact that she was catching on. She said, "And you said that the cabin Lydia and Paul owned is one of the cabins at that place in Coal Creek, too, right?"

"Bingo," I said softly, and just then the red light that signaled the arrival of Diane's patient flashed on. We both turned our heads to it. I stood up and said, "We'll talk more later."

"You can count on that," said Diane.

I paused at her door. "Before the day is out, Diane, I think certain files should be moved to safe-deposit boxes at local banks."

"I'll do mine," she said, staring at me.

"And I'll do mine," I said. "But what about Paul's?"

"I don't think anybody knows they're here," she said as she fumbled with something on her desk. "And besides I haven't read 'em yet. And I'll be damned if I'm gonna go sit in one of those little rooms at the bank while I read the damn things."

36

I didn't know whether my headache was the result of a hangover from the concussion, reverberations from the conversation with Diane, or annoyance at the fact that my beeper was shorting out from the volume of calls from the media, who suddenly wanted to know my life story, especially the part about the avalanche. I got calls from the *Star,* the *Enquirer,* and *People.* Even forgetting that my well-being was dependent on giving Merideth an exclusive, I was disinclined to cooperate with the media anyway. The press had not, in my opinion, been very gracious about the notoriety I had received the previous year.

I saw a couple of patients before lunch and then drove over to the hospital to see Randy, who, the staff told me, wasn't doing quite as well as he had been.

The previous evening had been "family night" on the unit. The kids' families were invited in for visiting and for unstressful recreational activities. Randy hadn't expected his aunt and uncle to show up at all. But Geoff Tobias surprised him and did show up. The purpose for the visit wasn't recreational, however. Apparently the purpose was to encourage Randy to change doctors. That is, to dump me.

The nursing staff said that Randy flew out of control during a chess game with his uncle and had to be restrained by staff. Randy screamed at his uncle, threatened him, and then hid behind the furniture, cowering.

By noon the next day, when we sat down for our regular session, Randy remembered none of the previous evening's events.

He said, staring at the floor, "They told me what I did last night. I'm sorry."

"No need to apologize, Randy."

"The nurse said he wants me to change doctors. Can he make me get another doctor?"

"I don't think so, but I'm not certain. You're seventeen, and in Colorado that gives you the right to make some treatment decisions, I think. I'll have to check the law. But I don't think he can make that choice for you against your will. But he can probably make your life pretty difficult."

"Yeah, that'd be a change," Randy said.

We spent the rest of the time talking about what it would mean for him that this rift was finally quaking into the open between him and his guardians. About his feelings over his aunt and uncle's sudden interest in his life. About his feelings over the possibility of not seeing me anymore.

It was a good session.

I drove home and slept most of the afternoon, getting up just in time to take advantage of the blustery afternoon and do twenty hard miles on my bike in the hills of eastern Boulder County.

Lauren had called while I was asleep, and I returned her call when I got back just before five, but she was in a meeting.

I phoned Merideth and was told she was at a courthouse in Marin County and wanted me to call her on her portable phone. In a voice that sounded histrionic and frantic, the secretary said, "Ms. Murrow said to tell you it was urgent. She says she's been trying to reach you for *days*. You just have to call her right away. You just have to." I jotted down the number as he dictated it and realized I was relieved I hadn't reached her. I didn't call the number of her portable phone. Although I did manage to generate some guilt over the anguish of the poor guy who was Merideth's secretary, I wasn't in the mood to be interviewed about the avalanche. Or to be reminded of the pull I felt every time I talked with my newly compassionate, pregnant, almost ex-wife.

My answering machine had surrendered. It was playing about two-thirds of my announcement message before it beeped and then was allowing four seconds of message space before abruptly hanging up on the caller without bothering to record the remainder of what they said.

I wondered if I could patent it and retire.

I sat drinking a beer and watching the darkness ooze over the mountains from the eastern plains, snuffing out the fires of sunset. I jumped at the sound of my doorbell, and as I ran to the front of the house I swore I would disconnect the damn thing. Sam Purdy stood at my door carrying a pizza box.

"Eaten yet?" he asked, and then handed me an envelope. "Found this stuck in your door."

"Hello, Sam, come on in," I said, reaching out my hand to take the business-size envelope. The envelope was unaddressed. I guessed it was a note from Adrienne, who had grown frustrated with my anemic answering machine.

Sam paraded right to the dining room, spied the beer bottle that I had left on the coffee table in the living room, and said, "Got any more of those?"

I threw down the envelope and went to the kitchen and grabbed a couple of more beers from the refrigerator and a couple of plates and napkins and carried everything to the dining room. Sam was sitting at the head of the table. I sat next to him. He opened the box to reveal a white pizza, all fresh tomatoes and cheese and garlic and basil.

"This looks great," I said.

I took a few bites and he ate an entire slice before he said, "I met with the special prosecutor today. She's sharp. She's the new DA from Jeffco, knows your personal Saint Bernard, Casey Sparrow, real well, and already knew the whole story about the snowplow from hell."

"And?"

"And I wasn't as disappointed with what she told me as I thought I'd be. Listen, you not only didn't hear any of this from me, you didn't hear it at all. But the grand jury wasn't—isn't—looking into anything too sinister. A venture capital company was kicking back some money to some local lawyers and accountants who were in a position to direct retirement funds into some risky ventures. A couple of old ladies lost their nest eggs and complained to the DA. That's the whole nut."

"And Russ London was part of it?"

"Must've looked like it to the Boulder DA or he wouldn't have handed the case off to the special prosecutor. But she's been suffering a rather severe case of witness attrition lately, and before she goes back to the grand jury and reconvenes, her staff's spending its time and energy trying to put together a document trail that's half as convincing as the witnesses were gonna be before their untimely deaths."

"How does it tie in to Marilyn London's murder?"

"That's the only disappointing part. The answer is the special doesn't know and I don't know. It might not tie in at all."

"What do they think Russ London did?"

Purdy smiled. "This feast is my way of thanking you for that, Doctor. What Russell London did—if he did what the special thinks he did—was direct the investment of some serious trust moneys into one very risky business deal. And it looks like he may have played both ends of the street. He not only got a kickback from the venture capital people, but it looks like he took a piece of the business deal for himself, too."

"How much money in all?"

"A quarter to a half a mil. He purportedly took fifty off the top. And they think he's got five percent of the pie."

"What was it? Biomed? A computer start-up?" I was sure Diane's husband, Raoul, would be able to fill me in on the principals of any high-tech start-up in the county. For a fleeting moment I feared that TelSat, Raoul's latest industrial adoptee, was involved.

"Nope."

"So I don't get it. Why do I get the royal treatment?"

"The start-up was a risky restaurant called Pain Perdu."

He watched my eyes light up. "That's right—the new mecca for the rich and frivolous. And because of the list of property owners at Mirabelle that you gave me, I happen to know that the majority owners of that restaurant, this couple named Tobias, also happen to be part of the inbreeding at Mirabelle."

I didn't know how to put all this together. So Geoff and Erica Tobias were not only tied in to dead psychologist Paul Weinman through Mirabelle, they were also tied in to ex-Mayor Russell London and, because of him, to Deputy DA Elliot Bellhaven. And it sounded as if the Tobiases were also tied in to whatever investment fraud the special prosecutor was investigating.

Purdy must have watched my brain cells misfire. "Yeah, the pieces are all starting to fit, my friend. See, this little group of mountain buddies has conspired to find a way to finance this incredibly risky restaurant business using slightly illegal means, and as the pieces of their little conspiracy have started to unravel, people have started to die in significant numbers. All I need to do now is begin to understand who has the most compelling motive to have the dead people out of the way. And then I will solve one—two—maybe three murders."

"Where does Elliot fit?"

"He doesn't seem to. I assume he knows all these people from growing up with them. But the special says his name hasn't come up in connection with any ownership or property records at the restaurant. So for right now I don't know where Elliot fits."

"Sam, why are you telling me all this?"

"I still need you. The prevailing wisdom in the department is that I should solve the heinous murder of Marilyn London and not waste time trying to turn the investigation of a domestic murder-suicide and an accidental house explosion into a crusade. So I need your continued assistance—mostly with the widow Templeton. Because"—he paused long enough to swallow a mouthful of pizza and take a long pull on his beer—"it seems that dead Larry owned a piece of the culinary palace on the hill, too."

That shouldn't have surprised me, but it did. "I don't think Rita knows about it, Sam. She told me that the life insurance company finally agreed to pay on the death claim, which wasn't that much, and then told her that Larry had recently borrowed a lot of money against the policy, so the accumulated value was almost entirely borrowed away, too. She says she hasn't been able to find out what he did with the money since so many of his papers were destroyed in the explosion."

Sam sighed. "Well, I know what he did with it. He bought a piece of the Tobiases' restaurant. A pretty big piece. I have somebody checking on the other Mirabelle owners to see if they did, too. In the meantime I want you to go back over this whole Templeton thing and see if you can discover anything, I mean *anything,* new. Right now, I'm starving, and I smell garlic and I smell hops. But most of the time, these days, I still smell dogshit."

"Okay. I'll keep looking until Scott tells me to stop."

"Don't worry about Scott Truscott. This isn't costing him that much, and he wants me in *his* debt for once. And he doesn't want it to turn out that the coroner's office missed something important in all this, anyway."

Purdy grabbed another slice of pizza, and I walked into the kitchen to get him another beer, pondering whether I could introduce Paul Weinman into Sam's thinking without telling him things I didn't have any right to tell him.

I decided I could. Sort of.

I sat back down and said, "Sam, I think I might have some idea about how the burglaries at the office and at Diane's house and the assault on her and the attempt to kill me might be related to this restaurant stuff."

He chewed his mouthful of pizza deliberately and swallowed with exaggerated effort. He said, "You 'think' you 'might' have 'some' idea?"

Meekly I said, "Maybe I'm a little more certain than that."

He sat back in his chair and focused his attention on his second beer, delaying the renewal of his assault on the pizza. "Go on," he said.

"First, a question. Did any other names come up during the investigation of the partners in this restaurant venture? Like Knorr?"

He thought for a moment before he said, "Knorr's one of the Mirabelle owners. But it's not on the preliminary restaurant investors list. But we're not done looking." It was apparent from his tone that Sam Purdy liked answering questions about as much as insurance companies like writing checks.

"What about Weinman?" I asked.

"I don't know from Weinman."

"Paul Weinman was a psychologist—"

I was briefly interrupted by Purdy moaning and muttering, "Ah, shit."

"—a psychologist who died over the holidays after he skied into a tree at Breckenridge. It turns out, Sam, that not only do a number of the players in this little drama own mountain property together and not only do they own a restaurant together, it turns out that a number of them also saw this particular psychologist for psychotherapy at various times over the years."

Purdy got interested and seemed to be remembering something. "Oh. I got it now. So this is the shrink who saw Russ London?"

"I think maybe. They knew each other. They both owned cabins up there."

"And, wait a second, is this the shrink you think might have been seeing Marilyn London?"

Quickly, perhaps too quickly, I said, "I don't know about that."

Purdy eyed me suspiciously, then continued, "Let me guess—you think that somebody is after something in this skiing shrink's files? And you have his files?"

"Not actually. But, yes—I think somebody's after his files. But that's only part of it."

He was getting annoyed. "What's the rest of it?"

"Well, Diane and I each have a file that people in this group might be interested in having, too. Diane, of course, has a file on Claire Draper—the woman who was shot in her office. That file would probably be of some interest to this group of suspects that you're assembling since she was also your primo grand jury witness. And I have a file that might be of some interest to them as well." I didn't have any legal rationale to disclose to Purdy Marilyn London's visit to me. So I didn't.

Purdy immediately detected my ambiguity. "Shit. Here we go again. You're gonna start keeping secrets. Aren't you? Fuck."

"Sam, before you get bent out of shape, listen to a few things. Okay? I don't know what's in Diane's files and Paul Weinman's files. I haven't read them. They could have nothing in them. And the only file I have . . . well, I would feel much better if I could just tell you what's in it, but I can't."

"You haven't read Weinman's files? Why not?"

"They're not my files."

"You have them—they're yours—go read them."

I think he half expected me to pick up my coat and drive downtown that very minute. "There's actually another small complication, Sam. They're not 'my files.' Paul Weinman's files are in Diane Estevez's custody."

His face tightened as if he'd just been poked with a syringe. "No. No. Don't tell me that. Not her. You I can work with. Her? She's . . . she's—"

"Stubborn?"

"Like a statue of a mule."

I was beginning to get anxious anticipating Purdy's arguments about why he should get to see all the files in question. I picked up the white envelope off the table and began to open it as a diversion.

Purdy said, "I hope all these files are secure."

I nodded.

He laughed. "As if anything you or she has is secure these days."

The envelope I opened held a single sheet of medium-weight bond. The lettering was by electronic typewriter or letter-quality printer. The words started a third of the way down the page.

WANT TO COUNT ON BEING LUCKY TWICE?
STOP WHAT YOU'RE DOING.

Purdy watched my face grow ashen and took the paper from my hands.

Exasperated, he shook his head slowly and with the beginning traces of a smile on his face said, "Amateurs. My God, we're dealing with amateurs."

37

Diane, too, had received a note.

Purdy, of course, confiscated the apparently identical sheets of paper from each of us for analysis and promised us that our police protection would be intensified, although he was "almost a hundred percent sure" that the note was intended merely to intimidate us.

Diane actually snorted when she heard Purdy's assurance.

I checked in at the coroner's office to see Scott Truscott the next morning, and as Purdy had predicted, Scott told me the coroner had approved my continued investment of resources in the Larry Templeton investigation. Truscott reminded me that my charter was to focus on the medical and psychological data that could help establish manner of death. The rest, he told me pointedly, was police work. He'd heard about the snowplow. I told him about the threatening note. He told me that he would understand if I chose to resign and didn't seem at all troubled by the prospect of my departure. He said that he expected to have a full staff on board by the end of the following week.

I congratulated him on his recruiting success and responded to his suggestion about resigning by asking to see, once again, the medical records that had been accumulated from Larry Templeton's physicians. He shook his head in mild exasperation and called one of his assistants into the office and told her to find the file for me.

Although I doubted that I would have missed them during my earlier examination of the medical record, my first pass through the file this time was to see if there were any records from Paul Weinman or any other mental health professional. There were not.

The second pass was much more tedious, deciphering scrawled progress note sheets and trying to make sense of laboratory data findings, X-ray reports, and consultation records. I was hoping to find evidence that one of Larry's physicians had sent him to Paul Weinman for a psychological consultation.

Laboriously, what I learned about Larry's medical history was that he had been operated on twice in the previous ten years; once his right knee had been scoped, once he'd had something obscene done to one of his sinuses.

I was hoping to discover some wisdom in the disjointed records and wasn't finding any. I jotted down some passages that contained words I didn't understand so that I could run them by Adrienne for her translation, and then I packed up the pile of paper. Scott Truscott was standing by his secretary's desk when I returned the file.

"Anything?" he said.

"Not that I could see. I was hoping I'd missed seeing a referral from his internist to a psychiatrist, or a mental health consultation report back to his internist, or something. But I didn't find anything."

Scott patted me lightly on the back and turned back to his secretary.

Lauren and I had lunch at the James Pub. She seemed distracted and short-tempered with me, but when I asked she denied that anything was wrong.

Everywhere around me I felt that clocks were ticking down.

After lunch I walked down Broadway to the hospital for my appointment with Randy. He was quiet and unresponsive and uninterested in doing any work. Talking with him that day was as arduous as walking through thigh-high snow.

I walked back to my office. My beeper chirped.

Merideth's voice was light and engaging. Her message on my Voicemail expressed concern about my safety. She said she wasn't at all sure the police were adequately protecting me. She hoped to be able to get away from the murder trial in Marin in a few days and return to Boulder with her crew to wrap up the taping of the Cech story and to look at the developments in the Russell London morass. She asked me to promise not to talk to anyone else about the avalanche before I talked with her.

I promised.

Adrienne's garden had yielded bushels of delicious Roma tomatoes the previous September. With my share of the bounty I'd made sauce to stock the freezer and carry me through the winter.

I invited Adrienne and Peter to join Lauren and me for spaghetti that night. Lauren phoned to cancel a half hour before she was due to arrive.

"I'm tired," she said.

"Is that all? Is something going on?"

"No. I just get tired sometimes. That's nothing new."

"Are there any new symptoms, honey?" I asked gently, fearing that her MS had flared anew.

"No. I'm just exhausted. I don't think it's an exacerbation."

"Would you tell me if it was?"

"Right now, I don't know," she said.

Here we go again, I thought.

Adrienne sat at the kitchen table and bitched about having to drink a nonalcoholic beer simply because fetuses "can't hold their liquor." Peter stage-whispered that she hadn't had a very good day and then resumed helping me chop and sauté garlic, shallots, and roasted peppers to add to the tomatoes. Every time I turned my back he would shake more red pepper flakes into the simmering sauce. Peter had arrived with an Italian red in a brown glass bottle, and I poured a glass for him and for myself and added a healthy slug to the sauce. From the corner of my eye I watched him wince as he noted the wine go into the sauce. It apparently hadn't been table wine that I dumped in. I should have known better.

Adrienne was tapping her toes on the floor to keep time

with her impatience. "Do you have anything to eat? Like appetizers? A person could starve watching you two cook."

I held up a loaf of crusty Italian bread with sesame seeds. "Want some?"

"That's it?" Adrienne said. "No melons, no prosciutto, no antipasto?"

Peter smiled a warning at me but kept his mouth shut.

"I have some carrot sticks. We're having a salad, too."

"I'm trying to feed a goddamn family here and you're offering me carrot sticks and lettuce? Next time I come here for dinner I'll try and remember to bring myself a snack."

I walked over and gave her a big hunk of bread and a little hug. "Ten minutes, Ren. I promise. You and Pinocchio will eat in ten minutes."

I tilted my head toward the stove. Peter took the cue and dumped the dried spaghetti into the boiling water on the back burner.

Adrienne pouted and took a bite of her bread, then said, "What? No butter? Pinocchio needs fat."

I held up a bottle of olive oil and a saucer.

She rolled her eyes and said, "Not a chance. The kid needs saturated fat. American fat."

I found a stick of butter in the refrigerator and placed it gingerly in front of her. Peter was busy with the pepper flakes and a wooden spoon.

"I need a consult, Doctor," I said to my cranky friend the urologist.

"I don't do friends," she said with her mouth full. "You'll have to take your pecker to someone else."

Peter and I turned to each other and laughed. But through the thick haze of her hormone-induced irritability, Adrienne was having trouble understanding what was so funny.

I tried to remember the notes I'd taken to remind me of questions I wanted to ask Adrienne about Larry Templeton's medical record. I said, "What's Gantrisin for?"

"It's for eye shit. I don't do eyes."

"And what's a dysplastic nevus?"

"It's a skin weirdness. I don't do skin, either."

"And anosmia, what's anosmia?"

"Inability to smell. And, no, I don't do noses." She was starting to smile just a little. "Is this a test?"

I said, "Just what *do* you *do*, Ren?"

She swallowed a mouthful of bread and looked right at me. She said, "I do dicks, dickhead. I do dicks."

Adrienne's mood improved somewhat as she ate. She ate enough, however, that by the time she was finished she should have been euphoric. But she wasn't. Her primary contribution to the dinner table conversation was a sharp, "You'd better have plenty more of this," halfway through the meal.

I was grinding beans for after-dinner coffee before I realized the implication of what Adrienne had said about the definition of anosmia. Larry Templeton had suffered from anosmia. Larry Templeton couldn't smell. He couldn't smell his wife's cinnamon muffins. He couldn't smell freshly cut grass. He couldn't smell gas. So even if the gas leaking into his house had been scented with a warning odor, Larry Templeton wouldn't have known he had to get out fast.

Larry Templeton had not killed himself. Which meant his death was either an accident or murder. I was making progress. Sam Purdy and Scott Truscott and Rita Templeton would be pretty pleased with me. And whoever had written the note suggesting that I refrain from further investigatory activities would probably be pretty displeased with me.

I weighed the relative judiciousness of continuing to participate in Purdy's criminal inquiries as I placed three cups on the table and sat down to wait for the coffee to drip. Adrienne was deflecting some of her residual aggravation about her day into a harangue against the driver of a blue Volvo who had tailgated her the entire length of the Boulder Turnpike that afternoon. She was describing to Peter the design of an anti-tailgating device she wanted him to install on her Land Cruiser.

The device she'd concocted would consist of a cylinder

of compressed odoriferous gas mounted under the rear bumper of her car. A blast of the contents of the cylinder could be released via a switch or button mounted on the dash of the car. The cylinder would contain the compressed scent of skunk, or sulphur, or something "rural and dairy in nature," like "eau de Greeley." Greeley was a town an hour north of Boulder that was home to one of the world's largest feedlots.

"When somebody was tailgating me all I would need to do would be to press this button and—voilà—the offender would get a whiff of whatever I had loaded in my cylinder that day. And they would back off."

"Or shoot you," said Peter.

Adrienne's look was cold enough to freeze boiling water. Evenly, for Adrienne, she said, "But that's the beauty of it—nobody would know where it came from. They would just know that when they got too close to my car, the inside of their car smelled like cowshit." She looked real pleased with herself.

"I even have a name for it," she said. "I want to call it 'Car Farts.' Maybe we can start a company and make a fortune."

Neither Peter nor I had any confidence in Adrienne's sense of humor that night, so each of us put our heads down while we laughed.

"I'm serious," she said.

Without looking up, I said, "Of course you are."

After Peter and Adrienne trudged back to their house up the hill, I climbed into my little rental and drove across town to check on Lauren. I parked behind a big black BMW in front of her house and had walked halfway to her door when, through the window, I saw her move across her living room in front of her pool table with a cue stick in her left hand, lining up a shot. I paused, surprised she wasn't resting. I took another step and watched as a tall, thin man moved into view. I stopped again. The man held a cue in one hand, a glass with ice and brown liquid in it in the other. I glanced back at the gleaming black car and guessed single-malt Scotch.

I quickly decided that Lauren looked just fine. And, since she seemed to have a full quota of visitors, I tiptoed back to my rental car.

On the return drive home, the car began to sound as if a small bird were living in its dashboard practicing sparrow diction. I silenced the noise by shaking the frame of the dashboard with my right hand. I pulled my hand away to discover that my fingertips were covered with a sticky brown substance that I was tempted to draw toward my nose for identification, but I quickly decided I didn't really want to know. The warbling resumed to mock me.

I was alternating between full-blown rage at Lauren's deception—breaking a date with me to have a man over to her house—and full-blown remorse over my inaction—fear that my ambivalence over Merideth had finally pushed Lauren away. I also reminded myself a dozen times that I might be overreacting—all I knew, after all, was that there was a tall, thin, handsome man with a cocktail in Lauren's living room at ten forty-five on a weeknight when she'd been too tired to have dinner with me.

It might not mean anything at all. Just like the red warning light that was flashing on the dashboard of my rental car might mean nothing at all.

The next morning my pager interrupted a discussion with a clerk at the rental car agency about the flashing red light on my car. The clerk was college-aged and lanky, and his skin hadn't recovered from adolescence. The agency apparently insisted he wear a tie, and unfortunately for him, that meant a dress shirt as well. His was one of those necks that hadn't yet grown to a sufficient thickness to do justice to a buttoned collar. He looked like a semiformally attired chicken.

My request to switch cars was making him anxious. "Sir," I said in my most sardonic voice, "I'd like a different car. I'd like the new car that you give me to be clean and well-running, and I'd like it to have been built no earlier than the date you graduated from high school. Excuse me—while you do the paperwork—I have a phone call to make."

My speech would have been almost perfect if I hadn't had to return fifteen seconds later and ask the kid for change of a dollar.

The Voicemail computer that answered my phone told me that my most recent call had been from Sam Purdy. Twenty cents later a woman answering the phone in his office said he'd like me to stop by to see him as soon as possible.

I walked back to the counter, dropped my coroner's ID under the clerk's nose, and said to him, "Listen carefully. I'm with the coroner's office, and that"—I jerked my thumb at the pay phone across the room—"was Detective Purdy of the Boulder Police Department requesting my immediate assistance with the investigation of a homicide—that means a *murder*—and I—need—a—car." With the difficulty the kid had swallowing, one would have thought his collar was too tight. He took a half step back from the counter before he handed me some keys and a folder of papers and told me I was looking for something new and red called a Sundance. It had Utah plates.

I found the car, which was clean and started right up. No extra lights flashed from the dash. I was due to see my first patient in a little less than an hour and quickly decided that if I hurried, I could squeeze in a visit to the Public Safety Building.

I also decided that there was no way I was ever going to give my coroner's ID back to Scott Truscott.

Purdy was expecting me and had me escorted to a part of the building that housed various forensic laboratories. He was bent over a microscope and was mumbling questions to a woman next to him who was looking intently at a photograph. She looked up from the picture when I entered the room and said, "Your guy's here," to Purdy.

He sat upright and swiveled around on the tall stool on which he was sitting. "Come here. You gotta see this," he said to me.

I was trying to read his expression. It wasn't easy. His face was composed in the neutral, unreadable countenance I'd seen when I had first met him and he was interviewing me about a dead patient of mine. I checked the face of the woman standing next to Purdy holding the picture, hoping to increase my data base. She looked uncomfortable. That made at least two of us.

Purdy got up and said, "Sit here."

I did and swiveled toward the microscope.

"We just got some stuff back on a rush job from the ballistics people at CBI that I want you to see. This is a comparison microscope," Purdy said, "so you'll be seeing two different images, side by side. The idea is to compare them for similarities and differences." I pulled my head back and looked for a focusing adjustment.

The woman took my left hand and placed it on a chrome knob. "Use this one here," she said.

Purdy said, "This is Katy Conover. She's head of the crime labs here. You're looking at slugs."

I raised my head and said, "Hello, nice to meet you," and turned back to the microscope. "You mean like bullets?"

"Yeah, like bullets. The one on the left is from Marilyn London's body. It's a little deformed from glancing off some bone. Now look up here. Katy?"

Katy Conover's voice was resonant and gravelly. She held the photograph against her chest face out toward me, and she was pointing at it from above. "This is called a photomicrograph, and it's a microphotographic image of the comparison you were just looking at. It's the image on the left on which I would like you to focus your attention." Her manner was professorial. "Notice these imperfections." She touched some markings on the photograph with the tip of a pencil. "And notice them here, as well, on the right side. Now see if you can identify them in the microscope."

I felt as though I were receiving instructions from a teacher in a high school science lab but turned back to the microscope as ordered. I had little trouble seeing the markings. I guessed that I was supposed to conclude that the bullets had come from the same gun.

"Fired from the same gun, right? What"—Oh, so *that*'s what this is about. "Is the one on the right the one you pulled out of the wall at Diane's house?"

Purdy was about to answer, but Katy Conover spoke first. "No, that one was too deformed from hitting the stud to get any meaningful comparisons."

"So where did you get the right-hand bullet?"

Purdy's face looked sad as he said, "From the gun that was in your office. The one that you gave me for safe-keeping."

By the time we had walked upstairs to his office, I was able to muster a little indignation to cover my humiliation at inadvertently incriminating my own patient. "What right did you have to fire that gun?"

"It was in my custody. I didn't need a warrant. You gave it to me voluntarily."

"But it wasn't mine."

"But it was given to you voluntarily, wasn't it? And you gave it to me voluntarily, didn't you?"

"But—"

"Alan—" Purdy held up both his hands and thrust them toward me with his fingers spread. "The pooch is screwed. Okay? There's no point in arguing whether the gate should have been closed. Let the lawyers argue about whether I dotted all my i's. Let's you and me move on. I'm not stupid and you know I'm not stupid. I already know which of your patients gave this to you, so I don't need you to tell me that. Which is fortunate for our friendship because the Lord knows what a stubborn jerk you can be about shit like this anyway. And the Lord knows how relentless a jerk I can be about shit like this. So let's move on."

"How do you know who the gun belongs to?"

"I guessed, then I checked the registration. For chris-sake, Alan, it's registered to his dad. This wasn't one of my more inspired investigations."

I sighed. "What are you gonna do?"

"I'm gonna talk to him. And I'd like your assistance."

"Me? What for?"

"Alan, I checked with his guardians this morning. You've got the kid in a locked unit in a psychiatric hospital. I'm assuming he's a little fragile."

I was angry. Not particularly at Purdy. But angry. "You're also assuming he's a little guilty."

"Well," is all Purdy said to that.

"He needs a lawyer," I said.

"Yes, I imagine he does."

"What are you gonna do now? Just walk into the hospital and bust him?"

Purdy sighed deeply and waited ten seconds or so before he spoke, giving us both, I assumed, some time to calm down.

He said, "You know me better than that."

And then, though I tried to ignore it, another realization struck me and filled me with sorrow. "And you know what else, Sam? He's going to need a new psychologist, too."

Purdy looked indignant. "Alan, this kid's going to need you more than ever now. You can't quit on him."

"Sam, I have no choice. I'm a part of this investigation. I've been helping the coroner. I've been helping you. I've had somebody try to kill me because of all this. Now that he's part of this mess, too, I can't treat him anymore. It's unethical. It's called a 'dual relationship.' There's a strict prohibition against it. It's intended to protect patients from their therapist having conflicts of interest." I paused and shook my head and looked at Sam Purdy. "How many times is this kid gonna get screwed by life, Sam? How many times? Sam, he's not a killer. He's a victim. He's a goddamn victim. Again."

My breakfast was in my throat. The taste was bitter and acidic.

I stewed while Purdy again called the Tobiases, this time to inform them officially that their charge was a suspect in the murder of Marilyn London. I sat across the office from him and listened to the detective's half of the conversation and watched him make exasperated faces at what he was hearing. Erica had answered the phone and ultimately assured Purdy that they would get Randy a lawyer.

I used Purdy's telephone to call the ward chief at the adolescent psychiatric unit and explained Randy's predicament. I also explained my conflicting roles so that he would be prepared for the transition of Randy's care to a different therapist. I then called the nursing staff and told them that I would be in to see Randy at lunchtime and to please have him available.

Purdy asked me what the consequences would be of moving Randy to jail. I told him that psychologically it was risky at best. He told me if they developed any more evidence, and he was pretty sure they would, he would probably have to risk moving Randy.

I was perplexed by his caution and told him so. "Why don't you just go and get him now, get it over with?"

He understood my conflicting interests at that point, and he seemed to hesitate before he spoke. "The problem is access to the gun. Obviously, the kid knew where it was —he gave it to you. But did he break into your office without being detected, get the gun, shoot Marilyn London, and go back into your office and put it back? You've just told me that his aunt and uncle knew you had the gun. And that Diane Estevez knew you had the gun. Your office had been broken into at least twice before the murder, so maybe some burglars saw the gun in there. See my problem? Too many people knew about this gun sitting around in your office.

"My other problem is motive. We don't have one." He paused for a long five count. "Yet."

"You think he did it, Sam?"

He shrugged his shoulders and said, "I don't think he didn't. You know where he lives, Alan? On Eleventh just south of Baseline. Two blocks from Chautauqua. Two blocks from the scene of the murder." Purdy shook his head. "I like it best when my criminals are slime. Cheap slime, middle-class slime, elegant slime—I'm not picky— I get to feel righteous when I bust slime. I hate it when my criminals are victims themselves. So if for some reason that I don't know yet it turns out this kid did shoot Marilyn London, I'm gonna end up having to bust a kid who has survived a plane crash that killed his whole goddamn family. And I'm gonna hate it. I'm not gonna not do it, but I'm gonna hate it."

I stood and turned to leave Purdy's office before I remembered what I had learned the previous night about Larry Templeton.

"This seems suddenly trivial, Sam, but Larry Templeton had a medical condition called anosmia. It's an inability to smell, in his case caused by some virus or something. If there was gas leaking in his house, he wouldn't have smelled it. He could have set off the explosion himself without ever knowing he was in any danger.

"So I think it rules out suicide," I concluded.

"But not homicide?"

"Seems to me if somebody knew the guy couldn't smell, it would have been a great way to kill him. That's what I'm gonna tell Scott Truscott, anyway."

"Or it could have been an accident," Purdy said.

I nodded. "That's right, I forgot. People do die accidentally, don't they, Sam?"

"Yeah," he said. "Mostly they do."

"Then maybe it was an accident, Sam. Maybe it was an accident."

38

Although I was being vague to Diane in describing my dilemma about not being able to continue to treat Randy Navens, my words were pure clarity in comparison with her elliptical responses. Propriety was required because neither of us wished to reveal my patient's name to Raoul, who was sitting in the room with us. Diane asked me if I thought my "patient"—Randy—could have done "it"— killed Marilyn London.

"Could have, sure," I replied. "But why? He's never even talked about her in treatment. What's his motive?"

"He *has* been having dissociative episodes, Alan. She could have been somehow involved with him in those. It's likely he wouldn't even remember."

"Again, Diane, that could be true. But the fugues seem to be confined to something having to do with this group of vacation cabins in the mountains. There's been nothing in them involved with Chautauqua. Nothing."

"You don't really know that. And anyway, didn't you say that the Londons owned one of the cabins at that place in Coal Creek?"

Raoul looked up. He'd been to "that place in Coal Creek."

I said, "Yeah, I did say that. Although I'd like to—I guess I can't pretend that 'my patient' wouldn't have had some contact with Marilyn London. Even though he has no memories of his family visiting the Tobias cabin growing up, his return there when he's dissociated certainly argues that he must have. So he could have gotten to know Marilyn London there, when he was a kid."

Raoul was intent now, as if trying to grasp the pieces of a brain teaser being presented to him verbally.

Diane ignored my rationalizations. "I agree. He must have been up there at some point when he was growing up, or he wouldn't have the sense of familiarity he has when he emerges from the fugue. Let's face it, the odds of his randomly breaking into his uncle's cabin during a dissociative episode are pretty astronomical." She paused. "And he knew where the gun was in your office," she said.

"Yes, he certainly did."

"So it doesn't look too good for your patient," Diane said to me.

"No, it doesn't."

Diane looked across the room at her husband, who was leaning left and then right, dodging a sharp ray of sun streaming in through a southern window, and said, "Raoul, it's time we stop being chickens and start being pigs."

Raoul was in the process of breaking open a new package of Chiclets. He stopped fumbling with the cellophane when his wife addressed him.

We were all in Diane's office. After I left police headquarters I had driven to my office, where I saw a couple of patients who didn't get all of my attention, and then had gone in search of Diane Estevez for some professional counsel and moral support. Raoul was in her office, fiddling with the wiring of the panic button he had installed in the floor next to her chair. I told them that one of my patients was a prime suspect and relayed the details of Purdy's latest revelations about the gun that had been stored in my filing cabinet.

Raoul scooted one seat farther down on the couch to elude the predatory ray beaming in the window and nodded his concurrence to Diane's obtuse metaphor about barnyard animals.

To both of them I said, "What the hell is that supposed to mean?"

Diane turned to me and said, "It's about level of involvement. It's about bacon and eggs. With bacon and eggs, you see, the chicken is *involved*. But the pig, the pig is *committed.* From the beginning, Alan, we've been involved. People have tried to kill us. They've tried to steal from us. They killed one of my patients. Now one of yours is at risk. And so far what have we done? You've snooped around some for the cops. I've gotten depressed and laid around in the hospital and eaten too much chocolate. Raoul's fixed the gate after the fox ate the chickens. We've done squat. It's not enough. So now it's time to get committed. It's time we stop being chickens and start being pigs."

Raoul emitted some Iberian derivation of "oink, oink."

I found myself encouraged by Diane's speech and amused at her husband's Spanish-language imitation of a porker.

"So what next?" I said.

"We need to do what we can to protect this kid. It's safe to say, Alan, that at the moment you are the only resource he's got left. So Raoul and I will join your team. Call it child advocacy."

Raoul looked at Diane and said, "In my case you may call it revenge."

"And how do we go about protecting him? I can't see him for treatment anymore."

Diane smiled and said, "You're asking *me?* I'm brain damaged, remember."

Raoul shrugged his shoulders.

I sighed, considered my new teammates, and said, "I think I may have some ideas."

My first idea had to do with transferring Randy to the best therapist I could get to take his case. Diane, since she had been assaulted and was now on "my team," was out of the question, unfortunately. But she and I concurred that any of two or three people in town particularly expert in posttraumatic stress disorder would be fine choices. I placed calls to all of them to check on their availability.

I was being ripped apart by the prospect of not being Randy's therapist any longer. Fulfilling my ethical responsibility—that is, transferring him to someone else —felt like desertion. Diane was right—I was Randy's last resource. And I was about to tell him I could no longer be in his corner.

Some resource I was turning out to be.

My next idea had to do with using data unavailable to the police.

My files.

Diane's files.

Paul Weinman's files.

The trick was going to be to discern, somehow, what information in those files was valuable enough to somebody that he or she would commit felonies to sneak a look. Knowing who wanted the information *that* desperately would then provide a list of people with a motive to break into our offices, to break into Diane and Raoul's home, and, perhaps, to kill Larry Templeton and/or Marilyn London.

And a motive—who knows?—to shoot Diane and shove me over a cliff with a snowplow.

Once Diane had culled Paul Weinman's records to come up with a list of people potentially interested in her files, we would simply need to correlate it with the list of people who knew enough about Randy Navens and his gun to frame him for Marilyn London's murder. And then all we would have to do would be to correlate the new list with the list of people who had a reason to want Marilyn London dead.

It didn't sound that hard.

I explained my strategy to Diane. Raoul commented critically on the passive nature of his proposed role. Diane said she would go over Claire's record with a fine-tooth comb and seriously consider reading the Paul Weinman files that were in her custody. She asked me to remind her of the names that seemed to be part of this mess.

I said, "Larry Templeton. Geoffrey Tobias. Amanda Bellhaven. Their charts are all in the box under the stairs. And if you can find his old record, we need to know about Russell London, too."

At first Randy seemed to be instantly resigned to my announcement that I would not be able to continue as his therapist. His aunt had already phoned and informed him that the police were investigating his role in the murder of Marilyn London, so he was staggering from that news before my arrival. He had suffered so many recent losses that my announcement of my impending exit seemed about as surprising to him as is the forecast of rain to the residents of Seattle.

"Okay," he said, looking at his feet.

"That's it? Just 'okay'?" I said.

"I've been a pain in the ass."

"That's not it, Randy."

"They wanted you out, you're out. They wanted me out, I'm out."

"I'm forced to do this because of my conflicting roles, Randy. Your uncle and aunt have nothing to do with it."

"Will I go to jail?"

"I'm afraid that it looks possible. The gun you gave me was used to kill her. Your fingerprints are on it."

"You the one who gave it to them?"

"Yes," I said, "for safekeeping." I started to explain the circumstances of my decision to give the gun to Purdy but realized the futility and self-serving nature of my rationalization. Regardless of my motive, the act of giving Purdy the gun had turned out to be a betrayal to Randy.

Randy exhaled through his nose and shook his head a tiny bit. Another loss calmly noted.

"I don't think I know her. The dead lady. But those things I have, those fugues—who knows? Right?"

"I guess that's what they think. The fugues."

"A lawyer's coming to see me."

"Good."

"I'm in trouble, Dr. Gregory. Big trouble. And what good are you now? Parents are supposed to protect kids, aren't they? What fucking good are you?" His words were full of rage, but his affect was as flat as a lake at dawn.

My natural inclination was, of course, to defend myself, but instead I just said bland words that would encourage the continued expression of his rage and his resentment. I'd been waiting a long time for him to mine the fury he felt at his family for not surviving that crash. To deny him a taste of that now would be yet another betrayal.

His words stayed livid for almost a minute. His affect never matched them. I pointed that out. He just stared at his untied shoes. I waited, hopeful, for the angry words to resume. Or even better for his feelings to parallel the rage of his diatribe. They didn't.

I explained that I would help him find a new therapist and that I would work with that therapist while he and I took some time to say good-bye. I promised that I wouldn't just disappear. The word psychotherapists use for ending a therapeutic relationship is "terminate." I couldn't bring myself to use it with Randy.

"If they arrest me," he asked finally, his voice cracking, using the cotton on the shoulder of his Georgetown sweatshirt to wipe away tears, "will I have to wear handcuffs?"

I fought a temptation to be sarcastic. What I was thinking was that handcuffs would be redundant, that shock and humiliation would have Randy totally incapacitated. I said, "I don't know. I'm sorry."

I was so sorry.

When it was time for me to say good-bye, I too had tears in my eyes. I stood and hugged him. His slack muscles had the dreary tone of a dirge.

At four-thirty Purdy dropped by my office. After he failed to beckon me by flicking the waiting room annunciation switch on and off repeatedly, he resorted to pounding on the connecting door from the waiting room until I went out and opened it. He followed me down the hall to my office. I sat at my desk, intent on ignoring him. He stood in my open doorway and asked me if I would like to accompany him to the hospital while he arrested Randy for the murder of Marilyn London.

I felt petulant. I wanted him to say "please." And I wanted to say "no." There was no reason to volunteer to be a spectator at this tragedy.

Except that Randy needed me. If anyone could cushion his anguish and terror over what was about to happen to him, it was me.

I was, for the time being, childless but imagined my internal conflict was similar to the ambivalence a parent might feel at being asked if he would like to assist in his child's anesthesia prior to surgery.

So I said I would go.

"Good," Purdy said. He then sat down across from me. "It doesn't look good for him, Alan."

He had learned something new. "Tell me," I said.

"First you tell me something. How old is he?"

I thought for a moment. "Seventeen. Almost eighteen, I think. Why?"

"Just data." He paused. "Listen, this isn't easy for me. Understood? Randy's a hiker. I've got a half dozen witnesses who can place him regularly on the path that leads away from Chautauqua up toward the Mesa Trail. Nobody remembers seeing him that night—the night of the murder—but we're still canvassing. At this point I won't be at all surprised if we can find a witness who can place him there around the time of the murder.

"And—his uncle told us that the night of the murder was the night of one of his fugues. So the kid's got no alibi. None at all. Unless he can remember where he was and get somebody to corroborate it.

"We got a warrant and we searched his room, his house. The house, like I told you, is just a couple of blocks away from the trailhead. And it turns out he would walk right past the London house on the way to Chautauqua. Anyway, we search his room, and in a locked metal box that's not very well hidden behind some books on a bookcase we find—God, this is hard—we find a big envelope stuffed with clippings about the crash. You know, the one in Iowa. A videotape, too—he'd apparently taped some reports off the news and even had the crash itself on tape. He had some family pictures in there, too.

"And in that metal box he also has a nylon ass pack with a can of mace and Marilyn London's driver's license in it." Purdy paused and watched my face absorb the news. A blip emerged in my forced calm, then my serene mask took over again.

"He's dead meat," I said.

"Yeah," Purdy said. "And there's more."

I felt as if the water in every cell in my body were, at once, vaporizing.

"His trust? Randy's trust?" Purdy said. "Russell London was the trustee. You and I shouldn't be too surprised at that, should we? Maybe we should even have guessed. Randy's dad had been on the planning board years ago. Did you know that?" I slowly shook my head, not to indicate to Purdy that I wasn't aware of Randy's father's position on the planning board, which I wasn't, but rather in anticipatory exasperation at what I knew Sam Purdy was going to tell me next.

"During the same time period Russ London had been mayor. They apparently got to be friends." Purdy paused. "The kid's trust has over four million in assets. Lot of life insurance, a hefty settlement from the airline, flight insurance from the credit card company. A few years' interest by now. Four, five million. Lot of money."

Purdy stood up and moved over to the French doors, his back to me. I tried to remember if I'd ever even noticed who signed the checks from the trust that paid for Randy's treatment. I was pretty sure it wasn't Russ London. I'd have noticed the name. Instead, the signatory was probably an anonymous somebody in his old law office. I started tapping the eraser end of a number two pencil on my desk, counting the taps, timing how long it would take Sam Purdy to get to the next part of the story. The part I didn't want to hear.

"Russ London invested a ton of Randy's money in Pain Perdu, Alan. I had Lauren look over the documents for me, and she says it's a clear violation of the fiduciary restrictions of the trust."

I only got to six. I set the pencil down. "So is it fraud?" I asked.

"The nature of any criminal activity in this financial swamp is a little murky. That's part of the problem the special prosecutor has been having all along. See, although the trust language prohibits the trustee from investing assets in speculative or high-risk business ventures, the reality is that Pain Perdu is making money hand over fist, and the investment has probably appreciated a minimum of twenty-five percent in one year. So what do you do? Censure an ex-mayor, current county commissioner, for making an astute business decision for a poor kid who's lost his family in a terrible plane crash? Nope. What most of his political buddies would probably do is slap him on the wrist, just for propriety's sake, while they're whispering 'Good move, Russ' in his ear."

I was full of questions. "So tell me why Randy would kill his trustee's wife, Sam? Even if Randy knew all about all of this, why would he kill Marilyn London? He sees how busy the restaurant is, if he's bright enough to figure out that a chunk of his trust is tied up in it, he's also smart enough to see he's making money by the Dumpsterful. That is, if he was at all interested in making any more money, which I can tell you he isn't."

"He had means and opportunity, Alan. As for motive, let's not forget that the kid is crazy."

My reflex was to defend Randy's sanity. But in Purdy's tone I recognized that his categorization of Randy's mental state wasn't an accusation. In Purdy's words lay a gift. I said, "That, Sam, sounds like an attorney proposing a defense strategy."

"Hey, I'm just tired. You're just listening to the musing of one tired old detective. I mean—this kid, this poor kid—there's the crash, and losing his parents and his sister, the trauma, the memories, the wicked guardians, the stress, the fugues, you know, so who could blame the kid for being a corner short of a square?"

I was touched by the magnanimity involved in Purdy tipping his hand about the nature of what he would be encouraging Elliot Bellhaven, the deputy DA, to believe about Marilyn London's murder.

I said, "Randy's aunt and uncle could be part of all this, Sam. Shit, it's their restaurant that the money was invested in. And I find it hard to believe that they haven't read the trust documents. So they've got a conflict here. And given that conflict, they're certainly in no position to make any decisions in their status as Randy's legal guardians."

"Yeah, we know. Absolutely. I agree. Elliot does, too.

He's already suggested to the court that the kid needs a g.a.l. He should have one appointed by morning." He rubbed the heel of both palms hard into his eyes. I could hear the grating from across the room. "I suggested to Elliot that Casey Sparrow might be a good choice to act as the kid's guardian ad litem. I thought it would be a good idea to get a lawyer without any ties in the county to act as his g.a.l.—somebody with no allegiance to the ex-mayor, with no favors owed to the DA's office—and, given the circumstances, it won't hurt to have somebody who knows a little something about criminal defense. You know?"

I knew. I was relieved that Sam Purdy was looking out for Randy.

"Thanks, Sam," I said.

"It's nothing," said Sam. "Just doing my job."

My tension had lessened just enough so that I was suddenly aware that the tendons in my neck were in danger of petrification. I rubbed the cusp at the base of my skull with my right hand and said, "You're not sure he did it, are you, Sam?"

"All I get certain about is evidence. And I got a lot of evidence. Sometimes I think I got too much. Know what I mean? But with adolescent perps sometimes you get so much evidence you think you been visited by Santa Claus." He yawned. It was the first time I remembered seeing him more tired than hungry.

Purdy made every light on the short drive to the hospital. I couldn't remember ever making five straight lights in Boulder. Why this time, when I wished the ride could last forever?

Purdy said, "I have an ambulance waiting to transport him to the jail for booking. A patrolman will go with him. You can ride with him, too, if you would like."

I didn't respond to his offer. Reminding myself of the fear Randy expressed to me about restraints, I said, "You're not gonna have to use handcuffs, are you? I'm sure he'll cooperate."

Purdy paused and said, "Yeah, handcuffs aren't pleasant."

I nodded once in defeat.

Purdy put on his cop face and parked the car in a no-parking zone near the hospital entrance. We took the elevator to the top floor and walked down the corridor to the locked entrance to the adolescent unit. Two patrolmen were waiting for us. Purdy raised his hand to push the buzzer to be allowed into the unit.

I said, "I have a key."

I started to unlock the door, and Purdy said to one of the patrolmen, "You guys wait here, Tom," and then to me, "I'm as sorry as you are that I have to do this."

"I know, Sam," I said. "Please, for Randy's sake, imagine you're arresting Simon."

At the image of incarcerating his own son, Purdy said, "Whoa," under his breath and led me into the unit.

Where the staff was in absolute chaos.

No kids were visible. Given the late afternoon hour, the kids would normally be back on the ward after their school day. The quiet hallway probably meant that for some reason they had been confined to their rooms.

There were five phones in the glassed-in nursing station. Someone was on every one of them. Down the parallel hallways to the patient rooms, two hospital security guards—one man, one woman—were frantically checking doors and windows.

In sudden terror I scanned everywhere I could see for a crash cart and ran down the corridor to Randy's room. A short, strong-looking kid of sixteen or so sat on one of the beds beneath a poster of an emaciated man with long blond hair and tattooed flames on his abdomen. The other bed was vacant.

"Where's Randy?" I blurted out.

The boy was stocky and had crew-cut red hair with a long rat's tail. A self-inflicted tattoo covered his left wrist. He said, "He's gone." The kid's Metallica T-shirt was full of holes.

"Gone?"

"He ran. Busted out."

"Thank God," I said. Then to the kid, "Thank you."

"He was a cool dude. Hope he makes it."

I turned to head back to the nursing station. Purdy was behind me. He waited until we'd walked a few feet from the room, and said, "What's with him?"

"Who knows. He said Randy's gone. He ran."

"And to that you said 'Thank God'?"

"Sam, I thought he had killed himself. I'm not happy he ran. I was afraid he was dead."

I trotted behind Purdy to the nursing station. Everybody was still on a telephone.

Purdy planted himself in the middle of the small room, held up his badge, and said, "Whichever one of you is trying to call me—and one of you had *better* be trying to call me—hang up the goddamn phone and tell me what the hell is going on." His voice cracked into the room like a dropped plate into a quiet dining room.

Everyone stopped speaking and looked his way. My beeper went off. Two nurses hung up phones.

"That's probably me," one of the nurses said to me. "I just paged you, Dr. Gregory."

The head nurse, Nancy, said, "And I've been on the phone to your office, Sergeant."

"Detective," Purdy corrected. "So where is the kid?"

"He bolted after school."

"Bolted?"

"Took off, ran. On the way back to the unit from the classroom he took off down some fire stairs and we couldn't catch him. One of the kids says they saw him out their window, thinks he was running across North Boulder Park." The head nurse was the one answering the questions, telling the story. She was accomplishing the difficult task of looking authoritative, defiant, apologetic, and meek simultaneously. Too much time around adolescent psych patients, probably.

"What's he wearing?" Purdy asked.

A different nurse answered him. I chimed in that Randy had a limp from his broken toe.

Purdy grabbed a phone and called in Randy's description to a dispatcher and ordered that a search be started.

I turned to the head nurse. "Nancy, was he dissociated?"

"Hadn't seemed to be, Doctor," she said pleasantly, as if I'd asked if he'd finished his dessert after lunch.

Purdy's presence was certainly causing everybody to act formally. I couldn't remember the last time anybody on the nursing staff had referred to me as "Doctor." Not twice in one minute, anyway. I said, "So how did he look this afternoon?"

"His affect has been flat, maybe occasionally teary, since you saw him earlier. He got a phone call from his aunt— no, his uncle—and that left him upset for a little while. But that was before school. He hadn't talked about it with anyone—refused to have a one-on-one. Since then—flat." She shrugged her shoulders.

"Why wasn't this kid on a shorter leash?" asked Purdy.

Nancy, the head nurse, jumped at that one. "His doctor"—everybody looked my way—"hadn't reduced his privilege level. The patients' doctors determine the level of restriction of their patients."

Purdy glared at me.

"It looks, Sam," I said, "like I may have miscalculated."

Purdy continued his glare. "Uh-uh. No. Miscalculating is something you do on your taxes. What everybody in this room has done"—he paused and made definitive eye contact with each individual in the nursing station, me last— "what everybody in this room has done is *fuck up.*"

39

Purdy stranded me without a ride when he stormed off the unit to organize a posse to find Randy. I desperately needed some support and wanted to see Lauren—maybe even needed to see Lauren—but she didn't answer her telephone at work, and her answering machine was on guard duty at home.

After trying Diane's house and getting yet another machine, I finally reached her on her portable phone while she was returning from dropping Raoul off at Denver's airport so he could head back to Huntsville on satellite business. Diane was in the fast lane near Broomfield as I began to fill her in on Randy's escape from the adolescent unit and on Purdy's plans to arrest him as soon as he could find him. Her questions and my answers continued until she was caught in traffic on Twenty-eighth Street in Boulder. When I asked for a ride back to the office from the hospital to get my rental Sundance, Diane eagerly offered to take me to dinner; memories of what had happened to her during Raoul's last trip to Huntsville made her grateful for the company.

She pulled her car under the canopy outside the ED of the hospital, and when I climbed in she immediately inquired whether I had a preference as to where we ate.

I said, "I haven't thought about it. I don't care."

She said, "Good, I was hoping you would say that."

She surprised me by turning west up toward the mountains, and in a couple of minutes she had her car going way too fast up Boulder Canyon. She downshifted abruptly about three miles up the canyon and slowed as she guided the car onto a bumpy bridge that led over Boulder Creek into the parking lot of the Red Lion Inn. "They have an early dinner menu," she said as though that explained something important about her choice of restaurants.

At that early hour, besides having an early dinner menu, the usually crowded Red Lion Inn had no customers. The host wanted to seat us in the main dining room. Diane had other ideas. She wanted "the corner table in the porch overlooking the swimming pool cemetery."

The host looked to me, hoping to find a face of reason. Not a chance. He was on his own. "We prefer to serve our early diners downstairs," he said pleasantly. "We have a very nice window table overlooking the lawn."

Diane smiled a wonderfully warm smile and said, "Oh, I'm sure you do. But I'm sure you can accommodate this one little tiny request. See"—she sighed and raised her eyebrows—"it's the table where we were engaged." She took my hand and led me up the stairs to the second-floor sun porch of the century-old converted hunting lodge that was set back thirty yards from the banks of Boulder Creek. The host followed reluctantly.

I said, "What's the swimming pool cemetery?"

"This place used to be a lodge-slash-resort-type place with a pool out front, like some architect decided that a blend of the rustic western and California motel looks was just what the Front Range needed during a renovation in 1953. The current owner bought it in the sixties. He got tired of the pool after a while and just buried the damn thing to get more parking." As we sat down in the corner table of Diane's choosing, she said, "It's right over there." I couldn't tell where she was pointing. "The owner and Raoul are poker buddies. They're both expatriates. And they both like Neiman, too. Believe me, it's not a pretty sight when it's our turn to host the poker games."

I glanced out. There was no tombstone to mark the swimming pool's demise. I decided to accept her word for its existence and not press for more evidence. I was mostly afraid she would provide it.

Diane gazed once at the menu, set it down, called the waiter over, and ordered a half bottle of wine, straightened her skirt, pressed her shoulders back to perfect her posture, and looked at me.

"I took a peek at those files," she said. She sat calmly, as if she had just lobbed a big stone into a still pond and had all day to wait for the ripples to reach me on the shore.

"Will it help Randy?" I asked.

She ignored my question.

She said, "Paul Weinman knew some stuff—maybe even *enough* stuff—to make him a suspect in some of this mess. He's lucky he's dead. Now *there's* an alibi you can take to the bank."

So far Diane was just being tantalizing and hadn't quite registered the fact that I was in no mood for a slow seduction. But I also knew that if she was going to tell me confidential data from Paul's files, she would do it at her own pace. Pressure from me would be counterproductive. Technically she could share the information with me in the form of seeking a clinical consultation or an ethical consultation. But she was going to need to get there on her own.

Diane continued, "But since Paul *is* dead, that rules him out."

"Unless he was feeding this information—whatever it is—to somebody before he died."

The waiter arrived to pour wine. With surprisingly little effort he broke the cork off in the neck of the bottle and walked sheepishly away from the table. Diane smiled a compassionate smile until he turned away and then shook her head in disdain.

"Who else has had access to the files, Diane?"

"Me," she said, smiling. "Paul's attorney for a while. Cybil Malone, his girlfriend, still has some of them in her basement. Maybe she knows how to pick locks. You"— she smiled again—"and Raoul. And some burglars. That's it."

"No, it's not," I said. "First, the burglars don't count. A lot of this crap had already happened before the first burglary. If the files are tied into this, they have to have some relevance to the initial crimes, too. Claire's murder in your office. The house exploding—maybe. The financial shenanigans at Pain Perdu. So the burglaries probably have had to do with removing preexisting evidence of something. But I don't know what.

"And second, there are a couple of other people who had access to Paul's records. The weekend he died—remember?—there were rumors and rumbles that one or two of his office mates went through his records to contact his patients so that they wouldn't just show up for appointments or hear about his death on the news." She looked dubious. "You remember, don't you?"

Finally Diane said, "I'd forgotten, but, yeah, I remember now."

"I wonder who they were. The people who went through the files."

"Me too. But there are at least a half a dozen therapists in Paul's old office that we have to choose from."

"Anyone you can ask?"

Diane knew everybody in town. "Clancy Coates is in that suite. I know I won't ask him."

"Diane. This 'innocent until proven guilty' stuff has some merit. So far Clancy's only been accused, not convicted."

"You're entitled to your standards. I have mine."

This was an argument I wasn't going to win. "What about that new Ph.D., Eric Petrosian—you know, the one who came to me for supervision for a few weeks after Paul died. He's part of Paul's old group. At least he was. And he was in your supervision group when Claire Draper was killed, wasn't he? Can you ask him if he knows who went through Paul's files?"

Diane liked the idea. "Yes, I can ask Eric. He owes me a favor or two."

The waiter returned with a fresh bottle of wine and wanted to take our food order. I was recalling with some unease my meal with Peter and Adrienne at Pain Perdu and the confrontation I witnessed between Eric Petrosian and Geoff Tobias, and I wasn't paying any attention to the menu. When the waiter turned to me with his pen poised I told him I would have whatever Diane was having.

He nodded and seemed to be fighting an impulse to click his heels together. He didn't. He left.

Shaking her head and whispering, Diane said, "You just ordered antelope, Alan."

"I did? It's okay. I'm not hungry anyway. But I don't think you should ask Eric Petrosian about the files. You *like* antelope?"

"Yes. I like antelope. I like elk and deer. The whole family of stealthy forest creatures. Each one I eat, it's one less beast to destroy my garden. And why shouldn't I talk to Eric?"

"Isn't it gamey? Like liver?"

"About Eric? Please."

I explained about the run-in at Pain Perdu between Eric Petrosian and Geoff Tobias.

"Eric might not have liked the service. Young Eric can be pretty arrogant. Some people say he's so arrogant at times that he acts like a young psychiatrist."

I suddenly had a hunch. "Did you find Russ London's file?" I asked.

Diane handled the change in direction as artfully as a Golden Glove infielder handles the short hop. "No. It must be an old file. I assume it's stored in Cybil's basement. I've only read some of the files that are at our office downtown and at home. In those boxes, remember?"

"Yeah. Can we go to Cybil's to look for Russ's file tonight after we eat?"

She nodded and shrugged simultaneously.

I sipped some wine and said, "Thanks."

When the food came she ate both portions of antelope.

Cybil Malone lived in town. We called her from Diane's car and drove to her house right after dinner. I was growing enamored with cellular phones.

Cybil's house was a pre–World War II bungalow on a tiny lot above the university not too far from Lauren's house. The inside of Cybil's home was awash with highly polished darkly stained oak, which was set off against a sea of stark white—walls, furniture, art, rugs, Cybil. She answered the door wearing white flannel lounging pajamas, offered us coffee that we declined, and accepted our renewed condolences about Paul Weinman's death before leading us down to her basement past an immense gravity furnace that had been converted from burning coal to burning natural gas. Octopus-like arms snaked all over the basement from the top of the igloo-shaped furnace. Cybil opened the door to a storage room, flicked on a light, and waved us in.

Paul's file cabinets sat on the side of the packed storeroom and looked undisturbed. As in covered with dust. Diane quickly unlocked the three cabinets and removed the steel bars that ran vertically to the padlocks at the top.

I stood back, waiting to be invited to help. Cybil intuited that she wasn't to be part of the search party, excused herself, and went back upstairs.

Diane said, "Help me find the file. Then I'll read it and decide whether I want a consultation about what's in it."

I started at the bottom of the most distant cabinet. Diane started at the top of the closest. I yanked on a reluctant drawer, which opened with a squeal. The first thing I discovered was that Paul Weinman's files were not particularly well organized. But I didn't find Russell London's patient record.

Diane said, "Voilà," after about ten minutes and pulled out a thin manila file. She moved across the room to a 1970-ish recliner covered in an absurd shade of orange vinyl that was eternally cast somewhere between pumpkin and persimmon, swept some dust off the seat, and sat down to read.

"Nothing amazing here," she said after five minutes or so that I spent sorting through twenty-plus years of Cybil Malone's book collection. She had a first edition *Our Bodies, Ourselves* and a mint-condition *Whole Earth Catalog*, as well as an impressive collection of Stephen King in hardcover.

"Looks like Russ was depressed about his marriage. Complained his wife was too critical, they had communication problems, intimacy problems, who takes out the garbage problems, who isn't getting enough problems, where does all the money go problems—all that ya ya.

There's a single session from 1987 that says nothing but 'Reviewed 1981 incident with patient.' And wait a second"—she flipped a page—"there's a referral to Clancy Coates for a med eval. Clancy apparently prescribed some sleepers for our mayor." She shook her head. "Paul should've just forced Russ to attend city council meetings. Puts everybody else in town to sleep." She closed the file. "That's it. Nothing politically sensitive."

She stood up and returned the thin file to its place in the drawer.

"When was all this?"

"Last session was four years ago," she said.

"How long was he in treatment?"

"Almost a year. Not weekly, though. Maybe twenty sessions total."

I shrugged and said, "Oh, well, my car's at the office."

"Let's go say thanks to Cybil and I'll take you to it."

"How carefully did you read the files in that box under the stairs at the office, Diane?"

She stole her eyes away from the Ninth Street Bridge over Boulder Creek and made a suspicious face in my direction. "Just skimmed them, just read them to get the gist."

"Would you have noticed a missing page or two?"

"Don't know. Maybe. Maybe not."

"Will you look again?"

"If I agree to do that, will you go someplace with me and have dessert?" I knew she didn't want to go home alone. "And pay?"

"Deal."

She parked the Saab in her usual place in front of the garage, and we entered the building through her office. I went into the kitchen and disarmed the alarm. She had the closet under the stairs unlocked by the time I got there. I slid out the heavy box and pulled open the lid. She grabbed a file, leaned back against the wall, sat down, arranged her skirt around her, and started reading. I sat on the floor opposite her and reread all the names on the labels of the files to see if any new ones grabbed my attention.

None did. My beeper went off. It startled both of us. We were sitting on the floor of the hallway of a building we both owned and Diane was reading a file she had every legal right to be reading, yet we were feeling exceedingly illicit. I left Diane alone to read and used her office phone to access my Voicemail.

Purdy. They hadn't found Randy. Had I heard from him? I phoned the police department and told them to tell Detective Purdy that the answer to his question was no.

Diane was still reading when I sat down again.

"No luck with Randy," I said. "I hope they find him. He'll be much safer in jail."

Diane reached out and reassured me with a light touch to my arm without removing her eyes from what she was reading.

"What are these?" I said, pointing to a couple of files at the front of the box.

"Would you please stop interrupting me?" she said, and glanced at the box where I was pointing. "I don't know. Take a look. If they're clinical, put them aside and I'll read them when I'm done with this one."

The first file had a handwritten label that read "DSS Report Log," the second a typed label that read "Consultations and Referrals—To Be Filed."

I started with the "DSS Report Log" file and recognized quickly that it was a record of Paul Weinman's phone contacts with the Department of Social Services regarding reports of child abuse and neglect he was required to make under Colorado law. There were six pages, each with a different date. Three of the pages had names on them, three just initials, none of which I recognized. I didn't read them. The forms recorded the outcome of conversations with DSS caseworkers regarding generic questions about the law and what he might and might not be required to report under the child abuse reporting statute.

The "Consultations and Referrals" file contained about twice as many pages as the other one. Its contents seemed to be a record of referrals and consultations made for inactive patients whose closed files were not stored in Paul's downtown office. He apparently placed them in this "To Be Filed" file until he got around to moving them to their proper homes.

The last page in the "Consultations and Referrals" file took my breath away. It was dated only fifteen months before. Paul's handwriting was cramped and difficult to decipher. It took me a minute.

> pc from M. London seeking therapy for herself. Given past treatment of her husband, told her I would not see her. She was angry and asked for other names. Gave her three: Clancy, Diane, Eric.

I read it again. And again. "Diane," I said.

"What?" she barked.

"Look." I held the sheet of paper out to her.

Annoyed, she snapped it out of my hands and held it while she continued to read the file that was already in her hand. After about a minute she turned her attention to the sheet I had handed her and read it. Her eyes opened wide. She whistled without using her lips, just her tongue against the top of her mouth. "I'm not sure I like the company I'm being included with here."

"Well, Diane, according to Marilyn London one of the three of you was sleeping with her and toying with her self-esteem. Or—who knows—maybe she was just jerking me off. I don't know what's true anymore."

"You can slim your list to two, honey. I'm not that flexible. If I was going to start assaulting patients sexually, I can guarantee you the odds are long against them being named Marilyn."

"Should we flip a coin?" I asked.

"Sure," she said. "Heads it's Clancy Coates." She grinned an evil grin. "And tails it's Clancy Coates."

My own deductions were chasing me in a different direction. "Diane, Diane, Diane. Don't be so quick to accuse Clancy. Stop for a minute and think. There's another connection. You haven't told me yet what Paul had in his files. But even without knowing what's in there, I do know that Paul, Clancy, and Eric were all in your supervision group, right? And didn't you tell me you presented Claire Draper's case to the group just before she was killed?"

"Yes, I did," she said in a hollow voice that anticipated the destination of my train of thought.

"So all of them knew from your case presentation how desperate Claire's husband was to find her and about his threats to murder her, right?"

"Yes, but I don't use last names in my case presentations—none of us do. So they couldn't have known—"

"Unless they already knew the Drapers' story from Harlan Draper, or from Russ London—Claire was London's secretary before he became a county commissioner, wasn't she?—and just put two and two together when you mentioned this desperate battered patient."

"Whom I identified as 'C.' "

"Whom you identified as 'C.' "

Diane's bottom lip quivered. Then her shoulders shook. "Alan, I may have set Claire up to be killed. God. Oh, my God. I can't believe it—it's like I handed the loaded gun to that bastard." She was staring at the blank wall in front of her, shivering as if she were terribly cold, hugging herself with both arms, rocking gently, rhythmically.

I moved across the narrow hall and draped an arm around her.

When she stopped sobbing I said, "There are pieces missing. I still can't figure out how anyone—Paul, Clancy, Eric—found out about what Russ London did with Randy's trust money at Mirabelle."

Diane said, "There's some things I haven't told you yet. Paul knew a little of it. He knew bits and pieces from Larry Templeton. It's all in Larry's chart. Larry was an initial investor in the restaurant. His stake got diluted when some big dollars came in, and he got pretty furious. Complained about it to Paul, so Paul knew at least some of it. And somebody, some therapist—Clancy, Eric, *somebody*—probably heard plenty of details from Marilyn London.

"And the rest? I think the rest was easy for whoever was abusing Marilyn, because the rest probably came from Marilyn London's pillow. So all we need to do is find out which of these fine therapists was screwing Marilyn London and we'll know who was blackmailing people with information from Paul's files.''

Diane stood and straightened her clothing. She wiped carefully under her eyes to spare her remaining mascara. Then her whole upper body shook once more, and she buried her head in my chest and resumed her tears.

In the midst of her crying she turned her head aside and said, ''Elliot Bellhaven is HIV positive, Alan. It's in his sister's chart. This city's politician of tomorrow is infected with the AIDS virus.''

I waited until her tears seemed to have been replaced by sniffling. ''So maybe Elliot's being blackmailed, too?''

''Maybe. It's certainly rich material to use against somebody with political ambitions.''

I wanted her to tell me on her own, but impatience won out. I asked, ''And what's in Geoff Tobias's chart, Diane?''

She managed a little laugh through the thin film of tears. ''I couldn't see a thing in there worthy of blackmail. Paul wasn't very fond of him. It looks like he was being treated for being a greedy, sniveling wimp—kind of an entitled narcissistic pygmy.''

I chuckled at the image. Shaking the referral record I still held in my hand, I said, ''You know, if this piece of paper tells us what we think it tells us, Clancy or Eric may have tried to kill us.''

Diane's response was quick. ''But why? It makes no sense to hurt us. How likely were we to figure this mess out? If they hadn't kept pushing at us, the burglaries and trying to kill us, we would've just left it alone. It makes no sense. No sense at all.

''And anyway,'' she said, her face all scrunched up in consternation, ''if this someone, Eric or Clancy, already knew what was in these files, why the hell did he need to keep breaking into our office to read them again?''

Of course, I thought. ''That's it. Diane. You've got it. It wasn't Clancy or Eric breaking into our offices. It couldn't have been. Whoever broke into your office up at your house ignored Paul's files, which were in plain view. They didn't want to read Paul's files. They were after *your* files. There's something in your files that someone doesn't want exposed. Somebody besides Eric and Clancy.''

Diane was again staring blankly at the walls. She turned to me acutely and said, "They broke into yours, too, hon. There must be something in your files, too. What the hell do we know that we don't know we know?"

It took us about five seconds to decide to go ask Clancy and Eric that very question.

40

Diane and I spent fifteen minutes trying to reach Eric Petrosian, Ph.D., and Clarence Coates, M.D., through their answering services, without success. Diane had their home numbers in her directory. No one answered at Clancy Coates's home. Eric Petrosian was less fortunate; his number was busy.

Diane said, "I don't think he's married or living with anybody, so he must be home. Let's go."

She laughed when I asked her if she wanted me to drive.

A minute later I reached over and turned down the music on the radio and said in a quiet voice, "How is us going through Paul's files any more defensible than Clancy or Eric or whoever going through Paul's files? You know, you and I are sharing case information—yours, mine, and Paul Weinman's—like we have some special dispensation."

Diane swallowed before she answered. She said, "One of us, either you *or* me, has the legal right to every bit of information we're discussing. Technically, we continue to consult with each other. In my heart, though, I guess I think it's different only because we're different." Her voice sounded metallic and hollow.

"So you're troubled, too?" I said.

"To the bone."

"If anybody else was doing what we're doing, we would both be judging them pretty harshly, you know."

"Yeah, I know." She exhaled loudly. "Let's just say that this time, Alan, we're grading on the curve."

"Maybe there's another way."

"Maybe. Like?"

"Don't know."

"Me neither."

I said, "We could leave this investigation to Purdy, to the police."

For a few seconds Diane was quiet. Then she shook her head. "They may figure out what's wrong up at that restaurant and they may figure out what's wrong up at that place in the mountains, and they may even figure out who really killed Marilyn London. But they're never gonna figure out *why* without a peek at Paul's files."

I didn't know what to say. I wanted to argue and couldn't find an argument anywhere. I felt defeated. On a previous case I'd spent a year of my life defending the ethical standard of confidentiality, and now I couldn't find a good rationale not to trash the concept of privilege myself.

I adjusted the volume on the radio again and told Diane how cold Lauren had seemed since she got back from New York. And about how considerate Merideth suddenly seemed to be. I asked her what she thought.

She seemed relieved that the subject was changed. "What I think is that you're being a fool. You've had a day in the sun, Alan. But you're too fond of it. Contrary to your apparent assumption, however, you are not valuable enough that either of these women is going to wait around forever for your decision."

"You think I should make up my mind?"

"No. I think you should recognize that your mind is probably already made up. You just don't like your choice because it doesn't give you everything you want. Anyway, I think Lauren has been patient with you beyond expectation. I'd be fed up with you if I were her, too."

"The baby complicates things," I said.

"I'm sure it does," she said, her voice compassionate again. "But it's not a compelling reason to reunite with Meri."

"I know," I said, "but letting go of her is not something I'm very good at."

"Yeah, I've sort of been noticing that for the past year and a half," she said. After checking her mirrors, she turned to face me for a split second. "Listen, I'm biased.

You choose to go back to Merideth, you're gonna end up having to move to the Bay Area to keep her happy, I'm gonna lose one of my best friends, I'm gonna have to take in a new partner, who will probably drive me crazy, and I'm gonna have to listen to Lauren vilify you for what you've done despite the fact that I'm still gonna love you even though you've been a jerk to her, she'll probably quit my softball team for revenge, I won't be able to find a decent second baseman, we'll lose the league championship, I'll get depressed and develop an alcohol problem, Raoul will divorce me and I'll have so little money I'll have to rent your crappy little house on the Kansas side of Boulder, and Peter will try and make me his new best friend."

"So you do have an opinion?"

"Honey, have you ever known me *not* to have an opinion? Just remember, it's not advice. I don't do advice."

"Diane, your softball team has been in last place for the past three years."

"I have a couple of promising rookies. Young, strong. Long-ball hitters." I started to laugh. "Don't laugh," she said. "This is our year. Don't screw it up for me, Alan. Second basemen who can hit over two fifty and turn the occasional double play are not easy to come by."

I knew better than to laugh again, so I smiled to myself in the dark car. We rode in silence the rest of the way to Eric Petrosian's modest house.

At the final turn Diane said, "Now *there's* an omen," and pointed at the street sign. It read "Hemlock Way."

I said, "I don't want to do this. We're arriving at his door, unannounced, at ten o'clock at night to ask him if he's dabbling in unethical behavior, burglary, or attempted murder. Maybe even real murder. This man's not gonna be happy to see us."

Diane wasn't hearing any of it. She had completed whatever moral gymnastics were necessary for her to resolve her ambivalence about proceeding on our questionable crusade. "Remember the avalanche. Remember my head. Remember Randy. Let's go."

Randy. Yeah, Randy.

Dr. Eric Petrosian's home was an abundantly land-scaped little fifties ranch with a two-car garage. A couple of interior lights were on, but the front of the house was not illuminated. He wasn't expecting guests.

I knocked. Diane watched the lack of vigor in my stroke, made an exasperated face, and punched the doorbell with the middle finger of her left hand. We could hear the chimes inside playing some insipid tune that I couldn't identify. Diane would probably know what it was, but that would piss me off so I didn't ask. We waited. The air was chilly and, atypically for Colorado, moist. I wondered about fog by morning.

Diane pushed the button again.

I said, "Maybe he's still on the phone." She ignored me.

A bundled person of indeterminate gender walked by with a standard poodle on a leash. I turned to watch; Diane stared at the door as if her determination alone would force Eric to answer it. From the sidewalk the big brown dog growled at me and then emptied part of its bladder on Eric's small lawn. I waved to the dog walker, who responded by tugging on the leash and moving on.

We waited.

I suggested that I go back to Diane's car and use her portable phone to determine if Eric was still home.

Diane didn't respond right away. I could hear the drone of traffic from a nearby boulevard. Finally she handed me her keys and said, "Okay," and recited Eric's number.

It took me three or four minutes to manage to get the car unlocked, the interior lights on, and the phone powered up and dialed. I was hoping it would ring and ring and ring and that we could leave and reconsider our plan. Instead the line was still busy.

From the curb I called the news to Diane by the door. I could have simply walked over to her with the portable phone in hand, but given her mood the distance between us felt like a reasonable buffer. She pounded her left foot twice and blew a balloon of steam from her mouth.

After turning off the power on the phone, I walked back

to join her. She said, "He knows we're here. And he knows why we're here. He's not answering the door."

"Sometimes I don't answer the door when I'm on the phone," I said.

"Bullshit. He's avoiding us. Which means he knows we know something. Which means we're right." She pounded on the door with the side of her fist. I realized with some resignation that she wasn't going to give up.

I went back to the Saab and called the operator. I identified myself as Dr. Alan Gregory and told her I had an emergency I needed to discuss with a colleague, Dr. Petrosian. I explained that his line had been busy for over thirty minutes and could she please check and see if it was operative, and if it was to please break through and notify him of the emergency.

It took her about a minute to tell me that his phone was off the hook. "Sorry," she said.

"You and me both," I muttered to myself as I clicked off the phone.

I walked back to the front door and told Diane what the operator had said. Diane replied, "Bullshit."

I said, "You're being truly stubborn."

She said, "I know he's in there. I'm going to look around. Coming?"

When I started to protest, she said, "What's he gonna do? Call the cops? Hardly."

I followed her down a narrow cement walkway that ran past the side of the garage and into the backyard. The rooms at the back of the simple house were brightly lit. Diane turned and sneered an I-told-you-so smile. Maybe because we were now officially trespassing, the sough of the distant traffic seemed even louder.

The first room we came to on our stroll was the kitchen. The unshaded windows revealed that Eric had removed the doors from the kitchen cabinets and painted them a rich yellow. One entire shelf seemed covered with nothing but a huge selection of various olive oils and vinegars in tins, bottles, and straw-bottomed cruets.

It all seemed so domestic. "He's a cook," I whispered to Diane as if that were a reason to curtail our surveillance.

"So what? Ever see 'Sweeney Todd'?"

I was about to chuckle when I saw the blood.

Diane saw it seconds after I did and raised one hand to her mouth. Splatters and droplets stained the lower cabinets and extended up one wall. A large pool of red was puddled at the side of the room in front of the range and had begun to seep under the stove. The edges and surface of the pool were elastic and taut and had begun to darken. Linear streaks of a rustier red led to a side door, as if someone had used the floor of the short narrow hall to clean a paintbrush that had been dipped in the kitchen mess.

Diane calmly pulled on her leather gloves and tried the handle on the door that led to the kitchen from the yard. The door was unlocked and swung open with a screech.

My heart was struggling to find space next to my esophagus.

Diane said, "We have to see if whoever it is, or was, is alive."

I nodded dumbly. But what I wanted to do was go back out to the car and call the police.

"Don't step in the blood. Don't touch anything," she said.

I said, "Actually, Diane, I was planning on leaving a note." She shot me a hostile glare. I lowered my voice and said, "Diane, I'm not sure this is a good idea."

"And what if it's Randy?" she said.

I sighed. Thirty–love.

I followed her around the bloodstains to the perimeter of the room and scooted sideways down the side of the short hall to the cheap birch door to the garage. Diane pulled open the door and looked into the dark room.

She seemed fearless. She reached inside with her gloved hand and flicked on a light. The overhead glare seemed unusually stark. The far side of the garage housed a Japanese pickup, the near side a Rototiller, a lawn mower, and domestic junk. The path of smeared and dripped blood extended to the edge of the closed garage door. I stepped carefully over the wet, rusty path and peered inside the cab of the pickup and onto the bed in back. Empty. I'd been holding my breath. I exhaled.

Diane whispered, "I think somebody was dragging him. Must have pulled him out to the driveway and put him in a car."

"Let's get out of here," I pleaded.

"Maybe we should check the rest of the house?"

"Diane? Do you *really* want to find whoever might be in the rest of the house?"

"Now there's something to consider," she said. "But what if it's Randy hiding back there?"

"You think he did this?" I asked, pointing at the blood.

"Alan, I don't even know this kid. I just know what he's been through and what he's been accused of. None of it's pretty.

"I'll go first," said Diane. "My head trauma is less recent."

I countered by saying, "But much more severe," and tried to move in front of her.

But she took off before I could pass and repeated, "Don't touch anything."

Despite the confines of the unimaginative architecture, Eric Petrosian had done nice things to his house. It would have been easier to appreciate his decorating efforts if the bulk of his accent pieces, furniture, and art weren't strewn around the rooms in destructive disarray.

"This place has been thrown," Diane whispered.

"Tossed," I said. "This place has been *tossed*."

"Whatever," she said, hating, as always, to be corrected.

At the far side of the living room the carpet began to squish beneath our feet and provide fossilized records of our footprints for future generations of crime scene investigators. All the way down the hall we walked—squish, squish—to find each of the bedrooms in similar disarray. In the master bedroom we discovered the source of the flood—Eric's water bed had been slashed open and the huge bladder folded back so someone could search underneath it.

"Can we go now?" I pleaded.

"Let me check the bathroom first," Diane said.

She walked in, closed the door behind her, and re-emerged a minute later, the sound of the toilet flushing preceding her return.

"I really had to pee," she said.

I couldn't believe it. "Diane—they'll know we were here!"

"What?" she said. "They gonna use butt prints?"

God help me.

I waited for Diane to precede me, and we retraced our steps through the house to the backyard and then back around front. I stopped and pointed out the continuation of the path of blood on the driveway. "Diane, we're screwed. We stepped in it already. On our way around the house the first time."

She looked down at the sticky drops, which in the dim light were barely distinguishable from ancient oil stains on the asphalt. She shrugged, disinterested, and walked to her car.

"Don't you care?" I asked.

"Spilt milk," she said. The calm in her voice made me particularly uneasy. "Could you hurry it up a bit, Alan? I would seriously like to get away from here before the police arrive."

"Why? You peed in his toilet. We stepped in the blood. They'll know we were here."

She fastened her seat belt and started the Saab. "Don't be so histrionic. And stop perseverating. They'll know *somebody* was here, not us. I don't want to stick around and explain to them why we were skulking around Eric Petrosian's house."

"Why the hell not? We haven't done anything."

"Because they'll want to know why we wanted to talk to him. And the reasons we want to talk to him are all in Paul's files. And I don't want to have to fight with your big detective friend about whether he gets to know what's in Paul's files. Because he doesn't."

Two blocks away Diane slowed the car, dialed the main switchboard at the police department after requesting the number from directory assistance, and said in a voice that mocked her husband's heritage that it seemed somebody had been hurt badly in a house on Hemlock Way. She gave Eric Petrosian's street address and did the cellular phone equivalent of hanging up before the exasperated person on the other end could pry any more information from her.

When Diane became hypercalm like this, she seemed surgical in her manner and in her inclination toward arrogance. I didn't want to talk to her until she snapped out of it. When she was finished vexing the public safety receptionist with her curt report of the mystery of Eric Petrosian's kitchen, I snatched the phone from her and called Sam Purdy's extension at the police department. He wasn't available. I called the adolescent psych unit. They hadn't yet heard anything about Randy's whereabouts. I was terribly afraid that it was Randy's blood spread all over Eric Petrosian's kitchen.

I set the phone down on the seat next to me.

Diane said, her voice even, "So it seems our prey is Eric. Not Clancy."

I was silent. I wondered if our prey was already deceased.

"Why did Eric want Claire dead? I don't get it." Diane's voice crept up half an octave in tone, a vain attempt at keeping the affect from exploding from within her.

I touched her upper arm. "I'm starting to think a lot of it has to do with that damn restaurant. I keep remembering the argument between Geoff Tobias and Eric Petrosian at Pain Perdu. I think Eric's somehow mixed up with the Londons and the Tobiases in that restaurant. Marilyn London told me that her therapist was mixed up with her financially as well as sexually. So I would guess that's it—through the restaurant. Claire was going to blow the lid off something to the grand jury. Eric couldn't permit that, so he used Harlan Draper like a loaded cannon to stop her in order to protect whatever financial shenanigans were going on at the restaurant. It's the only way this makes sense. Either by blackmail or extortion Eric must have dealt himself into the hand at Pain Perdu somehow. Either through Paul's files or his abuse of Marilyn London. Or both. And he's been protecting himself ever since."

"Did Eric blow up the Templetons' house?" Diane asked.

"God knows," I said.

Diane turned to me in the dark car, shaking her head. "We don't have it yet. This isn't enough. There's something else going on."

I was thinking the same thing. And I was deeply troubled by my hunch that the something else going on had to do with Randy Navens, United Flight 232, and a mountain enclave called Mirabelle. And with whoever's blood was spilled all over the house on Hemlock Way.

I pulled my Day-Timer from my coat pocket and flipped pages until I found the phone number of Rita Templeton's cabin in Coal Creek Canyon. It was after eleven, but she answered after a single ring and sounded wide awake.

"Rita, it's Alan Gregory."

"Oh"—she sighed—"I'm so glad it's you."

"Randy may be having another one of those episodes. Like he did the last time. I was wondering if you've seen him."

"I know. I know all about it. The sheriff has been here. Twice. Looking around with flashlights and those bright lights on their cars. They've come by and asked me about him. My son thinks this is the most exciting thing ever." She was breathless.

"Have you seen him, Rita?"

She paused. "No. I haven't. But I feel somebody out there. You know. You ever get those feelings? Like you're being watched?"

"Maybe it's just the sheriff keeping an eye out for Randy."

"Maybe, I don't know," said Rita.

Diane kept looking impatiently across the front seat at me as she would if we were strangers standing at a street corner and she needed to use the pay phone I was chatting away on. I rotated on the seat and rounded a shoulder at her as she stopped the Saab at a red light.

"You think he's there, don't you, Rita?"

Another, longer pause from her. "Yes. Why are the police looking for him? Has he done something?"

My turn to pause. "They think he may have killed Marilyn London."

"Randy? The kid with the broken toe? That Randy?"

"Rita, may I come up, look around?"

No hesitation now. "Please. Alan, please."

I picked up my Sundance at the office and talked Diane into following me home. The whole time I was changing my clothes, Diane insisted vociferously through my closed bedroom door that she should come up to Coal Creek Canyon with me. I finally convinced her to stay in town in case Randy showed up in the city. I would be almost an hour away—and if he did show up, I would need her to be with him until I got back. She finally relented and told me to take her portable phone so she would have a way to reach me. It seemed like a good idea.

Talking her into going up the hill to Peter and Adrienne's house was more problematic. The bad guys all knew where I lived, and I didn't want Diane in my house by herself. She used her aversion to Peter as a ploy to get me to agree to let her stay in my house instead. I argued that her denial about the jeopardy she might be in bordered on the hysterical. She remonstrated with an identical charge about my planned trip up Coal Creek Canyon in the middle of the night in search of an accused murderer.

I ignored her. She ignored me.

"And," I told her, "you don't have anything to worry about with Peter. He could sleep through a day care center being set up in his living room. You'll never see him." But Diane was adamant. I felt as if I were trying to persuade the Mississippi River into detouring through Nebraska.

I couldn't waste any more time arguing with Diane, so I picked up the phone and called out the heavy artillery.

Adrienne.

Minutes later, as I was climbing into the Sundance to head to Mirabelle, Adrienne was urging Diane up the hill, one arm around her, concurring that "of course he's an asshole, honey. That's not news." Adrienne's other little hand was behind her back, shooing me away.

Get. Get.

I loved having the cellular phone. And I was terribly anxious. I used the phone to try to allay my anxiety on the drive up the mountains. I called my Voicemail and reviewed my messages. I called time and temperature. "Eleven forty-two and twenty seconds. Current temperature thirty-seven degrees." I thought about calling Purdy and letting him know what I was doing but assumed he'd tell me not to do it, so I didn't call him. I thought about calling dispatch again and giving them some more details about the bloodbath at Eric Petrosian's house. But I didn't do that, either. By then, I decided, Eric's place had been descended upon by patrol people, detectives, technicians, and, most likely, the media. They didn't need my help.

I noticed patches of fog in low-lying areas by the road, and I tried to remember what dew point was.

Traffic was light going south out of town on Highway 93. At the top of the crest of the first big hill, the dim lights of the dining room at Pain Perdu glowed through the mist of the developing fog. I wondered with sadness and anger whether Erica and Geoff Tobias were at all concerned about the mess their nephew was in.

An unfamiliar electronic chirp filled the little car near the turnoff to Coal Creek Canyon. I mumbled, "Shit," and examined the dashboard, looking for a warning light or gauge to inform me what essential system of my rental was forsaking me in my hour of need. No light. No warning.

The chirp returned. I know that rhythm, I thought. For the first time in my life I was *getting a telephone call in my car*. Well, not exactly *my* car, but I quickly decided it still counted. I was pretty excited and almost dumped the car off the shoulder of the highway while looking at the tiny buttons on the handset, trying to figure out how to answer my call.

Adrienne was on the phone. "Why the hell did it take you so long to answer? What, you were in another room? Had to finish taking a leak?"

I took a deep breath. "Adrienne, hello. For your information, unlike physicians, clinical psychologists don't have the luxury of receiving cellular telephone operating training while at tax-deductible medical junkets in Boca

Raton. I'm a novice. Bear with me—I couldn't find the right button. So what's up? Just call to chat? How's Diane?"

"Hardly. Diane's been filling me in on your latest felony. What do you think? Should we call it leaving the scene of a crime? Failure to report? Criminal trespass? Don't worry, I'll chair the committee to raise funds for your legal defense. I think we'll call it 'Free the Hemlock Way Two.' And Diane's sound asleep in the guest room."

By that point in the conversation the curves of Coal Creek Canyon Road were bending in earnest. And I wanted both my hands back. "Get to the point please, Ren."

She huffed at being rushed, "The cops are all over the little crime scene you guys discovered. The radio news has picked it up. Some serious consternation about the lack of a body. Unconfirmed opinions that the quantity of blood left behind doesn't bode well for the life span of the leaking container."

"That's it? Any news on Randy?"

"No, that's not it. That's just the good news. And there's no word on the kid. What's the matter with your phone? You sound like you've crawled inside the trunk."

"The canyon's pretty deep here, I'm surprised there's any signal at all. Oh, fuck!" I dropped the phone, pounded the brakes with my right foot, hit some ice, and immediately began to spin. The doe I was trying to avoid stayed motionless, apparently content to watch me through the side window of the car as I slid by backward. The deer then bounded across the road in a single graceful leap and disappeared into the misty darkness. The Sundance completed a 540-degree spin and finally came to a stop in the correct lane but pointing in the wrong direction.

I turned the car around to face the right direction and plucked the phone from the floor. "You still there, Ren?"

"I'm still here. You all right, what happened?"

"I almost hit a deer. Listen, honey, I obviously need both hands. What's the rest of your story?"

"Merideth's back. She called me looking for you after she went to the crime scene on Hemlock, she knows your patient escaped from the hospital, and she's gonna call me again and ask me where you are at any moment."

"Lie."

"Lie? *Moi?*"

I said thanks and tried to remember how to hang up the damn phone.

41

A sheriff's deputy flagged me down as I slowed the car and began to turn into the entrance of the Mirabelle compound. He shined a searchlight in my eyes until I skidded the car to a stop on the dirt shoulder. I could almost feel my pupils shrivel in response to the whiteness of the light. Although I hadn't had a drink since my glass of wine with dinner, I was reflexively apprehensive that he was going to ask me to take a roadside sobriety test.

"Driver's license, please," said a hoarse voice a moment later. In the darkness behind the diffuse beam of the flashlight he was pointing into my face, the cop's body wasn't well defined. He looked more like an apparition than a person. Probably just what he intended.

I dug my license out of my wallet and handed it to him.

"Business here, Mr. Gregory?" he asked a moment later, his eyes and his torch sweeping the backseat, looking for Randy.

"I'm a friend of Ms. Templeton. She's freaked by all the activity around here. Wanted somebody to be with her."

"Mind opening the trunk?"

"Not at all." I was pretty sure that there was a lever inside the car that would do the trick, but I wasn't sure which one. I fumbled around until I found one on the floor beside the seat and flipped it up.

"That's the gas cap compartment, sir," said the deputy in a tone that was about twice as polite as was necessary.

I stepped out of the car with the keys. "It's a rental," I said. "My car got wrecked."

I unlocked the trunk and was relieved to find nothing incriminating in it.

He stepped back and took a good look at me again. "Your friend may have already told you," he said, "but we're looking for a male adolescent who may be dangerous and may be heading up here. You can go on in now, but give us a holler if you hear anything out of the ordinary."

For some reason feeling as though I'd just talked my way out of a speeding ticket, I smiled pleasantly, nodded, and got back in the car.

Rita Templeton was waiting at the door to her cabin, wearing black wool trousers and a tight yellow turtleneck that wasn't quite long enough to reach her crotch. A single carved wooden pendant hung on a long leather rope between her breasts.

Her eyes were full of hope, and she smiled and raised her arms as if she wanted a hug as I walked up. I offered to shake her hand instead. In another circumstance I wouldn't have had so much reluctance admitting to myself that she was an attractive, desirable woman. The events of the day precluded that, though, and the inadvertent smear of coral lipstick on her front tooth helped, too. Frank Sinatra's voice drifting in from some distant room sealed it.

Inside, she had tea waiting in the kitchen. Freshly baked raisin bread sat in a gingham-lined basket in the center of the table, its aroma saturating the room. The wood stove was stoked, and the radiant warmth felt good. Since I'd pledged my dinner antelope to Diane my last true meal was but a digestive memory, and I helped myself to a large hunk of doughy bread. Rita looked thrilled at my appetite.

"This is delicious," I said.

"Thank you. I like to bake. It's like therapy for me."

I thought for a second, then said, "Larry didn't appreciate it much, did he?"

Her mug of tea was at lip level, and she let it hang there with my words. "How did you know that? One of the kids tell you?" she finally asked.

"He couldn't smell. Had a condition called anosmia.

Some viral problem, apparently. Probably why he didn't smell the gas. Can't smell, can't taste . . ." I watched her eyes. "You didn't know, did you?"

She looked away from me and said, "There's a lot about Larry I didn't know, I guess. I just found out I own part of the Tobiases' restaurant. Larry bought it with the money he borrowed on his life insurance. Apparently it was a pretty good investment, the place is doing well." Her voice dropped off.

I watched her struggle to use her denial to wall off the reality that was so uncomfortable. I sat without speaking. I was tempted to tell her that one of the things she didn't know about her husband was that he, too, had been a patient of the community shrink, Paul Weinman, Ph.D. I didn't. Instead I just waited, permitting the silence to act corrosively on her defenses.

It didn't take long for the walls to crumble. "I'm not fooling you, am I? Larry and I weren't doing too well." She picked at her sweater and rearranged the pendant. "Not true. He's been dead, what—six weeks?—you know I haven't had sex in six months? Maybe longer. . . . It's easier if you don't keep track. I'm lying—I do keep track. I made love for the last time on August fourteen last year. My birthday. I'm thirty-seven. It feels old. It doesn't need to. I have friends who are thirty-seven and they're not old." The lines in the corners of her eyes and mouth seemed to sag into new definition. "I'm sitting here waiting to start to cry. But I don't have any tears left about this." She shook her head a little and struggled to keep her gaze away from mine. "Hey! You asked a question. About Larry not caring about my cooking. So how long did he know about this not-smelling thing?"

"Since last fall."

"That fits. No. He wouldn't have told me. He didn't like the phrase *I can't.*" She scratched the back of her neck and fluffed her hair. "He needed to get reading glasses a few years ago. Put it off forever. I would ask him why he didn't read as much as he used to. 'Just don't feel like reading. I read enough at work,' he'd say. He never told me he got the glasses—I found them in the pocket of a

sports coat I was taking to the dry cleaner. No, he wouldn't
have told me he couldn't smell. Nope—old L.T. wouldn't
have told me. He wouldn't have told me that."

Rita stood and walked over to fuss at the sink, mostly
to be alone for a few seconds.

I felt a surge of empathy for Rita's pain right then but
knew I couldn't provide whatever undefined response she
wanted from me. I refocused on Randy. "Rita, I want to
go outside and take a look around for Randy. If he's up
here, I'm hoping I can talk him into coming in," I said.
"Do you have a flashlight I could borrow?"

She hadn't yet turned back around to face me. She said,
"Yes. Of course." And walked out of the room.

When she returned her tongue was darting beneath her
upper lip, scrubbing at her front teeth. Apparently she had
passed by a mirror. A small, thin metal flashlight was in
her right hand, and as she began to speak I could see the
lipstick smear was gone. "Larry liked tools. Always the
best for Larry," she said as she held out the high-intensity
flashlight to me. She stared at me, and I noticed her hazel
eyes were two different shades. Then Rita said, in a manner that invited no response from me, "I think he was
having an affair."

At my house I'd changed into sneakers, jeans, and a
heavy black jacket. I had shed the jacket in Rita Templeton's kitchen and stood to pull it back on and to tug on
some rawhide gloves before I took the flashlight from her
outstretched hand. I shoved the flashlight into an outside
pocket of the jacket opposite the one that held Diane's
cellular phone. I said, "I shouldn't be gone too long." Rita
pressed her lips together tightly and nodded.

"Is there a back door?" I asked.

A loud knock at the front door precluded her answer.
They've found him, I thought.

I followed Rita as she raced back through the living room
to the front of the house. She turned and faced me before
she pulled open the heavy door.

The woman at the door said, "Hello, Alan." Then she
nodded a greeting to Rita Templeton.

Rita looked back at me. I said, "Rita Templeton, this is Merideth Murrow . . . my—wife."

Rita said, "Your wife?"

Merideth said, "We're separated."

Rita said, "You're separated?"

In a few seconds Rita remembered her manners and asked Merideth inside and led us into the warmth of the kitchen. Rita said, to me, "Would the two of you like a few minutes alone? . . ."

I spoke before Merideth could voice her assent. "Rita, I don't think that's necessary. I think Merideth is here on business. She's a news producer."

Merideth glanced, or glared, my way, nodded an acknowledgment to Rita, and then said to me, "It looks like the kid who's missing may have assaulted someone in town tonight. The police are checking out the scene. They haven't said so, but I think they may have a witness, too."

A witness? I thought of the person walking the poodle. I'd already guessed that Randy might have been involved in the fracas at Eric Petrosian's home and was, ironically, relieved at Merideth's supposition about the earlier events. Her report of the working hypothesis of the police at the scene was much better news than the alternative—finding out that Randy was the victim of whatever happened at Eric's house.

I said, "Oh."

Merideth and Rita looked first at each other, then at me.

I said, "How did you know I'd be up here?"

"I told you. I've got a source. And I put some pieces together."

"You've been talking to Purdy?"

"Can't reveal my sources, now, can I?"

"I was just on my way outside to look around for the kid. Why don't you keep Rita company for a few minutes. I'll tell you what I can when I get back. Okay?"

Merideth saw a rich vein of information in ready access to the widow Templeton, so she concurred.

Rita led me through the kitchen to a screened-in porch and then to a door that led to an immense redwood deck that faced the Continental Divide. I climbed down some narrow steps into misty blackness and made my way behind three other cabins on my way to the Tobias place. I was reluctant to use the flashlight, fearing that the deputies on the road would mistake me for Randy, so I traversed the hundred or so yards slowly and clumsily.

I was the loudest thing in the woods.

A promontory of thick pines and huge craggy boulders separated the Tobias place from its nearest Mirabelle neighbor, and I either had to climb it or return to the common area in the front of the cabins and risk exposing myself to the sheriff. I climbed. At the peak I paused to browse. The mist had settled into the depths of the steep ravine below the high outcropping, and the dark shadows of the craggy mountains in the distance were visible below the crisp dots of the night sky. At my feet were the charred remains of campfires and the miscellaneous detritus of others who had spent inspired evenings in this place.

I saw a light flash through the mist. Two seconds, no more. I stared at the spot in the fog where I had seen it and held my breath as though my breathing would extinguish the light as if it were a flickering candle flame. Nothing.

Then the light beamed on again. Almost five seconds this time.

Suddenly I was sure: Randy was hiding somewhere in the deserted mining camp below the compound.

42

While I was trying to still my pulse I tried to remember where the dirt road was that Raoul had used while wandering around Mirabelle during my first interview with Rita Templeton. The road was east of the Tobias cabin, I thought, and I began to descend the promontory in that general direction.

The flashlight, I knew, would startle Randy. My footsteps would startle him, too. Calling out to him would alert the deputies and bring them my way in an instant. I had to find a way to get close to Randy without spooking him with my approach, or he would bolt again and I would lose him and I might be robbed of my only opportunity to help him out of this hole he seemed intent on digging deeper and deeper.

The road was where I thought it would be. But it wasn't much of a road, maybe ten feet wide, uneven, full of holes. Someone had graveled it once, years ago, and the scattered rocks crunched with every step I took. Patches of crisp, honeycombed snow marked off areas shaded from the sun. I gravitated to the shoulder of the road, seeking some softer dirt, and walked slowly, carefully, down the hill into the ravine. Terrain and stands of ponderosa pines blocked any view of the place where I had seen the light. I had to hope Randy wasn't moving around; if he was, I would never find him. I was about as proficient at mountaineering and tracking as Sam Purdy was at dieting.

After I plodded carefully down the road for ten minutes it looped around to the left, toward the general area where I had seen the light. I stopped in the middle of the bend and listened. Nothing. Then a quiet, scratching sound, then nothing. *There,* again.

What is that? The wind. Maybe.

No.

The heavy air had condensed and seemed thicker and smokier the deeper I descended into the little valley. I could see nothing. Every ten feet or so I stopped and listened and assured myself that I really was hearing something. At times I couldn't discern the direction of the source of the sounds. Above me? Below me?

I stopped. I heard nothing.

Except, I worried, the still drum of someone listening for echoes of me.

Could I risk calling out to Randy? How close to him was I? I didn't know. I started walking again, hopeful, frightened, willing my feet to find quiet.

The fog thinned, and I spotted the light again. More noise, the same pattern of light. On for a few seconds, then off. Distance was difficult to judge, but I guessed I was within fifty yards of him. That scraping sound resumed, with increased definition now; different sounds—long scrapes, short scrapes, each scrape followed by longer interludes of foggy winter night silence. Then a sound from above me. *Above me?* An echo? An acoustical quirk of the little canyon?

Scrape, scrape.

Across the ravine the light came on again. A few seconds. Off.

The sound above me again. Or to my right. It was close. I froze. I felt surrounded.

A voice whispered, "Alan, it's me." Suddenly a hand gripped my right wrist.

Was that "me" or "Me"?

Then the soft, feminine whisper again: "Did you find him?"

I was about to say something like "Goddamn it, Merideth," but a smooth arc of harsh light rotated toward us, illuminating the fog all around me and finally spotlighting me like a deer frozen in headlights. I dropped to crouch from the intrusive brilliance and my right foot failed to find purchase, and I slipped down the soft earth of the shoulder at the edge of the road.

Eighteen inches I fell; maybe two feet, no more. Merideth slid down beside me.

The noise we made may as well have been a symphony playing fortissimo.

The beam from across the narrow canyon probed the night like a saber, the fog suddenly my ally, my only armor. I bent over Merideth—over the baby—and froze, begging my body to be silent, certain the echo of my manic pulse was filling the entire valley. If I called out, would Randy believe I was alone? I had to risk it, or he would run and I would lose him. Or he would shoot.

I opened my mouth to say "Randy," but the word was lost in the explosion of a gunshot. Objectivity about the speed of bullets aside, I waited a few seconds for the slug to cross the short distance and bury itself in my body. Mostly I prayed the baby would be spared.

By the time my shock permitted it, I was hearing footsteps, the sound of someone running up the hill, back in the direction of the compound. A moment later I heard shouted instructions. I guessed the voice was from the sheriff's deputy up at Mirabelle. I heard the acrid *bleeeeeep-whooooooop* of a siren. I heard Rita Templeton scream, "Alan's out there somewhere. Help him!"

I called out, "Randy, stop! It's Alan Gregory."

He didn't.

I pulled Merideth's face close to mine and with a hand pressing on each of her cheeks said, "Stay here. He doesn't know you. Stay down! Damn you." She started to protest, and I said, "For the baby—Merideth, please." She started to speak again, but I darted off into the mist and followed the retreating footfalls back up the road.

In no time I lost the trail of sound.

A few seconds later a searchlight from the deputy's car began to probe the fog in vain. On a loudspeaker the deputy called, "Mr. Gregory? Ms. Murrow? This is the sheriff. *Mr. Gregory?*" The deputy apparently didn't know about the existence of the old mining road, and he stayed up on the ridge as he scanned the depths of the deep ravine for the spot where the shot had been fired. Within a few more minutes I was back at the top of the hill, out of breath.

Merideth, some fear in her voice, called out, "I'm down here." I watched the light probe the area near where I had left her.

The deputy yelled, "Stay where you are and stay *down*."

I hadn't found Randy.

The sheriff's car remained on the other side of the promontory, still scanning the darkness for Merideth with its searchlight. A voice still called out for me. The shrill whistle of a siren pierced the night air as reinforcements hastened up the canyon to join the chase.

Rita Templeton screamed, "Alan? Alan!"

I stayed quiet and determined. I wanted to find Randy. And I wanted to find him first. I surprised myself with my calm as I walked to the rear of the Tobias cabin, certain that's where I would find Randy. Uncertain how I would talk him into surrendering to the police. Uncertain how I would keep him from using that gun he seemed to have grown so fond of lately.

Geoff Tobias hadn't bothered to fix the broken lock on the garage door. Or maybe he had attempted to have it fixed, but with Mirabelle's on-again, off-again caretaker off again in Costa Rica, maybe he couldn't be held responsible for the shoddy maintenance. The lock rested in the dirt by the door, the door partially open, just enough, it turned out, for me to slide into the absolute darkness of the garage.

The gun?

Wait a second, the police had the gun; I'd given it to Purdy. Where had Randy gotten another gun? Then I remembered. He had said that his father had two, a matched pair that he and his wife used for target shooting. But the keys to the gun cabinet were in the bag I had given to Purdy. Anyway, Geoff Tobias had said he was going to padlock the case. But on the garage door to this very cabin I had just seen how reliable Geoff Tobias was about padlock replacement. Had Randy gone home and retrieved another gun? It didn't seem possible that he could have eluded the police near his home. They would certainly have been watching his house.

Sudden doubt sent a chill through my body. I had been on the verge of deciding to call out to Randy and walk casually into the house, intending to interrupt his dissociative tour into the outtakes of the tragedy of the DC-10 in Sioux City. I expected to find him crouched into the cabinet he had described hiding in during his previous fugues, an experience that I assumed was somehow linked to the position the flight attendants had instructed him to assume prior to and during the crash of Flight 232. But my doubts told me I really didn't know what I'd find. I redoubled my efforts to be silent as I moved past the stored patio furniture through the garage.

When I arrived at the base of the stairs that led up to the house from the rear of the garage, I heard footsteps in some distant part of the house, their squeaky timbre a clear counterpoint to the outside sounds of voices shouting, radios squawking, engines revving, brakes braking. The footfalls moved closer and then with sudden determination accelerated straight to the room at the top of the staircase. I backed into the deep recesses of a cobweb-infested alcove that was filled with hoses and rusted garden tools. The door at the top of the stairs opened briskly.

My senses registered just sound, no additional light, not even a flashlight beam. The clump-clump of footsteps descended the stairs. A shadow, something darker than dark, passed by the landing at the bottom of the stairs.

He's leaving? I worried about my breathing being too loud, and I worried about the gun. I thought about stepping out of the closet and identifying myself. But if Randy was in a fugue or some other dissociative state, there was no guarantee that he would recognize me. And even if he did recognize me, he might be prone to shoot me in panic.

A racket erupted in the closed space of the garage, a chaos of sound. Crashing noises. Banging noises, breaking glass noises. Sliding, grunting, more crashing. Metal, wood. Finally, silence. Some steps back my way. Then the shadow passed by me again. I felt an insect crawl down my face, and I wanted to scream. When the door at the top of the stairs opened and closed once again, I flailed at the imagined insect below my ear and at the cobwebs that had entombed me and ran back out of the alcove toward the garage.

I risked a second of illumination from the flashlight.

As I feared, the huge pile of patio furniture once stored on the side of the garage had been shoved, pulled, and thrown in front of the garage doors. The mountain of twisted furniture peaked somewhere near the ceiling and ran the width of the room.

There was now no longer a silent way into this garage.

And there was no silent way out.

I sat on the edge of a redwood picnic table bench that had somehow landed upright and pulled Diane's cellular phone out of the inside pocket of my jacket. I stared at it and couldn't decide whom to call. Or what to say.

The reality was that I was trapped inside a cabin in the mountains with an accused murderer, and we were surrounded by an ever-growing squadron of police. If a dissociated Randy heard me talking on the phone, he might open the door, walk down the stairs, and shoot me.

Or he might invite me up for a Coke. There was no telling.

I placed my bet, returned the phone to my pocket, and crept up the stairs to confront my maturing doubts. I stepped whenever I heard noises outside that might serve to mask the squeaking of the old stairs. Near the top of the staircase I stopped and listened. There were no sounds emerging from inside the house.

Finally a phone started ringing. The sound was loud and old-fashioned and distinct. It rang and rang, the silence between rings seeming to extend longer with each interval. I counted the rings to fifteen and then stopped counting. Footsteps announced that someone finally entered the room at the top of the stairs. The person picked up the receiver, waited a second or two, and apparently without speaking replaced it back on the cradle.

Ten seconds later the ringing started again. And almost simultaneously I saw a wash of bright light under the door at the top of the stairs.

This time the telephone was picked up immediately.

An overwrought voice said, "He says to cut the damn spotlights or he'll kill me. Please do what he says. Please." He hung up.

The voice wasn't Randy's.

So who was it? Was that Geoff Tobias? Was Randy the "he"? Was Randy holding his uncle hostage? What the hell was going on here?

Shit. I supposed that it made some sense. Although Geoff's restaurant was making Randy's trust a ton of money, Geoff was, otherwise, a complete jerk in his treatment of Randy. Or maybe, I thought, Geoff was just a hostage of convenience. Somebody available when Randy needed a shield after doing whatever he had done to Eric Petrosian.

But why would Randy hurt Eric Petrosian?

I reminded myself that the possibility of Randy being in some altered state of awareness made most of the cards in this deck wild cards.

Slow down, Alan. *Was* that really Geoff's voice? I wanted to hear the sound again.

The light that crept under the door flashed off. The phone rang once more. And again. On and on. No answer. Then the lights came back on in order to motivate somebody to pick up the phone. The apparently aversive stimuli worked just as Skinner had predicted it should.

The voice said, "He's not kidding, turn off the damn lights."

Geoff?

Yes, Geoff.

The lights went off. But this time I didn't hear the sound of the phone being hung back up.

A moment's silence. The faucet sputtered and some water ran. I guessed I was on the other side of a door that led to the kitchen. Then, "I'm his uncle, his guardian,

Geoffrey Tobias. He won't let me say anymore." More silence, during which I assumed Geoff was listening to a voice at the other end of the line. "No. He says he'll talk to you when *he's* ready. He's afraid you'll shoot him through the window if he comes to the phone. He'll tell you what he wants when he's ready. Not before." A pause. "No—yes, of course I'm frightened. I have to hang up. He doesn't want me to talk." He hung up and, I assumed, accompanied his footsteps out of the room.

The noises from outside were muted but persistent. Shouts, tires rolling on frozen earth, radio squawks, a distant helicopter. I tried to listen through the diffuse sounds to hear Geoff recount to Randy the details of the phone call. But despite straining, I couldn't hear any voices and concluded that the pair had retreated to a remote corner of the house. I tried to conjure an image of Randy holding a gun on his uncle as they walked together from room to room, but it all felt absurd.

Remember the fugue, I thought, remember the fugue.

I didn't think much about my next move. I just did it. I walked through the door at the top of the stairs into a kitchen in need of serious remodeling. The room was large and dark and cold. A single, deep sink of rust-stained porcelain filled most of the solitary counter under the window. An old Norge refrigerator sat alone on one wall, its cord hanging unplugged from a junction box dropped from the ceiling via conduit. The door I walked through opened against an old gas range. A swinging door stood open to the rest of the house. Beside the swinging door another open door led inward to a walk-in pantry with feeble stocks of ancient food and evidence of many mice.

I stepped into the pantry and crouched behind the open door. I heard nothing but my heart and the sounds of the troops mobilizing outside.

The phone rang again. The telephone was an old Bell wall model in bright yellow. It had a dial and hung on the narrow slice of wall between the pantry door and the door to the rest of the house. An unrecognizable voice pierced the silence from a distant part of the house, and then a single set of footsteps preceded Geoff Tobias's return to the kitchen. As he lifted the receiver I could see the swell of his abdomen through the crack of the open door from the pantry to the kitchen.

Why didn't Randy follow Geoff on these trips to the phone? Maybe he was monitoring his uncle on an extension. Maybe he was afraid of being shot. But what was to keep Geoff from crashing out a window and taking his chances on a ten-foot fall to relative safety?

Geoff answered my questions for me. He said, "I told you he doesn't want you to call. *Be patient.*" And as he hung up the phone with his right hand, I saw a gun at waist level in his left hand.

At first I couldn't make any sense of what I saw. Then I knew.

Of course.

Geoff wasn't Randy's hostage.

Geoff Tobias was holding *Randy* hostage. All of this stuff on the phone was a charade. I wondered if Randy was even in the house. Or if Randy was still alive. And whom had I tracked down to the old mining camp, Geoff or Randy?

From outside, the abrasive lights flashed on once more. Immediately the phone rang again. Geoff Tobias anticipated it. In an angry, agitated voice, he said, "He says he'll shoot out the lights if you don't turn them off. Got it? I'll take this damn thing off the hook." He hung up again. The lights stayed on. The phone began ringing relentlessly.

It rang. And rang. I felt naked in the light seeping into the pantry, the darkness in the house had been my shield. Ironically, it was Geoff's, too. If the sheriff and police outside could see inside, they would see Geoff moving freely through the house. And maybe even see the gun. He couldn't permit that.

I searched the pantry for something—a pen, a pencil, a bar of soap—that would permit me to scrawl a note to hold up to the window to the police about the actual state of affairs in the cabin. Nothing.

I needed a better place to hide. Next to me, on the back

wall of the pantry, was a wide cupboard topped by a broad shelf of painted pine. I wondered if I could fit inside. I opened the door and peered in. The cupboard was empty. On the far side, however, were etched-glass panels framed in darkly stained oak—doors that led into the adjacent dining room.

Suddenly I knew where I was. I had just stumbled onto Randy's dissociative lair. I climbed into the "weird cabinet" that Randy had described hiding in, yanked the door shut behind me, folded myself into a sitting position, and pulled out Diane's phone. The kitchen telephone continued its relentless ringing. I started to punch the numbers for Sam Purdy's office, but the damn phone chirped with every punch. I fumbled with the volume control and reduced the screech, squinting the whole time through gaps in the etched glass for any sign of Geoff's return.

A female voice answered Purdy's phone. In a whisper I said, "Tell Sam it's Alan. It's an emergency about Randy. Hurry. Can't talk."

She started to ask some reasonable questions. I interrupted once, "Just find him . . . now . . . dangerous . . . please." I tried to talk only when the telephone was ringing. The cellular phone signal was spotty and weak. I could barely hear the woman in Sam's office through the static.

I think she said, "Okay. Hold."

It wasn't as though I had anyplace else to go, but it was a long, long time before I heard Sam Purdy's voice.

"Better be good, Alan." That was how I translated the cracks and pops I heard.

I watched Geoff Tobias walk into the dining room and head toward the kitchen. I said, "Can't talk," during a ring, and I waited.

Purdy said something like "Well, if you can't talk, why the hell did you call?" He heard the phone ringing in the background, "What? Got somebody on the other line?"

Geoff answered the kitchen telephone. I held the cellular phone to the cabinet door and hoped Purdy could hear Geoff talk. Geoff cooperated by arguing loudly with somebody about the lights for about thirty seconds. I pulled the phone back to my face.

Incredulously Purdy said, "You're inside?"

I tapped the phone once.

"And he doesn't know you're there?"

I tapped once.

"But he could hear you if you talked, so you're tapping your answers."

Tap.

"The sun sets in the east."

Tap. Tap.

"Got it." Sam was a quick study; his next question was, "Are the lights a problem for you?"

Tap. Thank God.

Five seconds later they went off.

Geoff hung up the kitchen phone and walked away. I watched his silhouette as he ambled through the dining room to another part of the house.

To Purdy I said, "It's Geoff, not Randy."

Purdy said something I couldn't understand.

I said, "Geoff has Randy hostage. Not the other way around."

Purdy sounded skeptical and said, "What?"

I just waited.

"Geoff Tobias has the gun?"

Tap.

Purdy said something to someone else. Then to me, "He's pretending he's a hostage?"

Tap.

Again he spoke offstage before getting back to me. "Is Randy okay?"

I waited.

"You don't know?"

Tap.

"Hold on."

Tap.

I needed to pee. I shifted my position to see if I could relieve some of the pressure on my bladder. My pupils had finally begun to adjust to the available light. Fearing Geoff's return, I kept my eyes peeled on the dining room, and that's when I noticed the lace.

Everywhere. The tablecloth on the claw-footed table.

The lining on the curtains on the window. Even the pattern of the etching on the glass.

Lace.

I realized how wrong I had been.

Oh Randy, what the hell happened in this room?

43

In the best of light I was no expert on crystal. I thought the vase that I peed into was one of the cheap ones in which florists deliver symmetrical bouquets of predictable flowers. But the crystal I discovered in the dark recesses of the cramped cupboard could just as easily have been Waterford and my voiding, therefore, sacrilegious. Regardless, the vessel barely held the contents of my bladder. It felt so good to pee that my eyes watered.

I had turned off the phone before I began preparations to relieve myself. Purdy was taking an inordinate amount of time to resume our conversation, and I was growing concerned that the battery power required to stay on the air would drain off any reserves I would need to reach him again later. When I called back he would probably be vexed with me for having hung up. But by conserving the battery, I at least kept my options open.

At the time I didn't have much more to say to him. No noise came from the rest of the house. My view from the cabinet left me no idea where Geoff and Randy were. I remained unconvinced that Randy was in the house at all.

I thought about the lace.

My revelation about the lace was that my cramped roost was on the perimeter of a dining room where something so terrible had happened that the delicate pattern of the lace was etched indelibly in Randy's memory. I replayed psychotherapy sessions in my head, trying to remember a clue that would tell me whether whatever had happened in this room happened to Randy or whether he was a mere witness to horror. The event, whatever it was, had already begun the arduous, twisted process of circumventing the protective shield of Randy's repression, the emerging memory fragments escaping and fueling Randy's dissociative returns to this canyon, to this cabin, to this room.

The lace.

I'd obviously underplayed the importance of Randy's splintered memories about the lace. With regrettably errant wisdom I had narrowed my search for clues about the trauma responsible for Randy's dissociative disorder to the physical and emotional wreckage of Flight 232 and its horrible consequences. I had never allowed that the source of his recent dissociative pathology might be more ancient.

But the lace was *here*.

So maybe—probably—the trauma, at least the first trauma, had been *here*. In his uncle's cabin.

Had Geoff Tobias been involved? In what? What had he done to Randy?

What?

And what about the gun with Randy's fingerprints on it? Geoff, I decided, perhaps too hastily, could have killed Marilyn London. And the burglary that Diane and Purdy and I thought was to take something *from* our offices could just as easily have been a burglary to leave the murder weapon *in* our offices.

To exchange it for the one I'd taken from Randy.

Who knew the gun was in my filing cabinet? Geoff Tobias knew it was there. I had told him myself.

Who would have had easy access to plant evidence in Randy's room? Geoff Tobias certainly would have.

But I didn't know a motive why he would.

I conjectured belatedly that it had to do with the lace. And with Randy's fragmented memory. And with something unknown to me that Eric Petrosian had learned in his examination of Paul Weinman's files. Something that Eric was now using to blackmail Randy's uncle, Geoff Tobias. Something so damning that Geoff Tobias was willing to kill in order to keep it from becoming public.

What was it?

The spilled blood at Eric Petrosian's house was compelling evidence that Eric might have underestimated one of the men he was blackmailing. Geoff Tobias, it seemed, traveled through life having his resourcefulness underestimated. The choreographed charade here at the cabin was a case in point—an elaborate production intended to insure that Randy would again be assigned the blame. And that Geoff would not.

My unrelenting apprehension as I crouched in the cabinet between the pantry and the dining room was that Randy was already dead somewhere in this cold house. Because, for this subterfuge to be successful, Randy could not be around at the end to recite his version of the story. Geoff, I feared, had either already killed Randy or would kill him soon.

The damned floodlights flickered briefly outside, then flashed back on with new intensity. Given that the dining room window faced the courtyard of the Mirabelle compound, the glass-fronted cupboard where I was hiding was particularly well lit by the monsoon of light from outside. I felt displayed like a pastrami in a deli case and was furious that Purdy would be so cavalier with my safety. And I was livid with myself that I hadn't bothered to ask for his cellular phone number.

I punched out the number of his office in Boulder and waited an interminable amount of time to be patched through to Purdy in Coal Creek Canyon. Seconds after I heard the connection go through, the klieg lights outside went off.

"We thought you had been discovered. Are you all right?"

Tap.

"Good. You hung up before?"

Tap.

"Battery problems?"

Tap.

"Do you know how much time you have left?"

I was tempted to acknowledge the innuendo in his question with some sarcastic retort but couldn't figure out a way to do it with my binary code. I replied with two taps.

"Anything new?"

Tap. Tap.

Purdy dictated his direct number and asked if I wanted it repeated. I tapped no.

When I looked up, my heart accelerated like a Ferrari. Geoff Tobias stood on the perimeter of my range of view, and the focus of his dark gaze seemed to go right through me. The gun was in Geoff's right hand, and I felt as if I were already dying from its slugs. Geoff turned his head slowly to the left and then equally slowly to the right, the long strands of hair he combed to cover his balding head hanging limp over the frame of his glasses. My pulse quickened as he took two steps directly toward the dining room cabinet, toward me. Fearful that Geoff would hear Purdy's voice, I was set to flick the phone to "off" but then decided that my only chance of survival might be to allow Purdy to eavesdrop on Geoff's discovery of me.

In some tiny part of my consciousness I was monitoring Sam Purdy's words as he asked me questions about the layout of the house. But I wasn't concentrating enough to generate any taps. I poised my right foot so it would be in position to kick open the pine doors on the pantry side of the cupboard when Geoff suddenly veered from my vision toward the kitchen.

Despite the deep chill in the house, my armpits were sodden and a drop of sweat was migrating between my shoulder blades. Seconds passed, deceiving me into premature relief, before one corduroy-covered leg and then another sidled back directly in front of the etched-glass doors on the cupboard in the dining room, inches from my face. I lifted the vase full of urine and imagined what it would be like to be splashed in the face with it. Warm, disgusting, and distracting were the best outcomes I could hope for.

A cabinet door opened and closed above me. The long-neglected hinges squealed. Then a drawer slid open reluctantly, and another. God, I thought, he's looking for something, and what he's gonna find is me.

When he opens the glass doors to this cabinet, I will throw a pint of urine in his face and then I will die.

Some shuffling-around noises filled the little cabinet. A drawer was stuck, then it slammed. Another opened. I'm next, I thought. I watched the upper border of the glass door for signs of Geoff stooping to discover me. Oh, how surprised he'd be. I readied the urine and prepared to bolt the other way into the pantry.

But finally the chubby corduroy thighs moved away from the glass doors in the direction of the kitchen.

I breathed.

Purdy said, "He's there?"

As Geoff's footsteps disappeared toward the kitchen, I tapped once.

Seconds later the phone rang in the kitchen. Thank you, Sam. Thank you.

"Yeah, it's me. What, you think we have an answering service? No, he still won't talk to you," Geoff Tobias said a moment later. After a pause he continued, "No, just listen this time. He wants a bulletproof vest. He wants a helicopter. And he wants his trust funds moved to a Swiss bank. . . . No, he's not kidding. . . . What? What do you think he knows about banking, he's just a fucking kid. Yes, he seems in control of his faculties. . . . No. He doesn't want you to know where he is in the house. And there's only one phone. . . . Yes, he's watching me right now. No more questions. *No!* No more questions. . . . He says you have ten minutes to give him an answer. *No!* That's it. Ten minutes." Geoff hung up and walked back across the dining room, the gun in one hand, some candles in the other, his head shaking slowly back and forth.

I figured I had ten minutes to find Randy. In ten minutes Geoff would leave Randy alone long enough to make another call. I tapped three times, hung up the cellular phone, and eased myself from the cabinet into the dining room. In a few short steps I was in the adjacent pine-paneled living room. A huge, inviting cut-rock fireplace and hearth interrupted one long wall of huge windows on the far side of the room. The wooden-paned windows extended from knee level almost to the ceiling and in daylight must have provided an inspiring view of the divide. But heavy curtains were pulled across them, and the whole room smelled of must and moist ash and postponed maintenance.

The front door breached into the house on the other side of the dining room wall from where I had been hiding. From the living room I could see that Geoff had pushed a heavy buffet in front of the door and piled sundry smaller pieces all around it. The furniture that remained in the living room was Early American and cheap. I crouched behind a glider sofa adorned with cushions covered with fabric of yellow flowers on a background the color of dry dirt and watched the connecting doorway that apparently led down a hallway to the rest of the house. I saw nothing that would indicate where Geoff was holding Randy. I listened for voices. Nothing. I moved closer to the hall and stood next to the doorway, my back flush against the wall. The cotton of my jacket seemed to roar as it scraped against the paneling.

I turned and looked down the hall. More varnished pine. Old, filthy rag rugs on a wooden floor. Closed doors lined both sides of the hall. One open door on the right. I moved to it and looked in. The bathroom, empty. I listened to the night and to the muted chaos of the police mobilizing in the yard and stepped into the cold, dirty room.

The bathroom floor was covered in tiny black and white hexagonal tiles. The sink was small and wall hung, the toilet stained and ancient. A claw-footed tub was jury-rigged with a shower, and a filthy vinyl curtain hung from an O-shaped ring suspended from the ceiling. A cupboard for linens was built into the wall by the door. The toilet gurgled and dripped.

I climbed into the tub and sat down, slowly pulling the curtain back around me. My plan was simple: When I heard Geoff walk down the hall to return to the kitchen to use the phone, I would slip down the hall and find Randy. And use my trusty phone to call in the cavalry.

I wished I'd had the foresight to find a weapon when I was in the kitchen. The bathroom was devoid of suitable objects. Briefly I was tempted to return to the kitchen and search for a knife. But the roar of footsteps coming down the hall precluded any such action on my part; instead I gripped the handle of the thin metal flashlight Rita had given me and prepared, once again, to be discovered.

Geoff Tobias walked into the bathroom and stepped to the toilet and began to urinate. The shower curtain was closed, so I couldn't see whether he had his gun with him. I tried to imagine a safe method of simultaneously urinating and holding a loaded pistol and couldn't conjure one. Maybe he had set the gun down. Maybe it was stuck in his belt. Maybe I could jump him. And maybe if I tried to jump him, I'd get tangled in the damn shower curtain and he would get the gun out in time and shoot me.

Geoff whistled while he peed. He whistled melodically and possessed a powerful stream of urine that splashed into the bowl with sufficient force to have brought a smile to Adrienne's face. The tune he whistled was something sprightly from *Les Mis*: "Master of the House"?

His footsteps signaled his return down the hall. I counted. Three steps? Four? A door opened and closed. I waited. And I played with the pieces of the puzzle.

Was Geoff the driver of the renegade snowplow? Made some sense. He *had* been trying to get me removed as Randy's therapist. Killing me was one way to do it. Now I had to wonder if he was worried that Randy had either already told me something or was about to tell me something that Geoff couldn't afford to have me know. If that was true, Randy and I were dangerous to Geoff for the same reason. And if Geoff was the snowplow driver, he had already tried to kill me to insure my silence. Was that why he was about to sacrifice Randy? To insure his eternal silence? About what?

The lace.

And who had broken into Diane's house and whacked her over the head? Geoff? Looking for what? Geoff had been in treatment with Paul Weinman, and Paul's charts weren't disturbed. But Diane's were. If Geoff had indeed broken into her house, what was he looking for in Diane's files?

Then I remembered something else: Diane had referred Randy to me for psychotherapy. And she *had* been treating Randy's sister, Lily, before her death in the crash of Flight 232. Could Geoff have been worried about what was in

Lily's chart? Hadn't Diane said it had been an innocuous treatment? . . .

A door opened down the hall from the bathroom. Reflexively I stood and prepared to move. The door closed, and Geoff shuffled down the hallway toward the kitchen. I lifted the rings of the curtain off the suspended rod, cracked an opening I could slip through in the curtain, and stepped onto the tile floor. The toilet gurgled. Drip. Drip. On impulse I raised the heavy porcelain lid off the tank and held it in both hands like a Louisville Slugger. Would this thing stop a bullet? No, probably not. I peeked out the door and saw Geoff standing at the end of the hall, surveying the house for intruders. I waited until he walked off toward the kitchen, and then I edged down the hallway in the opposite direction.

Randy was in the room behind the second door I opened.

Geoff had gone to elaborate lengths to insure that the fact that Randy had been bound would not be discernible on physical examination. Or autopsy. Randy lay on his back on a bed, his ankles and wrists bound together by multiple rounds of fiber-reinforced packing tape on top of thick towels, which were in turn taped to the steel frame of the bed. A heavy wool blanket lay folded on top of his body, and long strips of tape encircled the blanket and the mattress at six-inch intervals to keep Randy from arching and struggling. A gag in his mouth was held in place by another towel, by more tape.

Randy's open eyes were so dull that I feared he was already dead. Finally his chest rose to strain against the tape. I swallowed.

I tiptoed over to him and realized immediately that it would take me way too long to free him without a blade to cut the tape. I leaned over his face and said, "It's Alan Gregory, Randy, I'm here to help you. But I need to find something to cut the tape. I'll be back." I retraced my steps back out of the room, unable to come to a rapid determination about Randy's mental status. I wasn't even certain he had recognized me.

The door across the hall led to a small storeroom packed

with outdoor equipment. The vintages represented varied from fifties Boy Scout to nineties REI. There were tents, backpacks, canteens, sleeping bags, cross-country skis, snowshoes, a cookstove, lanterns, tennis rackets, and, at my feet, to one side, a cardboard box full of decrepit kitchen utensils relegated to camping use. The collection included a rusty paring knife with a wooden handle. As I bent to pick it up my phone rang.

Oh, Adrienne! I thought as I yanked the door shut, fumbled the phone from my pocket, and frantically poked buttons in the dark to find the one that would silence the bleeping. For a full minute I listened breathlessly for sounds of Geoff backtracking down the hall, certain he must have heard the phone, and finally identified the sound of his footsteps returning down the hall. I grabbed the paring knife and waited. A door opened and closed. Was Geoff looking for the source of the sound of the phone, or had he gone back to Randy to kill him? I waited for a count of thirty and then edged open the door of the storage closet and poked my head into the hall. No Geoff.

I was certain I was running out of time.

And I was right. Through the now closed door across the hall, I heard Geoff say to Randy, "I'm going to begin to untie you now. We're getting near the end. Don't fight me." His voice emerged tense and full of energy.

I held the cellular phone to my ear. It sounded dead. God, I thought, how am I going to reach Purdy? Then I realized I had turned it off when I was trying to silence the damn bell from ringing. I waited two anxious minutes in the hallway to allow Geoff some time to release Randy's restraints, briefly retreated into the closet, and then I punched the power back on and dialed Purdy. The sound quality was awful.

I said, "Lights! Noise!" as sharply as I dared. Nothing happened. I said it again.

Purdy said, "You want some commotion?" or something like that.

Tap.

"You got it." *Ou ot t.*

In seconds I saw lights flood the perimeter of the house.

I moved quickly back into the confines of the storeroom. I heard sirens and I heard voices shouting on loudspeakers. The phone rang in the kitchen. Geoff stormed from Randy's room and lumbered down the hall for another contentious telephone conversation with the authorities.

I busted out of the storeroom and darted across the hall without bothering to check on Geoff's progress toward the kitchen. Geoff had almost finished cutting Randy free. I cut the last of the tape that secured Randy to the mattress and laboriously sawed the dull knife through the thick band of tape binding Randy's ankles. As fearful of Randy's unpredictable mental state as I was of Geoff's imminent return, I left the thick wad of tape in place around Randy's wrists. And I left the gag over his mouth to preclude him from making any noise that might accelerate Geoff's return down the hallway with the gun. Randy's eyes were difficult to read as he permitted me to guide him across the hall into the storage closet. I moved in there with him, closed the door, and pulled out the phone. To Randy I whispered, "Police." Into the mouthpiece of the phone I said, "Geoff's got a gun. Randy and I are in a storage closet at the back of the house. Come on in *now*."

Purdy said, "I can't hear. You want us in?"

I tapped once.

Geoff Tobias said, "Where the fuck are you, kid?"

Was I too late in calling in the police? Seconds later I was poised and ready when Geoff's search for Randy reached the closet and he yanked open the door to our hiding place. I swung the toilet lid at him as if his head were a hanging curveball I was trying to drive into the dirt. Instinctively he raised his right hand and twisted away from the blow. The wide porcelain bat first cracked into his wrist and then smacked against his right shoulder with a crunch and splat that sounded like someone throwing a carp against a wall. Geoff's glasses flew from his head as if they were winged. The gun clanked to the floor and skittered away as it fell from Geoff's badly damaged wrist and hand. He screamed in pain and shock as he looked at the splinter of a bone protruding from his wrist but immediately took off after the weapon in a lopsided gait down the hall, a full step ahead of me as I fought to disentangle myself from Randy and the clutter in the small closet.

Just as Geoff scooped up the gun with his left hand and lumbered awkwardly into the living room, I heard the distinct sound of the front door crashing open. I dropped to the floor of the hallway, right on top of Geoff's eyeglasses, yelled at Randy to stay put, and slithered ten feet to the entrance to the living room to act as a sentry. I feared if I returned to Randy in the closet, Geoff would corner us there and shoot us both.

The huge pile of furniture blocking the front door had barely been budged by the cops. Across the room I saw the top rung of a ladder and a silhouetted form crouching against a dining room window. Shouted instructions cracked from amplified voices outside. I vaguely registered the racket created as the huge pile of patio furniture was shoved around in the garage. The sound of glass breaking seemed to come from half a dozen places at once.

With great despair, for the second time that winter, as I looked frantically around the room for signs of Geoff, I felt the cold, hard chill of a gun barrel being stuck into my cheek.

Geoff Tobias said, "Don't-move-you-fucking-asshole."

I stilled, realizing immediately that Geoff's need for a hostage had not been at all diminished by my heroics in freeing Randy. I also realized that I absolutely did not want to be between Geoff and the police when the barricades came down and a big bunch of heavily armed, scared cops tried desperately to figure out who the good guys were.

Geoff stood behind me, slightly to my left, the gun in his left hand. I twisted enough to see that his wounded right hand and bloody wrist hung limply from his injured shoulder. As I rotated he admonished me, "Don't move," and rammed the gun up harder under my cheekbone.

We stood together on the edge of the living room, near the hallway entrance to the bedrooms, each of us breathing heavily, Geoff yanking his head first to the location of one new sound and then to another. Slowly, deliberately, I raised my right leg until my shin was parallel to the floor and then kicked my foot up and back as hard as I could until I felt the minimal resistance of Geoff's limp right wrist.

As I kicked I fell off to my right side, away from the gun, rolled to the floor, and heard, simultaneously, the disparate sounds of Geoff screaming in agony and the sharp crack of his gun discharging. I couldn't tell where the bullet went. But all the cop noises—all the glass breaking, all the furniture bashing, all the shouted orders—seemed to stop at once. Without hesitation I rolled toward the shelter of the furniture stacked by the front door and raised my head in time to watch Geoff turn to me and raise his pistol and fire again.

After the explosion it took me three or four seconds to accept that his diminished vision and faulty left-handed aim had forced the bullet high and wide. Geoff seemed to hesitate momentarily, and I scurried farther into the barricade as another shot fractured into the cheap furniture. I prayed desperately for the police to get inside and put an end to this.

In seconds the furniture by the door behind me finally started to budge, and across the room two darkly uniformed cops came flying out of the kitchen door, screaming, "Sheriff!" their guns drawn and ready, their faces tense and frightened, their bodies prone on the floor.

Through a crack between two pieces of furniture I watched Geoff meekly drop his gun. From my hiding place I said, "That's your kidnapper," raising an arm and gesturing toward Geoff, who had backed away to the far side of the living room and was now silhouetted against the harsh lights emanating through the windows from outside. "The kid's in back. He's okay, I think."

"On the ground, hands where I can see 'em. Both of you. All of you," one of the deputies yelled. I pulled myself out from behind a bureau and started to raise my hands when, in the periphery of my vision, I saw Randy taking measured steps down the hall, his hands and mouth still bound with tape and towels. The hard, unfamiliar chill in his eyes told me he was on another planet, oblivious of everything in the room but his uncle.

And his memories.

I yelled at him to stop and then jumped to fill the space between him and his jittery rescuers before they could exercise their trained reflexes to shoot at threatening-looking people who weren't heeding their instructions. Across the room Geoff, who had begun to drop to the floor and was on his knees in front of the windows by the fireplace, eyed Randy's entrance warily. Geoff's injured arm and shoulder caused the right side of his body to sag to the hardwood like a branch heavy with spring snow.

Randy was stepping purposefully toward his uncle. "Don't shoot him," I screeched at the increasing number of cops in the room. I raised my hands and darted quickly to block Randy's progress toward his uncle. "It's over, Randy. It's over," I implored.

A cop yelled, "Halt." One more step and Randy did. Finally he shifted his face from his kneeling uncle and stared directly in my eyes. I locked his gaze with my own and spread my arms out to my sides.

The tension in the room eased as if air were being freed from an overfilled balloon.

The cabin was crammed with cops when a lifetime later I risked a brief turn to face the room, hoping to find an ally in Sam Purdy. "Somebody pull the kid away from there," cracked an authoritative, unfamiliar voice, and one of the cops used long strides to cross the room toward Randy. With absolutely no warning or hesitation, Randy leapt like a great cat away from the cop toward his uncle, screaming in otherworldly rage. Geoff's hands were now cuffed painfully behind him, and he was an easy prey for his catapulting nephew. As Randy lunged, Geoff awkwardly tried to pull himself up from his knees to back away to safety.

The cops all started moving toward Randy at once. I was closest to him and pivoted and dove after him, straight out like a freestyle swimmer off the blocks. Both of my hands locked around one of his ankles. Together we fell heavily to the hard floor.

In a frantic retreat from Randy's assault, Geoff Tobias stumbled as he reached his feet, tripping backward over a basket of kindling, then against a floor lamp, his cuffed hands no help in retarding his fall. Finally he fell hard into the curtains behind him. Dust puffed out, wood cracked in a loud pop and then splintered in discrete little bursts, glass snapped sharply, and the old curtain fabric ripped reluctantly and loudly from its rod. The officer closest to Geoff lunged out for him as Geoff hung suspended for a moment against the disintegrating glass wall, but Geoff's cuffed arms, his substantial weight, and every bit of luck he had in this world were all behind him, and with a terrible shriek he tumbled backward into the night.

Cops tore out the door after Geoff. Somebody screamed for paramedics.

Sam Purdy walked out of the crowd of law enforcement types and gently helped Randy and me to our feet.

"Cut the kid's hands free and then cuff him. And get that gag off him," he said quietly. "And would somebody please pick up that gun." A dark-suited deputy reached down for it, and Purdy barked, "*Carefully.* Humor me, pretend it's evidence." When he turned back to me the expression on his face was difficult to assay, but I thought I sensed some appreciation and some absolute bewilderment.

I said, "May I have a few minutes with my patient, Detective?"

He smiled a smile I couldn't interpret and said, "It's fine with me, but then this ain't my show." The smile faded, but he continued to stare at me enigmatically. "Is it?"

44

Randy and I met in a small bedroom across from the one where he had been held captive by his uncle. A sheriff's department sentry accompanied us down the hall and left me no doubt that he would be guarding the door while we talked. The furniture in the drab room was sharply angled and covered in a blond veneer. Chips and cracks scarred virtually every corner of the bureau and nightstand. I was reminded of my parents' bedroom set when I was small.

A beat-up captain's chair with a red vinyl cushion was pushed into a corner by the foot of the double bed. Randy took it without hesitation. I plopped down on the dusty surface of the often stained mattress, disturbing the accumulated residue of years of neglect and raising a visible cloud of dust motes perfumed with the distinctive aroma of enuresis. Randy watched me sit with a glare in his eyes that seemed intensified by the tautness of his jaw and the almost involuntary repetition of his swallowing.

As if ordered to, he closed his eyes and seemed immediately to drift off to sleep, his unbound wrists on the armrests of the chair, his head back against the wall. He was dressed in jeans and a sweatshirt from Brown University. His pants and white socks were covered with filth and what appeared to be dried blood. He needed a shave.

As he drifted off I reflected that he could not have been more distant from me had he been immured in a tomb.

But I knew where I was now, I knew this territory. I knew what to do.

It wasn't complicated. I waited.

Although his breathing was regular, I was unsure

whether his withdrawal was defensive or whether he had
simply been overcome by the horror of the day.

So I waited. But not long.

In a moment, in a voice at once childlike and hypno-
gogic, he said, "He did it right here. This is where he
brought her after dinner, after the lights. This is where he
did it." His eyes opened, and their sadness filled the room.
"I feel real weird," he said.

I sat as still as a memory.

He looked up and searched my eyes for something. Finally I said in a careful, hollow voice, "I saw the lace."

His eyes flashed, and then the flame extinguished as
rapidly as it had erupted.

These next words tumbled from him fast like pebbles
down a chute. "When he made her dinner I was supposed
to be in bed but I wasn't I'd gone back outside to try and
see some bats and I had to sneak back in through the
garage and the kitchen because I couldn't reach the window I had crawled out of and I heard them in there and
I hid in the cabinet and I could see them through the glass
and I saw the lace and their legs and he was next to her
and he was already touching her when the other man came
in. He kept telling the other man she wanted to do it, not
to worry. And then I watched them finish eating and I
watched them set up the lights and do it with the other
man's camera. At the end she was crying and she looked
scared and when the other man left he took her down the
hall and they came in here—this room—and I heard her
crying and then she got quiet. And I went to bed."

He exhaled and closed his eyes and held them shut for
a three count and opened them again.

"Lily?" I said.

He swallowed and wiped his eyes with the backs of his
hands even before the tears appeared and said in a voice
that quaked with the unrelenting force of a returning memory, "Ohhh, Lily." Randy began to rock now. "Where's
my mom and dad? Why did they let him do it? Why did
I let him do it? Where are they? Where are they?" His
voice was small and afraid and full of bafflement, not fear.
Then a scream, sharp, cohesive, contained: *"Lily!"* And

Randy began to cry. "I should have stopped him. I should have killed him," he said, a child.

"What other man?" I said, so afraid that Randy was going to tell me his father had been part of whatever had happened.

"I don't know. The other man just wanted the pictures."

"Of?"

"Lily."

"Did she have her clothes on, Randy?"

He closed his eyes and shook his head at the memory. He covered his eyes with the backs of his hands, his fingers spread to the sky like spikes.

He saw. He didn't want to see. But he saw.

I moved gingerly to the end of the bed and rested a hand on his shoulder. He leaned into it like a forlorn dog into a scratch. I stood and pulled him toward my chest as the rot of the frozen memories slowly melted into the cruelty of his consciousness.

When I walked from the room Randy was again asleep in the chair. I was prepared to argue with whoever was in command that Randy was too fragile for whatever they had planned for him. But the first person I saw after passing the deputy guarding the door was Casey Sparrow. Webbed flames from her hair seemed to fill the space at the end of the hallway.

She said, "So how's my client?" It was the middle of the night and there was not a dot of makeup on her face, yet she looked as bright as the sunrise after a week of rain.

Through my own sadness I said, "Badly in need of a good lawyer."

She said, "Think I'll do?" with some whimsy in her face.

"Ms. Sparrow, I think you'll do great. Your reputation for defending the downtrodden precedes you."

"Not to mention my proclivity for raising the dead," she said.

"Not to mention that," I said.

She and I quickly decided that she would make a case for Randy's return to the hospital. I told her I would like to accompany him wherever they ended up taking him.

Walking from the hallway into the main part of the cabin, I could see through the open front door that the media serving the Denver metropolitan area had set up a miniconvention in the common area in the front of the Mirabelle cabins. Crime scene tape held back their perimeter thirty yards. The zone in between was militarized. Police, fire, and rescue vehicles of every sort filled the brightly lit area.

Weaving through the various rescue vehicles, I went in search of Merideth. She found me before I found her. As we embraced I noticed how nicely our bodies fit together. We kissed.

I said, "Is the baby okay? Are you okay?"

She said, "God, I love you, Alan."

I said, "I love you, too, Me." I kissed her again, this time on the nose, and without a second of contemplation surprised myself to find my ambivalence resolved. I said, "But, you know, it's not enough." A day's tears—a year's tears, a marriage's tears—pressured my eyes, and suddenly I had to work not to cry. "I wish it was, but it's not enough."

She sucked in a huge amount of air and pressed her perfect lips together tight. She nodded and kissed me lightly. "I know," she said. "I've already decided the same thing."

The night air turned our breath to mist. Behind us, radios crackled and law enforcement types repacked their equipment. Spotlights flashed off, one by one.

Merideth's tears were full now, her eyes beginning to redden in the fading light. She pulled back from me and stared into the fog before she said, "I—um—lost the baby. It happened earlier in the week. I didn't want to tell you on the phone. And so I'm—here."

"Oh, Merideth, I'm sorry."

"No, no," she said, actually trying to smile. "It's for the best. It wasn't fair to her—I never told you I was sure it was a girl—and we, well, we—you and me—we don't love each other right. And I couldn't do it by myself. That's hard to admit. But I can't. I'm not—what?—generous enough, maybe, to be a single mom."

As softly as I could, I said, "No, hon, you're not."

"That was gonna be your job, you know." Her tears came now. "Being the perfect dad. Being the career woman–feminist's dream. I thought I wanted you back, but we still wouldn't have found a way to make each other happy, would we?"

"No." I didn't think there was anything left to feel that night. But the loss of the baby tore new sorrow from me. I said, "We couldn't, you're right." Merideth reached up and dabbed a tear from each of my eyes. "We never loved each other right."

"No," she said, somehow finding another smile, this one more sincere. "But we had some good times trying, didn't we?"

"Yeah. We had some great times trying, Me."

She gestured toward the Tobias cabin with her head. She sighed once, deeply, trying to recompose, and said, "So do I get an exclusive?"

I said, "Sure, if you want." I swallowed, eager to follow her from the intimate tragedy to the version that would be created by the media. "As this mess unfolds, though, it seems it's just a routine tale of personal trauma spiced with sexual exploitation, greed, and a healthy dollop of professional megalomania. Nothing worthy of your attention, just the standard, lurid fare of the local news."

"It's okay. I'll get the story while I'm here and feed it to the affiliate and collect another IOU. Never know when you'll need one."

"No. You never know that." I paused and said, "You and I have some papers to sign."

"I just don't want to," she said.

"Sign?"

"That, but also"—she looked everywhere but at me—"see, if the marriage isn't over, then I don't have to look at what part I played in this—debacle? I'd rather it be just your fault. When I left you I was convinced it was all your fault. But it isn't. When I said 'I do' to you, I actually thought that being smart and pretty and funny and sexy would just about fulfill my responsibilities in marriage. I need to take a look at what might have been missing, and the prospect doesn't sound like fun."

I said, "Maybe your therapist—Maja?—can help?"

She shook her head and wrinkled her nose at me. "No. She can't. You were right, Alan. Maja's a flake." Then with some petulance she said, "Don't you mental health people screen each other to keep out the flakes?"

I thought of Eric Petrosian and Clancy Coates and, reluctantly, Paul Weinman, and half a dozen other therapists I knew, and I said, "No. Not very well. Not very well at all."

Before we parted we made plans to meet late the next afternoon to sign the divorce papers.

45

Sam Purdy walked up behind me with a measure of stealth that surprised me and politely asked me to follow him. I did. We squeezed onto the backseat of a sheriff's department 4 × 4, and a deputy drove us down the gravel road to the abandoned mining camp below Mirabelle. A soft-spoken man with a lot of blond hair sat on the passenger side of the front seat. I wasn't introduced to anyone.

The fog had lifted, and spotlights were pumping sufficient light into the narrow ravine to play a night game. Despite my journey into this territory hours before, none of the terrain looked familiar.

Purdy was silent.

The deputy driving the 4 × 4 pulled it adjacent to two identical vehicles parked down a harshly rutted, ice-encrusted trail. At the end of the trail everyone got out of the car.

Purdy said, "Over here. Watch your step."

The shaft of the mine was lit by spotlights held by black-suited deputies. On a wide ledge twelve, maybe fifteen feet down was a crumpled body wearing clothes that were now burnt red and dusty brown even though they had once been other colors. One pant leg was pushed up to the knee, and the skin that was exposed was the gray hue of the sky on a day with high clouds.

"Can you identify him?" asked the man with the blond hair.

"Not from up here."

I knew who it was.

The man with the blond hair said to his deputies, "Almost ready to bring him up?"

"Two minutes, Sheriff," was the reply.

It took ten.

Purdy said, "Somebody tried to dispose of the body down the shaft. The fog probably kept them from seeing that it had fallen onto that ledge." For a fleeting moment I actually feared that he suspected me of being the "somebody."

When they got the body off the ledge, they turned it over, and I was relieved to find that he hadn't been shot in the face. I said, "It's a psychotherapist named Eric Petrosian."

The sheriff turned to Purdy and said, "I owe you a beer, Sam."

Sam Purdy said, "Yup."

Then the sheriff said to me, "You don't sound too surprised."

"I'm beyond surprise," I said. "I followed somebody down here earlier tonight. I thought it was Randy. I was going to try to talk him into giving himself up. I heard a lot of noises. It was foggy. I never saw anybody—just a flashlight beam. I guess now it was Geoff, trying to hide this body."

Purdy and the sheriff waited.

"Did Geoff kill Eric?" I asked.

Purdy said, "Possibly." He looked at me with eyelids that drooped over his irises in some blend of fatigue and cynicism. He continued, his lips barely moving. "Seems there *was* some kind of accident with a firearm at this guy's house tonight. Bit of blood."

I nodded. I didn't want to talk about Eric Petrosian's house.

"Sheriff," I asked, "what are you going to do with Randy?"

"Well, Doctor. The good detective and I are trying to deal those cards right now. Decide which *live* bodies get dealt to what county, which *dead* bodies get dealt to what city. But I think the kid's gonna go to Boulder. Right, Sam?"

"Yeah, I'll take the kid."

"But this guy"—the sheriff gestured at the remains of

Eric Petrosian—"this guy's more perplexing. He had the ill manners to be shot in one county and be found dead in another."

"Paperwork," said Sam Purdy.

"Paperwork," said the sheriff.

Purdy turned to me and said, "You wouldn't know anything about the circumstances of a crime being reported at a certain house on Hemlock Way in Boulder, would you?"

I stared at him dumbly.

"Didn't think so," he said. "Small town, Boulder. It's funny. I'd spent some time on Hemlock recently. Some *professional* time. Know who lives right next to this Petrosian guy? Claire and Harlan Draper used to live right next door. Lot of tragedy for one little street, don't you think?" He started walking back to the 4 × 4 and draped a heavy arm across my shoulders to keep me close to him. His voice became a stage whisper. "This Eric guy just *happens* to be in your office the day of the Harlan Draper massacre. He *happens* to own a house right next door to the battling Drapers. And he *happens* to show up dead in a mine shaft behind a bunch of cabins owned by just about everybody else I've had any reason to investigate in the past couple of months. Astonishing coincidences, don't you think?"

"Yes, astonishing," I said, mentally fitting the new piece into the puzzle. So *that* was Eric's connection to the Drapers.

"Isn't it?" said Purdy. "You recall, way back when, after the Draper massacre, I told you there was something funny about the interview we had with Dr. Eric Petrosian?"

"I remember."

"What was funny, what I could never make sense out of, was that he said that at some point after old Harlan busted into your office, you told him—Eric—to call 911. When we interviewed you—you told us the same thing. Well, Dr. Eric told us he called all right, got a connection to the emergency folks, and started to report what was going on, then hung up because he heard the sirens and figured we had already arrived. What didn't jibe is that the tape recorders and the computers at the dispatch center couldn't find any evidence that he actually did call." Purdy shook his head and tightened his grip on my shoulder. "Hard to misdial 911. You know? So given that Dr. Eric is appearing to be more messed up with this the longer it goes on, and seeing that somebody lost a whole lot of blood at Eric's house last night, I've been wondering, among other things, if Eric ever did make that call to 911."

My stomach started to shrivel at the implication of what Purdy was revealing. I said in a hollow voice, "You think Eric Petrosian told Harlan Draper where he could find Claire?"

"Yeah. That's just what I've been thinking. And you know what else? I had somebody downtown pull Dr. Eric's statement out of the Draper file. When he gave us his address, he gave us his *work* address, on Spruce Street. And I didn't catch it, didn't catch that it wasn't his home address. Since then, I've read that damn statement five times, maybe more, and I never caught it. Not once. If I had, I would've noticed that our murderer, our murder victim, and one of our witnesses were all next-door neighbors. I sure would've wondered about that. Yeah, that would've been dogshit. But Dr. Eric—he pulled one over on me. Know the feeling?"

I nodded. I knew the feeling.

Purdy squeezed my shoulder paternally and said, "Anything you want to tell me while you got a hundred percent of my attention? Any revelations? Like maybe why this Eric guy might want Claire Draper dead?"

I wanted to tell Sam Purdy that Eric probably knew something from Paul Weinman's files that he was using to extort his way into the ownership clique of Pain Perdu. And that Claire's testimony would have interfered. I wanted to tell Sam Purdy that Eric was probably screwing Marilyn London, one of his patients, who just happened to end up shot twice in the back after telling me on the phone that she was going to try to get some leverage on some unnamed psychotherapist, who it turned out was Eric Petrosian. And that Eric Petrosian in turn probably killed her or sent Geoff Tobias out to do it for him. But that I wasn't sure. And I wanted to tell Sam Purdy that Paul Weinman's files were under the stairs in my office and that the keys were in my coat pocket.

But I didn't.

So in response to his question, I said, "No, Sam. Nothing."

The police moved Randy back to the hospital. A private room this time. Police guard.

I stayed with him until he was settled in, received his permission to share with the police the outlines of his ancient memories of what happened in the cabin, and then sat in an empty conference room at the hospital to be reinterviewed by Purdy. When Sam was finally through with me, I drove my rental Sundance to my office in the gray light of dawn and walked straight to the closet under the stairs.

I thought I knew the whole story by then, but there was still one piece at which I could only guess.

Who was the other man in the cabin in Mirabelle with Lily Navens?

Paul Weinman's files would tell me if my guess was correct.

I knew I didn't have any right to look at Paul's files—and by then I didn't care.

The files were just as Diane and I had left them. I went right after the one that was labeled "DSS Report Log." When I flipped to the third page in the file, I shook my head and fought an impulse to scream.

My forbidden scream became a loud "Oh, shit!" at the *bleep bleeeep bleeeeep wooooooop woooooooop* of the siren.

It took me a second to realize I hadn't disarmed the burglar alarm. I ran to the kitchen and silenced the damn thing and then walked to my office to wait for the monitoring company to call to substantiate a break-in. The phone rang. I answered. A bored voice asked for the code word. I gave it to her. I wished all life's violations could be handled so easily.

I cursed Raoul's wizardry and my pulse began to subside

as I returned to the floor of the hallway. As quickly as I could I scanned the other file labels and yanked out the case file with Geoff Tobias's name on it. I turned the pages, frantically scanning the dates on Paul's notes of Geoff's treatment to find a progress note that matched the date on the piece of paper I had removed from the "DSS Report Log" file.

There was no match.

The date on the DSS report had no mate in Geoff Tobias's file. But the sequence of dates showed that the date of the DSS report would have fit right into sequence with a gap in the dates of Geoff Tobias's psychotherapy.

A page was missing.

Eric Petrosian had taken it in the confusion after Paul Weinman's death.

And Sam Purdy probably had it now. Or would soon.

I looked again at the DSS report. The initials at the top were lonely and sad. They read "LN."

Lily Navens.

Paul had jotted down a brief note after he called the Department of Social Services with a question about the statute of limitations on the requirement that psychologists report child abuse. The child who was abused was Lily Navens. The patient who admitted the abuse was then thirty-four years old. The patient was Geoffrey Tobias.

History of abuse: 34 y.o. male pt. reports repeated sexual mistreatment and molestation, of niece (LN), now 18. Last incident when victim was 8—1981.

DSS caseworker replied that statute of limitations on the reporting requirement is ten years. A report is welcome but not required. Will inform patient at next session.

I was so engrossed in Paul's succinct summation of the tragedy of Lily Navens that I failed to hear the footsteps behind me.

Diane said, "Just to cover your ass—may I please have some consultation on what to do with those records?"

Without looking up I said, "Yes, you may. How did you know I was here?"

"Raoul has the alarm rigged to call me right after it calls the monitoring station. I called them and they told me you tripped it." She looked over my shoulder at the sheet of paper in my hands. "Would you like to show me exactly what I need this consultation about?"

I handed her the DSS report.

Diane scanned quickly and said, "Oh, my God. Lily."

I said, "Yes. Lily."

Diane slid gracefully to the floor next to me, rereading Paul's note. "My own patient. How did I miss it?"

"It wasn't there to be seen yet. Repression's a black hole. You're good, Diane, and you know Lily was doomed to remember sometime. But she wasn't there yet. And you know what else? Paul's progress note from the date that would correspond to that page is missing from Geoff Tobias's file."

"You think Eric took the note from Paul's files after Paul died?"

"Yeah, that'd be my guess."

Diane was silent for a moment. "Right at the beginning. When Paul died," she said again, mostly to herself. "So Eric rifled Paul's files and was blackmailing Geoff Tobias about his abuse of Lily."

"Yeah. He was using that progress note from Geoff's chart to steal a piece of Pain Perdu. That's why he told Harlan where to find Claire. Eric didn't want her to testify to the grand jury about the financial shenanigans at the restaurant—something that would be sure to slay his new cash cow."

I walked Diane through everything that had happened at Mirabelle since I had left her with Adrienne the night before. She didn't interrupt me once.

When I was done she said, "So, if I understand all this right, the burglar at my house was Geoff Tobias searching for Lily's chart to find out how much I knew about the abuse."

"Yes. But Randy says there was another man there, too. That night. The 'incident in '81.' The photography session."

"Not photography. Pornography."

"Right. Pornography."

"Was Paul the other man?" Diane said, disbelief in her voice.

"No, I don't think so."

"Who then?" she asked.

I shook my head.

Diane said, "I could kill Geoff for fucking Tobias. That asshole better live."

"I think you'll have to stand in line. And he'll live. He has a badly broken wrist, a broken collarbone"—I bowed from the waist, taking credit for those injuries—"broken leg, and the ever-popular closed-head trauma."

"Good. What about the other break-ins?"

"The first one, here, I think, was Eric trying to find out if I knew about his sexual assaults on Marilyn London. The other one here at the office was so Geoff Tobias could switch guns to incriminate Randy for Marilyn London's murder."

"The snowplow?"

"I think Geoff began to worry, or suspect, that Randy somehow knew about what Geoff had done to Lily. And Geoff wanted to insure that Randy wouldn't recover any memories about all this and tell somebody. I think he was hoping Randy would kill himself, but when Randy started to dissociate and return to Mirabelle, Geoff panicked, realizing that the memories might be emerging. When I hospitalized Randy, Geoff started to improvise. Tried to get me taken off the case. When I resisted that, he tried to use the snowplow to do it more permanently. I'm guessing, of course."

"Why was the mayor's wife murdered?"

"Marilyn? Purdy'll have to get that from Geoff. I would guess that Eric convinced Geoff it was necessary to kill her to protect the restaurant. Maybe Marilyn was making threats against Eric for his sexual assaults during therapy, or was threatening to expose her husband for who knows what. I think Marilyn thought she could run with the big dogs. But I don't know who actually pulled the trigger of the gun that killed her. Both Geoff and Eric are cowardly enough to have done it."

Diane's eyes began to tear, and she raised her knees up to her chest. "Know how this started? I presented Claire Draper's case to a supervision group of my peers. And look what's happened since. She's dead. Her husband's dead. Her kids are orphaned. Her lawyer's crippled. Her neighbor's dead. Marilyn London is dead."

"It's not your fault."

"I know that. These tears aren't guilt, sweets. I'm crying at the damage we psychotherapists can do. Look at what Paul started by breaking a simple little ethical standard. He saw a bunch of people for psychotherapy whom he knew socially. That's all he did. A pissant little ethical standard that tons of therapists ignore. The single cell that starts the tumor. Then Eric. Malevolent goddamn Eric Petrosian. He used one of his own patients *and* a few of Paul Weinman's, and killed a couple more just to make a few thousand bucks. How the hell do these slugs get Ph.D.'s? What's wrong here? What are we missing in this profession? What the hell are we doing wrong?"

"There's plenty of evil to go around, Diane. It wasn't just Eric, and I don't think it was about money. Eric did it for control. That's my guess. And don't lay it all on Eric. Look at Paul. Look at Geoff."

"But I didn't sit next to Geoff Tobias and share the painful secrets of my patients' lives with him. I did with Eric. And I didn't see his evil. Paul didn't see his evil. You provided supervision to him, Alan. You didn't see his evil. Doesn't this frighten you? Doesn't it frighten you that we maybe didn't *want* to see the evil?"

I was silent.

She said, "And don't even get me started on incompetence."

I didn't get her started on incompetence.

"And," she said, wagging a finger at me, "you better not have lost my portable phone."

46

I left Diane at the office reluctantly. But she insisted that I go. She needed, she said, some time alone to digest her regrets and renew her sadness about the many tragedies of Lily Navens, and to reacquaint herself with the memories of all the damage that had been done so recently in the quaint Victorian space where she and I spilled so much energy trying to be healers.

Lauren was frantic with worry by the time I arrived at her door. I learned later that Elliot Bellhaven had jarred her awake with a phone call shortly after dawn and filled her in on the previous night's drama. In turn, Lauren had relentlessly hassled whoever was answering the phone in Sam Purdy's office until Sam finally returned one of her calls and told her his version of the events at Eric Petrosian's house and at Mirabelle. She had been trying to reach me since.

But I didn't know any of that as I steeled myself to knock on Lauren's door. I felt wary and was prepared to be penitent. She and I hadn't talked since the night I had made spaghetti for Peter and Adrienne—which was also the last time I had arrived unannounced at her door—the same night I had found her in the midst of some serious pocket billiards and cocktails with a tall, thin, attractive man who drove a car that cost about the same as a median-priced home in Missouri.

When she ran to the door in response to my knock and swung it open, she was already dressed for work. From the cut of her worsted suit I assumed hers was a day that included at least one scheduled appearance in court.

In contrast, I was dressed like a man who had been

up all night crawling around mining camps and stalking kidnappers.

I stood at her door like a beggar.

She leaned into the frame of the door as if she were using it to support herself. For a couple of seconds she just stared at me, then her upper body swelled with a cleansing sigh. "You really are all right," she said finally, and reached for me.

I leaned into her and buried my head in the crook of her neck and said, "I'm getting you filthy."

"It's okay. . . . You're okay. . . . It's fine."

We kissed. Neither of us closed our eyes. When we pulled back, each of us ran our tongues over our lips as if our tongues could determine some nuance that our lips hadn't deciphered.

"Are we okay?" I asked.

She nodded, her eyes moist and shiny. "Come in. Oh, Alan," she said, pulling me gently into her kitchen, sitting me down at the table, then efficiently searching out the things required to offer me a mug of coffee with milk.

She was standing at the sink, her back to me, when she said, "Do I have to ask about last night?"

"No," I said, and I relayed as much as I could about what had happened. I left out only the parts that came from Paul Weinman's case files.

As she listened she turned part of the way around to face me and seemed to pay special heed to the omissions in my story, probably because she had already heard a couple of other versions that made educated guesses at the facts I was deleting. "I think there are some pieces missing," she said.

"Yes. There are," I said. Then I smiled to myself. The smile was a selfish acknowledgment that I had a surefire way of distracting her from pressing me for details that I couldn't divulge. I sowed the seeds of distraction by saying, "Merideth was there. Up at Mirabelle." Lauren seemed unfazed and sipped from her mug, waiting patiently for me to go on. Before continuing, I hesitated, holding her attention the way Jack Nicholson pauses to insure that the camera remains on his face during a close-up. "She and I are meeting at four today to sign the final papers," I said. I watched Lauren's movements slow, then still.

Finally her head turned away from me. Looking west from her window to the sharp ascent of the Front Range, she said, "For real this time?"

"For real," I said.

"What about the baby? Merideth's baby."

"After I told her there was no future for us she told me she had miscarried."

"After?"

"After."

"You believe her?"

"About the baby, I'm not sure."

A few seconds for processing. "I'm sorry. For her," Lauren said, turning all the way toward me now, drying her hands on a dish towel that was as white as the orbits of her eyes. "And maybe for you, but I'll have to think on that."

"I'm afraid that you've gotten tired of waiting for me to get my head screwed on straight. About us."

"I have been a saint."

"I saw the saint having cocktails last week with a handsome man with a big black car."

She laughed. Smiling, she said, "He is handsome, isn't he? Were you jealous?"

"Sure. I was. And angry at myself for being so stupid about you."

"You have been stupid."

"Is he an issue?"

"The guy?"

"Yeah, the guy."

"That was Jacob. My ex. I invited him over to ask for some advice."

"About me?" I hoped.

"You *are* a little full of yourself. Such a hero you are. Yes. About you."

"And?"

"And he told me to have my cake and eat it, too."

"That's kind of his philosophy of life, isn't it?"

"Yes. That's Jake."

I took a long swallow of coffee, feeling it sear my throat, not minding. I said, "I think we should get married, Lauren."

She looked away from me and quickly back, smiling. "That sounds more like a statement of fact than an invitation, and before you get a chance to manufacture some romance and rephrase"—she held up her hand to stifle any reply from me—"let me say I agree with you. I, too, would like us to be married. Shhhh, I'm not done. But. I'm mostly concerned with us being married *well*.

"We've both tried just being married. It's not enough. So what I propose is that we act like people planning to get married for the next little while and see what we can accomplish."

"Like be engaged?"

"Like engaged. But I want to call it something else."

"Like what?"

"I don't know. When I think of the right word I'll tell you."

"For some reason," I said, "I feel like the fear-of-commitment ball has just bounced back to your side of the court."

"I don't think so. I'm ready for you, Alan Gregory. Yes, I am; don't doubt it. But first—first I'm going to New York. To kneel at the altar of the MS gods."

"You've been accepted."

She smiled and nodded.

"Congratulations. I'm happy for you. How long?"

"Six months to a year commitment to being in New York. Another eighteen months being followed elsewhere."

"Shit," I said, thinking, That's a long time.

"Shit?"

My eyes were slits from fatigue. "No, honey. I'm in. I love you, Lauren Crowder."

"And I love you, Alan Gregory."

I shook my head. "If I'm going to be without you for six months to a year, those damn doctors better not put you in the control group."

She smiled and nodded her agreement. "You can come visit, you know," she said.

"New York City? People litter there. And there're no bike lanes."

Lauren furrowed her brow and pursed her lips and said, "But there's me."

I stood and walked over to the sink and kissed her. She pressed herself into me and grazed my cheek with her left hand. She said, "So, have you shaved those legs any more recently than you've shaved this face?"

I fell asleep in Lauren's bed and woke up naked to find Sam Purdy standing in the doorway to Lauren's bedroom. Just like a nightmare. Except he was clothed, which tempered the horror a little.

He jingled a ring of keys. "She said I'd find you here. Don't you ever work?"

I growled and buried my head in one of the pillows on the bed.

"Get dressed. I'll meet you in the kitchen."

I pulled on the filthy trousers from the night before. Purdy had shaved and somehow managed to appear rested. He was wearing fresh clothing. I felt as if I'd just woken up in the middle of the afternoon after a serious drunk.

"You need a shave," he said.

I smiled, sort of. "I think I'm growing a beard."

"Your girlfriend just requested a leave of absence from Royal Peterson, our DA," Purdy said as he fumbled to find the combination of buttons that would coerce Lauren's microwave to heat up the dregs of the morning coffee.

I said, "Yeah—I know—from her job, and me."

"So then you probably know 'the personal reasons' she gave the DA for the request?"

I nodded. God, was I hungry.

"I don't," said Purdy, "and I hate not knowing things. I hate, for instance, not knowing who called into the department switchboard from Eric Petrosian's house. But I think I can live with that. If it really starts to bother me, there's about a thousand footprints over there I can use to make an ID." He glanced at me sideways, letting his eyes wander down to my bare feet before he continued. "And what I really hate is not knowing how this Eric guy knew enough information to blackmail all these other people. And what the hell was he gaining from all his inspired efforts? Although I can guess it has something to do with that stupid restaurant."

He tossed some photographs onto the table in front of me. Five-by-sevens. Color.

I glanced once at the photos and saw Randy's long face and dark eyes reflected in his sister's childhood image. I looked once at her youthful naked body sitting self-consciously on a ragged boulder against the backdrop of a small lake, her hands raised behind her head, her hairless vulva exposed. I swallowed self-consciously as I pushed aside the top photo. The next shot in the stack was set in the living room of Geoff Tobias's cabin. Well lit. By the fireplace. Lily's boyish body was dressed in lingerie that fell off one shoulder, exposing her chest but not even the hint of a breast.

The lingerie was lace.

I looked away. I fought an impulse to raise the backs of my hands to my eyes.

Purdy held up some more photographs and said, "Some of the others are worse. Wanna know where I got them?"

I was resisting a reflexive shiver. "Geoff's house," I replied.

"No. Not Geoff's house."

"What—*Eric's?*" My next guess was going to be Paul's, and I was going to be sick.

"Nope. See, I'm up all night chasing you through the mountains—which, by the way, is becoming a rather frequent occurrence these days—and I got plenty of time to think. I got time to think, for instance, about what all Geoff Tobias might have done to your patient's sister in that cabin. Randy, you told me, says he remembers that another guy besides his uncle was there and he remembers lights and cameras and since I'm still wondering what the fuck Geoff Tobias has on Russ London to get him to organize all these financial shenanigans for his new restaurant, I get a little suspicious. So I explain all this to a judge, who thinks that after all these years he's finally heard a half-decent reason for being woken up in the middle of the night, and he tells me I can go to Russ's house and have a look around. We find those pictures in Russ London's closet. I mean, in a box, right in the closet. There's a note inside this big envelope they're in that says 'Remember these?' That's all. Just 'Remember these?'

"So what I figure is that Geoff threatened to expose Russ London's moment of prurient weakness. I'm not totally sure Russ was part of it, the child pornography thing, yet. But it looks like he was. Let's face it—at the very least he knew about it and kept it to himself. And the fact that Russ kept these pictures all these years tells me maybe his interest wasn't transitory . . . but . . . I'll sort all that out.

"I was telling you what I hate, wasn't I? Well, know what else I hate? I hate that I think you and your anvil-headed partner know more about some of this than I do. I hate that the statute of limitations on child abuse and child molestation is so damn short. Now, there's no way this Eric guy could have known about this pornography thing, is there? Some paragraph about these pictures isn't sittin' in some file nobody'll show me, is it? Nah. That wouldn't be right. Wouldn't be *justice*. That wouldn't happen, no way."

Purdy wasn't even waiting for replies from me. He knew he was in the vicinity of the truth, and he knew I wouldn't confirm anything for him.

"Geoff Tobias is silent about almost everything. Hired some hotshot lawyer from Denver, who immediately performed your basic radical tonguectomy on his client. But we got plenty of physical evidence on the murder of Eric Petrosian and on the kidnapping of his nephew. Not to mention an eyewitness or two." He raised one eyebrow at me. "But prior to his attorney gagging him, Geoff did squeal on his buddy Eric. Said he thinks Eric blew up Larry Templeton's house. Says that Eric never admitted doing it, but kept referring to it so all the other pansies would think he was ruthless enough to do it. I'm not convinced Geoff isn't being a tad too modest. I'm beginning to doubt that Eric even had a motive to do Larry in. Now, Geoff, on the other hand, he had some motives. If Larry was threatening to go screaming to the DA about his share in the restaurant being diluted, it would have put Geoff's whole financial house of cards in jeopardy. Maybe after last night the feds will have enough new evidence to be able to sort it out, maybe not. Some mysteries, I've learned over the years, just don't get solved. My gut tells me that this Eric guy may just have been—what?—smart enough to take advantage of fate."

"Was Geoff driving the snowplow, Sam?"

"Probably. We finally tracked down that caretaker from Mirabelle—Janet whatever. Her ass-bite boyfriend was either wrong or was lying—she wasn't in Costa Rica, she was in Belize. Finding her wasn't easy, the friggin' country has maybe four working telephones. Anyway, she told us that Geoff *had* called her to do some work on his cabin, but she told him she couldn't—that she was gonna split for a while 'cause a cop was looking for her and she had this trip planned anyway and preferred to stay away from Mirabelle until this cop stopped hassling her. Says she thought we were trying to set her up. Makes some sense if you're the paranoid type—which she has every reason to be since she's got a couple of priors. One for possession with intent to sell, one for disturbing the peace in a protest out at Rocky Flats. Anyway, Geoff asked her what cops were looking for her, and she gave Geoff your name and my name. So he knew how to set you up. And his wife told us he drove heavy equipment in college, so he could've figured out the plow."

"What about Marilyn London?" I asked.

Purdy started rummaging around for sugar. I'd never seen Lauren use any and couldn't be of any help. "That's gotta be Geoff. Guy apparently would've done anything to save his restaurant or his ass. In that order. And we found all the evidence from her murder stashed in his house. Who knows, Marilyn may even have been trying to expose Geoff's blackmail of her husband. Or she might have been blackmailing Geoff about his role in all this in return. We'll find out."

I wasn't sure Sam would find out. Marilyn's intrusion into this swamp may have been through her illicit therapeutic relationship with Eric Petrosian. And I wasn't sure how the police were gonna find out about that. I wasn't at all convinced that Eric hadn't had a hand—directly or indirectly—in Marilyn's murder.

"The ex-mayor?" I asked.

"His political goose is cooked. The grand jury will definitely vote a bill." He gestured toward the obscene photographs. "I'd guess there'll be some rather prurient new charges, too."

"What's gonna happen to Randy?"

"That's more up to your therapeutic powers than it is up to me. I think the kid's innocent of everything but felony bad luck."

I smiled ruefully at that. "What about Elliot, Sam? His family owns a cabin up there, too. Is he part of this mess?"

Sam Purdy paused and looked right at me. "Not that I know of." He studied my face as if trying to discern something from my expression. "Unless you know something about Elliot you want to tell me?"

I shook my head. I felt relief that Elliot Bellhaven's HIV infection remained his secret.

Sam went on. "And, you know, a whole mess of lawyers are gonna be busy for years trying to figure out who really owns that damn restaurant outside of town. How come, no matter who loses, some lawyer always wins?"

"They write the rules, Sam. They write the rules."

"By the way. Scott Truscott says your contract's up. You're fired, I guess. Wants you to call him."

"At last, some good news."

"And I know who our elusive 'M' is. So you can write your last report." Purdy moved over and started an inventory of Lauren's refrigerator. "Doesn't this woman have anything to eat?"

"You do?" I said.

"I *do* what?" He sat back down at the kitchen table with a rolled-up slice of Swiss cheese that he'd dunked in a jar of mustard. "Larry Templeton was porkin' none other than Mrs. Tobias. Which, of course, is yet another motive Geoff had for blowing Larry's house down on top of his head. The 'M' apparently stood for Mirabelle, it was nobody's name at all. Mirabelle's where Larry and Julia Child met to perform their adulterous acts. In Larry's cabin, not Geoff's. Now—until last night I had never had the pleasure of meeting *Mrs.* Templeton. But now that I have seen her very attractive face and sampled some of her fine baking, I can't see being married to *her* and having an affair of the sheets with Mrs. *Tobias,* with whom I spent a very disagreeable hour quite early this morning. Go figure."

Go figure, I thought.

I stood up and walked over to the kitchen sink and threw some cold water in my face. I dried it with Lauren's pristine dish towel. I said, "Buy you some breakfast, Sam?"

He said, "Thought you'd never ask." He stood up and stopped in the doorway to the living room. He said, "I'm gonna shoot a little pool while you get showered and presentable. I want you to take me someplace *nice.*"

"Lauren won't be happy about your using her table, Sam."

"So tell me who is happy, hotshot. Tell me who is."

I spent ten minutes in the shower affixing blame for all this on Paul Weinman.

When Russ London told Paul during psychotherapy that he had witnessed or participated in the photographic sexual exploitation of Lily Navens—"discussed 1981 incident"—Paul was obligated—morally, ethically, legally—to report Russ London for sexual abuse of a child. But because Paul and Russ were friends, acquaintances, partners—whatever—Paul didn't report Russ.

Paul made one mistake by agreeing to see his friend for psychotherapy. That mistake led to his unwillingness to report his friend to the Department of Social Services for sexual abuse of a child. Once those two dominoes had fallen, the rest of this was out of Paul Weinman's hands. And into Eric Petrosian's.

Dr. Eric Petrosian. Eric used what was in Paul Weinman's records of the psychotherapy of Russ London and Geoff Tobias to blackmail his way into Pain Perdu and to exploit the advantage of his existing destructive relationship with Marilyn London. Eric in turn set Harlan Draper free like an assassin to target his wife, Claire. Harlan simply wanted to punish Claire for leaving him; Eric wanted to keep her from testifying to the grand jury about the restaurant. As the dominoes fell, Eric either blew up Larry Templeton's house or took advantage of it and either committed the murder of Marilyn London or got Geoff to do it.

And the whole sick scheme might have worked had Randy Navens's erratic repression of a long-forgotten night in a mountain cabin not become the wild card that trumped them all.

Dr. Paul Weinman made a couple of small ethical accommodations.

And the result was murder.

I prayed for Paul's soul.

And cursed his goddamn mistakes.

47

The morass in Mirabelle had sucked me away from my practice for too many hours, and I was forced to spend a lot of time on the phone over the next twenty-four hours rescheduling patients. Quite a few of them were angry about my recent erratic record of honoring appointments, and a few suggested they liked it better when my name wasn't in the paper with such regularity.

I dealt with their anger.

After I examined and reexamined my dilemma about whether I could continue to treat Randy, I finally decided that I could. Actually I called an old supervisor in Denver and ran the facts by him. He said I was on an ethical fence, and I could probably get off on whatever side I preferred. I decided to jump off on the side where I was able to continue to treat Randy.

With his memories emerging and the extent of his earlier trauma magnifying, it was clear Randy had a long road ahead of him in psychotherapy. My initial task was to help him see the recent events as part of a resolution and not merely as a new trauma. It wouldn't be easy.

Casey Sparrow stuck to Randy like a guardian angel. Orders from the court appointed a vice president of a local bank as the new trustee for his assets and granted temporary guardianship to the state of Colorado, for now through Casey. The issue of foster care was moot as long as he remained hospitalized.

Russell London resigned as county commissioner the day before the grand jury voted a nine-count bill on him.

While the lawyers worked to sort out who actually owned the place, Erica Tobias continued to run Pain Perdu as if Geoff had never been there. For the restaurant, the publicity around the scandal had the effect of a five-star review. I was ambivalent about the restaurant's success. But Randy was getting richer and Rita Templeton was getting richer, and that made it all somewhat palatable.

Merideth and I completed our divorce. Adrienne told me she thought that Merideth's miscarriage was a lie; she guessed she'd actually had an abortion. I'd already covered the same ground myself and felt some remorse wondering whether the abortion preceded or followed the final disaster at Mirabelle.

Merideth gave the whole story to the local affiliate. But I refused to either, one, go on camera, or two, talk about Randy—so when the story was finally aired in three parts during the spring sweeps, it didn't look like it was gonna shake up the Emmy committee.

Lauren went to New York for daily injections into her thigh.

And I went back to work.

Elaine Casselman took a few seconds to settle onto her chair. "We're back in session," she said.

I sat and wondered when she was going to get around to talking about the deep bruise that radiated through a thick crust of makeup on her right cheek.

She was jovial, the unusual jocularity another diversion, like the makeup.

"You know? The grand jury? And you know what? That special prosecutor gave us a speech about our responsibility to keep our mouths shut. Don't tell your husbands or wives. Don't tell your best friend. And then she says, 'Or your therapists,' and I swear she looked right at me. I almost stood up and told her I didn't have to tell my therapist—that my therapist already *knew* more about this than I did."

Elaine noticed me looking at the side of her face, and she raised her right hand to the bruise.

Her mood changed abruptly.

"Yeah. Max hit me." Her voice was quiet but determined. "Okay? Okay? And I told him if he ever hit me again, I would never see him again. Okay? Is that good enough?"

I felt tired. I just sat and listened, and I thought about Claire Draper and about Lily Navens.

And I feared for the woman across from me and wondered what had happened to Elaine Casselman as a child. I wondered what horror prepared her so well to be a victim.

"You seem angry," I said, my voice warm and dull.

The road stretched out farther in the distance than I could see.

You are invited to preview
an exciting excerpt from
Stephen White's new high-tension
thriller featuring Dr. Alan Gregory

SAINTS AND SINNERS

coming soon

Blythe Oaks preferred to run in the mornings. She always tried to time her workouts so that she was heading east just as the sun escaped the horizon.

Recently she had been running faster and farther than usual because when she was frightened, it was hard to stop running.

Today, as the sun lifted above the trees, she was on the Mall, in full stride, the Air and Space Museum on her right, the Capitol Dome framed ahead of her by the morning light. Minutes later she arrived at the edge of the Capitol Reflecting Pool. She stopped and abruptly pirouetted to examine the trail behind her.

The trail was vacant. No other runner was within a hundred yards.

Blythe jogged in place while she checked the progress of a distant runner and watched a renegade glide gracefully by on inline skates. Neither approached her. Neither even seemed to take notice of her. Despite the respite from her run, Blythe's pulse didn't slow. She glanced at her watch and crossed the Mall, striving to cleanse her mind of fear by concentrating on achieving good hip extension and not landing too far back on her heels. She quickly covered the long stretch of ground that extended west toward the Potomac.

Blythe Oaks ran fast when she feared she was being followed.

As she approached the street where she lived alone in a third-floor apartment, she prayed—she literally prayed —that she wouldn't find a flower waiting outside the front door to the building. She mouthed the words, the plea, her mantra to God, "Please, no flower, please, no flower, please, no flower."

Please, stride, *no flower*, stride.

Blythe Oaks had already decided that her stalker bought a fresh bouquet only once a week because each morning for seven days the single stem left by her door would be of the same variety. The flower was always wrapped in tissue paper color-coordinated with the hue of the bud. The flowers were always freshest on Saturday. So, she had concluded, the stalker bought them on Fridays. Maybe Friday night after work. But this past weekend, thank God, no flower. Before her run this morning, no flower.

"Please, no flower, please, no flower, please, no flower."

The car that had spawned Blythe's paranoia almost a month before was a blue Toyota Camry with D.C. plates. The first time Blythe had spotted the car it was parked on the street outside her apartment building, directly across from her own beige Taurus. Blythe remembered noticing the car that first time mostly because the person behind the wheel turned abruptly when Blythe looked toward the car. She recalled the long, dark brown hair, the suede jacket, a baseball cap—the Orioles?—with a plastic adjustable strap in back. Later that day, she thought she spotted the same Camry outside the Supreme Court building where she worked. The next day she saw it again, back on the street in front of her apartment. Sometimes she was certain she saw the car drive past her when she jogged.

Once the blue Camry had parked right next to her Taurus at the supermarket.

Blue Camry. Blue Camry.

After six strong miles Blythe turned the final corner toward her building and decided she liked her new Nikes. The clerk who had waited on her on Saturday and suggested this particular shoe apparently knew what she was doing. Blythe fantasized briefly about returning to the store and asking the clerk if she wanted to go for a run some time. Blythe shook off the fantasy. She knew she wouldn't ask. One reckless mistake was enough. More than enough.

A reflexive vigilance intruded as she neared her building. Blythe Oaks was becoming a car expert. She quietly called out the makes as she passed them in their slots along the curb: "Camaro, Buick, Honda, pickup, minivan, Saab."

Stride, stride. Stride, stride. "No Camry, no flowers. No Camry, no flowers."

One step up to the walk. Five more to the door.

With what felt like monumental effort, Blythe Oaks finally forced herself to look up. Immediately she started to cry. Such pretty blue buds. A note card of heavy gray paper. The beautiful cursive hand.

"Nice shoes! Soon everyone will know about us!" the note read.

Standing by the door, card in her hand, the flower at her feet, Blythe smiled awkwardly through her tears to greet a neighbor who was heading out the door to go to work. Inside, she took the stairs two at a time to the third floor, now crying in a desperately muted voice, "Please don't call, please don't call, please don't call."

In her mind now, she knew she was talking to the stalker, no longer to God.

She unclipped the safety pin that held her key to the waistband of her shorts, unlocked the door, and walked into her quiet apartment, trying not to sob, eager to be soothed by the silence of the telephone and warmed by the light drifting in through the living room bay.

Blythe Oaks had almost finished stripping off her running clothes when the phone finally began to ring. She started and flinched as she stared at the ivory-colored instrument, paralyzed.

If she answered the phone the stalker would say nothing. No breathing. No profanities. Nothing. As if the stalker's only wish was the vacant connection and the sound of Blythe's once confident, now hollow "Hello."

Soon everyone will know . . .

No! No one can know. She reviewed her options. Call the D.C. police. Or the Supreme Court police. Report the stalker.

"Why might a woman be following you, Mrs. Oaks?"

"Well, Officer, perhaps it's because I'm lesbian."

Right, Blythe. Not a chance. Maybe I should just leave. Go back to Utah. Give up my job. My dream.

Steam drifted from the shower. Water pelted the tile. The phone rang and rang. Standing naked but for her sweaty socks, Blythe Oaks cried again, loudly this time, sobs. She didn't know what on earth she was going to do.